Champagne Rules

Champagne Rules

SUSAN LYONS

APHRODISIA

KENSINGTON PUBLISHING CORP.

http://www.kensingtonbooks.com

APHRODISIA BOOKS are published by

Kensington Publishing Corp.
850 Third Avenue
New York, NY 10022

All Kensington Titles, Imprints, and Distributed Lines are available at special quantity discounts for bulk purchases for sales promotions, premiums, fundraising, and educational or institutional use.

Special book excerpts or customized printings can also be created to fit specific needs. For details, write or phone the office of the Kensington special sales manager: Kensington Publishing Corp., 850 Third Avenue, New York, NY 10022, attn: Special Sales Department, Phone: 1-800-221-2647.

ISBN 0-7582-1406-5

First Kensington Trade Paperback Printing: February 2006

10 9 8 7 6 5 4 3 2 1

Printed in the United States of America

To Mom and Ted,
for encouraging me to achieve my dream of being a writer.

Prologue—four years earlier

Suzanne balanced astride him, bracing her hands on his shoulders. Muscled shoulders, so slick with sweat her hands kept sliding. Sliding, like her body was sliding—up, down, as she rode him—their bodies making wet suck-and-slap sounds each time they came together. And each time they did come together, the burn, the ache, between her legs grew stronger.

Her body moved mindlessly, driving toward satisfaction.

But no, not yet. This was so amazing, so incredible, so unbelievable, she didn't want it to end.

So unbelievable . . . Like a dream, the whole afternoon was a dream. The dusky light in the cave, the dazzle of sunny blue sky outside. The earthy, tangy scent that combined sex, sweat, ocean, dust and something else, something male and exotic, something that went straight to her head and made it spin. The scent of the man beneath her.

The man. The sexiest, most gorgeous guy she'd ever laid eyes on. An athlete's body, lean and muscled. Skin like dark chocolate, hair the color of coal, a hint of the exotic in the short dreadlocks and neat goatee. His eyes, his smile, were bright flashes against the dim light.

She leaned down, letting tangles of long blond hair brush his nipples, touching her lips to his, feeling the slight tickle of his facial hair. But when he tried to deepen the kiss, she raised her head again, arching back, teasing him.

Teasing? Was this really her, acting like this?

Her head spun and for a moment she lost her rhythm, but his hands gripped her waist. Steadying, but not forcing her.

This incredible, powerful guy had surrendered control to her, put her in charge. The idea was so arousing, so erotic, she could hardly stand it.

She'd never felt this way before. She'd always thought of her body as healthy and reliable, but not exactly sexy.

Sexy. Oh man, this afternoon Suzanne Brennan was the epitome of sexy! Because *he* was, this fabulous lover of hers. For the first time in her life she was with a *man*—not a high school kid, not a college boy, but a real man. And every glint of his eyes told her she was a woman. A sexy woman.

She'd lost her virginity four years ago at the age of sixteen, but now she felt like it hadn't counted. Nothing in her sex life had counted until today, when she'd really become a woman.

A brand-new instinct told her to move faster and faster, to glide up and slam down against his hard body, grinding herself into him, twisting and twining around him, building that tantalizing ache, until they both exploded.

But another part of her wanted to hold back, to make it last.

She stopped moving, panting for breath, feeling his body shudder as he too sucked in air.

"You okay?" he murmured.

"Mmm." But when she nodded, her head spun again. Too much wine for lunch, on her last day on Crete. Too much sunshine. Too much man? No, never. "Want to make it last."

"Then distract me, woman. Distract the both of us." His

voice was sensual, deep and melodious. Sexy, to match every-thing else about him.

Distract them? From sex? "How?"

"Well . . ." He glanced around. "Look outside, down to the beach. What's happening?"

"Okay." She straightened a bit, lifted her gaze to the mouth of their cliffside cave. Sunshine, oh wow, it was bright! Tears sprang to her eyes as she squinted against the glare.

Dizzy again. Shouldn't have had so much wine.

But a soft breeze dried the sweat on her face and filled her nostrils with the scent of ocean and sun-warmed herbs. Gradually her head cleared, and her eyes adjusted to the light. "The sand's so pale it's almost white, and the water's a vivid greeny-blue. Like a postcard of paradise."

The kind of postcard she'd send to her big sister but defi-nitely not her parents. This particular paradise was a nude beach.

She smiled. "Some kids—young people—are dancing around in the shallow water, splashing and laughing." If she hadn't met him, she might be with them right now—if she'd had the guts to join in. "They're playing and it's kind of innocent, but it's provocative too, because they're naked."

His fingers stroked down the inside of her thigh, then back up again, coming to rest just below the spot where their bodies joined. Innocent, yet provocative. She shivered, a tremor that shook her from head to toe, outside and in.

His body tensed in response. "Don't move." His voice was rougher now. "Keep talking, give me something else to focus on."

Did she have so much power, that a mere shiver could threaten his control? An amazing thought—but then he had that power over her, this man who'd given her her first Big O.

Suzanne tried to hold still as she straddled him, her thighs hot and slick against his, her knees sore from the rough towel and the hard rock beneath it.

Her gaze roamed the beach. "There's a couple lying on a big red towel." Were they . . . ? She squinted. "Both men." That was one thing about a nude beach, there was no such thing as gender ambiguity.

"They're holding hands." She smiled dreamily. "Lovers. Letting the sun kiss them, waiting, being patient, feeling the anticipation build." Just as she and her lover were doing.

He reached out to claim her right hand, and brought it to his mouth. Gently, he nipped the mound at the base of her thumb, then took the tip of her index finger into his mouth and began to suck.

Her breath quickened. When she looked down, he shook his head. "No," he said. "Watch the beach."

Twenty or thirty yards below, gentle waves lapped the shore, receded, then lapped again. His mouth found their rhythm as he sucked, then released, bathing her finger in wet heat, then easing free so the cave's breath chilled her burning skin.

She'd never experienced—never even imagined—anything so sensual, so sexy.

Here she was, a voyeur, watching the people below on the beach, and at the same time this man was watching her, making love to her.

Suzanne couldn't stay still any longer. Her body picked up that same beat, the rhythm of his mouth, of the waves. She lifted off him, exposing his shaft to the cool air, then lowered herself, taking him back inside.

His teeth closed on her finger. He groaned, then released her hand as his breathing quickened. Inside her, arousal was building again. Hers, his, each feeding the other.

She moved faster, until his hips lifted off the ground.

But no, if she speeded up they'd both climax, and she wasn't ready for this to end. If she could, she'd make it last forever.

Forever?

She stopped moving, dimly aware of his frustrated groan.

Gazing down, she tried to make out his features in the dusky light, but only his eyes were clearly visible, slitted now as he struggled for control.

Forever? Confused, she shook her head to clear it, but instead the dizziness returned. She closed her eyes and held still, trying to think. This had nothing to do with forever. She was going home tomorrow, would never see him again. Her life was just starting, and forever was way down the road.

This man was her initiation into adulthood. He was teaching her about her own sexuality.

Yes, that's what this afternoon was about. That's all it was.

Feeling sane again, she realized his body was trembling, his fingers biting into her hips. "Are you all right?" she asked.

"The beach." The words grated out. "Tell me what's happening now."

He was so big and strong, yet he was letting her set the pace, using every ounce of will power to hold his body in check.

She turned her face to the sun, keeping her eyes closed a few seconds, then opening them slowly to the brightness.

Below, a couple strolled into view. "There's an older man and woman. Grey-haired, naked, walking at the edge of the water. Arms around each other's waists. They look like they've been in love forever."

Yes, here was what forever looked like. One day she'd find a relationship like theirs. "A love that survives highs and lows, that builds a family and a home, that starts out strong and grows even more beautiful each year."

"Or they're brand-new lovers. Just met each other this afternoon."

Oops, she hadn't meant to speak her thoughts out loud. Lucky he'd thought she was talking about the couple on the beach, not revealing her own dreams, or she might've spoiled the mood.

She replayed his words—such a different perspective from her own. "New lovers? Why not? This is a magical place."

What else could explain the force that had brought her together with this man? They'd met only an hour or two ago, at the special beach she'd discovered on the last day of her holiday. Only magic could have brought sensible Suzanne from Vancouver, Canada, to the adventure of a lifetime.

She sighed with pleasure, watching the sun glint off the froth that tipped the lazy waves. Never would she forget this afternoon. This man. Almost, she wished she knew his name, where he came from, what he did. But those were mundane details. They didn't belong in a magical fantasy.

His hand cupped her breast, his finger circling her nipple. Then his thumb and finger squeezed gently, and the tension between her legs built again.

" 'Magical,' " he repeated. "Good word. That's how it felt when I saw you walking toward me."

She nodded, remembering.

Bathing suit wrapped in a beach towel, sandals dangling from one finger, toes flirting with the lapping waves, she'd been walking into the sun. Her sunglasses were forgotten back at the restaurant, so her eyes squinted to see who was coming toward her. Feeling a little tipsy, more than a little self-conscious about being, for the first time in her life, naked in a public place. But everyone was; that's why she'd taken off her bikini. That, and the same wine-induced courage that had led her to venture onto a nude beach.

Already a few people had strolled past her, exchanging casual greetings, but she'd felt something different when this man came toward her out of the sunshine. A kind of spark, an energy that seemed to arc between them. Cretan magic.

As he'd moved closer, she realized how tall he was. So tall he made her feel almost petite, an unusual feeling for a girl who was five-foot-ten in bare feet. Then he stopped in front of her, head blocking the sun, and for the first time she saw him clearly. Her heart pounded as fast as if she'd jogged a mile under the hot sun. He was a statue of a Greek god come to life—except with sexy dreads and much better endowed!

Now his voice was a mesmerizing murmur as he said, "It was as if you were coming toward me out of a dream."

Yes, the whole afternoon, since she'd finished the second carafe of wine at that long, lazy, outdoor lunch, had the feel of a dream. Every girl's erotic fantasy. And yet, the body beneath her was hard and sweaty, her knees were beginning to tremble from tiredness, the scent in her nostrils was one her imagination couldn't possibly have conjured.

This was real.

Deep inside, her muscles convulsed and she tightened around him.

He groaned, a rough, masculine sound that made her clench again.

He stroked his fingers down the center of her body. Chin, throat, between her collarbones. Tracing her cleavage, gliding to her navel. And below. She arched back, the movement thrusting her hips forward.

He surged upward, catching her off guard as he plunged deep, and she cried out.

"They'll hear you," he warned.

Still, she couldn't hold back a moan of pleasure.

"What are they doing now? The people on the beach?" he demanded.

How could she focus on anything but the sensations he was creating? "One of the gay guys—"

She gasped and pressed a hand to her mouth as he gripped her hips and pulled her down, tight against him. "He's reading aloud to the other."

"What's he reading?"

She gave a surprised laugh. "My vision's not that good."

His fingers teased the curls between her thighs. "Your imagination is. Tell me what he's reading."

"I, uh . . ."

He twisted and twined her curls around his fingers, reminding her of a scene from a book her best friend's sister had loaned her when she was thirteen. A classic, the girl had assured her, then giggled and said that, all the same, she'd better hide it where her parents wouldn't find it.

His fingers drifted lower and her words came out in little gasps as she panted for breath. "It's *Lady Chatterley's Lover*, except he's changing it, because they're gay. He's saying it's Lord Chatterley who's having an affair with the gamekeeper. Oh, sorry, do you know the book?"

"Saw the movie. Sexy."

"There's a scene where the gamekeeper threads flowers into his lover's, um, hair." Okay, she might be sexy this afternoon, but she couldn't bring herself to say the word "pubic" aloud.

All the same, he seemed to catch her meaning. "No flowers. Just fingers." As he spoke, two of those strong fingers pressed gently against her clitoris.

"Fingers are—" She gasped at his touch, at the pressure building inexorably within her. "Fingers are good."

"Forget the beach," he commanded. "Look at us now. Look at how we fit together."

She turned her gaze downward, but her eyes, shocked by the transition from sunlight to shade, were momentarily blind. Disoriented, the only sensation she trusted was the solid heat of the man beneath her. Inside her.

But that was sensation, not . . . sense. What was she doing, making love—for the third time—with a man she'd just met? A man whose name she didn't know.

This was crazy. What had happened to sensible Suzie?

Yet, enchantment was in the air, and she was powerless to resist.

"Hey," he said softly. "You with me?"

Her eyes had adjusted to the darkness again, and she looked down at their bodies. "Oh yeah."

Long reddish-gold tendrils of hair dangled down, glowing even in the dim light, against her breasts. High, small breasts, almost white where her bikini normally covered them, compared to her holiday tan.

Contrasts.

Even her darkest tan was pale compared to his skin.

Her attention focused on the center, the place where their bodies came together. The golden curls of her pubic hair tangled with his black ones. She'd never been with a dark-skinned man before, never seen how beautiful the contrasts could be.

"Stop thinking," he whispered.

As if he'd clicked a switch, her brain shut off. All that was left was her body. A body that was pure sensation, nothing more, nothing less.

She savored the intoxicating musk of their lovemaking threading through the tangy Cretan scent. Her lips were open, gasping for air, moaning her pleasure, and on those lips she tasted the salt of her own sweat and the deeper, darker musk of his kisses.

Easing herself up, she watched as her body slid free of him, reveling in the sight of the rigid shaft that rose from his curly hair. She'd never seen anything so utterly male in her life.

Then she slid down again, engulfing him, feeling his length and breadth fill her to capacity, thrilling at the way her body opened to take him in. Glorying in the friction, the tension of his flesh sliding against hers, pressing deep into her core.

The sensations twined together, demanding her response, and inside her the pressure built, collecting itself and coiling tight, and tighter.

Suzanne squeezed her thighs together, clenched her internal muscles. She fought against the inevitable, but he was moving faster now and she couldn't hold back, she had to move with him. She whimpered with tension, pleasure, the need for release, the desire to capture and hold the moment forever.

He arched and cried out. His climax exploded into her, demanding her response. As he pumped, she threw back her head, shut her eyes, and the coil of tension sprang free, unwinding in waves that crashed against him.

Her body dissolved, melted, began to collapse, but his hands held her upright.

Slowly, she opened her eyes, to see the beach. Her head was spinning, her vision blurry, but still she could see sunbathers glancing around, turning to look up. She ducked quickly, feeling even dizzier.

"They heard us," she whispered, knowing her whole body was blushing as his hands loosed their grip and she slid bonelessly down to cover him.

He was still inside her as her eyelids drooped and sleep claimed her.

Everything after the cave had to be an anticlimax, Jaxon Navarre thought, as he and his sexy blonde emerged from the darkness and started down the goat trail to the beach. They were walking, step by step, back to reality.

Inevitable, but awkward. Easier to have gone when she fell asleep, but Jax wasn't a guy who'd leave a woman alone and vulnerable.

Not that he could imagine his blonde being vulnerable. She was the most no-holds-barred lover he'd ever had. And he'd had more than his fair share.

Yeah, finding sex had never been a problem. Finding a woman who didn't see him as some stupid stereotype was a different issue. He'd had girls throw themselves at him to prove they weren't prejudiced, to taste the exotic, to find out whether black guys really were better hung. They'd wanted him because he was the captain of his high school basketball team, then of his college team—quite a feat for a guy who was only six-foot-three—and now they wanted him because he was going to be a lawyer. A successful, rich one too, if he stuck to his plan.

This woman was different, though. She knew nothing about him, not even his name, and there'd been none of that artificial "Oh, are you black? Honest, I hadn't noticed" crap.

Too bad he couldn't pack her up in his duffel bag and take her home to San Fran.

He chuckled. Yeah, like that'd ever work. He would start articles with a very, very high-powered law firm next week, and he'd be on the line to prove himself. No sweat, though. He'd met every test so far, and he would meet this one too.

Tuning in to his surroundings, he saw they'd just emerged from a thicket of scrubby little trees that separated the nude beach from the next one over. He stopped and turned to his companion with a rueful grin. "Hell. Time to put our clothes on."

She swept a bold glance down, then up, his body. "Pity."

Juggling her towel, she tried to step into the bottom of her green bikini, and lost her balance. She would have tumbled if he hadn't caught her shoulders.

Staring into her flushed face, he thought again how gorgeous she was. With her striking features, cloud of wavy golden hair, small breasts perched high on a sleek, slender body, he was almost ready to believe she was a mermaid come to land for one afternoon to weave a spell around him.

Except, his mermaid definitely had legs and was having trouble finding them right now. And those pretty breasts were blushing with something that looked a lot like sunburn. "Are you okay?"

She tossed her hair back and almost lost her balance again. "Sure. Well, maybe a little drunk on wine and sun and sex."

"Wine? I missed out on wine?"

"At lunch. You have to have wine at lunch on Crete. At least on your last day." She gave him a dazzling smile.

That smile was a beauty, but her green eyes looked a little unfocused. The beginning of a hangover?

Or just too much sex? His own legs, legs that could play every quarter of a b-ball game without faltering, felt rubbery.

He took her towel and held her arm as she struggled into her bikini. She had trouble with the halter top, fumbling with the ties at the back. He turned her around, scooped her hair out of the way, and fastened her up. A bow, on a special gift. Too bad he wasn't unwrapping her rather than wrapping her back up. He buried his nose in the nape of her neck, and breathed in the scent of peaches and sex.

Whoa! He was getting horny again. Quickly, he stepped into his own bathing suit.

When he offered her his arm, she slipped her hand through, and they began to walk again.

"You said it's your last day?" he asked, not sure if he was glad or sorry. An afternoon like this couldn't have been repeated, could it?

"Yeah. Home tomorrow. How 'bout you?"

"I have a couple more days." He'd let a law school pal persuade him to come on this holiday, though he hadn't seen much of Chase since his buddy'd hooked up with that sexy redhead on the long trip over.

"My hotel's jush . . . just up there." She pointed.

She'd slurred her words. He frowned, thinking of the sun-flush on her skin, wondering how much wine she'd drunk. Earlier, she'd seemed in control, but now . . . Christ, he hadn't taken advantage of her, had he?

He tugged her to a stop and turned her to face him. "Are you all right?"

"Wonderful!"

"And, you're okay about this afternoon?"

"Oh yes! I," she announced firmly, "am sexy."

He chuckled. "That's the truth, woman."

"I am a sexy *woman*."

Or a sexy mermaid, he thought. "So, no regrets?"

"No way."

He'd been right all along. She was every man's wet dream—a gorgeous, uninhibited, sexy gal who knew exactly what she was doing.

They stood staring at each other for a long moment, and Jax wondered if she'd ask for his name, his number. His ego wished she would; his brain said he didn't need the complication.

"So, I guess this is it," he said tentatively.

She nodded, then giggled and held out her hand. "I forgot to say thank you."

Thank you? "Uh, you too." He took her hand gently, but she pumped his in a businesslike handshake. She was making it easy, but he couldn't let it go at that. He kept hold of that slender hand and squeezed it. "It's been great. Like . . . the best dream I could imagine."

She nodded. "Dream. Yes."

"We should keep it like that, right?" he probed.

"Mmm-hmm. Perfect dream." She yawned widely. "Time to go back to sleep."

And with nothing more—no kiss, no good-bye—she turned and walked a little unsteadily, but with hips boldly swaying, the last steps to her hotel.

Jax stared after her as she disappeared through the open door into the dark lobby.

Weird.

But then, the whole afternoon had been weird in the extreme.

As he turned to go, he realized he was still carrying her towel. He should leave it at the desk of her hotel, but . . . He snorted and shook his head.

Damn it, he wanted the souvenir.

1

"So, tell all, Suze." Jenny leaned forward, elbows on the table, pink flamingo earrings dancing. "What's the best sex *you* ever had?"

Around their outside table at Las Margaritas restaurant, three flushed female faces grinned at Suzanne.

It was Jenny Yuen who'd launched the topic, with her description of hot sex in her boyfriend Pete's double Jacuzzi. "It was the best sex of my life!" she'd exclaimed, brown eyes flashing. "I swear, Korean men beat Chinese, hands down."

"Ssh," Suzanne had said, used to the fact that Jenny's personality was twice the size of her petite body, but wishing she didn't always have to be quite so out there.

She wished she'd kept quiet, though, when Jenny turned the question on her.

"I, um . . ." Best sex? Suzanne barely suppressed a nervous giggle. That would have to be with her dream lover.

Jenny rolled her eyes, turned a pink sweatshirted back to Suzanne, and said to Rina Goldberg, "So, what's the best sex you've ever had?"

"Not with Marty, that's for sure." Tonight, at the Awesome Foursome's regular Monday dinner, Rina had already told them she'd called it quits with the man she'd been seeing for the last several months. Her heart definitely didn't seem broken.

"The best sex," she murmured. Looking like a gypsy with a fringed burgundy shawl over her usual black clothing, she pulled a wayward lock of curly black hair behind a multi-ringed ear as she sipped her second margarita and considered the question.

The others waited, munching from the platter of nachos locos—laden with everything yummy and fattening you could possibly imagine—and working on their own second margaritas.

Rina began to smile, and nodded her head firmly. "Yeah, I know *exactly*. The summer I turned eighteen, I went to a music school in Banff. There was this other student, Giancarlo, from Italy. He was a pianist and he had the most awesome hands."

The others oohed and aahed as Rina described the things Giancarlo had done with those hands, including making her come three times in a row atop the grand piano in a student rehearsal room.

Somewhere during the recitation, a third round of margaritas got ordered for everyone but Suzanne, who had a strict two-drink limit.

When Rina finished, Jenny turned to Ann Montgomery. "Your turn," she said, talking around a guacamole-and-sour-cream laden chip.

"You know I'm a conventional gal." But Ann's eyes were twinkling. "I'm not much into Jacuzzis or pianos. I like big, comfy beds. And a man who wears a tie."

"A tie? Bo-ring," Jenny scoffed.

"Not when there are four of them, all silk, and they're tying you to a four-poster bed."

"Bondage?" Suzanne frowned. "Ann, that's—"

"No, no!" Ann held up a hand to stop her. "I totally consented. And they were tied really loosely. He made slow, beautiful love to me, and all I could do was respond."

Jenny gave a skeptical frown. "I can't imagine you surrendering control to anyone. You're the control freak to end all control freaks."

Ann stuck her tongue out, then shrugged. "Okay, I concede your point. And yes, it surprised me too." She smoothed her short brown hair and straightened her shoulders inside the jacket of her navy suit. "I've never come so hard in my life. It was a little . . . scary."

As Suzanne glanced around the table, she thought how lucky she was to have found these women. They'd met last year at an introductory yoga course. The bonding began when, after the second lesson, they decided food, chat and alcohol were far better tension relievers than contorting their bodies into pretzel shapes. The four didn't have a lot in common, but that made the conversations even more stimulating. Strong ties of friendship had formed, and now the Foursome members were deeply loyal to each other and their Monday nights.

She stopped feeling lucky when Jenny turned to her with an evil grin. "Didn't think we'd forget you, did you, Suze?"

Oh God, after her friends' sexy tales, how pitiful to have to confess that her own sex life ranged between boring and nonexistent.

Except for her cave-sex lover.

The thought sent a thrill of excitement coursing through her. She slugged back the last of her second margarita and took a deep breath.

"Remember me telling you how I treated myself to a week package deal on Crete, after my second year of university?" They nodded. "Okay then . . ." She closed her eyes, letting the scene form.

"It's my last afternoon. I'm walking along a beach and this

man comes toward me, and it's like we're both struck by lightning. Immediate chemistry."

She opened her eyes, and saw she had their rapt attention. "Did I mention"—she paused deliberately—"that this is a nude beach?"

"Suzie!" Rina gasped, heedless of the salsa tumbling from her chip to the table.

"Our Suze on a nude beach?" Jenny said.

"We've established the man is nude," Ann said. "So get to the good stuff. What does this guy look like?"

"Tall, muscled, handsome. Absolutely perfect in, how shall I say this? Every dimension."

"In other words, he's hung," Jenny said, shoving up her sleeves and resting her pointy elbows on the table.

"You can say that again! I've never seen—" Suzanne broke off, then continued in a lower voice. "Yeah, definitely hung. Anyhow, then, somehow, we're holding hands, walking together, not even talking. Me, not talking. How weird is that?" She reached for her margarita glass and brought it to her lips, only to find it empty.

"Go on," Ann prompted, shrugging out of her suit jacket and leaning forward.

"We follow a path that leads uphill, through scrubby bushes. There's a zillion pretty little wildflowers dotting the ground."

"Skip the travelogue," Jenny demanded. "Like Ann said, cut to the good stuff."

"I'm shooting him these sideways glances, checking him out. And he's getting aroused." She grinned. "What a turn-on."

"Oh man!" Jenny said.

"We come across a cave. We step inside the mouth and suddenly we're kissing. He lifts me up, I hook my legs around his waist and we make love right there, standing up."

"Oh, my, God!" Rina fanned herself with the fringed end of her shawl.

"It's fast, explosive." And she'd had an orgasm for the first time in her life. Not just an orgasm but a mind-shattering one.

"Afterwards, we lie down on my beach towel and explore each other's bodies with our hands, lips, tongues. He makes me come with his mouth and I, you know . . ."

"Give him a blow job," Jenny finished, at the same moment Ann said, "Perform fellatio."

Suzanne felt her cheeks grow hotter. "He stops me before he comes, then he's inside me so hard and fast and deep, and it feels so amazing that I come again before he does." She cleared her throat and fiddled with her margarita glass, almost wishing she'd broken her two-drink rule, even as she remembered the reason she never would.

"Jesus, girl, I didn't know you had it in you," Jenny marveled, reaching for another cheese-coated chip and shoving it into the guacamole.

Suzanne closed her eyes, remembering watching as their bodies joined, separated, joined again. "Did I mention he's black?"

"You mean African-American," Ann corrected.

"Or African-African," Suzanne said. "Or from England. Lots of English people holiday in Greece. No accent, though. Yeah, probably American, you're right." Damn, doing this analysis had thrown her out of the moment, away from Crete and back to the restaurant.

"But definitely gorgeous, eh?" Jenny said. "And hung."

Suzanne nodded. "Yup. He was this delicious shade of dark chocolate and he had short dreads. His face was so striking. A sexy little goatee. His eyes were chocolate too, and sparkly. Vibrant."

"Wow," Rina breathed. "A chocolate man. How yummy."

"He was." Even now, she could remember that taste.

"And of course he was a fantastic lover." Rina sighed dreamily.

"He was a stranger, yet sex with him felt like the most intimate act I'd ever committed. For a moment I even found myself wishing our lovemaking would create a child." Suzanne gave a shiver. "Is that insane or what? Especially given my, uh, rather traditional feelings about marriage and kids."

"Traditional!" Jenny hooted. "Try archaic. Any woman whose deepest aspiration is to marry Ward Cleaver from *Leave It to Beaver* . . ."

"Well, he was awfully good to the Beaver," Rina said softly, wickedly, and this time they all hooted.

Ann sobered quickly, though. "Suze, what you said about creating a child? You did use a condom, right?"

Suzanne swallowed hard. She hadn't meant to reveal that particular bit of idiocy. "I was on the pill, but I know it was utterly stupid. I plead insanity. Plus too much wine, and I'd been out in the sun for hours and had sunstroke. That's why I—" She broke off abruptly, realizing she hadn't told them the rest of it.

Rina said, "Is that why you have a two-drink limit?" just as Ann demanded, "Why what?" and Jenny said, "So what was this demon lover's name anyhow?" The three of them burst out laughing, then turned challenging gazes on Suzanne.

And now they'd know what a complete idiot she was. She sighed, beckoned to a waitress in a red T-shirt, and said, "Could I have some ice water, please?" It was time to leave her fantasy cave, and come down to cold, hard Vancouver earth.

She waited until the waitress brought water for all of them, took a long, cold swallow, and spilled the truth. "Jen, I don't know his name. And I'll save all of you the trouble of asking the logical questions. The last thing I remember is falling asleep in his arms, in the cave. My memory picks up the next morning, in my hotel room, with the chambermaid and a doctor hovering. I had sunburn, heatstroke and felt like crap. I barely made my flight home. And . . ."

Another gulp of water, then she confessed the last bit in one long rush. "I'm not even surehewasreallyreal."

"Huh?" Jenny said, and Suzanne realized the other women wore baffled expressions. She'd spoken so quickly her words had all slurred together.

"I'm not sure he was real," she repeated flatly.

"But . . ." Ann frowned. "What are you talking about? You just told us what he looked like, everything you did together."

"I still dream about it every month or so." And, each time she did, she had an orgasm in her sleep. Way better orgasms than she'd ever had with any man other than her cave-sex lover.

She heaved a sigh of frustration. "Maybe it was just a dream in the first place. I'd drunk about a liter of wine. And yes, Rina, I've never had more than two drinks since then.

"Anyhow, wandering around in my alcoholic haze, I found that nude beach and felt so risqué, taking my clothes off." She thought of her own naïvety, and gave a snort. "Let's face it, it's more likely I fell asleep in the sun and fantasized the whole thing than that I had unprotected sex with a complete stranger."

For once, she seemed to have rendered her friends speechless.

Grimly she went on. "I've no idea how I got dressed again, or got back to the hotel."

"You don't remember saying good-bye to the nameless god?" Jenny asked.

Suzanne shook her head. "And if the whole thing really happened, we'd have had to say something, right? Like, good-bye, it's been a blast, let's leave it at that because we could never in a million years replicate the experience? That would make sense. I mean, he wouldn't exactly fit into my life. He's not the guy I want to marry and settle down with. I'm fine with everything"—especially those orgasmic dreams—"except not knowing if he was real."

"A dream lover," Rina breathed. "How romantic."

"Yeah, but how could you be fine with letting him go?" Jenny's brow was wrinkled. "If he was real, I mean. Maybe you couldn't—what was that amazingly literate phrase?—'replicate the experience'? But maybe you could, Suze. Wouldn't that be better than hot dreams?"

"Weren't you listening?" Suzanne said impatiently. "Even if he was real, I never knew anything about him."

"It's hard to track down a person when you have no information," Ann agreed.

"Hmm." Jenny drummed her fingernails—hot-pink, decorated with rhinestones—against the table. "How about a personals ad?"

"Oh sure, Jen," Rina said, "like there's any chance the chocolate man lives in Vancouver."

Jenny groaned. "Duh. Not the Vancouver paper, you twit, the internet."

Suzanne's breath caught. She used e-mail all the time, and the internet for veterinary research, but she'd never thought of using the worldwide web to try to track down her one-time, maybe lover.

Ann frowned. "That could be dangerous. Freaks and weirdos hang out on the internet."

Jenny rolled her eyes. "Suze wouldn't use her own internet address. We'll get her a free account with Hotmail or Yahoo. Anonymous. So what if she gets some flaky replies to the ad? She just ignores them."

"The odds of him seeing the ad are incredibly slim, even if he does exist," Ann pointed out. "This does *not* sound like the kind of man who needs the internet to find a date." Frowning, she ran her fingers through her hair, then suddenly gave an impish grin. "Still, there's nothing lost in trying."

Jenny and Ann were talking like this had gone beyond the

hypothetical. Suzanne's heart thumped nervously. She turned to Rina, who was staring off into space. "What do you have to say about this?"

"Hmm?" Rina said dreamily. "You know, sometimes we let people go out of our lives too easily."

Suzanne groaned. "This is *not* a good idea. I can't imagine marrying this guy, so what's the point?"

"Are you so sure he couldn't be your Mr. Cleaver?" Ann asked.

"I . . . Oh, come on, he was sexy and . . . outrageous. Definitely not husband material. I want a steady, reliable guy like my dad and my brother-in-law. Besides, I'm still in vet school, I'm nowhere near ready to settle down."

"Yeah," Jenny said, "so it's a perfect time to take a walk on the wild side. For once in your life."

"For twice, you mean," Ann, the stickler for accuracy, said.

"For twice," Suzanne echoed. The idea was tempting. Or maybe that was the second margarita talking. "I'll think about it. But if I do it, you guys have to help me."

Jax was standing at his secretary's desk discussing a file, when her phone rang. Caitlin answered, then put her hand over the receiver. She looked like a cheeky elf with her trendy orange-tipped hair, freckles and wide grin. "Your wife."

"Ex," he corrected automatically. Caitlin always teased that, because he rarely dated, she forgot he was divorced. "I'll take it in my office."

He closed the door to his closet-sized office, slid into his chair and picked up the phone. His marriage to Tonya might have been a mistake, but their hard-won friendship was something he valued. "Hey, you. What's up?"

"Just calling to say happy anniversary."

"Ouch," he said mildly. If they'd stayed married, it would

have been three years on Sunday. "Sorry I didn't send a card, but I figured Benjamin wouldn't appreciate it."

"He's cool. Especially now our marriage has lasted a whole month longer than yours and mine did."

They'd finally reached the point where the teasing was affectionate, even if occasionally barbed on her side.

"Double ouch," he said. So she and Benjamin had made seven whole months.

"So, I'm curious. Did you even pause a moment in your work to remember it was our anniversary?"

He smiled into the phone. Yup, there was a work barb. But it was kind of cute that, while she was happily married to another man, she didn't want her ex to forget her.

"Yeah," he confessed. "Found myself thinking about our honeymoon. Sonoma, the wineries, the hot air balloon ride. It was a lot of fun." It was also the last time he'd taken a week, much less a weekend, off work since he'd become an associate at Jefferson Sparks.

Actually, it had only been the second time he'd taken a holiday since he'd graduated from law school. The first time had been that trip to Crete with Chase, before he started articles.

Crete. Just the word conjured up unforgettable images.

"Yeah, it was great," Tonya said.

What? Oh right, he'd mentioned their honeymoon. Man, he was lucky she didn't know where that train of thought had led him.

"That balloon ride was awesome," she said.

"And our wedding night wasn't? That sounds like another ouch sent in my direction."

She chuckled.

And the truth was, while he remembered the balloon ride very well, he had only the vaguest recollection of making love on their wedding night, compared to that crazy afternoon in Crete. He remembered every single detail of that lovemaking.

No. Sex. It was just sex.

Sex so hot it had him squirming in his chair.

"Jax? You pouting, babe? Honest, I didn't mean to bad-mouth your skills in bed. The sex was always good with us, wasn't it?"

"Good?" There was a damn-with-faint-praise word to deflate a guy's dick.

Sure, once they'd been married a few weeks they'd started squabbling, mostly over the long hours he worked, and the bedroom became more a place for making war than love. But in the beginning, the sex had been pretty damned great.

He remembered when he'd finally given in and let his mom introduce him to her neighbor, the one who was taking cooking classes and was always looking for people to experiment on. The attraction had been immediate and mutual. There'd been lots of nights he and Tonya had planned dinner or a movie, taken one look at each other and ended up in bed instead.

Funny thing was, he couldn't call to mind any details of those nights either.

"Jax? You hang up on me?"

"I'm here. Seems to me, when we first got together, the sex was better than good." Crap, could he sound any more huffy?

"Ooh, bad word choice. Yeah, I guess it was. It's a while back, but I do remember some bells and whistles. But then we got married, and work came first for you."

Another barb.

He shot back. "You were working too, with all those cooking courses, those sous-chef jobs."

She paused, and when she spoke again, her tone wasn't snippy, but sad. "Yeah, but my work wasn't more important to me than our marriage."

And to that, there was no answer, because she was right. She'd been able to juggle career and marriage. He'd learned he couldn't handle both, and he'd had to choose. His career came first. Always had, always would.

"Oh shit, Jax, this really isn't why I called. I didn't mean to get into another rehash. You're doing what you want to do, and I've got my bells and whistles with Benjamin, and thank God, this time they've actually survived marriage. So you 'n' me are both happy, the past is behind us and I really do want us to be friends."

"Me too." He'd failed at marriage, and he hated to fail. He ought to at least be able to succeed at being Tonya's friend.

"So, let me tell you my real reason for calling." Now her voice rippled with excitement. "You want a new client?"

"Always," he said promptly, straightening and grabbing a pad of paper and a pen.

"God, Jax. You sound so . . . hungry."

"I am. Bringing in clients is one of the criteria for partnership."

"I know, believe me I know." But this time her voice was teasing, without the barb. "So I figured I'd do my bit to contribute to the game plan."

"You know someone who needs a lawyer?"

"Yeah. Me."

"You?"

"It's time. I've been looking around. Found a perfect place, a price I can afford, so . . . ." She gave a shaky laugh. "Yes, I'm doing it!"

She was going to open her own restaurant.

Damn, she wasn't a real client. Not for him, in the high-powered litigation department. He represented corporations fighting product liability suits, antitrust charges and so on.

Fuck. What an asshole he was, for reacting this way.

"Jesus, Tonya, that's great. Congratulations." This was her dream. She'd worked for it and he really was happy for her. "How can I help?"

"Oh, all that corporate stuff. You work with corporations, right?"

Had she ever really listened when he talked about his work? Or had he ever found the time to try to explain it to her, beyond telling her about all those billable hours he needed to put in?

"Space and equipment leases," she was saying, "contracts with employees and suppliers. Oh, and before I do all that, of course I'll actually need to incorporate."

He was scribbling as she talked, adding other tasks she hadn't mentioned. "Most of this work is done by paralegals, so we can keep the bill down."

"Thanks. And you can have dinner on the house any time. Bring a date too."

Yeah, like that was going to happen. Didn't sound to him like the recipe for a relaxing meal.

Not that he had time to date, anyhow.

Ever since he was old enough to understand the sacrifices his mom was making for him, he'd been determined to succeed. To make her proud, justify all she'd done for him.

If he stuck to work, ignored all distractions, he'd make partner in another year or two. Then, maybe, senior partner.

Just the thought of it made his heart pump. An immigrant kid from Jamaica, raised by a single mom who worked two minimum-wage jobs, becoming senior partner at one of the most prestigious law firms in San Francisco. Now there was a dream he could buy into!

But this was Tonya's day, not his. "When the incorporation comes through, I'm buying you a bottle of Dom Perignon."

"Sonoma bubbly will do me just fine. I'm a California girl and I absolutely refuse to get all pretentious."

"Not going to serve French wine at that restaurant of yours?"

"No way. I'm going to focus on local products. The cuisine'll be a blend of everything that's gone into the making of California. Kind of like me."

Tonya had been born here, but her grandparents truly were an ethnic mix, with roots in Africa, China, Scotland and Mexico.

"Jax?" Her voice was breathy with excitement. "I just thought of a name. What about 'Made in California?' "

"Sounds good to me."

"Gotta go. I'm going to call Benjamin and see what he thinks of the name." As always, there was a little fizz in her voice—a sexual one—when she said her husband's name.

He envied her those damned bells and whistles.

Caitlin tapped on his door, opened it and poked her orange-tipped head through. "Your next client's here."

Tonya had Benjamin; he had a client.

Bells and whistles? Yeah, sure. That'd be the day.

2

The Awesome Foursome had decided to hold their ad-drafting meeting at Suzanne's place, rather than a restaurant.

Her apartment was a renovated garage at the back of her parents' yard in Kerrisdale. Furnished with hand-me-downs and garage sale bargains, the cozy space was divided into a small eating-and-living area, an even smaller bedroom-and-office and a closet-sized bathroom. Suzanne loved its compactness, plus how it allowed her to have both closeness to and independence from her parents.

Tonight, though, she could have done with it being about a hundred miles rather than a hundred yards removed from her mom and dad's kitchen window.

She was nervous enough about what she and the girls were contemplating; she definitely didn't need parental scrutiny. Of course, chances were, after drinking a bunch of wine and tossing out a few silly ideas, they'd abandon the whole project.

Pausing in the act of opening the Yellowtail cabernet sauvignon Ann had brought, Suzanne glanced out her own window to see her mother standing on the back porch, saying hello to Rina.

Rina, in black leggings and gauzy black tunic top, with a red scarf draped around her neck, was a gypsy in an English country garden. She handed two pizza boxes to Suzanne's mom.

What on earth? Was she giving away their dinner?

Ah. Rina was rooting around in her tote bag and finally pulling out a brochure. For the Pacific Northwest Opera, no doubt. She played second clarinet, as well as teaching clarinet and piano to students of all ages.

She passed the brochure to Suzanne's mom and retrieved the pizzas just as Jenny joined them, bearing a pan that hopefully contained her decadent double-chocolate brownies. The three chatted cozily—and far too long for Suzanne's peace of mind. Jenny in particular was not noted for verbal restraint, and the last thing Suzanne wanted was for her mother to know about tonight's agenda.

With a touch of desperation, Suzanne went to the door, waved the wine bottle and called, "Anyone ready for a drink?"

That did it. Her friends said quick good-byes, and hurried over. Rina said, "Your mom's going to get tickets for PNO's next concert."

"Great." Suzanne took one of the Martini's pizza boxes. "You didn't tell her what we're doing tonight?"

"You betcha!" Jenny said loudly. "Told her we were pimping her daughter out to a Greek god." Then, "Jeez, Suzie, give us credit for having a little discretion."

Ann came in from the other room. "I'm hungry. I've laid out some deli salads. Would you guys get a move on?"

Jenny opened the pizza boxes. "I got a chicken-spinach-feta and a pepperoni-onion-mushroom."

"Good," Rina said, "I can eat everything but the crust."

She was always on a diet, saying she was too fat—though as far as Suzanne could see, what she hid under all those layers of clothes was the kind of curvy body men drooled over.

"And I brought retsina." Rina extracted a bottle from her

tote, eliciting a chorus of "yucks." She shook her head. "We don't have to drink it all, just spill a few drops. A libation to the Greek gods, so they'll bless this enterprise."

Suzanne gave her the corkscrew and Rina opened the bottle and poured a bit into all their glasses. They flicked a few drops around. Melody and Zorro, two of Suzanne's three cats, eagerly darted forward, took one sniff, then retreated, whiskers twitching in disgust.

"My feelings exactly," Ann said. She lifted her glass. "Okay, girls, a toast. Down the hatch. Then we can have some decent Aussie cab."

"To snaring a Greek god," Jenny toasted, and they all clicked glasses.

Ann popped a couple of pills into her mouth before drinking.

"You okay?" Suzanne asked.

"Just a headache. Missed lunch, stressful day." She grinned. "And it's no fun writing a sexy ad with a headache."

"You work too hard."

"Don't I know it." She pointed toward the door, where she'd dropped her briefcase on the way in. "Yeah, I can leave the office at six. But only if I lug about three hours work home with me."

"Sorry. God, Ann, you shouldn't be wasting your time on this silly stuff, then having to work to all hours."

Ann shook her head vigorously, then winced. "I needed a break anyhow. Besides, if a girl can't make time for her best friends, there's something seriously wrong with her."

Suzanne reached over to hug her. Then they all settled around the coffee table. After the first few nibbles and sips, they got down to work, tossing out suggestions.

"Notes," Ann said, putting down a half-eaten wedge of pizza and scrambling over to pull a legal pad from her briefcase.

Soon she was busy scrawling, crossing out, reading back. Finally, when they were into a second round of brownies—for all but Rina who'd only nibbled on her first one—she cleared her throat. "All right, children, I think this is it." She held up the pad and began to read, putting on a breathy, sexy voice that was completely unlike her normal speaking voice.

" 'Are you the man who shared sizzling sex with a hot blonde in the cave above the nude beach on Crete four years ago? If you feel like another erotic adventure, drop me a line. Be sure to tell me what you remember about that afternoon, so I'll know it's really you.' "

"Escapade," Jenny said. "Rather than 'adventure.' Comes from 'escape'—i.e., to escape restraint, inhibition."

"I keep forgetting you're a writer," Ann said, scribbling the change.

Jenny was a freelance journalist who scraped together a living researching and writing articles, mostly on human interest subjects.

"How flattering," Jen responded. "Just 'cause I'm little and wear pink, doesn't mean I'm a bimbette."

"I know, I know. It's just a surprise when you pull out the big words."

Jen leaped to her feet, swatted Ann's shoulder, then said, "Let's boot up the computer."

Ann handed the pad to Suzanne. "Final proofread?"

Suzanne stared down at the words. "Erotic escapade." That was so not her. And yet, they perfectly described the afternoon on Crete. Could she be that woman again? Did she want to be?

She held up a hand in a "time-out" gesture. "Hold on. This has been fun, but we're not really going to do it, right?"

"I did *not* skip out of work early, just for you to bail on us," Ann said.

"Suzie, we're just placing the ad," Rina said softly. "What're the odds of actually finding the man? And if by some wild chance he actually does respond, then you can decide what you want to do."

True. If he didn't answer the ad, it didn't prove he didn't exist. It didn't mean her afternoon of magic—of being the sexiest woman in the world—hadn't really occurred. And if, by some miracle, he did answer . . . Then the next step would be up to her.

Suzanne squared her shoulders. "Let's do it."

They crowded into her teeny bedroom and clustered round the computer that sat on a small desk by the window. Mouse, her little grey cat, who'd been sleeping on the keyboard as usual, jumped up. He shot her a dirty look and stalked out the door. Even though the bedroom window faced away from her parents' house, Suzanne pulled the curtains firmly shut.

"Jenny, you're the computer whiz. Do your stuff."

Her friend clicked and tapped deftly, then said, "All right, Suzie-Q, what's your alias?"

"Um . . . How about 'islandgirl?' "

"Cute," Rina said.

"Dull, dull, dull," Jenny said. "It makes me think of that movie *You've Got Mail*. Wasn't her e-mail name 'shopgirl'? Can you think of any better way of saying 'hello, I'm really, really boring'?"

But she *was* boring. Wholesome, traditional. She was a student who lived in her parents' backyard, shared her apartment with three cats, and dreamed of one day being a modern-day version of June Cleaver.

Of course, on that enchanted afternoon her behavior had been so out of character, so . . . " 'Outrageous,' " she said, her voice coming out husky, almost sexy.

"Now you're talking!" Jenny tapped away at the keyboard. "Oh damn, it's taken. The good ones are always taken. How about adding a number to it? We can try 'outrageous1,' 'outrageous2.' "

" '69,' " Suzanne said, then clapped a hand over her mouth

as her friends howled. "No, honestly, I didn't mean that. My evil twin made me say it."

"Your sexy twin," Jenny said. "It's perfect. Now, if only someone else hasn't thought of it." She tapped away then pumped her fist into the air. "All right! Suzanne Brennan, you are now officially 'outrageous69.' "

Before Suzanne knew it, the ad was placed and her friends were splitting up the leftovers and heading out.

By the time she'd tidied up the kitchen, Suzanne was having serious third thoughts. What was she thinking, pretending to be some outrageous, sexy, sizzling gal?

She was a twenty-four-year-old vet student who had her life mapped out. She was a firm believer in setting long- and short-term goals, and so far that approach had worked beautifully for her. Her summer and part-time work as a veterinarian's assistant not only paid her tuition, but assured her she'd chosen the right career, and even promised a job when she finally graduated.

She knew exactly what her husband would be like, because her dad and brother-in-law provided the perfect role models. Mr. Cleaver, as her friends jokingly called him, would have a job he loved—a meaningful job—but would work regular hours and put his wife and kids first, always.

Her friends teased her about being so old-fashioned, but Suzanne didn't care. She valued security and truly wasn't a risk taker. That's why this whole internet thing was so crazy.

Crazy, yet . . . kind of exciting.

Yes, it was exciting to think she might again experience amazing sex with a stunningly handsome man.

Then she shook her head. Let's face it, great sex and Suzanne Brennan didn't go together. In her cave-sex dream, she became a sexy woman, but somehow that image of herself never carried beyond the dream. She'd had a couple of lovers in the last few years, but every time things got hot and heavy, she just kind of . . . locked up.

The word "escapade" came from escape, as in to let go of inhibitions, Jenny had said.

If her Greek god really did exist and she found him, would she be able to escape her stupid inhibitions with him?

What if she couldn't? That was a scary thought.

After pulling on cotton pajamas, she stopped and stared at the computer screen. Would there be any answers yet? Why had she promised the girls not to look until next Monday?

Man, it was stressful, placing a personals ad. Kind of like throwing a party. What if no one came? What if too many people came? What if weird people showed up? What if the right guy didn't?

Expecting one man, somewhere in the world, to see and respond to her ad was sillier than casting a fishing line into the ocean in hopes of luring one particular salmon.

If that very special fish even existed. . . .

Jaxon yawned and rotated his head, trying to ease the ache in his neck and shoulders that had settled in an hour ago. What kind of guy had nothing better to do than sit at his desk doing research at eleven o'clock on Saturday night?

Answer: A lawyer who wanted to score brownie points with the senior partner. So here he was, spending his weekend researching a complicated point of antitrust law, so he could have a memo on Trent Jefferson's desk before Monday morning—a memo outlining a strong argument they could make to the charge that their client had violated the laws governing unfair competition.

Besides, what would he rather be doing? Sitting in a bar, making meaningless conversation? Twiddling his thumbs in front of a television? No, he was right where he wanted to be, plodding steadily forward on the fast track to success.

Plodding on the fast track. What was that, an oxymoron? Who cared? It was the life he'd chosen.

He stretched and took two steps to his office window. Outside, the city twinkled with moving lights. San Francisco was alive, but here on the thirtieth floor he was insulated from it. No sound reached his ears, and he viewed the world through tinted glass.

When had he last had a date? There'd been the lawyer he met at the continuing-ed course on intellectual property litigation. After they'd had to reschedule their first two dates, they'd both laughed ruefully and decided it wasn't worth the effort. That had been . . . what? Three or four months ago?

A date. He couldn't even organize a date. Yeah, he knew he couldn't afford the time for a relationship, but he wouldn't mind a date.

He chuckled at his reflection in the glass. "Fuck, man. What you really want is down-and-dirty sex." He was a physical guy, with physical needs. Putting in fourteen-hour workdays tired out his brain, but his body had a deep-down craving to get sweaty and satisfied.

Oh yeah, he was definitely horny. That dynamite blonde from Crete was back in his skull. Christ, it must have been, what? Four years? And it had only been one afternoon. Since then he'd fallen in love, been married, got divorced. But still, that blonde had a grip on him that had never let go. He thought of her at the oddest times, as well as the completely predictable ones like alone in his bed in the middle of the night.

Gazing down at San Francisco, he remembered how she'd stared out of the cave and down to the beach, describing what she saw. Her slim arrow of a body arched above him, those gold curls tumbling past her shoulders, and all the time he was buried to the hilt inside her. Burning with the desire to move, to make her shudder and moan, to find his release. But holding back, wanting the impossible, wanting to stay forever hard, forever inside this woman.

Even now, thinking about it, he was hard. The memory always had that effect on him. Even in the days when he and Tonya'd been making love daily, there'd been something extra-sexy about the thought of that afternoon on Crete. About that particular woman. He ran his hand down the front of his fly, remembering her touch.

Then he gave a growl of frustration and strode back to his desk. Where had he got to in his research?

He tried to force his attention back to the screen, but damn it, his brain wasn't functioning. What he wanted at this moment was to dream about hot sex in a cool cave.

He reached for the mouse, and gave in to his secret hobby.

In the time since he and Tonya had split up, he occasionally surfed the net, hunting for his sex goddess. He was a pro with internet research—enough to know his chances of locating her were slimmer than the odds of finding a needle in a haystack. The needle, at least, was actually there; diligence and persistence would turn it up. The woman existed, true, but she might not be in the haystack of the internet. The uncertainty somehow made the hunt even more compelling.

If he'd only asked her name, he'd have increased his chances a hundred percent. But at the time he hadn't wanted to know. She'd been a one-afternoon stand; the less he knew about her, the easier she'd be to forget.

What a pile of crap that had turned out to be.

With a combination of mouse clicks and keystrokes he Googled the words "Crete," "cave" and "sex."

Every time he did this he got hits: travel notes, personals ads, even the occasional erotic blog. He and his blonde weren't the only ones who'd indulged in cave sex on Crete. But the details and tone of the postings had never rung a bell, so he hadn't pursued any of the leads.

This time he skimmed the list of hits, clicking on one, then rejecting it, and going on to the next. Another sounded possible, so he followed the link to a personal ads website.

On his screen, words appeared.

Are you the man who shared sizzling sex with a hot blonde in the cave above the nude beach on Crete four years ago? If you feel like another erotic escapade, drop me a line. Be sure to tell me what you remember about that afternoon, so I'll know it's really you.

outrageous69

Adrenaline hit in a surge that had him leaping out of his chair. Goddamn! He thumped his fist against the desk. It was her!

Then practicality took over. *Maybe* it was her. His lover had definitely been a hot blonde, and the time frame was right. Why hadn't she given more details, like the color of his skin, the people on the beach below?

He sat down again, drumming his fingertips against the frame of his keyboard.

She hadn't given details because she wanted them to come from him, so she'd be sure of his identity. It could be dangerous for a woman placing an ad like this.

But then it could be dangerous for a woman walking off with a complete stranger to a cave in the hills. Having unprotected sex.

Yeah, like his hot blonde would worry about a little danger. She was gutsy, into excitement and adventure. Reckless. Outrageous. Outrageous69.

Sixty nine. Oh man, they'd sure shared some crazy fun.

His gaze snagged on the piles of paper, file folders and accordion files that littered his desk. What would she think of him now, with the brilliant but utterly conservative career he was so busily pursuing? She wanted a guy who was sexy, exciting, adventuresome. And he wasn't.

What he was was a lawyer obsessed with piling up more bill-able hours, impressing the partners, kowtowing to old clients and hustling new ones. Oh yeah, he could guess how out-rageous69 would view him. Sexy? Not a hope in hell.

Though his swollen cock was definitely ready and willing to perform.

Unable to resist the memories, he unzipped the fly of his jeans. She had stroked him with slender, deft fingers, and he'd felt huge in her hand.

Jax closed his eyes as his hand remembered her rhythm. She had stroked and teased, then she'd leaned down and all that sun-kissed hair had tumbled across his belly as she'd opened her lips and taken him in. She'd only managed to surround the first few inches of his length. But she'd compensated by caress-ing and licking, working her way down and back up, then down again, tonguing his balls until they tightened and clenched and he was ready to explode.

Then he'd grabbed her by the shoulders, pulled her away from him, thrust her onto her back. And he was on top of her, inside her, swallowing her cries with his mouth even as his own climax shrieked through him.

Oh shit!

Jax pulled his wet hand away from his body. It wasn't the first time he'd come, remembering her. But usually it happened in bed at night, or in the shower.

Thank God the office was deserted. Thank God he was wear-ing jeans rather than one of his good suits.

Praying the security guard wouldn't pick this moment for a surprise check, he stumbled on shaky legs to the men's room to clean up.

Back in his office, the message glowed at him from the com-puter screen.

He grinned and sat down in front of the keyboard.

3

Suzanne's friends had made her swear a vow in retsina not to check her outrageous69 e-mail until Monday afternoon. Then she was under strict instructions to print the replies unread and bring them to Maria's, the Greek restaurant the Awesome Foursome had chosen for dinner.

She could have cheated and they'd never have known. She was tempted many times, never more strongly than Saturday night when she had another orgasmic dream, but she resisted. For her, a promise, even a silly one, was a bond.

When she rushed home from the vet clinic on Monday and accessed her outrageous69 account, she was astonished to find almost fifty replies. "Don't people have anything better to do with their time?" she muttered as she clicked PRINT over and over again. Damn, she was going to be late for dinner.

As each new message came on screen, tantalizing words tempted her to stop and read: Hot time . . . sugarpie . . . most beautiful thing . . . caveman. She summoned her will power, averted her eyes, kept clicking PRINT.

Fuck me, baby!

"I don't think so, baby," she muttered. "Good old outrageous69 is a perv magnet." And what had she expected, with the wording her tipsy friends had come up with?

But her nerves zinged at the thought that, maybe, in those four dozen sheets of paper, she would find her mystery lover. Now that she actually held the replies in her hand, she was seriously tempted to flop down on her couch and read them.

"The girls would kill me." She stuffed the papers into a canvas tote and grabbed her car keys.

Ann was running late too, and they met on the street outside Maria's Taverna, under the blue-and-white awning. Ann ran a hand through her hair and said, "I swear, sometimes I wonder why I chose law. The clients are a pain, the partners are a bigger pain and the secretaries have chips on their shoulders the size of a Douglas fir."

"Bad day?"

Ann heaved a deep sigh. "Yeah, but what's new? One sort of highlight, though. Brad sent me a red rose with a card saying he was looking forward to our next date." She chuckled, though the sound was ragged. "I'm looking forward to it too, but with both of our crazy workloads, we'll be lucky if we can coordinate schedules before the new year."

"It's only July."

"And that tells you how busy I am." She raked her fingers through her hair again. Thanks to the short, practical style she wore, the locks fell back in place. "Sometimes I think the Foursome's Monday nights are the only thing that keep me sane. Definitely better than yoga. So, anyhow, Suzie, how did outrageous69 do?"

Suzanne patted her bulging tote. "The lady's hot." She only wished she, plain old Suze, was half as hot.

Perhaps Ann heard the ambivalence in her voice. She patted Suzanne's shoulder. "Honey, that lady is you. You were the girl in the cave, right? I mean, it wasn't Nicole Kidman."

Because of her hair, height and creamy skin, Suzanne often got compared to Nicole Kidman. Not that she saw much resemblance herself. The actress's features were sharp and pointy, her eyes blue rather than greeny-gray.

But had the Cretan god seen a resemblance? Maybe that's why she'd turned him on.

Ann poked her shoulder. "Stop it right this moment, Suze. I swear, you're as insecure as an articling student going to court for the first time. You're much prettier than Nicole is, and it's you the man wanted."

Feeling slightly cheered, Suzanne followed Ann through the blue-painted doorway. Jenny and Rina were settled at a table by the open French doors, with a large carafe of Greek wine. A waiter hurried over to fill two more glasses and ask if they'd like to order appetizers.

"What do you say, gals?" Ann said. "That gigantic appie platter, to share, plus a large Greek salad to make sure we get our veggies?"

They'd been to Maria's enough times that no one needed to open a menu. Everyone nodded approval, and the waiter said, "It'll only be a few minutes."

Jenny turned to Suzanne. "Well? How'd we do?"

Suzanne reached into her bag, brought out a small handful of papers and handed them to Jenny.

"Crap, I expected more." Her friend scowled at her suspiciously. "Did you read and pre-screen?"

Suzanne shook her head, fighting back a smile. She reached into her bag and withdrew another batch, which she handed to Rina. Another handful went to Ann, and she kept some for herself. By this time everyone was grinning.

Jenny rubbed her hands together. "Okay, that's more like it! Now we read them aloud. We'll each take a turn. I'll start."

Suzanne took a deep breath. Glancing around the room, her gaze snagged on the paintings and photos of Greece. Sun-drenched white buildings, fishing boats on a beach, yes, they called up memories. Was her Greek god a true memory? Would she find out tonight?

"Hey, Suze?" Jenny was waving a piece of paper in her face. "You with me?"

"Go ahead."

"Okay, this one's from 'imahottie.' " Jenny wrinkled her nose. "Tell me this isn't your guy."

"Better not be, or my fantasy will be ruined." Oh my God, she'd never thought of that. What if the guy did answer, and he was some kind of jerk, not the sex god she dreamed about? She wanted to grab those e-mails back from her friends, but knew they'd never let her.

"So," Jenny went on, "imahottie says, 'Hey blondie, if you're looking for a hot time, I'm the guy for you. I've got a seven-inch dick—' "

Jenny broke off, hooting with laughter as the others joined in. When they calmed down, she said, "Someone ought to tell dickhead what he can do with his seven-inch dick. Anyone want to hear the rest of this one?"

They shook their heads, and Ann took her turn. "This is from 'johnboy.' He says 'I'm a sensitive new-age guy—' "

"Groan," Jenny broke in.

" '. . . new-age guy,' " Ann persisted, " 'who loves Greece and good sex. I'll be up front and say I'm not the man who shared that cave, but it sounds like fun. I've been told I'm a good lover, and I believe in always satisfying my partner. How about giving me a chance to satisfy you?' "

She turned the paper facedown. "Give the man points for trying."

"I wonder how big his dick is?" Jenny said.

Rina swatted her with another sheet of paper. "My turn. This one's from 'sugarpie.' 'If you think sex with a man can be good, just wait until you've tried it with a woman.' " She broke off. "Oh my, I do believe you've hooked yourself an inhabitant of the isle of Lesbos, outrageous69. And that island was in Greece, right? Anyhow, sugarpie says, 'No man can ever understand your body the way I can. No man will ever respect and worship it as I will. No man will—'"

"No dick at all," Jenny broke in, and they all laughed.

"Enough," Suzanne said. "I freely confess I'm looking for a dick and—oops!" She broke off as the waiter appeared, bearing a huge platter of food.

Everyone took a moment to admire the presentation of spanokopita, calamari, those yummy little meatballs, dolmathes, pita bread and hummus and tzatziki dips. They each took a favorite, as the waiter added a big bowl of Greek salad to the table.

Suzanne popped a bit of hummus-laden pita into her mouth, then glanced down at the first sheet on her own pile of replies. What she saw made her choke and swallow the wrong way. When she could talk again, she said, "This is freaky. 'Young woman, your feet are on the wrong path. It's time to return to fundamental values.'"

"A religious nut," Ann commented.

"Listen to the rest. 'But first you must atone and be punished. Submit yourself to me and I will oversee your salvation.'"

"A sadistic religious freak. He wants to tie you up and whip you," Jenny said. "That sure wouldn't turn my crank." Then she smirked at Ann. "But maybe you should reply. You're the one who likes being tied up."

Ann stuck out her tongue. "Silk, tied very loosely. And he definitely wasn't whipping me, at least not with anything more than his tongue—and his eight-inch dick."

"Oooh!" Rina sighed, fanning herself with her stack of e-mails. "Eight inches. Imahottie just doesn't measure up." She stuck her fork into a stuffed grape leaf, lifted the neat, sausage-shaped bundle close to her mouth and ran her tongue suggestively around her lips. Then she took a large chomp, and the other three burst into laughter.

It was the most food Suzanne had ever seen Rina put in her mouth at one time.

The four of them carried on, taking turns reading, until Suzanne said, "This is depressing. The world is full of some very strange people."

"Don't despair," Rina said, holding up a sheet of paper. "This one sounds interesting. 'I remember the cave. It was above the bay, where people sunbathed nude.' "

"That was all in the ad," Suzanne broke in.

Rina held up her hand and read on. " 'The sand was so fine, the color of milk. Like the skin of your breasts, where the sun hadn't touched them.' "

Suzanne sucked in a breath. "That's true. Oh my God, this could be him."

Rina continued. " 'You were the most beautiful thing I'd ever seen and it killed me to know you were my best friend's wife.' Oh! Oh my!" She glanced up, her eyes wide, then went back to the letter. " 'We agreed it would just be that once but I couldn't get you out of my mind and that's why, when we all got back from holidays, I left town. But if this is really you, Jaclyn, and you want to see me, tell me where and when and I'll be there.' "

She put the piece of paper down. "Tacky."

"Yeah. Messing with his friend's wife," Jenny grumbled.

Suzanne, who realized her mouth was gaping, closed it. "Yes, but . . ." Oh my God, what had she done? "You weren't there. That place was special. It cast a spell on me. Maybe it did on them too. I don't . . ." She took a quick gulp of wine. "I just realized I honestly don't know if my guy was married, single, engaged. It never occurred to me."

"That is definitely not like you," Ann said.

"That's what I've been telling you!"

"You hate adultery," Rina said.

"Of course I do," Suzanne snapped. And the thought that she might have committed it made her feel sick.

"Okay, okay, we all understand that our Suzie was temporarily insane, drunk and sunstroked," Jenny said. "Let's get back to the letters."

A busboy came to clear away the now-empty platter. They ordered coffee and baklava, then went back to reading—skimming now—aloud.

After another dozen losers, Ann held up the next. "This is from 'caveman.' What do you think, folks? Another cute and corny?"

Jenny turned to Suzanne. "How about it, did he whack you over the head with a ten-inch dick and drag you off to that cave?"

"No, Eros sprinkled us with magic dust and set our feet on the path."

Ann began to read. "'I was underneath you, hard inside you, as you stared out of the cave, describing the scene below.'"

Suzanne felt as if the cave had kissed her with its cool breath. Goose bumps pricked her arms.

"'Do you remember the gay lovers?'" Ann read.

"Yes," Suzanne breathed. "One was reading to the other."

"'One was reading to the other,'" Ann read, her voice trembling. "'It was Lord Chatterley's Lover.'" Ann glanced at Suzanne. "He must mean *Lady Chatterley's Lover.*"

Suzanne shook her head. "I said that the man who was reading was switching it, making it Lord Chatterley with the gamekeeper. Because they were gay, you know?" She put her hands to her cheeks. They were burning, though cold shivers made her whole body tremble. "It's him. My God, it's really him."

Ann thrust the piece of paper toward her. "There's more. You read it."

For a moment Suzanne couldn't force herself to reach out

and take the paper. When she did, it rustled in her shaking hand. She glanced first at the top part. "It came in on Saturday night." Had he been thinking of her when she was dreaming of him?

The waiter began to set coffee cups on their table, and Suzanne was glad of the excuse to scan the message before she read it aloud. It was so incredible, knowing her lover really existed, and had typed these words to her.

When the waiter left, she took a quick sip of coffee, almost scalding her mouth, yet needing the moisture before she could speak. Then she took up from where Ann had left off. " 'I've thought of you so many times. Yes, my outrageous lover, if you do want to meet again, tell me where and when. I'll walk toward you and you'll walk toward me, and we'll see what fate has in store for us this time.' "

Suzanne put the paper down, realizing she'd gripped it so tightly she'd crumpled the edge. She tried to smooth it out, pressing repeatedly against the paper until Ann said, "You can print another, Suze."

She gave a little laugh. "Of course. I wasn't thinking." Then she laughed again, louder, hearing a note of hysteria. "He's real. What am I going to do?"

"See him!" Jenny yelped, thumping her fist on the table.

Their waiter, approaching with plates of baklava, leaped backward and nearly dropped their dessert on the floor.

Jenny rolled her eyes. "Be careful with that."

He came forward in a timid rush, almost threw the plates on the table and took off again.

Rina leaned across the table and touched Suzanne's hand. "You wanted to know if you were dreaming. Now you do. So think, Suzie, will you be happier if you see him, or if you leave it like this?"

"I . . . I don't know."

"I don't want to be the party pooper here," Ann said, "but you took a serious risk that afternoon, Suze, and you've got a hole in your memory. You say it was sunstroke, but what if this 'caveman' drugged you?"

Suzanne shook her head. "We didn't eat or drink anything." "The next thing you remember is being in your room the next day, feeling awful. Could you have fallen, hit your head?"

"Or maybe he bashed me over the head with that ten-inch dick? No, Ann, I don't think so."

"Then why don't you remember? You must have repressed it. But why, if it was this idyllic, erotic afternoon, and the two of you made a sensible decision to leave it at that?"

"She got sunstroke and fried some brain cells," Jenny said. "Don't make such a big deal of it."

Suzanne realized her head was throbbing, full of her friends' words, and her own worries and fears. She closed her eyes and tried to focus, to remember. After a moment, she said slowly, "You know what I think? Now that I know he's real, that I really did it—did all those things that were utterly out of character— I think my brain, my conscience, tried to forget. Sex with a stranger, not knowing if he was single, not using a condom." She shivered. "I couldn't come to terms with what I'd done, yet I couldn't manage to forget."

"You remembered the sex but not the conversation?" Ann said.

Suzanne shrugged helplessly.

"If you got so angsty about it the first time, then maybe you shouldn't repeat it," Rina commented, and Ann nodded her head firmly.

Jenny clapped her hands to her cheeks. "I can't believe this! You can't let this guy slip away again. God knows where he lives, and he's offering to come here and meet you. That's absolutely awesome. Come on, Suze, what's there to get angsty about? Just make sure he's not married, and then go for it. With a *condom*. Sex is a perfectly natural bodily function, so why not have great sex and just enjoy it? Without agonizing over it, for Christ's sake!"

"Ssh," Ann warned Jen, as Suzanne pressed both hands to her aching head.

Jenny took a long, noisy breath and continued in a quieter voice. "We all agreed to write the ad, and now everyone wants to bail out? No way. Look, here's what we're going to do."

"We?" Suzanne said.

"Yeah, we're in this together." Jenny giggled. "I mean, not the actual sex, but getting you together with this guy. So, Suze, you reply to caveman, ask him if he's single, and set up a meeting in some nice safe public place. And the rest of us'll be there when you meet, to blow the whistle if something goes wrong." She thrust her face toward Suzanne's. "What do you say, Suzie Q?"

Suzanne sucked in a long breath. Across the table, Rina's eyes were wide with concern. To her left, Jenny's impatient scowl challenged her to action. To her right, Ann's crinkled brow counseled caution.

She took another deep breath and her headache began to lift. How wonderful that these women all cared. They'd never let anything bad happen to her.

"I'm torn," she admitted. "I'm busy, I enjoy my life, I have my long-term plan to eventually find and marry—yeah, Jenny, Mr. Cleaver. This . . . caveman is definitely not Mr. Cleaver."

"But you're torn?" Rina prompted.

She sighed. "I sound so middle-aged and boring. Like Jen says, what's wrong with one more afternoon or evening of fabulous sex? This time I wouldn't drink too much. I'd know the memories I was creating were real."

Jenny, who was systematically demolishing her baklava, nodded vigorously.

"I'd go into it with my eyes open, and take a bunch of precautions," Suzanne went on. "Besides, we might meet and not even be attracted to each other this time."

Or she might be attracted to him, but he'd see plain old boring Suze. Now there was a dismal thought. She gripped her head with her hands, realizing her headache wasn't gone after all. "Oh, I don't know. I have to sleep on it."

"Of course you do," Ann said, her eyes still troubled. "But I'm against setting up a meeting. At least right now. E-mail him back—and be sure to do it from outrageous69 not your regular e-mail account—and ask him about himself. I'd consider even asking for references."

Jenny raised a brow. "To say he's still a great lover?"

"No!" Ann glared at her. "To say he's a trustworthy person."

"I agree you should play it cautious," Rina said, "and sleep on it, Suzie." She stood up. "I have to go, I've got an early morning." Her expression suddenly went dreamy. "But here's something to think about. Should I try to find Giancarlo, using the internet?"

Jenny grabbed her hand and yanked her back down. "What? You mean we're going to write another ad, for the magic fingers piano-man who made you come three times on top of a piano?"

Rina freed her hand and stood up again. "Or I could use the normal internet search tools. After all, I do know the guy's name." She shot a pointed look at Suzanne.

"Oh!" Suzanne picked up the e-mail printout and read it again. No, he hadn't mentioned his name. He hadn't said where he lived, or what he did for a living. Or if he was single.

She toyed with her baklava, then put her fork down.

"You eating that?" Jenny demanded.

Suzanne pushed her plate over, and Jenny, whose hundred-pound frame never gained an ounce despite the huge amount of food she consumed, dug in.

* * *

Later that night, Suzanne's caveman came to her again in a dream. Afterwards, her body damp with sweat, the throbbing still pulsing through her, she smiled at knowing the memory was true.

And what the hell was wrong with great sex?

Suzanne left the bed to Melody and Zorro—a tangled heap of gold and black atop the pale green duvet—and went over to turn on her computer. She hoisted Mouse from his sleeping spot, opened caveman's e-mail and clicked REPLY.

I remember Lord Chatterley, she typed. And I remember wishing we'd picked some of those tiny flowers that bloomed on the hillside. But you said fingers would do, and it was true. Your fingers were so amazing. You touched me with strength, yet never hurt me. You made my body sing.

Suzanne stopped. What was she doing? She should be asking for information so she could decide if she wanted to see him again.

She wished she could remember their final conversation. Had he told her his name, where he lived, what he did? Had he said he was married, and she'd gone into shock?

Whatever he might have said then, that was four years ago and the facts might be quite different now.

Mouse was insinuating himself across the keyboard. She nudged him away before he could click any keys, and typed: You could be anywhere in the world, yet you say you'll come to me.

She thought about the two of them walking toward each other. What if the magic really did belong to—depend on—that beach in Crete? Meeting again could be a disaster.

"Nothing can ruin a memory, Mouse," she murmured, stroking the sleepy cat. "If I decide to see him and it doesn't work out, I'll still have that first memory.

"And if I meet him in a public place, and don't give him my last name, address or phone number, I can't come to any harm."

Mouse butted his head against her hand.

Why would she want to see the man, if she had to take so many precautions? And yet, excitement fizzed through her. The element of mystery was in itself arousing. If caveman was just a perfectly nice guy, like the vets at the clinic, she wouldn't feel this same sense of adventure. She might, in the future, contemplate a loving marriage. But with caveman, what she had in mind was, as Jenny called it, a walk on the wild side.

Wild, but she honestly didn't believe it would be dangerous. If he hadn't hurt her in that cave, when she'd been so vulnerable, he wouldn't hurt her now. The only thing she really needed to know was whether he was involved with another woman. For her, adultery was taboo.

My name is Suzanne, she typed. I live in Vancouver, British Columbia, Canada, and I'm single. How about you?

She clicked SEND before she could have second thoughts, then shut down her computer. "All right, Mouse, the keyboard's all yours."

As she tumbled back into bed, she wondered how caveman would react to her garbled message, such a peculiar mix of sexuality and practicality. Of outrageous69 and boring-girl.

On Monday night, Jax got home from the office around eleven. He shared the apartment with Tod, a visual merchandiser—i.e., window dresser—at Saks Fifth Avenue, and Levi, an accountant with Rothstein Kass. One thing you had to say for him and his roommates: They worked in some of the classiest businesses in town.

Another thing you had to say: They weren't exactly homemakers.

He cleared Chinese takeout containers off the rickety coffee table in front of the wide-screen TV, and crammed the empties into the overflowing garbage bin under the kitchen sink. Then he opened the fridge door, and grinned. Someone had remembered to buy beer.

He cracked open a can and headed through to his bedroom, where he stripped off his suit jacket and tie and glanced at his computer.

Since Saturday night, he'd monitored his new caveman e-mail account obsessively. By now he was figuring it wasn't really his blonde. Still, he wished she'd reply, so he could stop wasting his time this way.

Oh, what the hell, just once more. No way would he get to sleep until he did.

And there she was.

He grew hard as he read her words. Yeah, he sure as hell remembered his fingers threading through her golden curls, teasing the moist, swollen flesh below.

This time he ignored his hard-on. Instead, he began to type.

Suzanne. What a perfect name for such a beautiful, sexy woman. My name is Jaxon. I'm single too. And as it turns out, we're almost neighbors. I'm in San Francisco. It would be easy to come visit you—or you could come here, if you wanted.

What was he doing? Wasn't he the guy who never took time off work? And yet . . .

Come. God, I want to come again, with you. I want to hear you come, feel you come around me. To caress your lovely breasts, see the pleasure on your face as I touch you. Just the thought of it . . .

He stopped typing. Should he be saying this stuff? Would she be offended? No, of course not, not outrageous69.

He resumed: . . . makes me hard. I want to taste you again, Suzanne. Everywhere . . .

He broke off again, so aroused he felt like he was going to burst.

He stared at the screen. A first draft. He should edit it; he always edited things before he sent them.

But that was the lawyer side of him. Tonight he was just a man. A horny man. Quickly he typed, Say you'll see me. I want more sexy memories.

He clicked SEND and stared at the screen.

Suzanne. Her name was Suzanne.

4

Suzanne couldn't get back to sleep. After an hour of trying, she flicked on the bedside light, tossed back the covers and again evicted Mouse from the keyboard.

Even knowing the odds were slim, Suzanne's breath quickened as the computer started up. She accessed her outrageous69 account and found three new e-mails, but none were from caveman. Idly, she skimmed, shaking her head in bemusement. Cave sex sure seemed to turn a lot of guys' cranks.

Damn, she hadn't cancelled the personals ad. She found the instructions Jenny had given her, and deleted her ad.

Just as she was about to exit from e-mail, a message popped up on her screen. From caveman! She gripped the mouse with a shaking hand and clicked the message open.

Jaxon. What a striking, unusual name. And he was single.

Suzanne started to read on, when a thought occurred to her. Was he still on-line?

Hurriedly, she clicked REPLY, then typed, Are you there, Jaxon? and clicked SEND.

Then she went back to his message and read it, feeling her

nipples bead. She pressed her legs together, savoring the burn of arousal between them. Good God, this man could turn her on, even via a computer. More than any other guy had done in person.

Another message popped into her in-box. I'm here. I can't believe it's you, Suzanne.

She beamed with delight. A real—or virtually real—conversation. Quickly she typed: It's me. Wow, San Francisco, I've only been there once, but it's a terrific city. She wanted to ask a thousand things. What did he do, and how did he like his job? What were his parents like, did he have siblings? What did he do in his spare time? Did he like animals? What should she ask first?

Her fingers faltered. Mouse regarded her with a steady gaze that seemed almost amused. Like he knew she was all set to gush like a teenager who'd just met a boy who might turn out to be The One.

Suzanne frowned. What was she thinking? This was not a teenage crush, nor was this her Mr. Cleaver—and she didn't want him to be. She was way too young to be thinking about marriage.

What was it she really wanted from caveman? Jaxon?

Sex. Excitement. Proof she could be sexy.

A new message popped into her in-box. Suzanne? Are you there? Did I go too far? Sorry if I offended you.

Now she knew how the conversation was supposed to go. She deleted her unsent comment about San Francisco. Like Jenny had said, skip the travelogue and get to the good stuff. That's what he'd expect. That's what he wanted.

You didn't offend me, you got me hot! Just like you do every time I remember what we did in that cave. SEND.

His reply was immediate. That was one wild afternoon!

She paused, fingers poised over the keyboard. She'd held herself out to be outrageous69. Could she deliver?

If the gals were only here to help.

The thought of the four of them brainstorming the wording of erotic e-mail made her giggle, which in turn relaxed her. This should be easy. All she had to do was fantasize about being with him.

But first . . . . On one side of her desk, family faces smiled at her from picture frames: her mom and dad in the garden; her sister, Bethany, with her husband and two kids surrounded by Christmas clutter. Suzanne turned the photos facedown.

Now there was only one face left, this one feline, gazing at her with a quizzical expression. She lifted the grey cat from her desktop and he gave a squall of protest as she set him on the floor. "Sorry, Mouse. Go sleep with Melody and Zorro. Trust me, you don't want to know about this." Then she began to type.

Remember how we walked up the hill, holding hands? Both naked, both aroused. Then we slipped inside the cave and it was so dark I could barely see you.

Imagine we're there. Feel me, Jaxon. We're kissing and our bodies are pressing together and then, suddenly, you lift me. I grip your shoulders with my arms and lock my legs around your waist, and we're still kissing. Are you with me?

She clicked SEND.

Waited.

Double-clicked eagerly on his response.

Oh yeah, I'm with you. I'm with you, and as hard as I was that afternoon.

Wow! Was he, or was he just saying that to be sexy?

No, this was her caveman. Of course he was hard. Beautifully, achingly hard.

For her.

And she too was intensely turned on, not just by the memory of Crete but at the thought of Jaxon, at his computer in San Francisco, aroused long distance. By her. Her words, and the memories they conjured.

She hadn't felt such a sense of female power since that afternoon four years ago. Yes, in this moment she really was outrageous69.

You are naked, aren't you? she typed.

His reply came. I could be. Do you want me naked?

Always! She typed back. But undress slowly. Undo your shirt buttons one at a time, and pretend those are my fingers, parting your shirt, slipping inside.

Shirt. Was he even wearing a shirt with buttons? Or maybe a T-shirt? She hadn't the slightest idea how the guy dressed.

He answered, Okay, but what I'd rather be doing is reaching inside your shirt. In my mind I can see those high, firm breasts of yours, each a perfect handful.

He liked her breasts. Even though, to be honest, you could fit the two of them together into one of those amazing hands of his.

Speaking of a handful, she typed, would you like to feel my hands on you . . . She stopped again, knowing exactly where she wanted her hands. If she left the message as it was, he'd be bound to pick up the innuendo, but . . . What the hell, this was Jaxon and he made her feel sexy and daring.

. . . your cock? Unzip your pants, pull them down, take off your underwear. And touch yourself, Jaxon, wrap a hand around that beautiful big erection, and imagine it's my hand. Sliding up and down, squeezing but not too hard.

She stared at the message on the screen. As much as she and the gals might have joked about gi-normous dicks, she'd never in her life typed the word "cock" before.

Oh, what the hell. SEND.

A message came back. And you put your hand between your legs, down among those pretty gold curls. Those are my fingers stroking, opening you. Are you wet for me?

She stared at the screen. Then down at her pink cotton pajamas, printed with a pattern of Siamese cats. Should she take them off? Did he think she was naked?

Her hand went tentatively to the drawstring bow at her waist, then stopped. No, she couldn't do this. Not here, with her parents sleeping just across the yard, her own cats on the bed. This was definitely not a cave on Crete.

But maybe . . .

Her hand slid lower, outside the soft cotton, down the seam that ran between her legs, trying to imagine it was his hand. Her body throbbed in response. She closed her eyes. Jaxon's hand, so dark against the pale pink fabric. Jaxon's fingers stroking the seam, creating friction against the tender flesh beneath.

She moaned, clenching her thighs against his hand. Her hand. Their hand. She wanted to keep the hand there, but, even more, she wanted to type to him.

Yes, I'm wet for you, she typed. But I want more than your hand. Remember how it was that first time in the cave, when my body was wrapped around yours? Remember how hard and hungry your cock was? How you plunged inside me, where I was all wet and wanting? That's what I want now. You, inside me.

Suzanne's muscles clenched as she imagined the act she was describing. She wanted to press her hand between her legs again, but right now she was inspired, on a roll, feeling like that sexy woman in the cave. She squirmed on her chair as she began to type again.

Now feel me sliding up and down on you, lifting my body, then moving down just as you thrust up. You're so strong, I don't know how you can hold me like this, but your strength is such a turn-on. Everything about you excites me, and now all my sensations are centering as you plunge into me even deeper and faster. You're so big and you fill me completely. The friction as you move is almost unbearable and I can feel the tension building and building and I want, I need you to give that one final thrust and pour yourself into me.

Do it, Jaxon.

Come now!

Breathless, she stopped typing and reached one shaking hand toward the mouse. Did she dare send this? It was almost pornographic. But then, what healthy red-blooded male didn't respond to pornography? She clicked the button.

And waited.

She reread his last message, then her reply. Her right hand hovered near the mouse, but her left one slid between her thighs and she caressed herself through her pajamas, imagining his touch.

He still hadn't replied. Had she gone too far? She removed her hand from between her legs. Worrying about his response was a turnoff.

Finally she saw the envelope icon. Hurriedly, she double-clicked.

Jesus, Suzanne.

I'm having trouble thinking what to say.

Oops, she'd gone overboard, blown her chance with him.

In fact I'm having trouble forming a coherent thought. Woman, you just blew my mind.

And that's not all you blew. You just made me come so hard it hurt.

Suzanne let out a sigh, made up of equal parts relief, pride and arousal. Now there was a turn-on!

And now it's your turn. Let's concentrate on your pleasure now. Are you ready?

She groaned. Was she? Could she really do what he was suggesting?

Yes. SEND.

Then be patient, give me a few minutes and I promise it'll be worth the wait.

She waited nervously. What was he typing? When the message came, she sucked in a deep breath, let it out slowly, then clicked it open.

Here we go, lover. Is your hand between your legs? Mine is there, in my mind, and let me tell you what it's doing.

She drew a shaky breath and let her hand drift down again.

It's stroking your silky, satiny, hot swollen flesh. As I stroke, your body moves with my hand, pressing against me, letting me know how you feel, telling me how you want to be touched.

We're both totally focused on the place where my hand meets your body. I'm limp from that earth-shattering orgasm you gave me, yet amazingly I feel my own body stir to life as I see the way you respond to me.

Oh! He'd left the Crete scenario and was creating something new.

It's the sexiest thing in the world, feeling how much you want my touch.

All I want to do is pleasure you, and your body is squirming, pressing, your hips are lifting and circling, you're telling me with every move that the tension is building.

I slip a finger inside you, feel your muscles contract around me, your body rock against me. I'm hard again and I know that's what you really want, so I take my finger out, suck it so I can taste you, then ease my cock into you, and your pussy is so tight and hot and wet all around me, and you're moaning, those little sighing, panting moans you make. God, Suzanne, I love those sexy sounds you make.

I reach down and with my thumb I press your clit and your body bucks, and now I'm circling that swollen nub as I thrust into you faster and harder, and you can feel the pressure building, the climax approaching, and you twist your body against me, demanding the release you need.

And I want to give it to you, Suzanne. I want you to come.

Now, Suzanne.

"Jaxon!" She cried out his name as her body clutched and spasmed.

* * *

"This had better be good," Rina grumbled as she dropped into the last chair at the sidewalk table at Sophie's Cosmic Café. "I had to move a clarinet lesson and deal with the dratted bridge traffic." She lived on the North Shore, over the Lion's Gate Bridge.

"Well, I had to reschedule a client," Ann said. "And catch a cab from Georgia and Burrard at noon, along with three dozen other businesspeople."

"I was free as the wind." Jenny grinned. "Being self-employed has a heck of a lot going for it." Her grin widened. "Plus, this could count as research. It could be fun to do an article on internet dating."

"Sex," Suzanne murmured, just as Ann said, "Been done too many times already, but—" She broke off. "Did someone say sex?"

Flushing, Suzanne leaned forward and beckoned them all to do the same. This wasn't a conversation she wanted anyone overhearing. "Internet sex. I've been having IM sex."

"IM? Instant messaging?" Rina queried, but Jenny's voice overrode her. "Holy crap, woman, tell all! With caveman?"

"Yes. With Jaxon. That's his name. Spelled with an 'x' rather than a 'c-k.' He lives in San Francisco."

"Obviously you decided to reply to his e-mail," Ann said dryly.

"Monday night. And we've been e-mailing back and forth and . . ."

"And having IM sex?" Rina finished, her dark brows drawn together in puzzlement. "How on earth do you have IM sex?"

Suzanne knew her cheeks were fiery by now.

Jenny saved her by saying, "Get a grip, Rina, use a little imagination. Think of how you have phone sex."

"Phone sex? What, exactly, do you do with the phone?" Rina asked with pseudo-innocence.

They all burst out laughing.

"Seriously," Rina said, "I've never had phone sex. But I can imagine. You talk dirty to each other?"

"Among other things," Ann said smugly.

"Aha!" Jenny pounced. "You have some experience."

"I dated a guy who lived in Toronto and we only saw each other every two or three months. But we did burn up the phone lines."

Suzanne stared at her friend. Why did she always assume Ann was as starchy as her tailored suits? "You've had phone sex? So, you mean he tells you what he'd like to do to you? And you, uh, touch yourself and . . ."

"I'd guess it's pretty much the same as cyber sex. Is that how you and Jaxon do it?"

Suzanne clapped her hands to burning cheeks. "I can't believe we're having this conversation. It's like something out of *Sex and the City.*"

"Never that," Jenny said. "We're way too stuffy for that."

"Inhibited," Rina said.

"Reserved. Discreet," Ann contributed.

"Canadian." Jenny rolled her eyes. "Only in New York are gals that out there."

Suzanne winced. "But don't you see, that's what Jaxon expects from me. I'm outrageous69. He doesn't know I'm this stuffy, inhibited, reserved, discreet Canadian. Well, he knows I'm Canadian, but he thinks I'm like Samantha used to be on *Sex and the City.* Completely concerned with sex."

"Let me see," Ann said mischievously. "The first time you meet the man, you end up in a cave, uh . . . Okay, let's call an apple an apple, like Samantha would. *Fucking.* Three times."

The word "fucking" made Suzanne flinch. But Ann was right, it had hardly been making love.

"Then," Ann said, "the next time you're in touch, you're both typing sexy suggestions and masturbating."

Suzanne winced again. Damn, how could she pretend to be

outrageous if words like "fuck" and "masturbating" embarrassed her?

Ann raised her eyebrows. "Correct me if I'm wrong, but I'm thinking Samantha would be proud of you, Suze."

"But it's not me," she admitted softly. "Not the real me."

"Then who is it?" Jenny asked. "That evil twin again?"

"No! It's not evil, it's . . ." She frowned. It sure hadn't felt evil, it had been so . . . "Sexy," Suzanne said, her confidence beginning to grow again. She gave a firm nod. "That's it, it's my sexy twin. And that's who has to go on my date with Jaxon."

"Suzie! You've arranged to meet him?" Rina spoke first, but all three of them gaped at her.

Their waitress interrupted, impatient to take orders. When she mentioned the daily special, some kind of fancy salad, everyone quickly ordered it. Jenny said, "And curly fries, we have to have a ton of those fantastic curly fries."

As soon as the waitress had gone, Jenny turned to Suzanne. "Okay, Suzie Q, spill. What's the scoop?"

"He's flying up on Friday and we're going to meet." She gulped. "I'm terrified." Because, after all, she really was Suze, the sensible, boring twin.

"What do you know about this man?" Ann asked. "What does he do? Are you sure he's not married? What about—"

Suzanne broke in. "I did ask if he was single, and he said yes." She frowned. "I have no way of knowing for sure, but why would he lie? Why would he think I'd even care?"

"Because you do," Ann pointed out.

"No! I mean, yes, I do, but that's the sensible twin. Why would he think outrageous69 would give a flying"—she swallowed and made herself say it—"fuck whether he's married? And no, I don't know what he does for a living. I didn't ask and he didn't say. And I didn't tell him what I do."

Ann's frown made Suzanne rush on. "Don't you see, that's not what we're all about, Jaxon and me? It's not one of those typical relationships where you meet the guy's family and friends, where he talks about his job, sports, whatever. Don't get me wrong, that stuff is great. That's what my life will be like when I'm a vet and I meet the right man, and we get to know each other, make sure we're long-term compatible, then get married, buy a house, have kids."

And in that moment, she realized that all the mulling—and IM sex—of the last couple of days had led her to a conclusion. She rested her elbows on the table and leaned forward. "But that's then, and this is now. I want what Jen said: a walk on the wild side. I want to be outrageous69, the sexy twin. Scrap all that *mundane* stuff, this may be the only opportunity I'll ever have to do something really daring."

"Or maybe dangerous." Ann rested her hand on Suzanne's forearm. "I'm worried. You don't know a single thing about this man. He could be a psycho. I understand your craving for adventure, but you have to be careful."

"Sspoilssport," Jen spat out, hissing the ess's.

"I'm not saying don't meet him." Ann glanced around the table. "But the three of us are going to be there."

Everyone kept quiet while the waitress delivered their meals, then Suzanne said, "Ann, I'm cautious enough to admit I'd love a security net, but on Monday you said you don't even have time to date your new guy."

"This is more important."

"She's right," Rina said. "We'll be there, won't we, Jen? What time? Where?"

Suzanne felt a surge of love for her friends. Whatever her life might bring in terms of romance—be it adventuresome or mundane—she would treasure these women's friendship.

"Early evening," she said. "I was thinking Spanish Banks? Kind of like the first time, walking toward each other along the beach."

"No caves at Spanish Banks," Jenny teased.

"I can't imagine we're, uh . . ."

"Going to leap into each other's arms and have sex?" Jenny finished. "Why not? You did the first time."

They had. Suzanne still had trouble believing she'd really done it. But she'd had too much wine, too much sun, hadn't really been responsible for her actions. On Friday, she would be.

"Why not just go to Wreck Beach, then you can both get naked?" Jenny said slyly.

Suzanne shook her head vehemently. "Not this time. I don't want to be *that* daring."

For the first time she glanced at her salad, a colorful, imposing composition. What on earth had she ordered? Something adventuresome, obviously, and wouldn't you know, she felt intimidated by it. She reached for a curly fry.

Ann finished a bite of her own salad. "Yum, that's great." Then she said, "Suze, if you go for a walk, stay where there are lots of people. There are some dark, deserted places up in Pacific Spirit Park. And absolutely do not get in a car with him." She snapped her fingers. "Walk over to Athene's for Greek food, and reminisce."

"Dinner . . . God, Ann, I honestly don't know what to expect. I don't know this man. This isn't, like, a normal date. As for reminiscing, the only thing we did was . . . Well, I can't see sitting in Athene's and talking about . . . you know."

"Fucking," Jenny said gleefully.

Rina sent her a chastising glance. "What about a picnic? Go to Granville Island and buy a bunch of delicacies. Put them in a picnic basket and leave it in your car." She grinned. "If things don't work out with Jaxon, you can share with us. But if you and he get along when you meet, you can picnic on the beach. Go wading in the ocean. Watch the sun set."

"That sounds better," Suzanne said. "But geez, are you three going to sit on a blanket watching the whole thing? That's too weird for me."

"If you stay on the beach, you should be safe," Ann admitted. "So we'll hang out for a little while, and when you feel comfortable with him, give us some kind of sign. Then we'll go get on with our own lives. Our *mundane* little lives."

5

Jax consulted his map and steered the rented Boxster toward the Burrard Street Bridge. He could have asked Suzanne to provide directions, just like he could have asked her for a hotel recommendation, but he didn't want her to think he was anal.

Especially because he really was.

He shifted up, gave the car a little gas, and it surged forward as if it had wings. Was he crazy to have splurged and rented a ritzy black Porsche? At home he didn't even own a car. Didn't need one, living and working downtown, with the Bay Area Rapid Transit making it an easy ride to his mom's place in Berkeley.

The breeze felt good against his skin. A convertible did give you a great sense of freedom. He could almost forget the guilt that had plagued him since he'd left the office this afternoon.

God, what a mess he was. Here he was, on his way to meet the sexiest woman alive, and all he could think about was his job. He'd better get a grip, or Suzanne would take one look at him and head straight in the other direction.

But the thought of work lingered in his mind. What about

her? She must have a job too. They'd never e-mailed about anything other than Crete, and sex.

He shook his head to clear it. An erotic escapade, that's what her ad had asked for, and promised. Jobs had no place in what they were doing.

She'd told him to meet her at Spanish Banks. Kind of a sexy name. Did Banks imply caves? He couldn't imagine she'd . . .

Oh hell, if she was anything like she'd been on Crete, he could imagine Suzanne doing just about anything. But would he, conservative lawyer-guy, be up to the challenge?

She'd said he should park in the last lot, then walk along the beach to the west, away from the city.

Again, they would meet on a beach. He liked the symmetry. But this wasn't a nude beach, thank God. Sure, he was in shape and women found him attractive, but he couldn't imagine having the guts to strip off his clothes and walk, naked, toward lovely Suzanne. On Crete it had been by accident, not design.

Could a planned meeting even come close? Maybe he should have settled for memories, and dynamite cyber sex.

The road got narrower and the breeze saltier.

Spanish Banks turned out to be a long beach lined with concession stands, volleyball nets and a series of parking lots. Lots of people around on this summer evening.

He pulled into the last lot and found a spot. When he turned off the engine, his heart was pounding so hard he could barely breathe.

How could he feel so nervous, when the scene around him was so wholesome? On the grass, a boy and his father played Frisbee with a golden retriever. A middle-aged couple cycled along a paved path and a pack of teenaged girls sped by on roller blades.

People were wearing shorts or jeans. He was slightly overdressed, in his black jeans and new designer T-shirt, but he didn't know where the evening would lead. He was aiming for casual, a little classy, versatile enough to go with whatever Suzanne had in mind.

Suzanne. Everything was so different this time. They knew each other's names. This wasn't a magical Greek paradise but her hometown.

Last night he'd come in his own hands, reading e-mail from her. And she'd done the same.

He drew in a shaky breath. Jax Navarre had few qualms about meeting with CEOs of multibillion-dollar corporations, but the idea of walking down the beach toward Suzanne gave him a serious case of nerves.

And yet, it turned him on.

Dumping his leather sandals in the miniscule trunk of the car, he removed the single tiger lily he'd chosen. Fiery, passionate, exotic. Like the woman he'd bought it for.

He walked across a strip of grass to the paved path that ran beside the beach, crossed it, and stepped down on the sand. The beach was a narrow strip punctuated with battered logs and rocky outcroppings. This sand was coarse compared to the fine white sand of Crete. Its grittiness abraded his soles and grains collected between his toes. It had been years since he'd walked barefoot in the sand, but it felt good.

A couple of kids splashed and swam. To his right, across a stretch of ocean, was a spectacular view of Vancouver. The setting sun created an eye-dazzling glitter on the windows of distant high-rises. At another time, he would have stopped to admire, but now he turned his back and began to walk.

Most people were wearing sunglasses, but not Jax. He wanted to see Suzanne without any barriers.

Had she cut her hair? How would she be dressed? He had absolutely no idea of her taste in clothing. Or in anything else.

Except sex. She liked it hot and wild.

* * *

Suzanne's legs were so shaky she could barely walk. But as her bare feet got accustomed to the grainy feel of damp sand and the breeze cooled her flushed cheeks, she gained confidence. She felt herself becoming the sexy twin, the woman who'd attracted Jaxon on Crete. Her head came up, her shoulders went back and she began to smile.

Up on the grass, her friends sat at a picnic table, eating KFC and pretending not to watch her. It was good to know she wasn't alone, though she was embarrassed that they'd witness her meeting with her mystery lover.

She'd taken forever deciding what to wear, and had ended up with a crop top in a shade of peachy cream almost her own skin color, and a long, gauzy skirt striped in yellows and oranges. The skirt opened at the front and she'd only buttoned it down to mid-thigh. A breeze teased her hair and tossed the filmy fabric of her skirt, peeling it back to show her legs, then floating it forward to wrap demurely around her.

Her jewelry was gold to match her hair: strings of dangly coins in her ears, a dolphin ring she'd bought on Crete on her right hand, a bangle bracelet on her left wrist.

People dotted the beach and her gaze moved nervously from one to the next. What would he be wearing? He'd had great legs, yet shorts seemed too casual for such a significant meeting.

Her breath caught. A tall man had just come down to the beach. All she could see from here was that he was black. From head to toe. Dark skin, dark clothes.

She knew it was Jaxon.

She wanted to run toward him as much as she wanted to run away. The muscles in her legs locked and she had to force herself to keep walking.

As she got closer, she could see the exact color of his skin, so warm and alive in comparison to the sexy black clothing.

Clothing tight enough to leave no doubt his body was still lean and firm.

He was clean-shaven now and the dreads had been replaced by short, tight curls, but the new look suited his strong features.

Her muscles became fluid again and she felt strong, sexy, powerful. They were magnets coming together.

When finally she stood in front of him, she smiled up and he smiled down.

"Suzanne." His husky voice caressed her name, making it beautiful.

"Jaxon."

He looked a little older, but even more attractive. Mature. His eyes, deep chocolate, full of light, were the same. Captivating. Her sexy, mysterious stranger.

He held out a tiger lily.

She smiled and took it. "Thank you."

Then he held out his hand, and she took that too, her own hand enveloped by heat, a throbbing pulse of sensation.

Wordlessly, they began to walk, strolling away from the city, toward the more remote stretches of Spanish Banks.

"I can't believe you're here." She tilted her head to gaze up at him. She had no idea who he really was. Part of her wanted to know everything, but another part said it would spoil things. Besides, if she asked him questions, then he'd be bound to ask her. She didn't want to lie, nor did she want to confess to being such a humdrum person. *I'm outrageous69*, she reminded herself.

"I can't believe we're together," he said.

Suddenly, he stopped and released her hand. He touched her shoulder, stopping her, then gripped her around the waist and lifted her effortlessly onto a chunk of driftwood, so now she was his height. "Beautiful Suzanne." He lifted a hand, traced the line of her cheekbone, then twisted a curl of hair around his finger. He touched her lips, outlining the top one, then the bottom.

Then he leaned closer and her heart stopped. Their lips touched. It was the gentlest of meetings, a hello and a question. But the moment the question was asked, she knew the answer. The magic was there.

She let out her breath in a soft sigh that parted her lips. His mouth moved, slanting against hers, kissing the corner of her mouth, nibbling her lower lip. His lips were firm, soft, full, utterly tantalizing and she smelled his slightly musky, very male scent.

Heat surged through her and she moved toward him, losing her balance and almost toppling off the driftwood. His arms came around her waist, steadying her, and hers came up to circle his shoulders. He moved a step closer, and their bodies touched.

She gasped. He was aroused. Already. And in the next breath she realized she was too. Beneath the filmy skirt, her new silk panties were wet.

She wanted to grind herself against him in mindless passion. On a public beach. Oh yes, she was outrageous69. It was amazing what this man did to her.

To her surprise, he didn't deepen the kiss. Instead, he lifted her down from the log and held out his hand. She took it and they began to walk again.

No, she didn't want to ask questions. For the moment, she knew everything she wanted to about Jaxon.

She gazed sideways at the front of his black jeans. If anyone spared them more than a passing glance, they'd notice his erection despite the fist he'd jammed in his pocket. But the people they passed seemed occupied with their own concerns, either packing up and heading home or spreading out picnic suppers.

The picnic basket was in her car, together with a rug. And she and Jaxon were walking in the opposite direction, strolling along the waterline, feeling the chilled Pacific lap their feet. Moving away from her friends.

He bent down and picked up something, then presented her with a fragment of abalone shell. She examined it, running her finger over the gleaming bands of blue, mauve and silver.

Jaxon caught her finger and brought it to his mouth. He sucked the tip gently, and she felt his touch through her whole body. Luckily, as a woman, her arousal wasn't so obvious. "What do you taste?"

"The ocean, and Suzanne. Enough to whet my appetite. I want more of you."

She imagined his tongue exploring her most private spots, and a shiver of desire rippled through her. "We want the same thing." Though her cheeks were burning at her boldness, her lust, she tilted up her chin and met his gaze.

He lowered his head and kissed her again, this time sliding the tip of his tongue across the crease of her lips. She opened readily and touched her tongue to his, inviting him in. He accepted, exploring her mouth, thrusting, then retreating, and she reciprocated.

The sun had almost hit the water now, the light was fading. She eased her mouth away from his and dropped her head to his shoulder, clinging tight. In the distance, her friends were rapidly becoming silhouettes.

Now that she was with Jaxon again, every instinct told her she could trust him.

Behind his back, she lifted a hand and waved, giving the signal. One of them waved back and she waved again, to confirm. They rose and moved in the direction of the parking lot. She'd just bet Ann was telling the other two they were crazy to leave her on her own.

Jaxon put his hands on her shoulders, easing her away. "What are you doing?"

"Chasing away a bug."

His grin was a flash of white. "A bug?" He glanced over his shoulder, then shrugged.

She guessed he didn't believe her. He probably knew she wasn't so foolish as to come here alone. And, even though she trusted him, she would keep her promise not to stray from the populated part of the beach.

She slid a hand down his back, feeling first the silky fabric of the T-shirt, then the coarseness of denim. Curving her palm around his butt, she wished her hand was on the inside of his jeans.

"It's getting dark," he said, "and I want to see you."

He added an emphasis to the last two words that made her think, *Naked.*

"The moon's almost f-full tonight," she stammered, "and it's clear, so there'll be stars. Our eyes will adjust. You'll be surprised at how much we can see." She forced herself to stop babbling. "I want to see you too." Yes, naked. But they couldn't do that here. Could they?

"Do you want to stay here?" he asked.

Yes, and no. If they didn't stay here, where would they go? His hotel? That didn't feel right, at least not yet. "I brought a picnic."

"Perfect."

His finger toyed with a curl of hair. "I wondered if you'd have cut it."

She often thought of having it styled short and practical, the way Ann did, but kept it long as a reminder of their lovemaking.

"You cut yours. And shaved the goatee." She tried not to make it an accusation.

He shrugged. "Getting older, I guess."

It suited him, though. Made him look more mature. Classy, rather than trendy.

He traced the low neckline of her top. "When I saw you walking toward me, for a moment I thought you were naked from the waist up."

She wanted to feel his hand on her breasts. Suddenly, nothing was more important. She reached under her top to undo the front hook of her bra, then eased the straps down over her arms and pulled the bra off. "Almost."

Jaxon sucked in a loud breath. Positioning himself between her and the path, screening her from passersby, he reached under her top to cup one of her breasts. Gently, oh so gently.

He circled a nipple with his finger. His head was bent and she leaned forward to kiss his hair, those tight, short black curls. His musky scent, a sexy contrast to the fresh ocean air, intoxicated her.

He bent further, took her nipple between his teeth, and began to suck.

Arousal was an ache low in her body, a weakness in her knees. She slid her hand across the front of his jeans, molding her palm to his erection.

Jaxon lifted his head, gave a groan of pleasure and pressed against her hand. "Feel how much I want you, Suzanne."

"I want you too." Inside her, please.

He removed her hand and stepped back. "Let's find a patch of sand and a couple of logs and have that picnic."

Was he talking about food, sex, or both? Sex, hopefully. Maybe after, she could think about food. Right now, her body was crying for release.

She turned toward the car, her new bra—silk and lace to match the lace-trimmed bikini panties—dangling from one hand. "No pocket," she said, and gave it to him.

He stowed it in a jeans pocket, then took her hand and they strolled back to the parking lot. The overhead street lamps were a shock to eyes attuned to the dim light of the beach. Suzanne blinked a few times, then studied Jaxon. Yes, he really was perfect.

"It's me. Remember?" he said.

"Every inch."

She led him to her car. Or, rather, Ann's—a sporty red Miata with the top down. Suzanne hadn't wanted to bring her own car, the old Volkswagen van she'd bought when she was seventeen. She loved the VW, despite its dents and rust, because it had space to transport friends, animals, vet supplies and the other paraphernalia she tended to accumulate. Yes, it was ideal for her real life, but it didn't fit the sexy twin image.

"You like convertibles," he commented.

"Love them." That was the truth, though they were, and would always be, utterly impractical for her lifestyle. Not to mention, way beyond her budget. Lucky Ann, with a lawyer's income—even if she did spend more time at work than enjoying her cute little car.

Suzanne unlocked the trunk, careful not to scratch the gleaming paint. She handed Jaxon the picnic basket and reached for the travel rug.

"No, not the rug."

She frowned. What was wrong with it? She'd washed it twice to get rid of the cat hairs.

"I've got something better," he said.

Curious, she followed him across the parking lot to a black Porsche convertible. "Oh my. Very nice."

He shrugged. "It's a rental. But I like convertibles too."

Was this what he drove, back in San Francisco? Probably so. Whatever he did for a living, he must be doing just fine.

If this was a normal first date, she'd already know the basic details of his life. She was definitely curious. Maybe he was a successful artist, a spy, a . . . She couldn't think of a job glamorous and exotic enough to suit Jaxon. Perhaps he had inherited wealth and was a jet-setter, a patron of worthy charities and arts.

Probably it was better not to know. After all, he might be an accountant. She studied his firm butt as he leaned into the trunk of the sporty car. Nope, that butt did not belong to an accountant.

He pulled something out and handed it to her. "Remember this?"

A striped beach towel. The kind of thing a person bought on holiday. Wait a minute! "That's my towel. From Crete." She gazed at him, dumbfounded. "How on earth . . ."

"You left it with me. Don't you remember?"

He was talking about the part of the afternoon she'd forgotten, and she hastened to cover her slip. "Yes, of course. But, you kept it all these years?"

"A souvenir."

She smiled and folded the towel over her arm. "Let's see if we remember what to do with it."

"I'd bet on it."

As they walked back to the beach, she thought about what she'd just said. Were they actually going to have sex on this towel again? On a public beach, with other people around, in only semidarkness?

The ache between her thighs told her yes. In some fashion, they were. They'd find a way, and it would be edgy and adventuresome and incredibly exciting.

Again, their hands joined as they walked past a few couples and groups who had staked out their own patches of beach. Neither spoke, but the air between them seemed charged with tension. Sexual tension.

Finally, Jaxon stopped. "Here."

A huge log would serve as a backrest—and a token privacy barrier. Spreading her old towel, Suzanne thrilled to the fact that he'd kept it. She sat down and looked up at him expectantly. A shiver flicked across her shoulders, caused not by the balmy evening air but by the anticipation of his touch.

Jaxon lowered himself to the towel beside her. He was all

shadows but for the glint of his eyes under the moon and stars. She reached out, touched his chest. Firm muscles, under the thin fabric. "Off," she whispered.

He hauled the T-shirt over his head and now she could run greedy hands over his bare shoulders, chest, flat stomach. She could trace ribs, tease nipples. She leaned forward and took one of those pebbly nubs between her lips. When she sucked, hard, his body clenched.

Then he reached for the hem of her crop top and eased it off. His hands gripped her shoulders and pressed her back until she was lying on the towel. Then he leaned over her, scattering kisses over her face, then down her chest, finally making it to her needy breasts.

Desire built again, a roller coaster making that long, slow climb to the top.

He rolled a nipple between his lips, flicked it with his tongue, circled it, then sucked, but more gently than she had. She held her breath, savoring the intense sensation.

Needing to touch him *now*, she fumbled with his belt, undoing the buckle, the button of his jeans, sliding down the zipper. When she thrust her hand inside, she gripped hard, pulsing heat.

He lifted his head from her breast and his mouth came down on hers in a hungry kiss.

She ran her hand up and down his shaft, and he moaned into her mouth. "I want you, Suzanne. Now."

"Yes!"

Her fingers still circled him as he ran his own hand up the inside of her leg. When he encountered the wet silk at her crotch he pressed his palm firmly against the curve of her body, then stroked her with a finger, through the silk.

It was her turn to moan and he murmured, "Ssh, lover."

He skimmed the panties down her legs and spread the sides of her skirt, then covered her with his body.

From a few yards away, up on the path, she heard hushed voices, a man and a woman chatting about what they were going to do on the weekend.

Jaxon's dark body wouldn't reflect the moonlight the way her pale one would. Surely no one would see them. Not if they were quiet.

He shoved down his jeans and underwear as he settled between her thighs. Their bodies shifted position, adjusting to each other. She felt the press of his naked maleness and spread her legs to welcome him, the sense of wanting almost unbearable now they were touching so intimately.

She heard something crackle and realized he was opening a condom package.

"Let me," she said. Then, awkward in the darkness, she fumbled to roll the sheath down his length. He held unnaturally still and she guessed he was as close to coming as she was.

The moment she finished, his mouth came down on hers again and she let her lips and tongue speak her passion. Her hips began to move, telling him she was ready. More than ready.

He ran a hand between them, stroking her moist folds, parting her, and the tip of his penis probed her entry. She wanted to cry out with sheer delight, but instead sighed into his open mouth.

She stroked both hands down his back as he eased slowly into her. Although she was soaking wet, she was tight, and he was the biggest man she'd ever taken inside her. Yet the friction was pleasure, far more than pain.

So much pleasure she was afraid she'd come before he was even fully inside.

Suzanne pushed his jeans down farther and gripped his buttocks, which had the desired effect of making him plunge hard and fast, filling her all the way.

Her body tightened around him, gathering itself, and she

knew that, if he moved again, right at that moment, she would shatter.

"Don't move," she whispered urgently.

She felt his body tense. "Why not?"

"I'm so close."

"Me too. I've been hard since I saw you."

"I noticed."

Voices approached again, this time not from the paved path but from the beach itself. This couple would pass within feet of them. Hurriedly, Suzanne hauled Jaxon's jeans up again, trying to cover his backside. As her hands brushed his naked butt, he shuddered and the movement rippled through her.

She felt her climax coming and tried to hold it off, but the force was too powerful to fight. Burying her mouth against Jaxon's shoulder and gripping his waist, holding tight, she let the blinding pleasure of orgasm take her.

And as her body spasmed, Jaxon moved too, sliding out and plunging deep and hard, just one tremendous thrust, locking his body to hers. His head went back in a silent cry. Clamped together, his hands on her shoulders, hers at his waist, their bodies trembled and shuddered silently. It seemed to go on forever.

6

Finally, Suzanne recovered enough to start taking in her surroundings. The stars shone serenely above them; the ocean
breathed in gentle sighs against the beach. The voices had
moved past them and were now just a murmur in the distance.

"Jesus, Suzanne." His hands loosened their grip on her
shoulders.

She peeled her own off his waist so she could stroke his
back. Her fingers trembled, and so did her voice when she
whispered, "I told you not to move."

He gave a soft chuckle. "You groped my butt."

She smothered her own laughter against his chest—hot,
damp, smelling of sex. "I was pulling up your pants, so those
people wouldn't see that fine butt of yours."

"Guess they saw a lot more than that," he said wryly.

No! "They couldn't see us," she said, wanting it to be true.
Or did she? Wait a minute, she was sexy Suzanne. Hadn't she
just proven that? She tried to infuse a Marlene Dietrich huski-
ness into her voice. "You think they saw us?"

His smile was a quick flash of white in the moonlight. "Dunno. I was occupied at the time."

This time she didn't bother burying her face when she laughed. "Yeah, I noticed."

"No, you didn't. You were busy too."

And how! "Women are capable of doing two things at once."

"Definitely the superior sex," he said easily.

Hmm.

While Suzanne was wondering whether he really meant that, he asked, "Would you care if they saw?"

There was only one way the sexy twin could answer. "Not unless they call the cops."

"God, woman, you really are outrageous."

She smiled with pride. Mission accomplished.

A residual tremor shivered through her and she kissed his shoulder. "That was incredible, Jaxon."

He buried his face in her hair and dropped a kiss of his own. "It was. There's something about beaches, isn't there?"

"There's something about you."

"About us together."

Her fingers danced across his back. "Or even us by e-mail."

His body shook with laughter. "Are you typing sexy messages to me?"

"Mmm." She typed quickly on his lower back. Then she pressed her finger into the hollow just above his buttocks. "And that was 'Send.' "

"Tell me what you typed."

"I said, 'Next time, let's make it last longer.' "

"Oh yeah!" He eased out of her, off her body, and she missed his heat. She sat up, pulling her skirt across her legs, hunting for her top, then slipping it on. Jaxon pulled up his jeans and fastened them. When he reached for his T-shirt, she put a hand on his arm. "Are you cold?"

"Don't want me to put it on?"

"I like looking at you. You have such a beautiful body."

"You're the beautiful one." Some men might have said it automatically, but the appreciative tone of Jaxon's voice told her he meant it.

People often said she was pretty, but she'd never felt beautiful. Only with him.

This evening was working out perfectly, as wonderful, in its own way, as Crete. And now she had enough experience to know how rare it was—at least for her—to have such incredible sex.

Sex, she reminded herself. That's all it was. Not making love, or anything foolish and romantic like that. Just sex. Utterly fantastic sex.

"Now that we've satisfied one appetite," she said, "want to work on another?" She opened the lid of the picnic basket. "I brought white wine. I wasn't sure if . . ."

"Sounds great."

She handed him the bottle and the corkscrew, then began to open the packages of Granville Island goodies, releasing the aromas of pepper ham, Greek olives, Italian antipasto, sharp cheddar into the night air. Soon they were sitting with their backs against the big log, toasting each other and sharing treats.

After the first few mouthfuls, Suzanne realized they'd reached a new stage, an awkward one. Now was the time for conversation, but what should she say?

Jaxon broke the silence. "This beach is terrific. Do you live near here?"

"No, I—" Wait, there was something wrong about this. It wasn't that she didn't trust him with her address; it was more that he'd asked a personal question and she was all set to answer. Was this going to lead to a chat about apartments, jobs, friends? The conventional first-date conversation, in which she'd be forced to reveal Suze, the sensible twin?

And did she really want to know whether he was an accountant or a cat burglar?

If she gave him a partial answer, perhaps he'd take the hint and not probe more deeply. The only probing she wanted from Jaxon tonight was physical, not conversational. "Further away from town," she said casually.

"I'm surprised what a short drive it was from downtown. Once you're out here, the city seems far away. I can't think of a comparable spot in San Francisco."

Relieved he'd accepted her evasiveness, she said, "I don't know San Francisco very well. I've only been there once, and I did the normal tourist things. Fisherman's Wharf, Ghirardelli Square, Chinatown. A boat ride over to Sausalito."

He chuckled softly. "Yeah, you hit the tourist biggies. Did you like the city?"

"Very much. It's colorful, attractive. I got the sense there's a bunch of interesting places and activities to discover, beyond the standard tourist stuff." She reflected. "Well, I guess that's true of most cities. They put on one face for tourists, but the locals learn a more personal one."

"Sounds right."

And that was what she was doing, Suzanne thought. Putting on a sexy face for Jaxon, in hopes he'd never look beyond it to the more personal, boring one.

He sipped the wine. "This is unusual, but I like it. What is it?"

"A gewürztraminer from a winery called Quail's Gate, in the Okanagan." She'd wondered if she should buy Greek wine, then decided Cretan wine was great on Crete but Vancouver called for BC wine.

"Okanagan?"

"In the interior of the province. The BC wine industry isn't as old as California's, but we have some really good wines." She wasn't a connoisseur, but having dinner with the Foursome every Monday had expanded her knowledge of all things alcoholic. "You can visit a number of the wineries and do wine-tasting."

"I did that in the Sonoma Valley once."

"Not Napa?" We can do this, she thought as she spread pepper cream cheese on a slice of baguette, and topped it with a couple of olives. We can make interesting conversation without dragging out the ho-hum personal details.

"Napa's too touristy. Sonoma's quieter, and the scenery is . . ." He paused, considering, then said, "Peaceful. Serene. Makes you feel like you could just sit in the sun, breathe in the air, drink some wine, sit there for hours. Or drift into the sky and see the whole thing from a hot-air balloon."

Wow! It sounded amazing, but not exactly . . . hot. Out of character, for him. "You did that?"

"Oh yeah." His expression, in the moonlight, held a strange combination of warmth and wryness, and suddenly she got it. He'd gone wine-tasting and hot-air ballooning with a woman. Just what was he remembering?

"That sounds like fun," she said, trying to sound carefree, not curious or jealous.

"Maybe you'll come visit one day, and we'll do it." He tickled her arm with something and she realized he was holding the tiger lily. "Ever had sex in a hot-air balloon?"

Was that what he'd been up to? Oh yeah, they certainly were avoiding the prosaic first-date topics. "I have to admit I haven't, Jaxon. But I'm game to try."

"I'd have to get my license to fly one."

Aha! Sounded like he hadn't actually *done it*—literally—with another woman.

"Unless you wouldn't mind having sex in front of the pilot?" he went on, one eyebrow cocked.

She shook her head quickly. "That's a bit much." Oh my gosh, had he done *that*? Did she sound hopelessly naïve?

"For me too," he said, to her relief. "It's one thing if people happen to wander by on the beach, on a dark night. . . ."

"Exactly."

He glanced out at the still ocean, then turned back to her, with that eyebrow cocked again. "So, outrageous69, what do you think about going skinny-dipping? This beach is pretty close to deserted."

"Oh! But Jaxon, the water's freezing cold."

"Kids were in swimming earlier," he teased.

"Kids never notice the cold."

"I'll keep you warm. Or are you chicken, Suzanne?"

Those were fighting words. Besides, she couldn't resist the thought of Jaxon naked under the stars. She skimmed her top over her head and undid the buttons at the waist of her skirt.

He gave a startled laugh and she paused. Perhaps he hadn't expected her to accept the dare?

Her fingers attacked the buttons again. So much the better. She wanted to astonish him, keep him off balance, give him the most erotic, exotic adventure he could ever imagine.

He was unfastening his jeans. She stood and let her skirt slide down her hips, wondering briefly where he'd tossed her panties. Jaxon froze in the act of pulling his jeans down, and stared at her. "God, you're beautiful. Are you a woman, or a mermaid risen from the sea?"

She glanced down. Her pale skin reflected the moonlight so much better than his. If anyone walked by now, they'd sure get an eyeful. But Jaxon's dazed expression told her that eyeful was something to be proud of. "Follow me in and find out," she dared him.

Then, without hurrying, she walked as gracefully as she could in the sand, to the edge of the water. Knowing his eyes followed her made her nipples tighten. The ache began again, low in her belly. He could arouse her just by watching her.

She toed the water. Had she said cold? Yikes, it was freezing!

She forced herself to take a few cautious steps in, feeling goose bumps rise on her whole body. Now there was a picture: female nude, with giant goose bumps.

Was he going to leave her standing here alone?

Jax watched, mesmerized, as Suzanne strolled away from him. She was breathtaking: straight-backed, that amazing mass of red-gold hair hanging halfway down her back, curvy hips and backside, then long, gorgeous legs.

Tonight, as the water lapped her knees, he could almost imagine those legs joining together, forming a tail. She'd flip her tail, swim out to sea, and he'd never see her again.

Instead, she turned, and, if such a thing were possible, the view improved. Graceful female curves in absolutely the right quantities. She crooked a finger, then turned again, and walked deeper into the ocean.

He cast a quick glance up and down the beach. Oh hell, he wasn't going to wuss out. He had a mermaid to catch.

Hurriedly, he dragged his jeans and boxer briefs down, struggling to free his erection. Then he strode the few steps to the waterline and splashed in. Jesus, it was ice! On the other hand, there was the sight of Suzanne to heat his blood. He was almost surprised the water around his legs didn't boil.

Trying to keep his balance on the pebbly bottom, he walked toward her. She held out her hand and he took it. He leaned forward so his breath tickled her ear and whispered, "You are one x-rated woman."

She gave him a cat-smile. "I'm not the one who's doing hard-core porn."

He glanced down. The water came to mid thigh, and its chill had done nothing to discourage his jutting cock. But he was positive he wasn't alone in this sweet agony. He slid a hand between her legs, making her gasp. "You're as turned on as I am."

"I'm not"—she sucked in a breath as his finger invaded her slick heat—"denying it," she choked out.

Suzanne reached for his penis, obviously deciding two could play this game. Jax didn't care. The great thing was, it didn't matter who won.

She caressed his length, then pulled away from his probing finger. Leaning down, she gathered a handful of water, then brought her hand back to his erection. He gasped at the shock of cold water against his heat.

When she dropped to her knees, he winced at the thought of the freezing water, the rough sand and pebbles biting into her flesh. But he didn't pull her up. He had to find out what she was going to do.

She bathed him again with icy water, then leaned forward and took him in her mouth. Her very hot mouth.

His hands came down on her shoulders, gripping convulsively. "Jesus, Suzanne," he hissed. "You can't—" He broke off as she swirled her tongue around the head of his cock.

Oh man. She could.

She sucked, swished her tongue around some more, nibbled with her lips, scraped her teeth ever so gently against his aching flesh, cupped his balls in her hands. Then she released him and gathered another handful of water. When she splashed him, his body bucked involuntarily, and it did again when she once more applied her mouth and hands.

His hips began to move as he thrust into her mouth. He forced himself to hold back, giving her only as much of his length as she could handle. But even that was too much for him and he could feel his body tightening, gathering itself, preparing to surge heedlessly toward orgasm.

He yanked on her shoulders. "Come here."

When she released him, he dragged her to her feet and into his arms. His body trembled as he struggled for control. "You call this skinny-dipping?" he managed to get out.

She laughed, pulled free and splashed a handful of water up his chest. "I'm just getting started. You'll see what you get for calling me chicken, mister." She turned and plowed through the ocean, heading away from shore. When the water reached her waist, she threw herself forward and swam a few strokes. He was right behind her, almost glad when the freezing water subdued his lust.

They romped, splashed, twined chilly naked limbs around each other, stole a kiss or two, until the cold drove them back to the beach.

Suzanne reached the towel first and flung herself on it, facedown. He sprawled on top of her, their bodies racked with shivers until they began to warm each other. His hard-on was growing again, and he pressed into her backside, letting his cock slip between her legs. She moaned and wriggled her butt toward him, curving it into his belly, encouraging him to slide back and forth between her thighs.

He moved her hair aside, a damp mass that covered her shoulders, smelling of salt water and some complicated mix of flowers and herbs, and kissed the nape of her neck. She tilted her head to the side and he took that as an offer to nibble her earlobe.

He slid an arm underneath her, lifting her even higher and she arched cooperatively. He fingered the folds between her legs, slippery with wet heat, and thrust a finger inside her.

"Jaxon," she murmured, "you feel so good, but I want all of you."

He found her female nub, in its own way as swollen as he was, and teased it, feeling his own arousal build just as if she'd been touching him.

She arched higher in a wordless demand. He eased back and positioned himself at her entrance.

And then he remembered. Protection. Damn! He hated to wait, and he hated wearing a latex sheath. He wanted to pour himself into Suzanne, to join his juices with hers.

Cursing silently, he eased away and hunted for his jeans. He fumbled another condom out of his pocket and got the damned thing on, though the size he always bought now seemed too small.

Finally, he was back in place. His hand circled her waist, snugging her body close to his, and slowly he eased his way in. She was so tight, the friction so delicious, it was all he could do to maintain a slow pace.

She rose slightly, to rest her head on her folded arms, and he eased back to hold her hips, bracing himself as he moved in and out. Almost all the way out, until the night air pricked the damp flesh of his groin, then all the way back in, reaching into her center, touching her secret places.

She shifted position again, freeing one arm, and reached back to touch his shaft, to circle the base, then to fondle his balls. He plunged faster, even deeper, and her body met his, pushing back against him, opening wide to him.

She was panting, moaning a little but pressing her mouth into her arm to muffle the sound.

He was close, so close, to losing himself, his movements were getting wild, uncoordinated. He wanted to bring her with him but didn't have much time.

Jax reached for her clit, fingered it, felt her buck under him. She moaned again, a high, wild whimper of sound, and it undid him. His balls tightened and he arched and thrust into her, finally letting go, surging into climax. Her own spasms sucked around him like waves and he wanted to shout out his pleasure but managed to hold in his cries.

With effort, he kept himself from collapsing on top of her. Gradually, her body folded down until she was lying flat on the towel, with him spread over her like a blanket. Still inside her. God how he wanted to stay there, and again he resented wearing a condom.

He kissed her shoulder. "Warm enough?"

"Mmm," she purred. "Toasty. How about you? Are you freezing your butt off?"

Now that she mentioned it, and the heat of sex was cooling, he was feeling chilled. Their adventure was coming to a close.

He wanted to invite her back to his hotel room or, even better, invite himself to her place. But he sensed that was against their unspoken rules. Did either one of them really want to face the dawn together? Morning breath and the need for polite breakfast conversation? This wasn't a conventional date, but an erotic escapade.

Still, he couldn't stop himself from murmuring in her ear, "Do you have plans for tomorrow?"

She paused—long enough to make him wonder if he hadn't satisfied her, if she had a date with someone else. Then she said, "I'm tied up during the day, but I'm free in the evening. You'll still be here?"

They hadn't planned past this one night. But feeling optimistic—and horny—he'd made his return reservation for Sunday, and brought his computer and a briefcase full of work, a fact he didn't plan to confess. "I'll be here. What time's good? Want me to pick you up?"

"Hmm." She stirred restlessly under him and he eased off. She began to sort through their clothes. "Okay, how about quarter past six, the corner of Fourth and Fir. From downtown you drive—"

"I'll find it," he broke in. "We'll go for dinner?"

Another pause and he wondered if the suggestion was too unimaginative. Maybe he should've thought up another wild picnic. But then she said, "Sounds good. Feel like Greek?"

He grinned appreciatively. "I have a special fondness for all things Greek."

She chuckled. "There's a little place called Maria's Taverna. It's nothing fancy but the food is great."

Dinner and conversation. What would they talk about? The more time he spent with Suzanne, the more convinced he was that this woman wouldn't be impressed by a buttoned-down, partnership-track kind of guy.

He could make up an intriguing autobiography.

No, he didn't want to lie to her.

Wait a minute. This should be easy. Women were the ones who liked to talk. He'd just let her go on about whatever interested her, and if she slowed down, then he'd ask a few questions.

Both clothed now, they got to their feet. When he stuck his hands in his pockets, he came across her bra, and handed it to her. She stowed it in the picnic basket, then bent down to retrieve the towel. After shaking and folding it, she handed it to him. "Yours, I believe."

"You don't mind if I keep it?"

"You're the one who collects sex souvenirs," she teased. Then her voice went soft, a little husky. "I like the idea of you having it."

He hoisted the picnic basket and, arms around each other's waists, they made their way to the parking lot.

"Your hair's wet," he said. "Want to put the top up on your car so you don't get chilled?"

She stowed the basket in the trunk. "I probably should."

She fumbled with the black top and he helped her secure it in place. Then she leaned back against the car and he leaned forward, aligning his body to hers. Her hair was a mass of tangled gold, her slender arms were cool under his hands, her nipples were hard buds against his chest. Even the artificial light of the parking lot didn't dull the glow of her cheeks, the sparkle in her sea-green eyes. "Thanks for tonight, Suzanne. It's been—" Try as hard as he could, the right word escaped him. Again, he'd done things with her that he couldn't have imagined himself doing.

"Yes, it's been that all right," she agreed. "I'm so glad you came, Jaxon." Then she gave a little laugh. "I mean, came to Vancouver."

He bent down and touched his lips to hers in the gentlest of kisses. "Sleep well, outrageous69."

"You too, caveman." She slid into the little car, started the engine, then blew him a kiss and drove away.

He stood, watching until her taillights disappeared, then slid into the sleek Porsche and found his way to the hotel. He was cold and damp, sandy and stiff—and he'd never felt better. Yeah, Suzanne had sure as hell delivered on the promise in her personal ad.

What would tomorrow night bring?

To Suzanne, it felt like Ann's Miata flew home on autopilot. She was so absorbed in reliving the night's adventures that she found herself pulling into her parking slot off the back alley with absolutely no recollection of the drive. She could only hope she hadn't run any red lights.

Glad that the windows of her parents' house were dark, she slipped into her converted-garage apartment, set down the picnic basket and headed into the bathroom for a long, luxurious shower. Much as she'd love to keep the scent, the feel, of Jaxon on her skin, the sand in her hair—and other, even less comfortable places—had to go.

Oh my God, what had she done?

Had sex on a public beach with a man she barely knew.

And yet, it had felt right. Amazingly right, to touch Jaxon and be touched by him.

As the water cascaded over her, she realized she was standing there with a loopy grin on her face. The man was fabulous. And with him, she was downright fabulous too. She laughed with sheer joy, and lifted her face to the shower's spray.

Tomorrow she'd see him again.

Was that wise?

Anxiety rushed in to replace the joy. And with it came the recollection that she'd promised the girls she'd phone Ann and report her safe return. It was late, but Ann had insisted she call, whatever the hour.

She dialed the familiar number. When Ann's voice said "Suzanne?" a little breathlessly, she said, "Yes, it's me. Were you asleep?"

"No! Not at all. I'm fine. I mean, I'm awake." And in fact Ann did sound remarkably wide-awake, if slightly unfocused. "Uh, how did it go?"

"Fantastic. And I'm home safe, and alone."

"Good."

She was surprised and relieved that Ann didn't press for details. By Monday, she'd probably want to share at least some of her adventure, but right now the memories were too fresh and personal. She wanted to hug them to herself.

"You're really okay?" Ann said softly.

"I feel wonderful. I want to thank you and the others for being there."

"Uh, you're welcome."

Ann was sounding distinctly odd. Was she uncomfortable with her friend morphing into the sexy twin?

"We can talk about it Monday." A self-satisfied grin snuck its way onto her lips. "Besides, there'll be even more to tell by then."

"What? Suze, you're not seeing him again?"

"Tomorrow. No, I guess it's tonight."

There was a pause, then, "What's the plan? Do you need backup?"

"No, we'll be out in public."

"Like tonight? Another dark, near-deserted place?"

Man, Ann really was stressed about this. "No," Suzanne hurried to reassure her. "We're going out for dinner. He's picking me up from work. Well, not from work exactly, I'm meeting him down the block."

"Down the block?"

"I'm trying to preserve the sexy-twin mystique. I haven't told him about my job, school, the stuff that would ruin my image."

"But, that's who you are, Suze. If you're seeing this man again, don't you want him to know who you are?"

"No." The answer was immediate, and it made her reflect. "We have something special going, and I don't want anything to spoil it. Besides, we probably won't even see each other again, after this weekend." She felt a twinge of regret. And yet, how long could she role-play sexy Suzanne?

"Oh Ann, I've done something dumb. I should have said I'd meet him later. Sure, I can take a change of clothes to work and grab a quick shower there, but how am I going to transition my psyche from vet assistant to sex goddess in under fifteen minutes?"

"You're asking the wrong woman," her friend said dryly. "Okay, so he picks you up, then what's the plan?"

Suzanne groaned. "Dinner at Maria's."

"What's with the groan? Maria's is great."

"Yeah, the food's terrific, the Greek atmosphere's a good thing, but . . . It's just a tiny neighborhood restaurant. I should have suggested—oh, I don't know, maybe a Japanese place with tatami rooms where we could pull the screens and have some privacy to fool around."

"You met in Greece, not Japan."

"We had sex in Greece. That's why Jaxon came to Vancouver. For sex, not food and chat."

"But he agreed to dinner."

"Actually, it was his idea." And what did *that* mean? Maybe he did want food and chat?

Ann sighed. "Suze?"

"Mmm?"

"You've made the date, and it sounds safe. So don't agonize over it."

"I guess you're right. Yes, sure, of course you're right. Thanks."

"You're welcome. And listen, I'm glad you're okay. Stay safe, eh?"

Suzanne hung up. Yes, agonizing was pointless. If things went downhill from here, she'd still have terrific memories of tonight.

She put the drooping tiger lily in a bud vase, rescued her bra, stowed the contents of the picnic basket in the fridge, then took the vase and the abalone shell into the bedroom. Her two bed-cats were a sleeping tangle of fur on the duvet, but Mouse gave a squeaky meow and hopped down from her desk to twine around her ankles.

"You've deserted the keyboard." She bent down to stroke him. "I should take advantage of that."

She didn't want to be sappy, but figured it wouldn't hurt to send a quick message to Jaxon, in case he checked his e-mail before she saw him again.

She accessed her outrageous69 account and started a message. Don't know when you'll pick this up, Jaxon, but I wanted to . . .

She stopped. What she wanted to do was gush about how wonderful the evening had been. She wanted to tell him how he'd made her feel like a sexy woman. That she'd again had that deep sense of intimacy when they joined, the feeling that their bodies belonged together, that they somehow completed each other.

How distinctly uncool.

As she stared at the screen, running her mouse aimlessly in circles on the mouse pad, she noticed the envelope icon indicating she had new messages in her normal e-mail program. When she checked, she saw notes from both Rina and Jenny.

Rina's said, I've been thinking of you all evening, Suze. I had a really good feeling about you and Jaxon. You seemed so natural together. And wow, I know you said he was gorgeous but I figured maybe your memory was exaggerating, and obviously it wasn't. Sure hope you had a good evening. Let me know, okay?

Suzanne clicked REPLY. We had an unbelievably wonderful evening, and I'm home safe and alone. I'm seeing him again tomorrow night. At a restaurant, as I've already reassured Ann. I promise to tell all—well, almost all—on Monday night.

Jenny wrote, I have one word for you, Suzie Q. Hottie! No, make that two words: major hottie! Hope the two of you got seriously down and dirty.

She wrote back, Very seriously! She grinned smugly, thinking how those two little words of her own would torture poor Jen, and clicked SEND.

Then she returned to her message to Jaxon, feeling better equipped to finish it. . . . I wanted to tell you I'm tingling inside, remembering the feel of you. You are so . . . incredibly . . . hot. Can't wait for next time. In the meantime, I wish you sweet—no, make that naughty—dreams.

Good. No schlocky romantic stuff. Just sex. Exactly the way both of them wanted it.

Suzanne woke late on Saturday, realizing she'd forgotten to set her alarm. Hurriedly, she rushed through her morning preparations, then grabbed her backpack and stared into her closet, wondering what on earth to take for tonight's dinner date. Maybe it was a good thing she had no time for deliberation or she'd have been there for hours. She selected a few colorful items, remembered to add earrings and hurried outside.

"Morning, dear." Her mother's voice made her spin around, feeling as guilty as a teenager sneaking in past curfew.

Her mom, grey-streaked blond hair tousled, clad in a pretty cotton bathrobe, was holding a pair of secaturs. There was a gardening basket on the lawn, half full of peonies in two shades of pink.

"You're up early," Suzanne said.

"You know it's better to cut flowers before it gets too hot."

"Right, sure." Yes, she knew, but guilt was cramping her tongue.

"We noticed you were out late last night," her mom said. "Your van wasn't back when we went to bed. But it seems you've traded cars with Ann?"

The joys of living in her parents' backyard. No doubt they'd done some speculating as they sat at the breakfast table, seeing Ann's Miata where the VW usually sat. "Um, yes." Avoiding an out-and-out lie, she said, "Sometimes a gal needs a bigger car. The Miata's fun, but not so practical."

"Yes, I've always been surprised Ann owns a car like that. I think of her as such a sensible girl, just like you."

Suzanne stifled a groan, but at least the sensible car/girl discussion beat facing questions about where she'd been to all hours. Her mother bent to pick up a handful of peonies. "You're working today? Why not take some of these to the clinic? My plants are flourishing this year, and the season's so short, let's spread the joy."

"Thanks." She accepted the flowers and buried her face in the fluffy, overblown blooms, inhaling the familiar scent—spicy, almost sultry.

"By the way, Bethany called last night to say she and Joel were offered theater tickets for tonight, so your dad and I are keeping the grandkids. Why don't you come over and join us for a video and popcorn?"

Just the kind of homey evening she loved. But not tonight. "Sorry, I can't. I'm having dinner with a friend."

"Oh?" Her mother's eyebrows asked, "Anyone I know?"

Suzanne evaded the question by glancing at her watch. "Oh

my gosh, I'm going to be late." She hurried toward the Miata, saying over her shoulder, "Thanks again for the peonies."

When she climbed into the car and started it up, she saw her mother hadn't gone back to cutting flowers. She was still standing, secaturs in hand, watching Suzanne. Although the distance was too great to be sure, she just knew her mom's eyebrows were still cocked high.

7

When she arrived at work, Trish, the receptionist, gushed over the flowers. "Peonies are so feminine and sexy."

And so am I, Suzanne thought, grinning like a contented—and yes, very feminine and sexy—cat.

In the clinic kitchen, Trish arranged the flowers as Suzanne fixed herself a cup of coffee. The younger woman rattled on about her Friday night movie-and-pizza date. Suzanne wanted to say, "Girl, if you knew how I'd spent the evening, it would knock your little pink socks off!"

When Suzanne pulled a lab coat on over her T-shirt and khakis, Trish frowned at her in puzzlement. "Have you changed your hair? You look different."

"Same old me," Suzanne lied blithely.

She certainly hadn't changed her hair; she was wearing only her usual minimal amount of makeup, and the clothes were her standard working attire—and yet the two vets and several of the regular clients also commented on how well she was looking. "What's your prescription?" old Mr. Abernathy, owner of an equally ancient Boston Bull, asked her teasingly.

Not figuring it was wise to say, "Sex on the beach," she substituted, "Fresh air and exercise."

He nodded approvingly. "It's so nice to see there are some young people who live healthy, wholesome lives. Listen to the news these days and you get the picture it's all drugs and computer porn."

Well, at least she didn't use drugs!

When she had a break, she checked her cell phone and found voice mail from Rina asking her to call, and a text message from Jenny, reading, Bitch! Gimme deets!!!

Finding a private corner to hide out in, she tried Jenny, got a busy signal, then dialed Rina.

"So," her friend said, "it was everything you'd hoped it would be, seeing him again?"

"And more."

"I'm so happy for you. And you're going out tonight?"

"Dinner at Maria's."

"Oh Suze, that's wonderful. It sounds so romantic."

"I'm not sure I'd say romantic. But definitely erotic."

"Dinner at Maria's is erotic? Nope, this whole thing of you and Jaxon rediscovering each other and starting a relationship, it's the most romantic thing I've heard since, oh, since I watched *Ghost* again last weekend. I'm absolutely puce with envy." She let out a long, sappy sigh.

"In *Ghost*, her love interest was dead, for Christ's sake. Besides, you don't get it. Romance isn't what we're looking for. And if Jaxon really did get to know me, he'd probably dump me like a hot potato. After all, potatoes are the most boring vegetable in the world."

"I love potatoes."

"Me too," Suzanne said gloomily. "Especially mashed potatoes and gravy, with roast chicken and those tiny baby peas Mom grows in the garden each year and sticks in the freezer to last through the winter."

She shook her head dismissively. "Jaxon is this sophisticated guy who lives in San Francisco. He probably goes to all sorts of fancy restaurants. Bet he hasn't eaten mashed potatoes since he was a kid. If then. He has such a . . . an innate classiness, it's got to be nature plus nurture. I'm guessing his parents are wealthy, successful, sophisticated, not plain old normal folks like us and—"

"Good God, Suze," Rina broke in. "Slow down. Why don't you stop guessing and ask the guy?"

"Because our relationship isn't about parents and history; it's very much in the present, and all about sex."

"Then stop obsessing over his parents and history."

"Oh, stop being so damned logical." Chuckling, Suzanne hung up.

Next she phoned Jenny, and this time got through.

"You had sex!" Jen screeched.

"More than once."

"Where? How? And does the Denzel guy measure up to expectations?"

The Denzel guy? What was that about? "More than measures up."

"C'mon, Suzie, don't torture me. Tell me, tell me, tell me."

"On Monday. With the rest of the Foursome. Besides, there'll be more details after tonight." At least, she hoped there would. Unless she managed to bore him to impotency over dinner.

"You are doing the safe-sex thing, right?" Jenny asked.

"He brought condoms."

"You left it to him? Hey, anything new and supercool?"

"I honestly wasn't noticing the condoms."

Jenny gave a wicked giggle. "Good point. If the condom's more interesting than the guy, you got a real problem. Still . . ." Her voice trailed off.

"Still what?"

"Nothing. Gotta go."

Hmm. It wasn't like Jenny to break off a conversation on sex.

Suzanne learned why an hour or two later when she went out to reception to get the next patient, and a grinning Trish handed her a brown paper bag. "A friend of yours dropped this off for you."

"For me? Who?"

"A tiny Asian woman, dressed in hot pink, with glitzy finger-nails."

Jenny.

Suzanne took the bag, peered inside, and promptly dropped the package on the floor, scattering condoms. As Trish giggled, Suzanne hurriedly scooped the contents back into the bag, then rushed to her locker and shoved the bag into her backpack.

When she returned to the reception area, Trish murmured, "Hot date tonight?"

"The hottest," she whispered back. Then, at normal volume, "Okay, who's next?"

She did find an opportunity later in the afternoon to study the contents of the paper bag. A note from Jen said, "Recom-mended by the condomologist at Rubber Rainbow. Enjoy, on the condition you report back <g>."

Wow, Jenny'd actually gone to the specialty condom shop, just for her.

And there was sure lots to enjoy. Tricolor condoms, and glow-in-the-dark ones.

Flavors: chocolate, cola and banana. Banana? On the theory that if it looked like a banana, it might as well taste like one? But if Jaxon was a banana, he was definitely a chocolate-dipped one.

Then there were textures: ribs and dots, spirals, ribs and studs. Studs? Hmm.

When she hurried into the bathroom on the dot of six,

Suzanne had to admit she did have a I've-had-great-sex-and-am-going-to-do-it-again glow.

She pulled on a shower cap and took a quick shower, then changed into the clothes she'd brought along: a lacy thong and demi-bra, a denim miniskirt, a skimpy teal tank top and an emerald-green silk shirt. Leaving the shirt unbuttoned, she knotted it at the waist and rolled the sleeves up her forearms. Then she added dangly earrings enameled in shades of green and blue, and took a deep breath.

A vigorous toothbrushing, a quick mascara touch-up. No point applying lipstick. With any luck, it wouldn't last long. Her hair was still wound back into a knot, the way she wore it for work, and she decided not to set it loose. Wild was good, but riding top-down in Jaxon's Porsche would result in crazy-lady hair, which wasn't her most attractive look.

Oh God, this was dangerous. She and Jaxon had shared two amazing encounters. Was it pushing their luck to try for a third?

When she walked into the reception area, Trish whistled. "Watch out, Nicole Kidman!"

"Thanks," she murmured, trying not to grind her teeth. She bent to stroke Honey, a golden retriever pup who'd been in for shots and was waiting impatiently as her owner paid the bill.

She stepped out the door and paused to remove a couple of blond dog hairs from her sleeve. "The sexy twin," she murmured, reminding herself.

Then she scanned the street and there he was, down near the corner. Jaxon lounged against the black Porsche, gazing in the other direction. His clothing was the opposite of last night's. Today he wore a crisp white cotton shirt, open at the throat and rolled at the sleeves. It was tucked into tan linen pants, belted in sleek brown leather that matched his stylish loafers.

He turned his head, saw her walking toward him and strode in her direction. He gripped her hands. "Suzanne."

She tilted her head up for his kiss, a soft, closed-lipped one that lingered against her mouth. Her knees turned to jelly and she stumbled slightly, leaning against him for balance. His arms came around her and she put hers around his waist. They leaned together, not kissing, just holding each other. Her body was completely aware of his and she delighted in the heat of his skin beneath the white shirt, the strength of his thighs.

Against her belly, she felt him harden. She pressed closer, feeling the response in her own body. How could the desire be so immediate, so powerful? But was his desire for her, Suzanne Brennan, or for a Nicole Kidman knockoff?

A passerby whistled, and she eased back slightly. "Jaxon?"

"I know," he said reluctantly, his arms falling away. "Even we wouldn't have the nerve to make love here."

Though, almost, she would have. Why had she worried about her ability to play her sexy-twin role? The moment she was with Jaxon, she slipped into that skin without conscious thought.

When they reached his car, he opened the passenger door for her, then went around and got in on the driver's side. In silence they did up their seat belts. She glanced across, saw the way his erection tented the loose trousers, and squeezed her thighs together. She wanted all that hard maleness inside her, but first she wanted a good, up-close and personal look. Last night, under the light of moon and stars, his body had been magnificent, but she wanted to make a more detailed, well-lit inspection.

"See something you like?" he drawled.

She smiled boldly. "So far, so good. Can't tell for sure until I get the wrapping off."

He gave a pleased hoot. "And you'll get your chance." Then his face softened. "You look gorgeous. Vibrant, exotic."

"Do you think I look like Nicole Kidman?"

"What? You mean the actress?" He narrowed his eyes and studied her again. "I guess maybe your hair, a little bit. But no, I don't think so. Are you, uh, trying to?" he asked cautiously.

She threw back her head and laughed. "No, I'm not. Most definitely not. Thank you, Jaxon."

He shook his head, and his bafflement was the highest compliment she could receive. It was clear he'd never seen a resemblance. It was her, just plain Suzanne, who stoked his libido.

"I got your e-mail this morning," he said. "Yeah, I did have naughty dreams." He leaned close and whispered in her ear, "You gave me a wet dream."

"Should I apologize?"

He grinned. "Not to me. Maybe to the chambermaid, but I did leave a big tip. Now, where am I taking us?"

She was more than a little tempted to tell him to head back to his hotel. But she could hear Ann's voice in her head warning her it wasn't safe.

The restaurant was less than a mile away, but she wanted a little time with him first. A scenic detour seemed in order. She directed him down to Cornwall, a narrow road that ran near the ocean, past Kits Beach.

He rested his hand on her bare thigh. "I like the short skirt." His fingers flirted with the hem, which had crept almost to the top of her thighs. A few inches away from where he stroked, the new thong she'd finally had the guts to wear was growing damp.

"You look wonderful." She touched his bare forearm. "Coffee." Then she plucked at the shirt sleeve. "With whipped cream on top." Finally, she put her hand on his leg, feeling the rough linen and the firm thigh underneath. "And a splash of Bailey's Irish Cream. My favorite liqueur."

"Thirsty, are you?" He released her thigh to shift gears at a stop sign, and she felt the play of muscles in his leg.

"Getting thirstier by the moment." She caressed his thigh, sliding her hand to the inside, and upward. The bulge in his pants grew and as it did, so did the tension between her thighs. She crossed her legs.

Through the thin fabric, she closed her hand around him. He sucked in a breath, then took a hand off the steering wheel and placed it over hers, squeezing down, encouraging her.

When he let go, she slid her hand up and down, feeling him respond. But this was too frustrating, touching him through two layers of fabric. She eased his zipper down and slipped her hand inside his pants and underwear, finding his nakedness and curling her fingers around him.

His pelvis tilted and he thrust upward, into her hand. She released her seat belt and moved closer. Then she freed him so she could see that beautiful dark shaft rising out of the creamy trousers. A chocolate Popsicle, just waiting for her to lick, suck. . . .

"Suzanne! We've got the top down."

"Oh yes, we certainly do." She began to stroke up and down.

He groaned. "My God, woman . . ."

"Tell me if you want me to stop."

He groaned again. "Don't stop. It feels too good."

It did. He felt so good in her hand that she was getting unbearably aroused too, just from touching him, seeing him. He was huge. Where imahottie had likely been exaggerating when he claimed seven inches, Jaxon had all of that, and a good inch more. She marveled that her body could encompass all of him.

Moisture beaded the tip of his cock and she used her index finger to swirl it around his velvety softness.

He squirmed in the seat, then cursed and said, "God, I can't take it."

She glanced up. They were on Point Grey Road now, a street of large, expensive homes, some set back from the road. She pointed toward a tree-screened drive. "There, turn into that driveway."

Jerkily, he obeyed, driving to a parking area beside a West Coast–style mansion, and turned the engine off. "That's . . . the restaurant?" Her hand kept up its rhythm and he could barely choke the words out.

"Nope." But, as she'd hoped, there were no other cars, and no sign of life.

She released him, hunted in her purse for a particular condom. "Chocolate," she said, opening the package. "Seems like the perfect match." She eased it onto him, bent over and locked her lips around him.

He came out of the seat, gasping, "Oh yeah!" Then he fumbled for a lever and his seat suddenly reclined, giving her better access.

Her taste buds were flooded with an odd, but not unpleasant flavor. Chocolate? Definitely not as tasty as a chocolate bar, but not bad. She explored every inch of him, sucking and flicking and swirling her tongue. And while her tongue played, so did her hand, circling his base, sliding up and down.

He squirmed, thrust, moaned, then gripped her head and tried to lift her away. "Stop, you have to stop or I'll come." The words grated out.

She smiled, reveling in her female power. "You don't want to come?"

He groaned. "Of course I want to. But it's so one-sided—"

Before he could finish the thought, she leaned down again and carried on where she'd left off. Her own thighs were clenched tight, against the mounting desire that had her too, on the verge of orgasm.

Jaxon's muscles were locked, resisting her. Then, suddenly, he surrendered. He began to move with her, then let go with a wrenching groan and exploded.

She could smell that special musk that was Jaxon's skin, Jaxon's sweat, Jaxon's essence, and wished she was tasting him rather than a condom.

Finally the spasms subsided and his body flopped back bonelessly.

After a moment, she raised her head.

His eyes were glowing with an emotion she couldn't read, but it was definitely positive. "You're going to kill me."

"You'll die happy." Without even trying, her voice came out Dietrich-husky.

"You're every man's sexual fantasy come to life."

All she cared about was being his fantasy, but that was something she probably shouldn't tell him.

He glanced down, then removed the condom, knotted the end, and slipped it beside the seat. "I can't believe you did that. I mean, here, in someone's driveway. You don't know the people who live here, do you?"

"Uh-uh. So, maybe you should zip up and we should move on."

His lips curved. "Not quite yet."

"But . . ."

He did zip up his pants. But then, rather than turning the key in the ignition, he leaned across her and fumbled for something. Suddenly her seat went back until she was almost lying down. "Jaxon!"

His hand slipped under her skirt. "Turnabout is fair play."

"Oh my God."

His fingers found the crotch of her thong, where she was soaking wet. "Pull up your skirt, Suzanne."

She obeyed, revealing her lower body, clothed in a skimpy triangle of black lace. He made a husky purring sound in his throat and leaned over, struggling with the steering wheel, trying to contort his body so he could put his face in her lap.

It just wasn't possible, so he raised himself up again and kissed her, running his fingers over the strip of silk between her legs. She shuddered as he somehow found all the places that were most sensitive. Her hips writhed as he tantalized her.

He slid the silk aside and now stroked the swollen, aching flesh. She lifted herself against him shamelessly, begging for release. He stroked faster and she squirmed, pressed, felt the tension building inexorably.

Their mouths were locked together, but she wasn't really kissing him, just panting her need against his lips.

And then he touched his finger to her clit and sensation exploded. She arched and cried out, feeling the spasms wrench through her and spend themselves against his hand. He held her until her muscles relaxed and she let out a long sigh. "Oh . . . my . . . God."

He laughed softly. "My sentiments exactly."

Then he eased away. "Should we go before someone comes along and catches us?"

"I suppose," she said dreamily. Then she pulled herself together enough to remember where they were. "Oh yes, let's get out of here." It was pure luck no one had discovered them yet.

In the tiny Greek restaurant, Jaxon studied Suzanne as she chatted with the waiter. She'd been here before, obviously. Many times. With other men? Well, of course.

He hated the jealousy that sprang up inside him. Why should he think he was special? Why would he *want* to be special? It wasn't like he was looking for a relationship. Been there, done that, failed miserably. Wasn't about to try again.

Even taking this much time off work made him antsy. But hell, he'd got a lot done today, and if he put in a long night when he got back to San Francisco tomorrow, he ought to be caught up by Monday morning.

Realizing he was frowning, he forced away all thoughts of the office. Instead, he concentrated on how vibrant Suzanne was in those vivid colors, with her glowing hair now freed from its knot to tumble past her shoulders.

The waiter headed for the kitchen and Suzanne turned her attention to him. "This place isn't fancy, but the food is great."

"I don't need fancy." He sipped the tart Cretan white wine

they'd decided on, and glanced at the painting on the wall across from him. "Brings back memories, doesn't it?"

"You bring back memories. When I think of Greece, I always think of you."

Nice. "That afternoon was wild. I remember it often myself." He gave her a quick grin. "And always get hard." He was now too, just from mentioning it. "And here we are now, going back on the decision we made four years ago."

She slitted her eyes slightly. "Decision?"

"To leave it at the one afternoon. Not exchange names and phone numbers, not keep in touch or see each other again."

She ran her finger around the rim of her wineglass. "I guess . . . we didn't want to spoil it?"

He frowned slightly. It was almost as if she didn't remember. It seemed their Cretan idyll hadn't been as mind-blowing an experience for her as for him. But then, being Suzanne, it would be the sex she remembered, not the talk. Truth was, he hadn't spent a hell of a lot of time replaying their conversation himself.

"That's what we said," he reminded her. "It was like champagne. If you drank it every day, it would lose its magic."

She leaned forward, bright-eyed. "That's exactly right!" Then she gave him a mischievous grin. "Though I think we've proved we can drink champagne more than once in our lives, without it going flat."

Jax thought of what she'd done to him in the car, and felt his erection grow. "Definitely not flat," he murmured, slanting a glance toward his lap.

Her eyes widened, then she gave a quick burble of laughter. "Not flat, eh? Um, let me guess. Round and hard, and getting bigger?"

Definitely bigger. Those loose linen pants were growing tighter by the moment.

She leaned farther toward him and whispered, "Do you ever wear boxers?"

"I do wear boxers. Boxer briefs."

"No, I mean plain boxers, the ones that look like shorts."

He was glad for the dark skin that hid his blush. He shook his head.

"Why not?" Her eyes were gleaming.

"They're, uh ..." What the heck kind of conversation was this to be having with a woman, over a restaurant table? He shifted as his erection strained against his fly. "They're too revealing. I might as well not be wearing underwear at all."

Her eyes sparkled. "That's not such a bad idea."

"Tell you what, when we're alone I'd be happy to ditch the undies. But in public, it's indecent."

Jax heard his own words at the same moment Suzanne began to laugh. "Of all the things we've done," she choked out, "I think that ranks pretty low on the indecency scale."

He had to laugh too. "True. But it's one thing to get down and dirty with you. It's another to walk around with my, uh ..."

"Attributes?" she supplied.

"Yeah, okay. Attributes hanging around for everyone to see."

"Nice attributes," she purred. "But I see your point. If a guy's well endowed, he is kind of hanging out there, in boxers. So—" She took a slow sip of wine, then ran her tongue suggestively around the edge of the glass. "I should never give you a pair of silk boxers?"

Silk against his skin, Suzanne reaching inside the fly, hauling him out, running that pointy pink tongue around him. He groaned.

Her eyes sparkled. "That didn't sound like a no."

He wasn't saying no, but he wasn't saying yes either. "How about you? If I gave you ... oh, how about a silk thong? Would you wear it?"

She tossed her hair back. "You didn't notice?"

"Notice?"

"Earlier, when you were, uh, inspecting my underwear, you didn't realize I was wearing a thong?"

A thong. His cock surged against his zipper. She was sitting there with a naked butt under that tiny skirt.

"Let's order dinner," he said gruffly.

She grinned happily, then beckoned him toward her and put her lips to his ear. She flicked her tongue out to touch his earlobe. "Am I torturing you?"

"God, yes."

"If it's any consolation, I'm just as aroused as you."

Yeah, it was a consolation, but mostly more of a turn-on. "Want to skip dinner and go park in another driveway?" he asked hopefully.

She chuckled. "Anticipation is fun, don't you think? Why don't we have dinner, and do some anticipating? The calamari is excellent here."

He drew in a deep breath and let it out. "Sounds good." If they could keep the conversation on food, maybe he'd get his boner under control.

He'd just taken a sip of wine when Suzanne said, "About calamari? Those little rings? Don't they always remind you of cock rings?"

It was all he could do to not spew wine across the table.

She was chuckling as she flagged down the waiter.

They decided to share calamari—which he'd never be able to eat again without imagining cock rings—followed by spiced roasted lamb served with rice, roasted potatoes and Greek salad.

Talking about food got his stomach remembering that he'd skipped lunch, too busy concentrating on work in his hotel room. Fortunately, the calamari arrived quickly, and he and Suzanne shared memories as they munched.

They ordered red wine to accompany the lamb, and when they were midway through the meal Jaxon realized it was past nine o'clock. The conversation had flowed easily and he was thoroughly enjoying Suzanne's company. He'd learned she had a way with words, a sense of humor, compassion and an interesting perspective. And he'd learned all that even though they had never touched on a subject more serious than the deficiencies of Greek plumbing.

What a novelty. He'd spent two evenings with this woman and she had yet to ask him about his job. They still hadn't exchanged last names or phone numbers, much less the ubiquitous business cards.

Four years ago, they'd decided not to see each other again. Would they do the same thing now? Would this weekend have to last him for the next four years, or even longer?

If he asked, he'd spoil the mood. Surely if Suzanne wanted more from him, she'd say something. She was the one who had chosen to break their self-imposed separation.

He'd love to see her again—if he could keep his job under control.

The second half-liter carafe of wine was almost empty when she said, "You're flying back tomorrow?"

"In the morning." He thought of explaining that he still had a ton of work to do, but he didn't want to be the first to raise such a dull subject.

He wondered what she'd be doing—and how she'd spent today. Maybe work, shopping with a friend? Could have seen another lover, for all he knew. Perhaps even a husband. She'd said she was single and she didn't wear a ring, but he only had her word for it.

No, he had her personality. Sexy Suzanne couldn't be married. She was far too wild and free. He couldn't imagine her ever being tied down in a marriage.

Her long lashes brushed her cheeks as she gazed into her wineglass. Then they fluttered upward and her green eyes stared levelly into his. "Are we playing by the same rules this time, Jaxon? Champagne rules?"

He tensed. This was a test, and he wasn't sure of the right answer. "I . . . I suppose so." He studied her face, which gave nothing away, and stumbled on. "I mean, nothing's changed. Has it?"

She gazed at him for a long moment, then smiled. "Great sex and no commitment? No, nothing's changed."

Unexpectedly, he felt sad. But why? This was what he wanted. A sexual interlude with no consequences other than a scramble to catch up with work. Not a relationship. He couldn't handle a relationship, and sure as hell wasn't going to set himself up for another failure. But sex? Hell, yeah.

"It's not exactly a conventional relationship," he said.

"That's for sure. Not conventional, humdrum, mundane. It's special."

He reached for her hand. "So maybe that's our pact. We can taste champagne more than once every four years, but we can't let it get mundane. How does that sound?"

She studied his face. "Four years is way too long, I agree. And mundane is definitely a bad thing." She gave a mock shudder. "One day I'll do that. Marriage, kids, the whole ball of wax, just like my parents and sister."

It was the last thing he'd expected. "Really? You see yourself getting married?" A mermaid who'd lost—no, given up?—her tail. He almost shook his head because he just couldn't see it.

Her eyes widened slightly, and he had the sense she'd said more than she had intended to. She shrugged carelessly. "Maybe. Who knows? It's years off. For now, I'm young and alive, I want to have fun, and you're a wonderful playmate."

"You too. And I sure know what you mean, about being young, having fun, not getting serious." In a way, he was glad he'd been married. The lessons he'd learned had come hard, but now he knew his own limitations. He sure didn't see any wedding bells in his future, not if he wanted that huge corner office with SENIOR PARTNER on the door.

Ceremoniously, Suzanne poured out the last of the wine, giving him the bulk of it, then lifted her glass. "A toast, then."

He raised his glass too.

"To the Champagne Rules." She clicked her glass to his. "Rules to have sex by."

He chuckled, and echoed, "The Champagne Rules." He lifted his glass in a salute, then drank the wine in one long swallow.

Across the table her hair was a tumbled mass of gold and copper threads, her eyes sparkled like emeralds, her smile made his whole body throb. Tonight, having hours to study her features, he'd seen a more mature woman than the one he remembered. Her face had lost its roundness and her features were stronger, more pronounced. As well as being beautiful, her face showed character.

He found himself wanting to know her better—to know who she was when she wasn't being a sex goddess. But asking might violate their new set of rules.

Yeah, of course it would. Right now, they shared the perfect fantasy. A fantasy wouldn't survive their trading details about their day-to-day lives.

He heard a scuffling sound under the table and suddenly her bare foot was in his lap, her toes probing his crotch. He sucked in a breath as, predictably, his penis sprang to immediate attention.

Suzanne gave a purr of satisfaction.

Trying to sound cool, he said, "Okay, I had no objection when you used your fingers and your tongue, but your toes?"

She grinned, her eyes alive with mischief. "You'd rather I climbed under the table and used my tongue?"

Oh yeah!

He was almost tempted to call her bluff. Then he thought, this was Suzanne, she might very well do it.

He frowned slightly. Was he keeping up his end? She wanted an exciting man, an adventuresome one. Not a guy who simply tagged along, following her lead.

Tonight, he had to be the one to come up with something new—and outrageous—to try. But how could a guy think, with Suzanne's toes tickling his package?

"Damn it, woman, let's get the bill and head out!"

8

Outside, the night was balmy. He didn't know the city well enough to suggest an activity—like perhaps going dancing at some dark, sexy club. Damn, he should have asked the concierge at his hotel for suggestions, but he'd been so caught up in work it hadn't occurred to him.

Crap. He just wasn't cut out to be Mr. Sexy.

As he pulled the Porsche key from his pocket, Jax thought about how much wine they'd drunk. Or, at least, he had. She was a sipper, and he'd put away more than his fair share.

Back in San Fran he rarely drove, so he wasn't used to having to worry about drinking and driving.

He paused by the car. He didn't feel impaired—except by lust—but no question he was over the legal limit. He wasn't about to endanger lives, much less his law career. "Feel like a stroll?"

"Sure. It's such a nice evening."

Arms linked, they headed down the block, quickly finding themselves in a residential area. On a summer Saturday night, many windows and doors were open. Light streamed out, accented by the sound of voices, music and TV programs. A few kids on bikes or roller blades streaked past, and occasionally an older couple walked by, or a young couple with a baby in a stroller.

This was the kind of traditional life Suzanne had talked about, when she said that one day she might get married.

Could he imagine her as part of this scene? His immediate reaction was no. But how could he say, when he barely knew her?

The women inside those windows didn't have sex on the beach at Spanish Banks. They worked all day, gave their husbands flak if they came home late from the office, spent their evenings chauffeuring kids to activities or helping with homework, and probably fell into bed too tired to have sex.

Hard to imagine Suzanne ever being too tired for sex.

Jax's arm was around her waist and his hand nudged the underside of her breast. It was getting late and the streets were quieting down. He curved his hand upward and teased her nipple to alertness. Her body snuggled closer, and she hooked a couple of fingers under the waistband of his pants.

She'd said she was wearing a thong.

Ever since she'd told him that bit of information, hours ago, the thought had been in the back of his mind. Now he checked to make sure there was no one else on the sidewalk, then slid his hand under her short skirt and cupped her naked butt.

Her hand made an advance of its own, sliding front and center, gripping his erection through his underwear.

He upped the ante, letting a finger trace the thin strip of thong down between her buttocks, to where the silk was damp with the dew of her arousal.

They were on a public sidewalk in a residential neighborhood. Where the hell was he going to take it from here?

Perhaps more to the point, where would daring Suzanne take it?

"Oh look," she said. "An adventure playground." She broke free and darted away.

He followed her into a schoolyard. The area was unlit but he could make out the colorful playground equipment and a wooden fort.

She plunked down on a swing and he went behind her to push, catching her waist each time she came back, holding her, lifting her, then releasing her to soar high.

When she tired of swinging, she eluded his hands and climbed the ladder to the slide. He positioned himself at the bottom to catch her, and she slid into his arms. He held her body tight against his. It was dark here, with the sun already set and the playground unlit.

He stole a long, breathtaking kiss.

Then he remembered it was his turn to take the lead, to find some new, audacious way to make out. He glanced around, then tugged on her hand. He led her to a wooden structure and climbed the ladder. "Come on up."

They stood on a kind of tower, with a sagging wooden bridge leading to another tower. He started to walk out on the bridge, feeling it sway up and down with each step. The motion reminded him of lovemaking. He beckoned her to follow, then caught her in his arms and, flexing his knees, made the bridge bounce a little.

He kissed her, gently at first, feeling their bodies slide against each other with the bridge's hypnotic rhythm. Her mouth opened to his and she invited him in. But when she tried to tighten her arms around him, he eased away slightly, glancing around to ensure they were alone. The dark playground was screened from the street by a row of broad, leafy trees.

He undid his belt buckle and unfastened his pants, sliding them and his briefs down his hips and letting them pool around his ankles.

Suzanne pressed close, setting that bouncing motion going again, sliding her body against him in a tantalizing friction.

He wanted to lift her up, hike up her skirt and imbed himself inside her, but his balance was too unstable on the swinging wooden bridge. Instead, he tongued her ear as wickedly as he knew how and whispered, "Lie down."

Quickly she obeyed and he kneeled between her legs, helping her tug her miniskirt up to her waist. In the dim light, her pale skin almost glowed, clad only in a scrap of black lace.

Optimistically, he'd tossed a couple of condoms in his pocket, but hadn't been on the ball enough to get anything more interesting than his regular style. "Got any other fancy condoms in your purse?"

"I'm tempted by glow in the dark, but that might not be a wise move. How d'you feel about ribs and dots?"

Oh yeah, trust Suzanne. "I think those ones are more about how you feel," he teased. "Sure, sixty-nine, go for it."

Besides, this discussion and her fumbled search of her purse gave him a chance to cool down. Maybe for once he could last longer than sixty seconds.

Jax sheathed himself, then eased down, trying not to rest too much of his weight on her.

He kissed her again, thrusting gently against the band of silk between her legs, teasing her through the thin barrier. The bridge reflected his motion, swaying up and down.

He reached a hand between their bodies, his fingers stroking her through the silk, heading for her clit.

She moaned into his mouth. "Inside, I want you inside me."

And suddenly, he had to be there. He didn't have time to slide the thong panties down her legs. Instead he pushed the silk aside and found her entrance, easing her open, and thrust into her moist heat.

Her hips lifted to meet him as he filled her, and the bridge bounced harder. He and Suzanne plunged together as the bridge fell, then rose, its rhythm fueling their passion.

One day, he wanted to make love to this woman slowly, taking more than a couple of minutes. But this wasn't going to be the time. The night air brushed his naked lower body and he felt outrageous himself, thrusting into Suzanne in a deserted playground in the middle of a nice middle-class neighborhood.

Dimly he was aware of the sound of a television from across the street, behind the fringe of trees. A car drove by, its headlights piercing the darkness, then disappearing again, reminding him that anyone could come along. Someone might choose this very moment to walk their dog in the park. Teenagers might come to neck in the darkness, and find him and Suzanne, making out like they were crazed adolescents themselves.

The notion of being caught like this was more tantalizing than frightening. He smothered a groan, then realized there wasn't much point to keeping quiet. The bridge creaked and jangled with each bounce.

Suzanne was panting against his neck, hot and quick, and he knew she was close too. What an amazing lover she was, always matching him when it came to passion.

"Jaxon!" Her voice was a whisper, a sob, a demand, against his neck.

He found her mouth and poured his passion into it, just as he thrust deeper, harder between her slick, heated thighs.

Inside him, his climax was building to the point of no return. He reached between their bodies, fingered her swollen bud and she gasped into his mouth. Her body clenched, holding still for a long, frozen moment. Then she spasmed, throbbed, pulsed around him, and he let loose, plunging into her, joining their bodies in the moment of orgasm.

It took all his will power to keep from collapsing on top of her.

As he slowly regained his senses, he realized what he'd done.

After wanting to show Suzanne what a sexy, worldly guy he was, he'd ended up humping her like a horny teenager in a playground. He couldn't help it, he just had to laugh.

The chuckle started down in his belly and built as it rose in his body, until it finally rumbled out of his mouth. Still trying to catch his breath after the frantic sex, he gasped and guffawed.

And then Suzanne began to laugh too.

When they finally calmed down, he touched his lips to hers. "You're one hell of a sexy lady. But I swear, one of these days you're going to get us arrested."

She tapped his shoulder. "May I remind you, this one was your idea?"

He grinned proudly. "You were the inspiration."

Another car drove down the street, and lights flashed again. This time the car stopped, rather than driving by.

"Stay still," he murmured. "They won't see us."

Lights strobed from the parked car, piercing the darkness of the playground.

"Keep down!" he hissed. "I bet it's teenagers."

The lights pinpointed them and he groaned. "They won't believe their luck."

The car doors opened and, for a long minute, the interior light illuminated enough of the scene for Jax to realize—"My God, it's the police!"

"What?" she yelped.

"The cops. Suzanne, pull your clothes together." Hurriedly, he lifted himself off her, trying with one hand to yank down her skirt while with the other he pulled off the condom. He grabbed at his pants and briefs, awkwardly hauling them up his legs.

Just as he zipped his fly, powerful flashlights illuminated them. Suzanne was on her feet too, and he took her hand as they stood, swaying, on the wooden bridge.

"Step apart from each other," a male voice ordered. "And come down from there. Now."

Ignoring the instruction to separate, Jax guided Suzanne to the ladder. Then, thinking about her short skirt and tiny thong, he climbed down first himself. As she followed, he used his body to shield her from the two officers.

He'd teased her about getting them arrested, and now it seemed to be happening. As a lawyer, he should be worried, but for some reason the whole situation was striking him as hilarious.

"Apart! Step apart. And hold your hands out where we can see them." This time it was a female voice.

"As if we're carrying hidden weapons," he murmured to Suzanne.

"Ah," she whispered back, "but you are, big boy."

A laugh sputtered out of him before he could suppress it.

"Step apart!" the male voice hollered.

Trying to act like an adult, he moved a foot or so away from Suzanne and they both walked forward, holding their hands up. The two officers turned flashlights on their faces, and Jax winced as his eyes began to water. "What's the problem, officers?"

"You're trespassing," the man responded.

He frowned. "It's a public schoolyard."

"It's closed to the public between dusk and dawn. Didn't you see the sign?"

"Uh, no, it was . . . dark." Another chuckle was building in his chest and he tried to hold it back, but he could hear it resonate in his voice.

Suzanne gaped at him, her face stunned in the harsh glare of the female officer's flashlight. He saw the exact moment when she too began to crack up.

Quickly he said, "Sorry, we didn't see the sign. We didn't mean to trespass and we won't do it again."

The female officer said, "And your reason for being in the playground was?"

Suzanne let out a splutter of laughter. Then she said, "It was m-my fault. I saw the swings and made a b-beeline for them." Her voice shook as she fought the giggles. "It's so long since I've been on a sw-swing. And then I had to slide down the slide, and then we saw the fort, and it was . . . you know, like being kids again."

The male cop said, "Not from where we were sitting, ma'am."

It was Jax's turn to laugh. He just couldn't hold it in anymore. And that got Suzanne going again.

"Neither of you seem to be taking this very seriously," the woman officer said stiffly. "Let's see some ID, folks."

Jax pulled his wallet out of his pocket and handed it to the male officer as Suzanne fumbled in her shoulder bag. He sure as hell hoped a bunch of kinky condoms didn't pick now to escape.

The male cop herded Jax a few more steps away from the women, and took his time riffling through his wallet, shining his flashlight on the contents. "Mr. Navarre, is this your current address?"

"Yes, I live in San Francisco."

"And you're here on holiday or business?"

"Just a quick weekend visit with my, uh, friend, Suzanne."

The officer pulled out a card and showed it to him. Damn, his State Bar card. "Guy like you ought to know better."

"Yeah, but . . ." He glanced over to Suzanne.

A few feet away, the woman officer seemed to be going through a similar rigmarole with her. He perked up his ears as she said, "Ms. Brennan."

Ah-ha. Now he knew Suzanne's last name. And, if she'd been listening, she knew his. It was a peculiar way to find out. There'd been no particular reason to keep their surnames secret, but the subject had never come up.

"You sure the lady's a friend, and she consented?"

The cop's serious tone brought Jax's attention back to him. The man was subjecting him to narrow-eyed scrutiny.

Ah. Of course the guy had to check that the sex was consensual. Jax sobered up quickly. "Yes, of course. Just ask her."

Duh. That's exactly what the female officer would be doing right now.

"And she lives in this neighborhood?" the officer continued.

"I . . ." He couldn't confess that he didn't know where she lived. "We were eating at a little Greek place a few streets over, and decided to go for a walk afterwards."

"A walk."

"Yeah. Then we saw the playground. We didn't see any sign, honestly."

"Okay, you stand right there, don't move an inch," the officer ordered. He went over to the women, and then the two cops went to stand a few yards away, conferring in hushed tones. Jax couldn't overhear a word.

He glanced back at Suzanne, ready to exchange a wry grin, but found her looking stunned.

What had that female officer said to her?

He took a step toward her, but she made a quick "stay away" gesture and he stopped. What the hell was going on?

After a few minutes, the male cop came back. "Okay. The lady confirms it was consensual. All the same, it was stupid." The man's lips twitched, but he straightened them quickly. "Acting like teenagers."

"I know." Jesus, didn't the guy realize he wasn't responsible for his behavior when he was around Suzanne?

He glanced over, saw Suzanne and the other officer deep in conversation again.

"You aren't really going to arrest us, are you?" he asked. "For, uh, acting like teenagers?"

The officer scratched his chin and Jax got the sense he was fighting laughter. "We'll let you off with a warning this time.

Seeing as you're a visitor in town, and all." He folded up the wallet and handed it back. "So, how you liking Vancouver?"

Jax couldn't hold back a snort of laughter. "It's got a lot to offer, from what I've seen so far."

"I just bet it does." The officer's voice shook. Then, unexpectedly, he shone the light in Jax's face again. "You two been drinking?"

"Wine with dinner, over several hours."

"Be sure to walk it off, or call a cab rather than drive home."

"Of course." Probably not a good idea to tell him that walking it off was what had got them here in the first place.

The officer joined his partner and they strolled toward their car, heads bent close, male and female laughter blending together.

Jax squeezed Suzanne's shoulder as they too walked toward the street. Under his hand, her muscles were tight. "Are you all right?"

"Keep walking, they're watching us."

The officers had climbed into their car but weren't going anywhere.

In silence, he and Suzanne left the park and started along the sidewalk. After a couple of minutes, the police car drove past them.

He waited until it was out of sight, then stopped and turned her to face him. "God, I'm sorry, Suzanne, this whole thing's my fault."

"No, it's not." Her voice was subdued. "And it's okay. At least we didn't get arrested. Let's keep walking, in case they come back."

Way to kill a fun, sexy mood, he thought as they continued on in silence.

"So, what did the lady cop ask you?" he finally said.

Under his hand, her shoulders tightened even more. It felt as though she was holding her breath. Then she exhaled loudly and her shoulders went down. "I'm not sure you want to know."

Oh yeah, like he could resist an opening like that? "'Course I do."

"Okay, to s-sum up," her voice shook a little, "she wanted to know if you'd raped me. When I assured her you hadn't, she wanted to know if I was a hooker and you were my pimp."

"What the hell?" Sure, the cops needed to know the sex was consensual, but that was going way the fuck too far.

Suzanne swung around to face him, and stared up into his eyes. "Because you're black and I'm white."

"Oh shit." He should've known. "Christ, Suzanne, I'm sorry."

"No, *I'm* sorry. I apologize on behalf of my ignorant, racist city. Damn it, Jaxon, it's so, so . . ." She shook her head vigorously, clearly unable to come up with the right word.

"It's racial profiling. San Francisco's not so bad. Guess we have more blacks per capita, but it still happens."

He was pissed, and yet he thought about what the cops had seen. "A couple fooling around in a playground, they'd have assumed neighborhood teens. Then they see us up close. Well-dressed black guy, beautiful blonde in a skimpy top and a miniskirt. Not what they'd expected, especially in a neighborhood like this."

"So they jump to all sorts of crazy conclusions, just because of how we look?"

"That's all they have to go on until they find out more. Suzanne, they wanted to make sure you were safe."

She looked indignant. "From you? But you'd never hurt me."

"And just how would they know that?"

Her eyes widened. "I can't believe you're defending them."

"I've been exposed to lots worse. Any black guy has."

"It's so unfair."

He sighed. It was sweet she was pissed off, but the lady didn't have a firm grip on reality. "Yeah, some of it's really unfair. But it is fair to make sure a woman's safe when she's in a vulnerable situation with a guy who's a lot bigger and stronger than her."

She frowned.

"You did that too," he pointed out. "Last night, you had friends at the beach to make sure you felt safe."

"You knew that?"

"Sure. Saw you wave them away."

"You know it wasn't because you're black, right? Mostly, it's because my friends were worried about me meeting a near-stranger."

"Good friends."

"The best."

He was glad she had them too. Suzanne had this crazy—delightful—penchant for doing outrageous things, and one day it might lead her into trouble. Nice to know she had folks looking out for her.

She sighed. "It's a tough world, isn't it?"

"Sometimes. But I've learned that getting mad's more likely to hurt than help." He smiled at her. "Besides, this world has lots of good things too. Like us, together." He bent to touch his lips to hers in a kiss that was friendly and reassuring, rather than passionate.

Finally, she seemed to relax. And was that a gleam of mischief in her eyes?

"The lady cop thinks you're a hottie," she said.

Good God. "What?"

"Once she was convinced there was no problem, that we were lovers, she wanted to know if you were as good as you looked. I said even better."

"A police officer wanted to know . . ."

"If you were a hot lover."

He shook his head. "Women!"

"I don't think that was racial profiling, I think it was pure admiration." She frowned slightly. "How do you tell?"

"Sometimes you can't. There are so many stereotypes."

"Well hung," she said. Then, "Sense of rhythm. White men can't jump; only black guys are good at basketball."

He couldn't hold back a chuckle. What would she think if she found out he'd played b-ball for years?

"I'm glad you can laugh about it," she said, a little stuffily.

"Oh God, sometimes you just gotta laugh. If you take this stuff too seriously, it messes with your head."

"I guess."

As they began to walk again, he said, "Think we could find our way back to that playground?"

"Don't you think that's pushing our luck?"

"Not for sex. Yeah, that'd be pushing it. But I left a used condom on that bridge. Don't want some kid to find it tomorrow morning."

"Good thinking."

"You'll have to stand guard, though. Warn me if the cops come back."

She snickered. "A different role for me. Keeping us from getting arrested."

Suzanne woke late on Sunday, her body aching in numerous spots. From too much sex? No, there couldn't be too much sex, not with Jaxon Navarre.

What a great name.

Had he overheard hers too? If so, he could look her up in the phone book.

But he wouldn't. It would go against the Rules they'd agreed on.

She eased out of bed and into the shower. As she soaped herself gingerly, she pondered the past two nights. Amazing sex, but all of it in the "quick and dirty" category. Never once had they made love in a bed—or even a comfortable setting—and taken their time about it.

And, if she was going to be accurate, making love was hardly the correct term.

She and Jaxon had committed to a sexual encounter, an erotic escapade. As Tina Turner had sung, "What's love got to do with it?"

Nothing, in this case, obviously. You couldn't fall in love with a person until you knew them really, really well. As more than just a fantastic lover. Which wasn't going to happen with her and Jaxon, because that was not what either of them wanted.

Suzanne ran the bath sponge down the curve of her hip and remembered the feel of his hand tracing that same line.

Then she thought of his face, animated, as they talked across the table at Maria's. Yes, they'd avoided personal subjects, but even so she was getting to know him. Jaxon was the kind of guy who'd drive his arthritic Cretan landlady to visit her husband's grave, to save her the painful walk. And he hadn't said it as if he was trying to score points. It was just one of several vignettes he'd shared as they reminisced about their experiences in Greece. Her heart had given a mushy flip-flop when he'd told her the story.

He was a man who'd give an overworked waiter a sympathetic smile rather than a sharp word when he had to remind the guy they wanted more coffee.

A man who'd go out of his way to retrieve a condom, so a child wouldn't discover it.

A man who even tried to understand and explain why the police had jumped to those horrible conclusions.

He was a good guy. Those small actions made her believe it. And that was reassuring if they were going to continue their relationship.

Relationship? Another questionable term. It implied emo-

tion. Yet they were definitely more than acquaintances. Or
were they? Maybe she should consider them acquaintances
who had sex.

But that sounded so cold. When they had sex, she felt a true
sense of closeness, much more than with the couple of other
lovers she'd had, even though she'd known those men much
better. With Jaxon, there was a feeling of intimacy.

Intimacy? Suzanne snorted and tossed away the bath
sponge. Good grief, they'd had great sex. That was what she'd
wanted, and what she got, and maybe would have again in the
future.

Future. Her *future*, several more years down the road, was Mr.
Cleaver. He'd be considerate, like Jaxon. With any luck he'd be
sexy too. So . . . Was there any chance Jaxon might be Mr.
Cleaver in disguise?

Suzanne leaned against the wall of the shower and considered that question. The timing was all wrong. They lived in different countries.

They were different races. That fact had been brought home
to her last night, with a vengeance. If they were a couple,
there'd be other nasty incidents.

And if they loved each other, they'd weather them as they
had last night. Other people's prejudices wouldn't drive them
apart, but bring them closer together. No, for her, race definitely wasn't a reason to avoid commitment.

But there was one really strong reason. The girl who wanted
to marry Mr. Cleaver was boring, sensible, old-fashioned.

And when she thought about it that way, she didn't see
Jaxon in the Mr. Cleaver role. He was a perfect match for sexy
Suzanne, but not for her sensible twin.

Nor, when it came right down to it, did she want to think
about all that future-oriented, settling-down stuff at the moment. This erotic adventure was as unexpected as it was amaz-

ing, and she wanted to revel in it for as long as she and Jaxon could sustain it. And she truly believed that required strict obedience to the Champagne Rules.

She climbed out of the shower, toweled herself briskly and put on a robe. In the kitchen, she fed the cats and made coffee. She toasted a whole-wheat English muffin, slathered it with her mom's homemade strawberry jam, and took her breakfast back to the bedroom where she booted up her computer. She hadn't checked her e-mail since Friday night.

There was a message from caveman, one he'd sent late Friday night after he'd received her own. He said: Naughty dreams? Bet on it. What other kind could I have, when dreaming of you? Can't wait to be inside you again . . .

Hmm. He hadn't e-mailed last night, or this morning. Well, it had been very late when he dropped her at the Miata, and maybe he'd had an early flight. But she had hoped for something. An e-mail kiss to say how fabulous the weekend had been. Confirmation that he hoped they'd be able to meet again next weekend, as they'd discussed.

Suzanne made a fist and bopped herself on the side of the head. There she went again, with the shlocky stuff.

Resolutely, she turned her attention to the rest of her messages. Most were from her Foursome pals.

Jenny had e-mailed yesterday evening saying, Wondering how those condoms are holding out . . . ☺☺☺

Suzanne clicked REPLY. FYI, chocolate's not as good as the real thing (candy or cock <g>), but ribs + dots work just fine. ☺☺☺☺☺

Rina's Saturday message said, Hope you and Jaxon are having a wonderful time. Can't wait to hear all about it. Drop me an e-mail and let me know you're okay.

Suzanne answered. More than okay! Yes, we had a great evening. I'll tell you all about it on Monday.

And then there was Ann, from eleven o'clock on Saturday

night. Damn it, I'm trying to avoid phoning to say CALL ME when you get home! I know, I know, you're a grown-up and I'm not your mom, but I'm concerned—and curious! Write and tell me you got home safe, and whether you learned any more about the mysterious Jaxon.

Suzanne typed, I'm home and fine, and we had a great time. She paused, then typed more slowly. Did I learn more about him? Yes, in one way. I learned he's considerate. But I don't know what he does for a living, I don't know about his parents, or if he's got siblings. I don't know his favorite color, favorite movie, Zodiac sign, what kind of books he reads. IF he reads!

She halted her flying fingers. She hadn't realized how bugged she was at not knowing these things. But how could she ask, when she wasn't prepared to share the details of her own life? Besides, knowing would violate the Champagne Rules, and she'd just finished persuading herself those rules were essential.

Decisively she grabbed the mouse and deleted everything after "considerate," then began again. I know his surname's Navarre, he has terrific taste in clothes, he's got an awesome body, he likes convertibles, and he's a FANTASTIC lover. What more do I need to know right now, Ann? I mean, this is just about sex. It's not about a future.

We've set up what we call "Champagne Rules." We'll see each other occasionally, for wild and crazy sex, but not so often the bubbles go flat.

She thought of Ann's reaction at reading these words. Her friends saw her as so conventional, and damn it, maybe she was, but she had a fun, exciting side too. Jaxon had proved that to her. She began to type again.

He is not my Mr. Cleaver. He's my fantasy. Every gal's entitled to a fantasy, isn't she? And when it comes to fantasies, on a scale of one to ten, he's a twenty!!!! ☺ 'Nough said?

There, that ought to tell Ann where things stood.

It was only after she clicked SEND that she reread Ann's e-mail to her. Hmm. Her friend had referred to Jaxon as mysterious, but she hadn't challenged the nature of their— Okay, she had to call it a relationship, there simply was no other term. So, why had Suzanne responded by being so . . . Yeah. Defensive was the only word.

As she finished her English muffin, she debated sending an e-mail to Jaxon. Nope, forget it. To date, she'd made the overtures. This time, she'd leave the ball in his court.

And hope he batted it back to her.

9

Jax, after having splurged on the Porsche in Vancouver, took the BART from the airport to downtown San Francisco. He made decent money, but had clear priorities: his mom's mortgage, and a wardrobe that said "success" to clients and colleagues. When he'd finished law school, he'd traded the student jeans-and-dreads look for a more conservative, professional one.

He walked the few blocks to work, waved at a couple of other lawyers who were in, then went into his office. His desk had grown a half dozen more piles of paper since he'd left on Friday. The message light on his phone was blinking and, when his computer booted up, the e-mail in-box was loaded.

Phone first. He set it to speaker and pressed the PLAY button, then scribbled notes as he listened to half a dozen messages. When he heard his mother's voice, he smiled and settled back in his chair.

"Hey there, son." You couldn't say she had an accent, exactly, just a sunny lilt that warmed his all-business office. "Figured there'd be more point callin' you at work than home.

Don' imagine you'll get back to your apartment any time soon."

Oh yeah, his mom knew her kid.

"Hope you had a nice little holiday this weekend. Any chance you'll tell your mama all about it?" She gave a rich chuckle. "I'll bribe you with dinner. Any night this week. Or next weekend, if you're not gallivantin' off again."

He picked up the receiver and hit her speed-dial number.

As the phone rang, he glanced past the piles of waiting work to the sunshine outside. Crap. Sometimes he hated how hard he had to work to get where he wanted to be.

But hell, he'd blown the weekend; now he had to pay the price.

When his mother answered, he said, "Dinner'd be great. If I work like crazy tonight, maybe we can do tomorrow." Experience told him Monday was his best chance; after that, the week would get even crazier. "Okay if I let you know in the afternoon?"

"Sure, hon. Call me at the shop soon's you know, and I'll buy groceries on the way home, throw together somethin' special."

After a day on her feet at the clothing store, the last thing she needed was a couple of hours standing in the kitchen cooking. "How about I take you out for dinner?"

"Save your pennies, I'll cook."

"Let me treat you, Mom. God knows I owe you for all the dinners you're always feeding me."

"God knows you do not owe me anything, boy. It's a mama's job, and her joy, to look after her baby."

Baby. He was thirty years old, a lawyer climbing toward partnership at a prestigious law firm, damn well determined to look after his mom in her old age—and still the woman wanted to take care of her "baby."

What could he do but love her? And take her to dinner.

"Let's both be lazy and let other folks wait on us. Isn't there some restaurant where the food measures up to yours?"

There was a pause, then she said, in a thoughtful tone, "You know, I think I'll take you up on that offer. You hang up now, Jax, and work hard, so's we can go for that dinner. We've got lots of things to catch up on."

Hmm. Sounded like something new was going on in her life too. And she, unlike he, was willing to share.

He hung up, cast a final longing gaze at the sunshine outside, then dove into the work on his desk. After a couple of hours, he realized he'd been even more productive than usual. Who knew that awesome sex would have this side benefit?

He ought to do it more often.

And, on the subject of Suzanne . . . He called up his caveman e-mail account. Hmm, nothing from her. Did that mean he'd failed to deliver what she'd been looking for?

Leaning back in his chair, he did a quick memory rewind. Nah, he was damned sure he'd satisfied her. Over and over again.

He whipped off a quick note. Hey, outrageous69, that was one hell of a fine weekend. Wore my poor old bod out, but I'm betting I'll be "up" again by next weekend, if that works for you. Hell, sexy lady, I'm already up, just thinking about you. So, what do you say? He clicked SEND.

Gotta love Suzanne. Any other gal would require some sentimental bullshit, which he sure as hell didn't have the time to make up.

Also gotta love the Champagne Rules. Her invention. She ought to write a book. Might not be many women who'd buy it, but every guy he'd ever met would be lining up, getting the hots just imagining being with a woman like her.

Hell, he'd hooked himself up with every man's wet dream.

But right now he was a lawyer not a lover, and shouldn't be

wasting billable time on dreams. He speed dialed for pizza delivery, then got back to work.

It was after two when he left the office.

Suzanne chose a long, loose skirt and a tailored blouse to wear to the usual Sunday family dinner. When she studied her reflection in the mirror, the woman looking back could have been applying to join a convent.

"Nope," she told her cat audience, "it'll make Mom suspicious."

She stayed with the long skirt, but replaced the buttoned-up shirt with a figure-hugging coral tee. Yeah, that ought to get her by the mom radar.

Before she left, she checked her e-mail. For, oh, about the twentieth time. Now, finally, she found a message.

Aha! So he was "up," just thinking about her. Her spirits were up too, now that she knew he was still turned on, and wanted to see her again.

Hurriedly, she typed, Up? Oh, I do like you "up," caveman!

If she had more time, she'd indulge in a little cyber sex. Oh well, his message had been brief, so she'd reply in kind. Her fingers flew over the keys.

That's a thought that'll give me steamy dreams, imagining all the things we can do when you're "up." There must be one or two we haven't tried yet, right? How about this? I'll come up with one, you come up with another (there's that magic word again <g>) and we'll try them out next weekend. My town or yours?

It would be pricy to fly down to San Francisco. He'd paid for the last flight, but he obviously had more money than she did.

She was curious about how he'd entertain her. Would he invite her to stay at his place?

No, that would break the Rules. She'd learn his taste in furniture, artwork, books, music. Maybe see family pictures. Besides, she couldn't stay at his place because she couldn't return the offer if they met again in Vancouver.

No way could Jaxon Navarre stay overnight in her converted garage, just outside her parents' kitchen window. Oh God, this was getting complicated. It would take ingenuity on both their parts to stick to the Rules.

"Suzanne?"

It was her sister's voice, calling from the garden. In a minute, she'd come through the open front door.

Suzanne's fingers flew as she added, Can't wait to see you again. She clicked SEND, closed out of e-mail and was just shutting down the computer when Bethany knocked twice on the doorframe.

"Suze, you here?" she called.

"Hi, Beth." Suzanne met her in the main room, and they exchanged hugs. "Just finishing up some e-mail."

Her sister grinned. "Remember the days before e-mail ruled our lives?"

"Nah, I was too young. It's only middle-aged folks like you who remember that," Suzanne teased. Bethany was eight years older, but definitely didn't look her age.

Beth ran a hand through short hair that was already tousled. "The kids are—"

The screech of happy childish voices cut her off as Krystina and Declan burst through the door and tackled Suzanne.

"Dying to see you," Bethany finished dryly.

Suzanne bent down and returned the enthusiastic hugs of her niece and nephew. Declan, at three, was growing so fast he'd caught up with four-year-old Krys. With their dad's dark hair and big brown eyes they almost looked like twins.

One day, she wanted a pair of her own, just as happy and healthy as these two.

For a fleeting moment, she imagined what her and Jaxon's

children would look like. Gorgeous, if they took after their father. But if they took after him, would they too suffer because of racial prejudice?

She shook her head, forcing away the thoughts. Not relevant. Pregnancy would definitely violate the Rules!

"You're looking especially good, Suze," her sister said. "Have you done something?" Bethany scrutinized her carefully. "Not a new hairstyle or new clothes. Looks like you got some sun, though—your face is glowing."

"I did spend some time at the beach this weekend," Suzanne said, biting the inside of her lip so she wouldn't laugh.

"Let's go, Auntie Suze," Krys said, tugging at her hand. "I'm hungry."

"Me too." She held out her other hand to Declan, who latched on, and let the two kids pull her out the door. "Do you know what's for dinner?"

"Chick'm," Declan said decisively. "And smashed 'tatoes."

"Mmm, my favorite." Her stomach growled affirmation. Oh yeah, she'd definitely made the transition to sensible Suzanne, the potato lover.

Over her shoulder, she said, "Beth, there's strawberry shortcake in my fridge."

"I'll bring it."

Sunday night tradition dictated that Bethany and Suzanne bring starters and dessert, while Jane and Michael Brennan took care of the main course and the housecleaning. Tonight, her dad must be the cook. He was a meat-and-potatoes kind of chef. Her mom tended to be more experimental.

Sure enough, when they went into the kitchen, it was her father who stood at the stove, his lean waist aproned, stirring gravy. She leaned in to kiss his cheek, then stole a taste from the wooden spoon and gave him an approving, "Yum."

Her mom poured milk for the kids, then picked up a wine bottle. "Suzie?"

"Please."

"You've had a busy weekend," her mother commented.

"Not really. Saturdays are always a little frantic at the clinic, but I pretty much vegged today. Caught up on some reading." And sleep, after the two late nights.

"It was the evenings I was referring to," her mother said, a twinkle in her eye.

"Evenings?" Bethany, about to drink from her own wineglass, paused. "So that's why you're glowing."

Oh damn. She wouldn't lie to her family, nor could she bring herself to be rude and say it was none of their business. She'd made a halfhearted attempt at working out a cover story; now she'd have to see if it flew.

"You are!" Beth crowed. "You're dating!"

"Not exactly." Dating. What a high school word for her and Jaxon's adventures.

"Seeing a heterosexual adult of the male persuasion?" her mother asked.

"When you put it that way." Definitely heterosexual, and two-hundred-percent male. "But we're not dating, as in beginning a relationship. Neither of us want that right now, so we're just hanging out and having fun. Like I do with the gals in the Foursome."

Her sister cocked a skeptical eyebrow. "Hanging out with a heterosexual man is never the same thing as hanging out with a girlfriend."

"No, but . . ."

Fortunately, Bethany's husband, Joel, saved Suzanne by coming into the kitchen and enveloping her in a big hug. "Hey, it's my favorite sister-in-law."

"You say that to all your sisters-in-law," she teased. In fact, he had three others, the wives of his brothers.

"The one I'm with is always my favorite at the moment," he

said peaceably. "And usually that's you, since my brothers are so nomadic."

"Yeah, you can trust the Brennan family to be nest-builders, not nomads," she said.

"Works for me." He put an arm around Bethany and hugged her to him. "I'm the aberration in my family, the only one who didn't inherit the gypsy spirit."

His parents were currently doing aid work in Africa, and his brothers and their wives were all over the world pursuing activities as diverse as photojournalism, medicine and art. In contrast, Joel, like Bethany, was a homebody.

"I think you're perfect," Suzanne told him. He was exactly the kind of man she wanted for herself. Though he had a good career as a high school teacher, Beth and the children always came first. He and Beth were a team: they were each other's best friend, always supportive and their skills complimented each other.

"Suze is seeing a guy," Beth told her husband.

"Uh-huh?"

Good old Joel, he'd never pry.

"Isn't dinner ready yet?" Suzanne asked.

Her dad laughed. "Good luck with that technique. Never works for me. But yes, dinner's ready. Who wants a drumstick? Declan? Krystina?"

When they were all seated with full plates in front of them, Suzanne picked up her fork and scooped up some potatoes and gravy.

"So, what's this guy like, Suze?" Beth asked, just as her mother said, "Where did you meet this fellow?"

Suzanne put her fork down. "I'm really not ready to talk about this right now. We've just met, I barely know the guy."

"That'll come," Beth said, "the more you see of, uh, Mr. Nameless Guy. Look at Joel. He was a stranger when he came into the shop to send flowers for his mom's birthday. Then we had coffee a couple of times, started dating, and after we'd known each other three years, we got engaged."

"Sounds ideal," Suzanne said, "but I'm not ready for my own Joel to come along yet. I'm only twenty-four, still in school. Right now I just want to have a little fun. Give me another three or four years. Then you can nag me about finding Mr. Right."

"Makes sense to me," her father said. "Don't be in any rush."

"Yeah, sis," Beth said, "sow some wild oats."

Suzanne picked up her fork again, relieved she could finally begin to enjoy her dad's wonderful meal.

"Sow oats?" Krys said, laughing. "Mommy, you sew clothes, not oatmeal!"

Joel gave his wife a mischievous grin. "Okay, Beth, want to explain about oats?"

"Absolutely. On Krys's thirtieth birthday."

The adults all laughed. Krys looked puzzled and her little brother chose that occasion to reach for the salt shaker and spill his milk in the process.

Sowing wild oats, Suzanne mused as she helped clean up the mess. Beth was right, that's exactly what she was doing. And it did make sense, as her dad had said.

She paused in mid stroke wiping the table. Oh God, she'd thought she was so risqué, seeking out an erotic escapade, and all along she was just being sensible Suzanne! A laugh escaped.

Everyone paused in what they were doing and turned to look at her.

"Hey, better to laugh than cry over spilled milk, right?"

Jax's alarm went off at five thirty on Monday morning.

He groaned, wishing he could cancel six A.M. racquetball, but Rick would be up and on his way to the BART. His pal lived and worked in Berkeley, and it was great that he was willing to make the trip downtown for their Monday, Wednesday and Friday matches.

An hour later, he wasn't so happy with Rick.

Jax floundered across the court, smacked up against the wall as the ball flew past him, and listened to his pal crow with glee. "Man, you're a lawyer-slug today."

The ultimate insult. He and Rick, both lawyers as well as former basketball teammates, had nothing but contempt for their colleagues whose asses got fatter and bellies rounder each year.

Jax retaliated by returning Rick's serve with a smashing stroke that sent it flying into a back corner. But Rick, damn him, flew over to intercept it as it dropped.

Used to be, Jax had been the better athlete. Playing college ball, he'd been the guy whose discipline and drive regularly made him team captain or MVP. Rick had been a great team player, an all-round fine athlete, but he didn't go the extra mile.

Jax was pissed that, over the past year, more often than not, Rick had won their racquetball matches.

When their court time was up, the two men headed for the showers. "You spend the weekend riding a desk as usual?" Rick asked.

Jax's foul mood lifted and he couldn't stop a grin. "Believe it or not, I took some time off. Had to make up for it last night though."

"Time off? Notice you didn't spend any of it coaching b-ball."

Rick was always after him to help coach the underprivileged kids he worked with. A weird pastime for a guy who'd been born into a well-off, third-generation African-American family.

"You still working out that guilt trip for havin' grown up so damned privileged?" Jax teased.

"You still trying to ignore your roots and pass for white?" his pal taunted back.

"Oh yeah," Jax said easily. "Still trying to figure out how to bleach my skin."

It was their same old shtick.

Later, as they were getting dressed, Rick said, "Come to dinner one night this week?"

No way, not if he hoped to see his mom tonight and free up time this weekend for Suzanne. "Can't. Thanks anyhow. Too much work." He shrugged into a pale blue cotton shirt that had set him back more than a hundred bucks. On sale.

"That excuse is getting stale." Rick put on his own shirt, blue and cotton as well, but casual denim. "Rosa's got to thinking you don't like her. That right, man?"

"No, Rosa's great, and so's Jase." It was true. Rick had married a Latina college teacher who was bright, gorgeous, sexy, sophisticated, and also warm, loving and fun. And their kid, Jason—what was he, about three now?—was lively and smart as could be.

Jax tied his tie and pulled on his suit jacket. "Honest, it's just work."

"You work too hard." Rick, who'd left his own shirt unbuttoned at the neck, hadn't brought a jacket.

And you don't work hard enough. "That's what it takes to get ahead." Which he would, and Rick wouldn't. All those privileges Rick had grown up with had worked against him, robbing him of the drive to succeed.

The other man shook his head. "Same old, same old. Different definitions of 'ahead.'"

Jax laughed. "Yeah, and we each think ours is right." Well, he damned well knew his was right, but a guy had to make some concessions to keep the peace.

"Maybe they both are," Rick said. "Mine—a general practice in Berkeley, little house, wife and kid—that's what works for me. Yours . . . Well, no one ever said you weren't ambitious. Whatever you want to be, Jax, you can do it."

Within reason, Jax amended silently. It'd be nice to think he could have it all, but a guy had to know his limitations. Like knowing he made a crappy husband, just like Tonya'd told him a couple months after they got married. Back then, he'd been pissed, challenged, tried harder, but he still couldn't hack it, not the firm and the marriage. She'd been right to bail, to find a man like Benjamin, who could give her what she needed.

Benjamin, like Rick, was a good guy.

But Jax would go farther in the world. It mattered more to him.

Sometimes Jax wondered why he and Rick had remained buddies all these years. When they'd met, it was natural to hook up, two black b-ball players both in pre-law. As they got to know each other, though, their differences became more apparent. Rick's assumption was that everything would come easily to him. Jax, the impoverished immigrant on an athletic scholarship, wasn't able to take one damned thing for granted.

As they walked out into the pale morning sunshine, Rick said, "Wednesday?"

"Sure." Then Jax said, a little awkwardly because they didn't talk much about personal stuff, "Why do we keep doing this, man?"

"Racquetball?"

"Yeah." Keeping in touch, he really meant. Fact was, though, it was only the racquetball that kept them in touch.

Rick slapped his shoulder. "So's you don't turn into a whitewashed lawyer-slug."

"Yeah, sure, that'd be it."

Rick headed off to catch the BART back to his office. Jax, feeling like he'd sweated off pounds, picked up a couple of fried egg bagel sandwiches and the tallest, strongest coffee available. He was at his desk by seven thirty, ready to pick up where he'd left off a few hours ago.

At nine every Monday, the litigation lawyers met to discuss their cases. After they'd gone the rounds, Trent Jefferson, the senior partner, said, "All right. New files. Family Friend's been slapped with a class-action suit alleging discrimination in employment practices."

Hank Campbell, one of the other partners, whistled. "That's got to hurt, with their wholesome image."

Family Friend, a major client of the firm's, was a huge department store chain that promoted itself as having a corporate culture based on Christian values. The company's popularity had risen immensely in post-9/11 days.

Jefferson glanced around the table, and his gaze landed on Jax. "You want to run with this, Navarre? Check out the claims, talk to the client?"

"Absolutely." This was the biggest file that had come his way. He'd have to work his tail off, but he could handle it.

"Most of these cases settle," Jefferson said.

And if it did, Jax would lose an opportunity to go to trial. But . . . "That's true, but maybe not this one."

"Why do you say that?" Campbell asked.

"It's true lots of giant corporations have faced allegations like this and settled. But they could afford to. And I don't mean money wise, I mean in terms of PR. They hadn't built their business around a good-guy reputation. If Family Friend settles, even with a confidentiality agreement and no admission of guilt, you know how the public will interpret that: guilty as charged. That could really hurt business. Look at all the flack with the allegations around Wal-Mart. Business has suffered, without anyone even proving the allegations are true. Seems to me, the best strategy here is to answer the charges in court, and win decisively."

There were nods around the table, and he gathered he'd passed the first test.

"You figure out a way to win this one," Jefferson said, "and you can sit first chair."

Lead lawyer, on a suit this big? Man! Jax could barely keep a grin from busting out as he gazed at the men who controlled his future. "Sounds good to me."

Jefferson handed him a file. "Copy of the complaint's in here. Read it, call Sam Miller, the CEO at Family Friend, do some research. Plan on starting in the San Francisco area, with the complaints against management at the head office and the local stores. If we decide not to settle—and I agree with your thinking on that—you'll need to interview managers all over the country."

Jesus, this thing really *was* big.

"Report back next week," Jefferson went on, "with a plan, a schedule, an outline of the firm resources you'll need. Bring Marianne in on it if you need assistance."

Marianne Bryant, who was at the moment staring all hungry eyed at the file in Jax's hand, was an associate. An ambitious one. Jax figured he wouldn't need any assistance. Why train the competition?

As Jefferson moved the discussion on to the next file, Jax was already making his plans. He'd set up a meeting with Miller, work through lunch, get all his ducks in order, then take off for dinner with his mom. Likely it'd be his one free night in the next couple of weeks, so he might as well enjoy it.

Oh fuck. Suzanne. He'd have to call off the weekend. Too bad, but hell, he knew his priorities.

10

At six, Jax joined a crowd of commuters and caught the BART to Berkeley. His mom lived in the same general vicinity as Rick and his family, in a two-story bungalow with a small garden. Not fancy, but prices were so damned high in any neighborhood that was decent.

When Jax first started work at Jefferson Sparks, he'd saved every penny other than what he needed to spend on rent, food and an appropriate wardrobe. First priority was paying off student loans; second was scraping up a down payment to buy a house for his mom.

Last year, he'd made it, though the mortgage was big enough to give him nightmares.

His mom managed a ladies' clothing store and rented out her upstairs to Berkeley students. She insisted she loved the company and said the kids, with whom she shared her kitchen, kept her young.

She wanted to help out with the mortgage, but he wouldn't let her. He'd never be able to make up for all her sacrifices when he was growing up.

Hard to believe the neighborhood was so pricy, he thought as he walked down the street. It was casual, friendly and most of the residents were young families and retired couples.

His mom's current boarders, Hannah and Clare, a lesbian couple, waved to him from the front steps where they sat sipping beer.

"Having a good summer?" he asked them.

Clare grinned. "Love the weather, but I'm not so happy about having to work for a living. It's way too grown-up for me!"

Hannah elbowed her partner. "If you can call being a research assistant working for a living."

"I work with my brains, because I happen to have some. Those who don't, have to rely on their brawn."

"Great for the muscle tone though, isn't it?" Hannah countered, raising a firm brown arm and studying it. An architecture student, she'd taken a summer job on a construction crew and the work did seem to be suiting her.

Clare turned her gaze from her partner's arm to Jax. "I hear you're taking Darissa to Rivoli."

Rivoli? It was popular, upscale, but reasonably priced. It just wasn't in Darissa Navarre to pick someplace expensive.

But he was already salivating in anticipation of a great meal. The last time they'd gone there—for her birthday earlier in the year—he'd had mushroom fritters that were incredible, followed by a lamb dish that was tasty and imaginative.

"And you're coming back here for dessert," Hannah said. "Last night she made that chocolate ginger cake of hers. We had to smell it cooking. Then she said we couldn't touch it until tonight when you get home from dinner. So don't be too late, okay?"

"No, ma'am."

He heard heels tap on the polished wood floor inside, and raised his head as his mother opened the door. He grinned at her. Darissa Navarre hadn't had an easy life, but you sure couldn't tell it from looking at her. Only fifteen when she'd had him, she was now forty-five, but looked far younger—and damn fine too, with her erect posture, striking face and cap of curly black hair.

"Hey, pretty lady, did you happen to see my mother in there?"

She laughed and opened her arms to him. "Come here, you flatterer."

He hugged her tightly, then stood back. "Classy dress." No follower of women's fashion, he had no idea what designer might have created it. All he could see was that its color—like ripe purple grapes—made her dark skin look even richer.

She winked. "Gotta love working in a clothing store."

After she and his step dad split, she'd had a variety of jobs, all low-end. There wasn't a hell of a lot a Jamaican immigrant could do in the States, not without her high school diploma, but she'd taken whatever she could get. All for him, so he could make something of himself.

In the last few years, she'd finally been able to concentrate on her own career. Passing her GED with top marks gave her confidence, and the needed credential to start looking for more upscale jobs. He wasn't a bit surprised when she found them. His mom was one smart lady and a great judge of character, not to mention having a quiet dignity and a warm personality.

Call him prejudiced, but he figured women didn't come any finer than his mom.

As they walked toward her ancient Honda, he thought of his rental Porsche. "You're going to need a new car before long. Ever thought of a convertible?"

Her eyebrows rose. "They aren't practical."

Practicality. The philosophy that had always ruled their lives.

"Fun, though," he commented.

She narrowed her eyes suspiciously, then grinned. "Yeah, I

bet they are. So, is that what you were doing this weekend? Ridin' around in some hot little car, maybe with some hot little honey?"

Should never have mentioned convertibles. He opened the door to the passenger side for her. "On the phone you said you had something to catch me up on?"

She was laughing when he settled behind the steering wheel. "Not noted for subtlety, are you? Okay, so you want to change the subject, and you know what, I'm gonna let you, because I have some news."

Grateful she'd accepted his clumsy diversion, he said, "Tell me," as he pulled away from the curb.

"I'm thinkin' about taking a part-time job, Friday and Saturday nights."

"Mom, you don't need to do that. You already work full time. Look, if you need more money—"

She touched his arm. "Hush now, boy, it's not about money. This would be for fun. 'Member how we were just talking 'bout that foreign concept?"

He glanced over and saw the gleam in her dark eyes. "Oh-oh, I'm not sure I like the sounds of this. You gonna take up stripping or some such thing?"

She hooted. "Now, if that isn't the finest compliment, for a boy to even think such a thing about his middle-aged mama. Fact is, Tonya and I've been talking about me working at her new restaurant."

He was happy his mom and Tonya had remained good friends after the divorce, but he was definitely not pleased about this bit of news. "No way, Mom, your waitressing days are long gone."

"Would you just listen? Who said anything about waitressing? She wants a hostess. During the week she figures she can do it herself, along with managin' the kitchen staff and the waiters and waitresses. But she's hopin' the weekends will be hopping, and she wants her customers to get the finest care and attention. She wants me to greet folks, make sure they get a table they're happy with, check on how they're doing and so on."

"Yeah, you'd be perfect. But wouldn't it be tiring, after working all day in the store?"

"My feet'll get sore, I'm sure of it, but I get energy from being with people, you know that. I like mixin' and minglin', making sure folks are having a good time. 'Sides, I'll have all of Sunday to put my feet up and rest."

He parked, and when they'd both got out of the car, she said, "There's another reason this appeals to me."

"What's that?"

"Tonya can't afford to pay a lot, but she'll make me a partner in the business."

"A partner? Really?"

"Oh, just an itty-bitty minor partner, but all the same, Jax, I'd be a part owner. There'd be Tonya and Benjamin, the chef, Consuela, and me. Just imagine, we'd have partners meetings and make decisions together."

"Wow, Mom, I'm impressed." He shook his head. His mother, a partner in an up-and-coming business. She'd always sworn America was the land of opportunity—for those who worked their butts off—and the two of them were living proof.

Ushering her into Rivoli, he saw the rather starkly-decorated restaurant was bustling, but they were in luck and got a table with a view of the back garden.

Jax picked up the wine list. "We have to celebrate." He thought of Suzanne, of how they'd talked about champagne. Keep it special, don't let the bubbles go flat.

He beckoned the waiter over and had a quiet discussion.

The waiter hurried away, saying, "I'll be right back with your champagne."

"Champagne?" his mom said. "Why Jaxon Navarre, where's the little boy I raised, who put every last penny of his allowance into his piggy bank?"

"I have more pennies now. I can afford to throw a few around." He gave her a quick hug. "Especially on my favorite lady."

"Your favorite lady?" she said. "You saying there wasn't a hot little honey this weekend?"

"I . . ." Where was that waiter?

"What's the big secret, Jax?" She narrowed her eyes.

He knew what that expression meant. She wouldn't be backing down any time soon. And if he didn't tell her, next thing he knew she'd be trying to fix him up with someone again, like she'd done with Tonya.

"Okay, yeah, I did see a woman." He couldn't hold back a self-satisfied grin. Maybe he had wanted to tell someone about Suzanne after all. "And yeah, she's pretty hot, if you really need to know stuff like that."

"Whoo-hoo, my baby's dating!"

"Don't get carried away," he said dryly. "I saw her once. Maybe we'll get together again." Or maybe not. He'd have to e-mail and cancel the weekend. Suzanne might write him off. Couldn't expect a woman like her to sit around waiting for him.

"Well, sure you'll get together again. Sounds like you had fun together."

"Yeah, but I don't have time for a relationship. You know that. It's the main reason Tonya and I broke up."

"I love that girl like a daughter, but she should've hung in longer, tried to work things out with you. Maybe I'd have grandbabies by now."

He shook his head firmly. "Nope. Tonya did try, we both did, but it didn't work. It was better to cut our losses. Thank God we *didn't* have children."

She frowned, her warm brown eyes concerned. "You've always been so driven. . ."

And where did he learn that? She'd worked herself past the point of exhaustion to give him a good education. They were a lot alike. Not dummies, but not so smart that things came easily to them. They both had to work damned hard for every single thing they achieved.

"Mom, you know that's what it takes to—" Jax broke off as the waiter finally appeared with their champagne.

The man deftly eased the cork out and poured. Golden liquid and fizzing bubbles rose just to the rim of each elegant flute, then subsided.

When he and his mom were alone again, Jax raised his glass and his mother picked up hers. "To your new venture," he said. "Here's to Tonya and Darissa's place."

She chuckled. "You make it sound like a country kitchen." She clicked her glass to his, then sipped the champagne. "Mmm. Delicious." She eased the bottle out of the ice bucket and read the label, then pulled a little notebook out of her purse and scribbled something.

"What are you doing?"

She glanced up. "I'm in the restaurant business. I have to pay more attention."

Aha. That's why she'd changed her mind yesterday, and accepted his invitation to eat out. "This place prides itself on using fresh local ingredients, right?"

"Sure does." She finished writing and grinned. "Rivoli's a competitor. I'm only here because I'm doing research."

"Want me to steal a copy of the menu?"

She rolled her eyes. "Like I didn't already read it on-line?"

Yup, this lady was just as success driven as her kid.

After she'd told him what she wanted him to order—in the name of research—she said, "How are things going at work?"

"My billable hours are higher than anyone else's. I'm starting to bring in new clients of my own, mostly referrals from existing ones. And the senior partner just gave me a major new file."

He'd spent the afternoon going over the papers filed by the National Association for the Advancement of Colored People, counsel for the plaintiffs. Tomorrow morning, he'd set up a meeting with Sam Miller, the CEO of Family Friend.

His mom's smile split her face. "That's wonderful."

"It's a big class-action suit, and can you believe, I might end up being first chair? If I can win this one, I'll definitely be in line for a partnership." Of course, the case probably wouldn't be heard for years; class-action suits seemed to go on forever. But if he could prove to Jefferson he had it under control . . .

His mom reached over and gripped his hand. "You'll do it, Jax. Whenever you set your mind on something, you make it happen. I'm so proud of you."

He knew she was, yet he never tired of hearing the words. He was all she had. He was the reason she'd left her family in Jamaica, married that American jerk and come to the States. Whatever he did, he did for her, to prove her right and make her proud.

The waiter arrived with their appetizers: goat cheese soufflé for her, smoked salmon for him. They tasted their own, tasted each other's, analyzed both and she wrote some more notes while Jax munched appreciatively.

When she'd closed her notebook and taken a couple more bites of her soufflé, she said, "Now tell me more about this girl you're seeing."

Should've known she'd get back there eventually. The woman really wasn't distractable.

"It's casual." He shrugged. "She seems nice, we have fun." Sexual fun. He tried to push that thought aside. He'd always suspected his mom could read his mind.

"Sounds like a good start for a relationship," she said. Was that a twinkle in her eye?

How could he explain? She just didn't grasp how much work it took to succeed in his area of law. He had to put in the hours, do his homework, build his connections.

Twice in his life, he'd made the mistake of overestimating his abilities. In high school, he'd dated the head cheerleader pretty seriously, but she'd cut into his study time and his marks plummeted so he'd had to call it off.

The second time was Tonya. He never should have married her, but he'd been in love and feeling like Superman. He could handle everything.

Except, he couldn't. If he'd settled for a less prestigious field, like Rick, he wouldn't have to work so hard. But then he'd be a middle-of-the-roader, and that wasn't good enough.

He was perfectly aware of being a typical immigrant child— an overachiever. Arriving in America as a little boy, he'd learned about his new country quickly, and one of the things he'd learned was what Americans valued in a man: money, status, power. Things that were harder—but not impossible—for a black man to achieve.

"What's her name?" His mother's question broke his train of thought.

"Huh?"

"The girl you aren't having a relationship with."

"Suzanne." A.k.a. outrageous69.

"Pretty name. What does she do?"

I don't have a clue. Instead, he said, "Mom, leave it alone, okay? It's just casual."

"Mmm. Black girl, brown girl, white girl, yellow girl?"

"White." Actually, she was golden.

"That a wise idea?"

"You being racist, Mom?"

"You know me better than that. But it's a fact, there's more stresses on a mixed-race relationship. Some people gonna look at you funny."

"We're not having a relationship!" And he sure as hell wasn't going to tell her about the playground, and what the cops had thought.

His mother gave an infuriating catlike grin. "I hear you, boy." And, clearly, didn't believe him.

He ground his teeth in frustration. "And when's the last time you went on a date?"

The grin became wider. "Saturday."

"You did?" Why had he thought his mother wasn't dating? "Who's the guy? Someone special?"

She seesawed her hand. "Nice guy, just casual. We have some fun."

Oh damn, she sure knew how to get back at him. "You never told me you were dating."

"Didn't know I had to clear it with my son," she teased.

He huffed out a breath. "Of course you don't. But I thought..." That she was hanging around the house cooking meals, chatting with her lesbian tenants and being celibate. "I can see why you'd want some male company. Aside from mine."

She reached over to squeeze his hand. "Jax, I've been dating ever since I was able to cut back on the hours I worked. Didn't you know? Sure, a woman can use some male companionship every now and then."

Did she mean sex? He *really* didn't want to think about that. "You've never introduced me to any of your dates." Could he sound any more childish and whiny?

"You haven't introduced me to yours. Likely for the same reason. They're not serious, just casual fun."

He wished she'd stop tossing his own words back at him. Was her idea of casual fun the same as his and Suzanne's?

His mom was a beautiful, desirable woman. Why hadn't he realized men would be after her? "You ever thought of getting married again?"

She shook her head firmly. "I'm used to my independence."
Another thing the two of them had in common.

The Awesome Foursome had chosen the SalaThai on Cambie
for this week's Monday dinner.

Suzanne was the last to arrive. She'd watched an emergency
surgery on a Weimeraner that had been hit by a car, and was
hyped up with excitement, relief that the dog would make it
and anticipation of one day operating herself.

On a normal night, she'd have been bursting to share all the
gory details, but she guessed her friends had a different priority—i.e., sex.

And yet, as she headed across the busy restaurant to the corner table they'd snagged, expecting sly grins and a lot of "wink,
wink, nudge, nudge" comments—she instead saw serious expressions on Rina's and Ann's faces. Jenny looked annoyed.

"Something wrong?" Suzanne asked.

"Some people have a warped sense of perspective," Jen said
darkly.

Clearly, her friends had been arguing.

Rina reached out to pat her hand. "Why don't you order a
beer, Suze?"

"Good idea." Had they been arguing over her and Jaxon, or
were they on some completely different issue?

A slender Asian woman in a red Asian-style top and a black
skirt with brocade trim took her order for a Singha.

"Jaxon is a beautiful man," Rina said. "You didn't tell us he
looks like Denzel Washington."

Ah, so that's what Jenny'd meant on Saturday. "Does he? To
me, he looks like Jaxon."

"Denzel," Jen said firmly. "When he was younger, of course."

"Denzel's still a damned attractive man," Ann said. "Jaxon
will age well too."

Probably true, but what Jaxon would look like at forty, fifty, sixty wasn't exactly relevant to Suzanne.

The waitress delivered her beer and Suzanne took a sip.

"Well, anyway," Rina said, "the two of you are a wonderful looking couple. And I'm sure you had a great time, but . . ." She fiddled with a dangly, wire-and-bead earring. "The truth is, I'm worried about you."

Suzanne smiled at her. "Thanks, but we've spent two evenings together now, and I'm pretty sure he's not going to murder me."

"Good to know," Ann commented dryly.

"It's your heart I'm concerned about," Rina said.

"My heart isn't involved. I told you, this is all about sex. Period. Just like Jen said. It's my walk on the wild side." She glanced toward Jenny, seeking her support.

"See, I told you!" Jenny waved a gem-studded pink fingernail at Rina. "Suze has her game plan all figured out. She knows what she's doing."

"Exactly. Jeez, guys, even my sister says I should sow some wild oats. I'm not looking for a husband, I want . . . a sex toy." Even as she said the words, she winced at the demeaning connotation. And yet that's really what she and Jaxon were to each other.

She gazed into Rina's worried brown eyes. "I'm not going to go and fall for him, honest."

Her friend frowned. "This really is unlike you, Suze. You hardly ever date, you've got this whole plan about marriage and a family, you're totally into your own family and your career. You're not a sex toy kind of woman."

She remembered the assorted condoms Jenny had given her, and grinned. "Suzanne the sexy twin is. And I like being her. Just for now, for a little while. My life plan hasn't changed. The find-a-husband part was always targeted to start in a few years."

Rina wasn't grinning back. "I don't want you to get hurt. Getting together with Jaxon once made sense, for fun and to test out that old Crete memory of yours, but now it's turning into something different. You're doing this romantic stuff, planning to see him next weekend. Suzie, you're starting a relationship."

"We're not doing *romantic* stuff and it's *not* a relationship. It's sex, and I won't get hurt. This is about my erogenous zones, and my heart isn't one of them." Suzanne glanced at Ann. "You're being unusually quiet tonight."

Her friend looked tired and stressed, as if there might be more on her mind than just the Jaxon issue. Maybe a problem at work? Come to think of it, she'd sounded odd when they talked on the phone Saturday night.

Ann's gaze slid away from her face, then, apparently with some effort, returned. "I'm with Rina. I'm afraid you're getting in over your head."

Suzanne shook her head. "I don't get it. Last week you were all egging me on, so long as I was careful. What's changed?"

"Yeah," Jenny chipped in. "Give Suze a break, girls. You both helped write the ad, so no fair dumping on her now."

Ann rubbed a hand across her forehead. "But Rina's right. Once is different than an ongoing relationship. And"—she scowled at Suzanne—"don't play semantics with me. Seeing a guy several times, having sex and talking, is a relationship. And this is a man you know next to nothing about. I think it's time you found out some information."

Although Suzanne had been growing increasingly curious about Jaxon, Ann's words made her defensive. "It's against the Champagne Rules." She glanced toward Rina and Jenny. "Jaxon and I have these Rules, about keeping things special. Bubbly and fizzy, you know. Not letting things get flat."

"You do know those Rules don't make any sense at all, right?" Ann said grimly. "Not to any sane person."

"They make sense to Jaxon and me, and that's all I care about." She leaned forward to rest her hand on Ann's. "Don't you see, I want this to be different. I want to be different. I want to be champagne, not a cardboard box of table wine."

"Yes, I've heard what you said." Ann closed her eyes and kept them shut for a moment. "Okay." She opened her eyes again. "I admit there's a certain appeal to a relationship that doesn't involve all those stupid trivial details of each other's lives."

"Well, I don't," Rina broke in, her voice soft but determined. "For me, I'm only going to invest time in a relationship if I can see it going somewhere. If I can see us getting to know each other better, growing closer, finding things to respect and admire about the other person, learning to trust—" She broke off, and gave an embarrassed shrug. "You get the picture."

"And I agree," Suzanne said. "That's exactly what I want, when I start thinking about settling down. But that's years off. I'm not ready."

"You've got acres of wild oats to sow first," Jenny said. "We all do."

"I do understand," Ann said, "and I'm not saying you need to find out his favorite color, or zodiac sign, or who his first grade teacher was. But don't you at least want to know his address and home phone number? What he does for a living?"

The truth was, Suzanne did. But she also believed in the merit of the Champagne Rules. "It's a slippery slope. Where do you draw the line? Besides, what would it change? I've spent two evenings with him, and I really don't believe he poses a physical threat." She smirked. "Except I've discovered muscles I never knew I had."

"Way to go!" Jenny said.

"As for my heart," Suzanne went on, "if you're worried I'm going to get hurt, don't you think there's more likelihood of that happening if I really get to know the guy? You don't fall in love with someone you just have sex with. You fall in love the way Rina said, by slowly getting to know him, and finding those things that are special about him and make your heart go all mushy."

"That's true." Rina had a puzzled frown on her face, clearly not happy about agreeing.

"I still think you need to find out more about him—" Ann started.

"Okay, okay." Jenny held up both hands. "Can we find a compromise? Suze, can't you find out some stuff without it ruining the sex?"

"If I could think of a way, maybe I'd do it," Suzanne confessed. "But if I ask him all those questions, then he'll ask me about myself. If I start talking about my family and my job, I won't feel sexy anymore. I'll become . . ."

"Boxed wine," Jenny said. "Nothing wrong with it, but it sure as hell doesn't compare with champagne."

After a moment, Rina said, "I guess this is one of the things we're just not going to agree on. Speaking of rules, we have a rule for that, right?"

"We do," Suzanne said with relief. "Agree to disagree, and leave it alone."

She collected nods, then said, "Can we order now?"

"Yeah," Jenny agreed. "Then I want to hear every single detail about your sexcapades."

She beckoned their waitress, and soon they had fresh beer all around and were digging into an aromatic selection of curries, stir-fries and pad thai.

Suzanne had the others' rapt attention as she related her weekend's adventures with Jaxon. Even with considerable editing, she had to admit it sounded even spicier than the food they were consuming.

When she told them about her calamari-cock-ring comment, they laughed so hard all the other diners turned to look.

"I don't even know what a cock ring *is*," Rina confessed in a whisper.

Suzanne added her own confession. "Neither do I, really, but I do read." She glanced around. "Jenny? Ann? Any experience with them?"

Ann, who was still being unusually subdued, shook her head.

Jen said, "This definitely calls for research. I feel a new article coming on."

Suzanne carried on with the story, all the way to the smoldering kiss when Jaxon dropped her off where she'd parked the Miata.

"Awesome night," Jenny said.

"Yeah." Except... "There was only one kind of icky thing," she said quietly.

Ann's hand jerked and she spilled yellow curry on the tablecloth. "Sorry. Icky, Suze?"

"In the playground, I told you the cops came, but I left something out. They did this racial thing. Because Jaxon's black and I'm white. They were pretty offensive about checking out whether it really was consensual sex." She gave a strained laugh. "They even wondered if he was a pimp and I was one of his, uh, ladies."

"A 'ho'?" Jen said. "You?"

"That's so obnoxious," Rina said.

"Racial profiling," Ann said. "Nasty."

"Yeah."

"How was Jaxon with it?" Ann asked.

"Not terribly surprised. He said he's had worse happen."

"I just bet he has." The words were Jenny's, and her tone was bitter.

They all stared at her.

"What?" she said. "It's whacked, but it happens. He's a person of color; of course it happens. Fuck, it happens to *me!*"

"Jen?" Suzanne said.

"Remember the SARS epidemic, and how it was associated with China and Chinese people? Well, I was driving into the States with a couple of friends—white friends—and *I* was the one who got taken inside at the border. It was my passport they checked and double-checked."

"It happens to me too," Rina said softly.

"You?" Suzanne said. "Because you're Jewish? But you're not even a practicing Jew."

Rina shook her head. "No, it's because I look . . . ethnic. Dark skin, curly black hair, big nose. People aren't quite sure what I am. Could be Iraqi."

"Shit," Ann said. "This stinks."

"How come you guys have never talked about this?" Suzanne asked. "I feel so naïve for not having realized."

Jenny and Rina exchanged glances. Jen shrugged. "It's dirty. Who wants to talk about dirty stuff?"

Although they hadn't the slightest qualm about discussing intimate details of sex.

But Jen was right, sex wasn't dirty. Prejudice was.

"That's what's so great about you and Ann," Rina said. "Our skin color doesn't matter in the slightest to you."

"Let he who is without sin, cast the first stone," Ann said quietly.

"Yeah, and do unto others, and all that stuff," Jen agreed. "You and Suze say you aren't religious, but you *live* it, you know? You're decent and caring, much more than a lot of those right-wing *supposed* Christians."

"This is getting way too heavy," Rina said. "Suze, I'm so sorry about what happened with the police. But if you're going to keep seeing Jaxon, be prepared for things like that."

"You don't think that would stop me?"

Rina reached over to hug her. "Of course not. Isn't that what Jenny just said?" Then she said, "It's late. Time to head home."

Quietly, they settled the bill and gathered up their belongings. Outside on the street, they exchanged hugs all around just as they always did. Except, tonight, the hugs were a little tighter.

Jenny and Rina headed off, then Suzanne dug out Ann's car keys. "Time to trade cars again. It was sweet of you to let me have the Miata."

"No problem."

God, they were both so solemn.

Trying to lighten the mood, Suzanne said, "My brother-in-law's absolutely green. He saw your car when they came over for Sunday dinner. Turns out he had a sports car, once upon a time, before marriage and kids."

"Can't lug kids around in a two-seater," Ann murmured as they swapped keys. "Look, keep me posted on Jaxon, okay? Let me—all of us—know when you're seeing him again. Please, Suze?"

Suzanne touched her arm. "Ann? Is everything all right? You've been awfully quiet. I know we disagree about the Rules, but it's no big deal, okay? I appreciate your concern."

Ann hadn't been meeting her eyes, but then suddenly did. Her cheeks were pink. "That's not why I was being quiet. I did something . . . kind of crappy. Oh damn, Suze, I have to tell you, this is driving me crazy."

"You did something crappy?" Suzanne shook her head. "I don't believe it."

"You haven't heard it," Ann said grimly. "Got time for coffee and a confession?"

"Of course."

11

Down the block they found a coffee shop and ordered lattes. When the coffee arrived, in bowl-shaped cups, Ann wrapped her hands around hers, her interlaced fingers rigid with tension.

"Just tell me," Suzanne said.

"Last Friday, you know we agreed you'd give a signal and Jenny and Rina and I would go home?"

"Uh-huh."

"I drove out of the parking lot, but I just didn't feel comfortable leaving you alone with a stranger. I parked in the next lot over."

"You came back? I didn't see you."

"I didn't want to ruin your evening." Ann's face was flushed.

"You . . . what did you see?" Suzanne could feel her own cheeks heat as she began to realize the possibilities. Oh God, could one of her best friends have seen her having sex? "Ann, how could you do that?" She'd known her friend had an overprotective, even controlling, streak, but she'd never thought Ann would spy on her.

"It's not as bad as you're thinking."

"How bad is it?"

"I saw you and Jaxon settle down with your picnic stuff behind a big log. I couldn't see over the log, honestly. I figured if you got in any kind of trouble, you'd call out and I'd hear. I didn't want to get any closer because you might see me."

"Yes, God forbid *we* might see *you*."

Ann winced. "I told you this was crappy."

Suzanne tried to steady her racing heart. Okay, it wasn't too bad. She and Jaxon had made love behind the log, and Ann hadn't seen them. They'd had their picnic and they'd . . . Her eyes widened. "You were there when we went skinny-dipping!"

Ann ducked her head and nodded.

"Jesus, Ann."

"I'm sorry, sorry, sorry." Then Ann looked up and shook her head. "No, wait a minute, I'm not *that* sorry." Her cheeks were still bright, but now she met Suzanne's gaze. "It's a public beach. I had a right to be there. I wasn't the only one either. You put on quite a show for a gay couple who were walking their dog. And I only did it because I care, and I was worried."

"I . . ." It was difficult to argue with Ann's logic, or her motivation. "I'm so embarrassed," Suzanne muttered. "It was tacky, what Jaxon and I did. But at the time it felt so right."

"It . . ." Ann paused, then said deliberately, "It looked right. It was . . . beautiful, Suzie. I should have felt embarrassed watching, I should have turned away, but . . ."

"Yes, you damn well should have!"

"It was like a movie." Ann stared into her coffee. "In the moonlight, you were silhouette figures. It wasn't really you, not someone I knew, just this female shape, together with a male shape. It wasn't so much sexy as sensual and . . . moving."

She looked up. "That's why I'm so worried about you. It's not just about sex."

"Of course it is. You should know that better than anyone, seeing as you watched the whole damned thing."

Ann shook her head. "There's a connection between the two of you."

"Sexual chemistry."

"More than that. I could see it. If I could see it, you must feel it."

"It . . . All right, when we make l— have sex, it feels like . . . we complete each other. That we touch each other deeply."

"Making love. You were going to call it making love, and that's what it is."

Suzanne shook her head fiercely. "It isn't. It just happens that we're very sexually compatible, so the sex feels more intimate."

Ann spooned up some of the foamy milk from the top of her latte. "I should have listened more closely when you first talked about him."

Suzanne told herself to calm down. "What do you mean?"

"When you talked about that afternoon in the cave, didn't you say the sex was really intimate, the kind of lovemaking that should create a child?"

"I . . . Yes, okay, that's how it feels. But Ann, apply your rational mind. I can't be in love with him, can I? To love, you have to know a person well enough to respect them." She thought about Jaxon helping the Greek widow, and going back to the playground to dispose of the condom. But she hadn't known those things—she hadn't known anything about him—when they first had sex.

She went on. "For love, you need a mental connection and an emotional one, as well as a physical one."

"That's what your mind says, but maybe your body knows better." Her friend gazed at her earnestly over the cup she cradled in both hands. "Maybe your mind and emotions will catch up with your body, and you'll find it really is love. That's why it's so important you know what kind of man you're dealing with. I know you, Suzanne. What if he's married?"

"He's single."

"He said so, and you believe him?"

"Yes! Why would he lie?"

"Because you wouldn't see him if he was married."

"He doesn't know that." And she did trust Jaxon. Didn't she? "We've already had this discussion." She stood up, having barely touched her coffee.

So did Ann. "Don't hate me, Suze."

She sounded utterly woebegone and Suzanne's heart melted. She gave Ann a quick hug. "I could never hate you. But did you tell Rina and Jen?"

"Of course not. I just said I was worried about you getting emotionally involved."

"I won't let myself."

Ann turned to go, murmuring something under her breath that sounded like, "You already are."

On Tuesday morning, Jax met for two hours with Sam Miller, a grossly overweight, bald man who energetically denied that there was any validity to the complaints against the Family Friend managers. The denial was reassuring, though it would have been more useful to have some solid facts.

Jax came away with a rough action plan in his head—one that would require him to put in at least sixteen-hour days for the next week and a half.

When he got back to the office and listened to his voice mail, he heard his ex asking him to give her a call. He buzzed Alan Cohen, the paralegal in Corporate who was handling Tonya's file, got a quick status report, then phoned her.

"Hey, girl, what's this about you propositioning my mother?"

She chuckled. "That woman's easy, Jax. She was willing to settle for a five percent share, but I talked her up to ten."

"So it's decided? You're really going to be partners?"

"It's a done deal, as of this morning. She said she spoke to you last night. Thanks for not trying to talk her out of it."

"You ever tried talking my mom out of anything?"

"True. You inherited pigheaded from her. So, anyhow, we'll need to revise the percentages in the partnership agreement. Darissa and Consuela for ten each, me and Benjamin both at forty."

They discussed the other details, then she said, "There's another reason I called."

"Oh?"

"We're going to have a dinner party to test out some possibilities for our menu. It'll be two, three dozen people. Wondered if you might come?"

"Mmm. I'd like to, but . . ." He and Benjamin had pretty much gotten over being awkward with each other, but some of Tonya's friends weren't so comfortable with it. Besides, he was going to be all-work no-play for at least the next ten days. "When're you talking about?"

"Haven't set the date, but probably a couple weeks time." She paused, then said, "Let me guess. You're too busy." He recognized the edge of bitterness in her voice. Just like when we were married, she was thinking.

"Might be some potential clients for you," she added, the bitterness sharpening.

"It's not that," he said, though in part it was, and he knew she knew it. For him, every social gathering meant the potential for garnering business. But damn it, he did want to support Tonya. "Let me know when you've got the date set, and I'll do my best."

"Really?" She sounded pleasantly surprised.

"Sure."

"You can bring a friend." Now there was a teasing note in her voice. "That is, if you're dating these days."

"Um . . ."

"Jax? You are dating?"

If it was a couple weekends down the road, maybe he could invite Suzanne to San Francisco. But would he want to take her to Tonya's dinner? Would she be interested? No, he couldn't. The Champagne Rules must prohibit it. "It's kind of complicated."

"Ooh, this is getting interesting. How so?"

He chose the stuff that was easy to explain. "She lives in Vancouver. BC, not Washington. I visited her last weekend. And we've only just, um, got together."

"Sounds serious, for you to be flying up to Vancouver to visit. How did you meet?"

He choked, and had to cough. "Happened a long time ago, before I met you. And then . . . our paths crossed recently."

"Jax, you have to bring her! I've got to meet her."

Introduce his sex goddess to his nosy ex-wife? Despite being curious about what each would think of the other, he couldn't imagine surviving the stress. Not to mention, his mom would be there too. He didn't want that woman getting any ideas.

"Oh Jax, I'll be nice to her," Tonya cooed. "After all, any friend of yours . . ."

Friend. Was Suzanne a friend? He guessed the Rules prohibited friendship too.

But maybe not. It was impossible to *not* learn things about each other. Even the most superficial conversation could be revealing. He knew Suzanne loved animals, flowers and sunshine, hated cold showers, male chauvinism and pollution. She didn't mind guidebooks, but preferred to talk to local people.

He was dimly aware of Tonya saying something about the dinner, but his brain was following its own path.

Up until now, with Suzanne, he'd been thinking with his cock. But now his big head was getting involved. He realized that, while they maybe weren't friends yet, it was likely to happen if they kept seeing each other. Was it possible to have a relationship that included both friendship and great sex? Or, if the friendship deepened, would the sexual sparks fizzle out? The champagne would go flat, and that's why they had their Rules.

Yet, for Tonya and Benjamin, the bells and whistles kept blaring even as their relationship deepened—through friendship, then love, marriage, even business partnership.

But Tonya and Benjamin managed to juggle careers and their relationship. He'd proven he didn't have that ability. Friendships involved time and energy, way more than sex did. If he tried to be friends with Suzanne, he'd fail, and failure was the thing he hated most in the world.

"*Jaxon Navarre!* You still there?"

He jerked upright. "Sorry. Yes, I'm here."

"That gal must really be something, hon. I've been calling your name for, like, ten minutes, and you were off in dreamland. So, what's her name, what's she do? Black girl, white girl, yellow girl, brown girl?"

Her words were an echo of his mother's. Suddenly everything clicked. "Mom's been talking to you about more than just the restaurant business." The two women had always done this—talked behind his back—and it drove him nuts.

"God, Jax, you sure can be slow."

"So why are you asking these questions, if you already know the answers?" he said, knowing he sounded huffy.

"'Cause Darissa said you were real closemouthed, so we decided I'd try to see if I could get any more out of you. And I did. You didn't mention Vancouver to your mom, or the fact you'd met this Suzanne years ago. Darissa did say she figured the girl has a sports car?"

"Red Miata," he confirmed grudgingly. "But that's all you're getting."

"Until I meet her."

"I didn't say I'd—" But Tonya had hung up.

And now, before he buckled down to work, he'd have to e-mail Suzanne and tell her he couldn't see her this weekend. Crap!

No, wait. He didn't want to treat Suzanne like another item of business, crammed into the middle of his busy workday. He'd wait until tonight, when he finally made it home.

There'd been no e-mail from Jaxon Monday night, when Suzanne returned from dinner with her friends. And she was too upset and confused to send off a sexy, superficial message.

She had Tuesday off—each week she took a day off in exchange for working Saturdays—and the day crawled by. She drove down to Granville Island for coffee, then took a long walk along the False Creek waterfront, ending up back at the island, where she bought groceries at the market. Back home, she put chicken, vegetables and spices in the slow cooker, read a couple of veterinary magazines, then did some weeding in her mom's garden and worked on her tan.

She only checked her e-mail about three dozen times.

After dinner, she chatted on the phone with a vet student friend, watched a couple of TV shows, then curled up on top of her bed with a novel—ears alert for the clunk of arriving e-mail.

This was ridiculous. Just like being a high school kid, waiting for a boy to call.

And obviously this one wasn't going to.

At eleven, she climbed under the covers and turned off the light. She drifted off to sleep, then woke two or three hours later, thinking of Jaxon. She'd never get back to sleep unless she checked her e-mail again.

And yes, now there was a message from caveman. It had come in only a couple of minutes ago.

Before reading it, she clicked REPLY and typed, If you're still there, Jaxon, don't go. I just got your message.

Then she read what he'd written. Damn, he couldn't get to-gether this weekend.

Why?

All he said was, he wasn't going to be able to make it.

Another woman? Or was he bored with her already?

Another message appeared.

Still here. So, you're a night owl too, Suzanne. It's damn sexy, thinking of us both awake, in different cities, when the rest of the world sleeps.

Can't stop thinking of all the things we did last weekend . . .

Okay, he didn't seem bored.

What's your favorite memory? she typed back.

I have to pick just one? he responded.

Let's start with one.

His answer came quickly. Then I pick skinny-dipping. When you kept splashing cold water on my cock, then taking me inside your hot, hot mouth. I've never felt anything like that.

Hot. Oh yes, she was definitely getting hot right now.

Eagerly she typed back, Tell me what it felt like. And imagine I'm doing it right now. Imagine my mouth circling you. I know you have a great imagination, Jaxon.

And for the next ten minutes they relived having sex at Spanish Banks, proving they both had wonderful imaginations.

Finally, warm with a postorgasmic glow, she left the com-puter and sank into bed, where her brain slowly regained con-trol over her body.

She'd sat waiting all night for him to e-mail. When he did, at *two* in the morning, he'd canceled their date. Then she e-mailed back and engaged in IM sex with him.

Great IM sex, yes, but all the same, maybe she was being too available?

He must think she had nothing better to do than sit at home all night waiting for him.

* * *

Suzanne was so disgruntled with herself, she almost didn't respond when she got Jenny's text message the next morning. Need 2 meet. 4sum. BG @ 12.

So, the Foursome wanted to meet her at the Bread Garden, and harass her some more, did they? Why should she opt into this?

Or maybe she was being paranoid. They'd all made their opinions clear on Monday night, and invoked the agree-to-disagree rule. Maybe one of the others had some problem she needed to discuss. She messaged back C U @ 12.

At five to twelve, Suzanne hurried the few blocks to the deli-style restaurant. Rina, coming out of a parking lot, met up with her.

"What's up?" Suzanne asked.

"Oh, uh, let's get some food." Rina waved toward a patio table where Ann and Jenny had their heads together.

Suzanne chose a Thai noodle salad, Rina went for Greek salad, and they took their trays over to join the others.

"What's going on?" Suzanne asked.

"We need to talk to you," Ann said quietly.

"Oh no, not again. We went through this Monday night. Leave it alone, okay?"

The other three exchanged glances. Ann had cut her veggie wrap into a dozen pieces, but didn't seem to have taken a bite. Jenny was picking at the embroidered design on her pink blouse. Rina couldn't seem to get the knot in her scarf tied to her satisfaction.

Finally, Ann sighed, shrugged out of her charcoal suit jacket and said evenly, "We've done something you're not going to like."

On top of her Saturday-night voyeurism? "What the—"

Ann held up a hand to stop her. "After we had dinner Monday, Rina called me and we talked, then I called Jenny. We're all concerned that you seem so bound and determined not to know anything about this man."

Suzanne shoved her salad away. "That's my business."

"You said you couldn't ask Jaxon questions, because then he'd ask them back, right?"

A horrible suspicion dawned. "You didn't go and check him out, did you?" Then she shook her head quickly. "No, you couldn't, you don't have enough information."

"It didn't take a lot," Ann said grimly. "Jaxon Navarre in San Francisco. That turned out to be enough."

Suzanne gaped at her. "You did! You went behind my back. I'm . . ." Her heart was racing and she couldn't find words.

They'd betrayed her. These women—her closest friends, or so she'd thought—had betrayed her. "How could you? Damn it, I . . ." She shoved her chair back from the table.

Ann reached for her hand. "Don't go. Hear us out."

Suzanne pulled away from her touch as Jenny said, "Suze, we thought you might like to know some stuff about him if you didn't have to come right out and ask him."

"Well, I *don't!*"

But that was a lie. She'd already been curious about Jaxon, and now her friends' anxiety made her nervous. Were they just feeling guilty, or had they found out something awful?

Her heart was still skittering, but she couldn't leave. And maybe she wasn't feeling so betrayed and furious anymore. These women really were her friends, even if their actions were misguided.

"Suzie?" Rina said. "Are you sure you don't want to know?"

Suzanne sighed, curiosity winning out. "Don't tell me," she tried to joke, "he's something awful like an accountant."

Ann shook her head. "Worse."

"An ex-con?" Suzanne asked fearfully.

"No, not that bad," Ann said. "A lawyer."

"What?" Her first reaction was, it was too conventional a job.

Ann rested her forearms on the table and leaned forward. "I did an internet search for his name. His firm has a website and it lists all the lawyers. It's a high-powered place called Jefferson Sparks. He's an associate, specializing in complex litigation. Prestigious work."

"Okay, I guess a lawyer's not so bad."

"Gee, thanks," Ann said.

"Well, it's not like you speak so highly of your colleagues," Suzanne pointed out.

"No. For the most part we're a bunch of self-centered workaholics."

"Ouch!" Jenny commented. "Then why the hell are you doing it, Annie?"

"That's a damned good question."

Her tone was so grim that the others all stared at her. She often joked about her career, but she'd never sounded so serious before.

Suzanne remembered how often she'd seen Ann take an overloaded briefcase home, drink high-test coffee so she'd stay awake to work late, pop pills for headaches or . . . What were all those pills Ann was taking?

"Ann?" Suzanne said, "Is everything okay?"

Ann's eyes widened. "Oh God, sorry, was I making this about me?" She shook her head briskly. "No, I'm fine, there's nothing new. All I'm saying is, law's a profession where it's hard to find your balance. There are a lot of hoops to jump through if you want to succeed, and it's harder for a woman. I'd bet it's harder for a man of color too, though I shouldn't assume that about Jaxon. Who knows, he may come from a family of lawyers."

"It wouldn't surprise me," Suzanne said. "The way he carries himself, the way he dresses. He's classy."

"So, maybe he's had the way paved for him. Maybe he doesn't need to be so work obsessed, like I am."

"He sure wasn't on the weekend." And that was all Suzanne cared about—how he was when he was with her. "So, I guess it's good to know he has a respectable job. Now I won't have to worry about it."

The other three exchanged glances.

Oh-oh. "*Is* there something I should worry about?"

"Jenny?" Ann said.

"Uh . . ." Jenny took a long swallow of Coke and Suzanne sensed she was stalling, which was completely unlike her in-your-face friend.

"Get on with it," Suzanne said.

Jenny put down her glass. "He's married."

"What?" Suzanne yelped.

Rina grabbed her hand. "We're sorry, Suze, but his secretary confirmed it."

"His secretary? You phoned his secretary and asked if he was married?" Suzanne's head was pounding with a jumble of emotions. Jaxon had lied to her.

No, wait, there must be some mistake. She couldn't see him as a cheat and a liar. But how could she judge? The girls were right, she barely knew him.

Jenny was shaking her head. "Give me a little credit. I'm a journalist, remember? I've got sneaky ways of finding information."

"Go on."

"I got his home number from directory assistance and called. Blocking the display, so no one could see my name or where I was calling from. Anyhow, I got a recorded message in a male voice that just repeated the number and said to leave a message. I tried a couple more times, same thing happened. Then I phoned his office and asked for his secretary. I pretended to be from Nordstrom's in San Francisco."

"Huh?"

"I said Mr. Navarre's wife had made a purchase last week and wanted it delivered, but I needed to confirm the details and hadn't been able to reach her. I said I'd left a message at her home number, but she hadn't called back, and I remembered her mentioning that Mr. Navarre was a lawyer, so I looked him up in the phone book. Nordstrom's is famous for customer service, so I figured the secretary might buy into a salesclerk going the extra mile."

She fiddled with her Coke glass. "I was expecting the secretary to tell me I had the wrong Navarre, because her boss wasn't married."

"What did she say?" Suzanne asked with trepidation.

Jenny sucked in a breath. "She said, 'You're calling here for Tonya?' "

"Tonya," Suzanne echoed flatly. Jaxon had a wife named Tonya.

"So then I backpedaled and said I had the wrong Navarre, the woman's first name was Mary. I apologized and asked her to forget the whole thing."

"Tonya," Suzanne said again. Then, "Damn him! He lied to me."

She was dimly aware that all three of them were touching her, patting her shoulder, stroking her arm, but she felt the weirdest combination of numbness and fury.

"We're sorry, Suze," Ann said. "But it's better to know, isn't it?"

"They could be separated," Jenny said. "I could hardly ask the secretary that, but she did sound surprised that someone was trying to reach Tonya at Jaxon's office."

Rina and Ann nodded too, and Suzanne found her own head going up and down in time with theirs. That had to be the explanation. He hadn't really lied. Lots of people who were separated thought of themselves as single.

"Suzie?" Rina said. "I know you'd never get involved with a married man, but how do you feel about a guy who's separated?"

How did she feel? So damned confused she couldn't think straight.

"Like, if they've actually filed for divorce and are just waiting for it to be finalized?" Jenny said.

"It's still infidelity," Suzanne said slowly.

"Oh come on," Ann said. "If a couple's made an absolute decision to split and they've filed the paperwork, they still have to be faithful to each other?"

"Oh God, I don't know," Suzanne said, sipping iced tea and trying to think this through. "You know how I feel about divorce. People shouldn't get married until they're sure, and then they ought to honor their vows. But if Jaxon and Tonya have already filed for divorce . . ."

"It's sure not like you're some kind of homewrecker," Rina said. "Though you'd need to be careful of the rebound effect."

True. But . . . "We're not dating, we're just having sex. Does it matter if it's rebound sex, so long as it's great sex?" She poked her fork into her Thai salad and twirled a few noodles around it. "It's so different for me, thinking this way. Like, if I was considering Jaxon as husband material, this would probably 'X' him off the list. He doesn't seem to take marriage as seriously as I do. But as it is, why should I care if he's been married?"

"What if he has children?" Rina asked softly.

Suzanne dropped the fork back to her plate. "Oh my God! No, he couldn't. He couldn't have walked away from his children. He's not that kind of man. I'm sure of it."

"Splitting up with your spouse doesn't necessarily mean abandoning your kids," Ann said. "And an unhappy marriage can be tougher on kids than a civilized divorce."

"They're both horrible on kids," Suzanne said with conviction. Memories of her long-ago best friend Liz always surfaced when the girls got onto this topic. Parents damn well *owed* their children, and they should never bail on that responsibility.

"You have really high standards when it comes to marriage," Rina said. "I'm not saying you're wrong, but it's an ideal, not reality. Couples split up all the time, whether or not they have kids. Roughly half of marriages end in divorce."

Suzanne glared at her. "If fifty percent of the men in the world beat their wives, that wouldn't make it right."

Rina exchanged glances with the other two.

Jenny snorted. "Same old, same old. We've had this discussion so many times, you guys, and the result never changes. Fact is, Suzie Q's holding out for the *Leave It to Beaver* guy."

Suzanne stuck out her chin. "Yes, I am, and I won't apologize for it. I *deserve* a man like that. Stable, responsible. Honorable." The kind of man who would *never* let his child down.

Not like Liz's father had done, back when they were teenagers.

Damn it, her emotions were too close to the surface right now. She felt tears begin to rise, and fought to blink them back.

"Hey, Suze." Rina put an arm around her shoulders and squeezed. "It's okay. We know how seriously you view marriage. We don't mean to criticize."

Suzanne sniffed. "Perhaps I *am* an idealist. But it's the only way I can be. Maybe one day I'll tell you why, but not today, okay?" She'd shared a lot of secrets with these women, but Liz's story was just too painful.

"You never have to talk about it if you don't want to," Ann said. "We don't have to see eye to eye on everything."

"Nah. Everyone just has to agree with me," Jenny chimed in, giving a goofy grin and tapping a Pepto-Bismol-pink fingernail against her cheek, "because I'm always right."

The others responded with giggles and snorts. Disagreement tended to be the norm, and usually Suzanne viewed their differences as stimulating and thought provoking. She just had trouble being objective when it came to her views on marriage.

"The thing that's great about the Awesome Foursome," Ann said, "is that we respect and care about each other. Right?"

"Right," Jenny and Rina chorused.

A moment later, Suzanne softly added her own, "Right." She realized she'd pretty much forgiven her friends. The information they'd uncovered made her feel stupid and naïve that she hadn't checked out Jaxon herself.

"Now," Ann said, "to return to the main topic, Jaxon. Suze, you need to find out if he's married or separated. Right?"

"Absolutely."

Or, maybe she should just break it off now.

He'd been deceptive about his marital status and canceled next weekend without an explanation.

Perhaps the erotic escapade had run its course.

12
_____

Suzanne didn't sleep more than an hour or two that night. She rose feeling exhausted, and still not sure what to do about Jaxon. The tiger lily in the vase by her bed was wilting, and perhaps that was a sign.

Thank heavens she loved her job. The moment she opened the clinic door, her spirits lifted. She greeted the first clients, a lugubrious-looking basset hound and his perky blond owner—no, pets and their humans didn't always look alike—and ushered them into an examining room.

Now she was in her element, each caress of a furry, silky or bristly coat sending a healing warmth to her troubled heart.

It wasn't until she headed out to pick up a sandwich at lunchtime that her mind returned to Jaxon.

Was she ready to give up great sex? Yes, for sure, if he was married. But if he was almost divorced . . .

She took out her cell and dialed Ann. "I know you're busy, sorry to interrupt, but I'm obsessing over what to do. Maybe I should just break it off?"

"Have you found out any more information?"

"No, but maybe there's no point. It's getting too complicated."
Ann sighed. "I'm not saying you should keep on with this
but, Suze, if you don't get the facts you'll always regret it.
Gather data, analyze it, then decide what you want to do."

"You see things so clearly."

"Don't I wish! And it's way easier when it's someone else's
life."

Get the facts. Her friend was right. The bottom line was, it
wasn't right to judge someone when you didn't have the facts.
She might not be a lawyer like Ann and Jaxon, but she did have
a strong set of values. "Thanks, Ann. Facts it'll be." Suzanne
hung up, feeling better.

Until she tried to figure out how to gather those facts. To
ask would break the Rules—besides, how would she know his
answer was the truth?

Inside the sandwich shop, she stood in line, trying to decide
what she wanted. When it was her turn, she stared at the containers of sandwich fillings. "Tuna. No, egg."

The moment the server, a bored-looking Asian girl, began to
scoop out the egg-mayo mixture, Suzanne wished she'd stuck
with tuna.

"Sprouts or lettuce?" the server asked.

God, her brain was nonfunctional today. "You choose."

The girl raised a pierced eyebrow, heaved an exaggerated
sigh, then scooped out a pile of sprouts and slapped them on
top of the egg filling.

Paying for the sandwich she didn't want, Suzanne realized it
was time to call another friend and draw on her expertise.

Outside, she dialed Jenny. "Help! You know how to gather
information."

"Tonya? I did check her name. It wasn't in the San Francisco
phone book, and I didn't get any hits when I Googled it."

"How can I find out his marital status?"

"I'm guessing there must be some kind of public records on

the internet you could search. Likely for a fee. I thought of doing it myself, but figured that would make you even more pissed off. Anyhow, isn't it easier to just phone his number and ask for Tonya Navarre?"

Duh, how obvious. But . . . "I can't, Jaxon might answer."

"So hang up. And of course you'd have to block the call."

"Block it?"

"So he wouldn't know where it originated." Jenny groaned. "You don't have a clue, do you? Okay, I'll do it. That way, if he answers, he won't recognize my voice and I can ask for Tonya Navarre."

"I owe you."

"Yeah. Big time, babe."

Suzanne heaved a sigh of relief. The matter was out of her hands, and she could relax a bit. At least until she heard back from Jenny.

Which she didn't, all afternoon.

After work, she went out with a couple of friends from vet school. They got together every two or three weeks for dinner and to chat. Mohinder was stuck working in his father's grocery store this summer. Tiff had at least scored a job working with animals, but it was with a pet grooming service. Both were deeply envious of Suzanne's job at the clinic.

With some reluctance, she turned her cell phone off and tried to concentrate on the conversation. But the moment she'd parted from her friends and was walking to her van, she clicked her phone on. No messages, and it was after ten.

She dialed Jenny.

"You've been wining and dining with your buds," her friend groused, "and I've been working up a hefty callous from hitting redial every hour. No one's answering. I can't keep doing this all night, Suzie Q."

"No, of course not," she muttered. Damn. Why wasn't someone home at ten on a Thursday? "Sorry, Jen. Thanks for trying."

"I have a breakfast interview tomorrow at seven. I'll try again when I get up. Someone's bound to be there at the crack of dawn."

In the moments when he wasn't working flat out, Jax had just one thought on his mind.

Phone sex.

After he and Suzanne had played cyber sex the other night, it had dawned on him they could have picked up their phones instead. He'd rather listen to her voice than read words on a screen.

She had a terrific voice. A little low, a little husky. Very, very sexy.

When they'd had sex the past weekend, they hadn't actually said much during the act itself. Some panting and moaning, but they'd always been in a relatively public place so they'd had to keep quiet.

He'd never heard her voice talking dirty to him.

Man, just the idea was a turn-on.

It was late Thursday night when he got home from work. Unlocking the door to the apartment building, he wondered if either of his roommates would be in. Both kept late hours like him—Levi with work and his girlfriend, Rachel; Tod with the gay bar and party scene. Be nice if they were out; he liked having the place to himself.

Especially if he was going to keep thinking about phone sex.

He took the stairs, for exercise.

Better to focus on phone sex, though, than the disturbing question that kept popping into his mind. What had Suzanne been doing awake at two in the morning?

Was she really a night owl? Or had she just come home from a hot and heavy date?

Would she have sex with two men in the same night, one in real life and one via e-mail?

God, she was Suzanne, she'd do anything. Wasn't that what made her so irresistible?

It was crazy to feel jealous.

He was so damned conventional. His brain had a hell of a problem coming to grips with the fact that this *thing* with him and Suzanne didn't follow any of the traditional rules.

It was governed by its own, very untraditional, Champagne Rules. And they included nothing about fidelity.

He really was a fucking caveman, if he needed to think of Suzanne as *his woman*.

He unlocked the apartment door and stepped inside, muttering, "Get over it."

"Over what?" Levi asked. He was sitting on the couch, notebook computer and beer can in front of him, TV tuned to one of those nature shows he liked.

"A girl. What else?"

"Tod could answer that better than me." Levi snickered. "In fact, he's in his bedroom right now with someone who definitely isn't a girl."

"Oh fuck."

"Yeah, that's what they're doing. That's why I have the TV on. I'm happier when I can't be sure if it's lions roaring or Tod and his latest conquest."

"How long have they been at it?"

"Dunno. I came home about an hour ago, the phone was ringing but I didn't get to it in time and Tod definitely wasn't answering. There were sounds coming from his room that I didn't want to hear."

Oh yeah, there were disadvantages to sharing an apartment. But rent downtown was horrendous. No way could he afford his mom's mortgage plus a place of his own. And, working the hours he did, he needed an apartment close to the office.

Jax grabbed a beer and went into his room, glad it neighbored quiet Levi's rather than noisy Tod's.

He knew Suzanne's surname. He could likely look up her phone number, but that was kind of intrusive. Better that he e-mail and suggest phone sex. Then, if she was into it, they could exchange numbers. He'd have to use his cell; the apartment phone was shared by all three of them.

Okay, how to phrase this, so he'd sound sexy without being crude. Hey, Suzanne, just got home and I'm thinking about that sexy voice of yours. You know something? We've never talked dirty to each other. Want to give it a try, over the phone?

After clicking SEND, he began taking off his suit, wondering if by any chance Suzanne was at her computer too, and would send a reply. Sometimes they had uncanny timing.

In the front room, the phone rang and he heard Levi answer it. He couldn't catch what he said, but in a moment Levi knocked softly on his door. "Jax?"

It was for him? It was really late; besides, everyone who knew him called the office or his cell. Suzanne? Had she gotten his e-mail, and called directory assistance for his number?

He rushed to the door and opened it. "That for me?"

"Sort of. Some woman asking for Tonya Navarre."

They exchanged puzzled looks.

"She hasn't gone by Navarre since we were divorced," Jax said.

"And she's never had this phone number. So, I said she'd re-married, was Tonya Keeler now. Said I didn't know her number but I could get it from you. The woman's still on the line."

"I'm not sure I should give Tonya's number to a stranger."

"Yeah, you're right, I wasn't thinking." Levi looked cha-grined. "I shouldn't have given her name either."

"I'll talk to this woman, find out who she is."

But when he picked up the phone, he got a dead line. He checked and said, "The caller number was blocked. Probably a marketer. All the same, think I'll e-mail Tonya, give her a heads up."

"Yeah, and tell her I'm sorry, okay?"

Jax went back to his computer and sent a quick message to Tonya.

Then he checked his caveman e-mail. Damn, nothing from outrageous69. Maybe Suzanne was out.

With another man?

"Tonya remarried?" Suzanne said to Jenny, who'd just called to report. "Phew, what a relief! But why didn't Jaxon's secretary just say that?"

"Maybe I took her by surprise when I called. Didn't give her a chance? Sorry, Suze, guess I screwed up."

"Well, you redeemed yourself tonight." Jaxon hadn't lied to her. She was right to trust him.

"Hold on," Jenny said, "I'm just going to Google Tonya Keeler, see if she turns up."

After a moment, Suzanne heard clicking sounds—Jen at the keyboard. How the woman could type so fast, with nails that long, Suzanne didn't understand.

Wow, he really was single. She was so glad she'd called Jen the moment his message had popped up on-screen saying he was home. She might actually sleep tonight.

"Hey, here she is," Jen said. "A short paragraph in a restaurant column. Tonya Keeler, head chef at Bijoux, is leaving to open her own restaurant. In partnership with her husband, Benjamin Keeler. I'll e-mail you the link."

"Thanks."

She'd checked the facts and now she knew. She could carry on having sex with him, if she wanted.

He'd suggested phone sex.

Could she imagine herself . . . ? Why did phone sex seem even more outrageous than real sex?

"Jen, have you ever had phone sex?"

"*Oh. My. God!* You're having phone sex?"

"Not yet."

"Girl, you are getting so far beyond me, it's not funny. I *really* need a new boyfriend. How about sharing Jaxon? He likes interracial relationships, right?"

Suzanne chuckled, knowing Jenny wasn't serious. Or at least being pretty sure about it. "Hands off, I saw him first."

After they hung up, Suzanne checked the link Jenny had sent, and read the article carefully. Tonya sounded successful. No picture, damn it. Was she gorgeous? And what was she like, the woman Jaxon had once planned to spend his life with?

What had happened to their marriage?

And why should she care?

Her fingers hovered over the keyboard. Should she e-mail him back now, and agree to set a date for phone sex?

No, better to sleep on it.

Sleeping on it meant dreaming about it. A hot, sexy dream.

As soon as she rose, she e-mailed Jax. A little "voice to voice" action? I could get into that. You're on, caveman. How about tonight?

Phone sex, tonight.

Could she really do it? In the bright light of a Vancouver morning, gazing out at her mother's English country garden, she couldn't imagine talking raunchy over the phone. Or at all! She'd always been pretty quiet in bed. Of course, pre-Jaxon, there hadn't been a whole hell of a lot worth talking about.

She could only hope that, when she heard his voice on the phone, sexy Suzanne would respond.

One try. She'd give it one, and if it didn't work out, then maybe it was time to call it quits and go back to being her real self.

Maybe around eleven? she typed. Seems like a fine way to finish off the week.

Driving to work, she thought about the information her

friends had uncovered about Jaxon. It was a relief to know he was single—but then, she'd believed him when he'd told her that, right in the beginning. It was only the girls' concern that had got her worried.

And he was a lawyer. Ann had said he did complex litigation. What did that mean? Maybe he represented people who'd been harmed by prescription drugs, tobacco, environmental pollution and so on?

She'd like to ask, but that would break the Rules. And she couldn't let on that she knew he was a lawyer, and divorced, because she'd learned the facts from her friends, not him. Damn. Her secret knowledge put a barrier of actual deceit between them.

It was one thing for them to agree not to share personal details. That wasn't deceit; it was choice. But this was different. She had to pretend not to know facts she actually did know.

If it had turned out he was married, she'd have been glad her friends butted in and found out. But he wasn't. He hadn't lied to her, so now she'd rather the gals had just kept their noses out of her and Jaxon's business.

She couldn't be mad at them, since she understood why they'd done it. If one of them had started behaving as . . . outrageously as she had, she'd likely have butted in too.

When she walked into the clinic, she must have been scowling because Trish said, "Ouch. Boyfriend troubles?"

"No. More like girlfriend troubles. Do you ever find yourself wishing your friends would mind their own business?"

Trish chuckled. "All the time. But they wouldn't be girlfriends if they did, would they?"

Suzanne had to laugh too. "Guess it comes with the definition?"

"Pretty much." Trish slanted her a mischievous look. "So, got a hot date with your guy tonight?"

Did it count as a date if they were in different cities?

"Bet on it," she said fervently.

* * *

Eleven o'clock tonight, she'd said.

Off and on all day, Jax wondered about Suzanne's suggested time. What did eleven mean?

She must have plans for the evening, but more like an early movie and a snack than a heavy date. Or maybe it wasn't a date at all, just an evening out with friends. Guy friends, or girls?

As for him, this Friday evening, he was deep into research on employment discrimination, getting his head around the legal issues involved in the Family Friend lawsuit. At dinner time, he dashed out to pick up a couple of Big Macs and a side of fries. Then he worked until ten thirty.

As he strode home, past packed restaurants and clubs blaring with music, San Francisco was alive with energy. So was he, thinking that soon he'd be hearing Suzanne's sexy purr.

The apartment was empty, which was a relief. Not much of a surprise, though, on a Friday night. Quickly, he stripped off his work clothes, took a quick shower and grabbed a beer from the fridge.

He closed and locked his bedroom door, then stretched out on his bed with a couple of pillows behind his back.

On the dot of eleven, he dialed the number he'd already memorized. His body began to harden in expectation.

The phone rang twice and he frowned.

Three times. She was the one who'd said eleven. Wasn't she back yet?

Four rings. He sat upright.

Five rings. He hadn't thought to check his e-mail this evening. Maybe she'd changed times, or even cancelled.

Six rings. His incipient erection had disappeared.

"J-Jaxon?"

No sexy purr. Instead, her voice was choked and wavery.

"Suzanne? Are you all right?"

"I'm . . . f-fine."

Either she had a rotten cold or she was in the middle of making love to someone else—in which case why the hell would she have answered the phone?—or she was crying.

Tentatively, he asked, "Is something wrong? Are you crying?"

"No, I . . . Oh damn, it's just that Bondi died and . . ." She gave a loud snuffle.

"Bondi?" Had a relative died, or a close friend? Another lover?

She said something garbled that ended in "Jack Russell."

A lover named Jack Russell, with the nickname Bondi? Oh crap, he'd called for phone sex and she was mourning another guy.

Okay, don't jump to conclusions. "This, uh, Bondi? Jack? was a friend of yours?"

"Friend? No, a dog."

Had she said . . . "Dog?"

"A Jack Russell's a type of terrier."

Her dog had died. He winced. Damn, that had to hurt. He'd never had a pet—he and his mom had never had the money or time—but he loved animals. As a boy, he'd always envied the kids who had dogs, cats, even hamsters. Except when the pets died.

"I'm sorry, Suzanne. He was your dog?"

"No, no, not mine. We operated on him this afternoon and I thought he was going to be okay."

Operated on him? Light dawned. "You're a vet."

"Studying to be one." She blew her nose. "I'm working as an assistant in a veterinary clinic."

If she was going to be a vet, surely she'd have to get used to having animals die.

Perhaps she read his mind because she said, "I'm not usually such a mess when a patient dies. But this was the first time I'd assisted with major surgery, and it went well. Later, though . . ."

Jaxon took a slug of beer. Man, was he out of his depth. When he'd phoned, the only thing on his mind was phone sex, and instead he had a weepy woman to deal with.

"It's not your fault," he said. "I'm sure you did everything you could."

"I know. Honestly, I know." Another sniff. Then suddenly she said, "Jaxon! Oh my God, what am I doing? I'm sorry, I'm a mess and I'm breaking the Rules."

Rules? Oh yeah, they weren't supposed to talk about personal stuff. "It's okay." In fact, he kind of liked that she was sharing things with him. He wasn't too keen on the tears, though.

"I'm going to hang up right now," she said, "and pull myself together. Then I'll call you back. Okay?"

He wished there was some way to help, but the fact was, the damn dog had died. He couldn't fix this. He was about to say, "Okay" when he remembered something his mom had told him. "Sometimes," she'd said, "a woman just needs to cry."

Her advice had stood him in good stead with Tonya when they were dating and first married. Before he'd let his job drive a wedge between them.

Besides, this was Suzanne. She was feeling shitty, and maybe he could help.

"No, don't hang up. It's okay. Maybe you just need to cry. For Bondi."

He heard a shuddering breath and then she wailed, "I . . . I . . ." He couldn't make out the rest of it, she was crying so hard.

He gripped the phone, feeling powerless. If he'd been with her, he would have offered her tissues. A beer. Anything, if she'd only stop crying. He'd have held her. "I wish I was there. I could give you a shoulder to cry on."

"I l-look like such a m-mess."

Trust a woman. "Everyone does when they cry. Besides, if

your face was buried in my shoulder, I wouldn't even see it. We could turn the lights out, if you wanted. Anything that made you feel better."

After a moment, she murmured, "I'm sorry."

"For what?"

"For dumping this on you."

"Hey, that's what friends are for."

After the words left his mouth, he realized what he'd said. Friends. He reflected, and knew he meant it. It had taken this for him to understand they were friends.

"Thank you. Can you hold on a minute?"

"Of course."

He heard her blow her nose a couple of times, then she was back. "I feel better." She gave a shaky laugh. "You have a great shoulder for crying on, Jaxon, even over the phone."

"Thanks."

"Most men bail when a woman cries."

He gave a rueful grin. "Yeah, that's the first instinct. Doesn't mean it's the best one."

"That's very wise. For a guy. How did you learn that?"

"Hate to confess, but my mom taught me."

"Bet your girlfriends have been grateful."

"I guess. And my ex."

"Ex? As in ex-wife?" Her voice sounded edgy.

"Damn, now I'm breaking the Rules too."

"No, it's okay. I'm . . . interested."

Curious, he figured. And that curiosity was flattering. "Yeah, I have an ex. Our marriage only lasted a few months."

"Wow, that's too bad."

"Just wasn't meant to be. We wanted different things."

"No kids?"

"No! God, no."

"How long ago did you split up?"

Oh yeah, Suzanne was definitely curious. "More than two years ago."

"Do you ever think of her? Your ex-wife?"

He lay back against the pillows. "Tonya? Sure. Look, it's not what you're thinking; it wasn't a horrible divorce. Yeah, we had our rough spots, but we've pulled a friendship out of it. In fact—" He broke off. He'd been about to mention the opening of Tonya's restaurant, and the dinner invitation. Nope, he wasn't ready for that. Quickly, he said, "In fact, I went to her wedding."

"She's married again?"

"She met Benjamin and three months later they were married. He's a nice guy." And a better husband. The kind of man Tonya deserved.

After a few seconds of silence, he said, "Suzanne? What are you thinking?"

"Divorced people aren't usually so well adjusted."

"I suppose not. We got lucky, Tonya and I." And he'd had to grow a thick hide to avoid being wounded by all those barbs she still kept jabbing at him. The thing was, he knew he deserved a lot of them. And it was easier to let her stab, than to rehash the never winnable battle about work priorities.

Without realizing it, he had relaxed. He reached behind himself to adjust one of the pillows. Too bad Suzanne wasn't lying here with him, her head resting on his chest, her fiery gold hair spread every which way.

"I don't mean to pry," she said. "Tell me if I'm being rude, but what went wrong with your marriage? The two of you still care about each other, so there must've been a strong bond."

He'd loved Tonya. He really had. Just not enough? "Not strong enough. Or, maybe, not the right kind. Our priorities were different."

"Really?"

"We were both working hard. Tonya was taking courses, learning how to run a restaurant, and I was just starting to build my practice."

"Your, uh, practice?"

He'd forgotten. On the weekend he'd been obsessed with not telling her he was a boring lawyer. Now, under the spell of late-night, long-distance conversation, he'd come close to spilling the beans. There really was a point to those Champagne Rules. "Sorry, I shouldn't be saying this stuff. Guess we should get back to playing by the Rules."

"We've already broken them so many times, let's just suspend them for the night. What kind of practice, Jaxon?"

Fuck. He couldn't lie. Voice flat, he said, "Law."

"You're a lawyer?" Her voice sounded stilted. Yeah, it was like he'd figured. She either figured lawyers were deadly dull, or pond scum. Or both. No one had ever said pond scum was exciting.

"Litigation."

"Like, suing people?"

"You don't want to hear about it, it's pretty boring."

"Boring? But . . . you like it, right? I mean, you wouldn't do it if you didn't like it."

He shook his head. Were things that simple for her? "You like veterinary work?"

"It's what I've always wanted." For the first time tonight, her voice sounded relaxed and happy. "When I was a kid, I patched up every animal or bird I could get my hands on."

For the first time, he focused on Suzanne being a vet, wearing some kind of smock or scrubs, in an animal-style operating room. And then on her as a little kid—had she maybe been called Suzie?—picking up birds with broken wings and trying to fix them. Then as a student packing a load of heavy textbooks.

This was his sexy lover?

"So, you go to school in the winter and work at a clinic in the summer?" he asked.

"And part-time through the year. Can't let my folks—" She broke off abruptly.

"What?"

"Now *I'm* being boring."

It wasn't blazing sex, but it wasn't boring. He was intrigued, trying to fit all this new information into his image of outrageous69. "No, I want to hear. What about your parents? Were you going to say they couldn't afford to put you through school?"

"They've helped a lot, but I do as much as I can. They're not rich. They have their retirement to plan for."

A considerate, loving daughter. He added that to the picture.

"It's tough going to school and working," he said.

"I manage." She paused. "You sound like you've been there."

"I went to college on an athletic scholarship and—"

"You're kidding!?"

"No. Why? Don't I seem like the athletic type?"

A pause, then, "Actually, you do. But I don't think they give scholarships for," she snickered, "the kind of athleticism I've seen from you."

He chuckled. "Nope, I'm afraid it was far more conventional. Basketball."

"Really?"

"I know, I'm not seven feet tall. I'm six-three and that's short for a player, but I did okay."

"So you played ball and studied. That would keep you busy."

"Had a part-time job too."

"Wow. And then law school, right? Was that on scholarship too?"

"Yeah, but not athletic. That one was scholastic."

"Wow again."

He groaned loudly. "Okay, you don't think of me as athletic, and you don't think of me as bright. Just what do you see in me, Suzanne?"

"Mmm," she purred. "I see lots in you, Jaxon. But I guess the first thing I saw was . . . Well, you have to remember it was a nude beach, and, well . . ." She paused suggestively.

Now this was outrageous69 talking! This was what he'd been anticipating all day. His cock stirred with interest. "So you saw my big brown . . . eyes?"

She gave a splurt of laughter. "It was definitely big and definitely brown. . . ."

"Keep talking that way, woman, and you'll make it even bigger."

"Wish I could do it in person. But seeing as all we've got is the phone line, I guess I'll just have to use . . . my . . . mouth."

He imagined that mouth wrapped around him and his cock struggled to spring to attention inside boxer briefs that were designed for support, not a hard-on.

"I'm imagining your mouth, Suzanne. Such a lush, tantalizing mouth." And now he wanted to envision the rest of her, as she was right now. "Where are you anyhow, and what are you wearing?"

"I'm lying on my bed, but you really don't want to know what I'm wearing."

"Clothes, huh?"

"Rumpled clothes I've been wearing all day." Outrageous69 had disappeared again. "I'm so sorry," she said, sounding exasperated. "This is just the opposite of what I'd intended for tonight. I was going to have a bath with some scented bath salts, then put on this little silk-and-lace camisole I bought and—"

"Do it."

"What? You mean, do all that stuff, then phone you back?"

"No, don't go. What I mean is, do it now. Do it with me."

"O-oh." Her voice was a long, slow sigh of understanding, sharpening into definite interest.

His cock was pretty damned interested too. "Is your phone a cordless?"

"It sure is."

"Okay then. So, what would you like first? Maybe a glass of wine?"

"That sounds wonderful. I have some in the fridge." He heard a squeak—bedsprings?—then she said, "I'm heading out to the kitchen." A pause. "Jaxon? Will you join me? Would you like a glass of wine?"

"Sounds good."

Abandoning the now-tepid beer, he left his bedroom, relieved Tod and Levi were still out. Now, was there any wine in the apartment? He found a bottle in the cupboard, unopened. Great. Whoever had bought it, he'd pay them back. "I have a shiraz cabernet from Beringer. How about you?"

"Pinot gris from Grey Monk. And there's a bottle of ice wine Jenny gave me for my birthday. It should be awesome, but I think I'll save it. For when we can do this in person." Her voice lowered, and went more seductive. "Sure you can't visit this weekend?"

Could he? No, what was he thinking? He'd be putting in sixteen-hour days on Family Friend. Maybe if he did that for the whole week . . . "I'll try for next weekend."

"You'll try *hard*?"

"Very hard."

She chuckled. "I'll save the ice wine for then."

What was she saying? "You're inviting me over?" For what? Wine and sex? Dinner and wine and sex? Or to stay overnight?

"Oh, I—"

Crap, he'd jumped to the wrong conclusion. She'd meant she'd bring the wine to a picnic.

But then she said, "Yes, I am. The next time you can come to town? For dinner? Is that all right? Not too mundane?"

He laughed, and it came out strained and shaky. "No way."

"Great. Okay, I'm going to pour myself a glass of wine."

He remembered what Tonya used to do, how she'd made a ceremony out of pouring wine. "Do you have some special wineglasses?"

"Rina gave me some cut-glass ones."

Rina. She had a friend—or relative—named Rina. And another called Jenny, who'd given her the ice wine.

"Use one of those glasses now," he said.

"Okay. How about you? Do you have special glasses?"

In this bachelor pad, where he and his roomies drank beer out of the can? " 'Fraid not, but we'll pretend."

He pulled down a cheap glass. "I'm pouring my wine. How about you?"

"I'm lifting my glass. Ready to make a toast."

He lifted his own. "What's the toast?"

"What else? To us, Jaxon. And this evening together."

"I'll drink to that."

He took a swallow. Good stuff. "Now, how about that bath?"

"Yes. By candlelight."

There wasn't a hope in hell he'd find a candle in this apartment. But Suzanne could light hers, and he liked the picture that was forming in his mind. "How about a few candles? All along the rim of the tub." Flickering across her naked body.

"Sounds good to me." Her voice was husky, breathy, sexy.

He rubbed a hand over the front of his briefs, pressing against his erection, wishing she was there to touch him. Now what?

He wanted her to run a bath and climb in, but should he do it too, or just lie in bed imagining her?

"Jaxon? Are you going to take a bath with me?"

"Do you want me to?"

"Do you need to ask?"

Thank God the apartment had two bathrooms. He hurried to the one with a tub and locked the door. Once they both had the water running, he said, "Time to take off your clothes."

"You too. What are you wearing?"

"A pair of boxer briefs." That were filled to bursting.

"That's all? Sexy. What color?"

"Navy."

"Not bad, but with your beautiful skin you should wear more dramatic colors. Black, white, maybe red."

"Red underwear? Gimme a break."

She gave that throaty chuckle of hers. "Red silk boxers. What do you say?"

He groaned. "Only for you, Suzanne."

"I should hope so." After a moment, she said, "I just took off my jeans and now I've got to put the phone down to pull my T-shirt over my head."

He waited, imagining her in a bra and panties. Maybe she was wearing a thong. Did she wear that sexy stuff all the time, or only on a date?

Or only when she was with him?

"Okay, now I'm down to my undies too," she said. "Ready to take off your briefs?"

"Woman, I'm busting out of them."

"Busting out? Just from . . . this?"

"From thinking of you, from your voice. God, I wish I was there. I want to touch you. I want you to touch me."

"Me too. But we've got our imaginations, our hands and each other's voices."

"Oh yeah! So, lover, imagine my hands on your body. I'm flicking loose the clasp to your bra and peeling it off, then cupping your breasts in my hands. Such beautiful breasts, each one a perfect handful."

"And speaking of a handful . . . Oh wait, my tub's full."

He'd completely forgotten about the running water. He cranked off his taps too.

"Jaxon? Are you still wearing those briefs?"

"Yeah."

"Don't you think it's time we took them off? I want to slide my fingers down each side and peel them slowly off you."

He did it himself, trying to imagine her fingers instead of his own. Must've worked, because his cock sprang free and aimed straight for the ceiling. "You still wearing your panties?"

"Yes, and they're all wet."

He sucked in a breath. She wanted him. Even long distance. She was just as into this as he was. Man, he was one lucky bastard.

He focused on her bath. "Do you have those candles? And what about bubble bath?"

"I've lit half a dozen candles around the tub, and turned the lights off. I tossed in some jasmine bath salts and the room smells tropical, a little sultry."

He could imagine the scent, the candlelight. "Ready to climb in?"

"Didn't you want me to take my panties off?"

Oh yeah, he'd lost his train of thought when she told him they were wet. "Please. Imagine me taking them off. I want you naked. I want to see your beautiful, naked body."

"Then look your fill. I'm naked now, in the candlelight. Let's get in the bath."

"Let me take the back, then you can climb in and lean against me. How does that sound?"

"Perfect."

He stepped into the tub and sprawled out, his knees up. His cock rose, seeking the surface of the water. "Come on in, the water's a lot warmer than on Friday."

She giggled. "Last Friday the water was stimulating."

"Last Friday you were stimulating. You always are. What are you doing now?"

"Lying back against you," she murmured. "Your body is so hard under me and . . . oh wait, I'm wriggling around until—"

"Slip my cock between your legs."

"You're so hard. You feel fantastic."

"I'm reaching around you to caress your breasts. Put your hands there, and imagine they're mine. Stroking your nipples as they harden. Teasing them while I kiss your hair, find your ear, and nibble on it. Can you feel my lips, my hands?"

"Oh yes. But I want to touch you too. I'm reaching down for your cock, taking it in both hands, curling my fingers around you. Do you feel me?"

He leaned back, closed his eyes and gave himself up to the fantasy. He reached a hand between his legs and touched himself, imagining his large fingers were her small, graceful ones. "How are you touching me? Hard, soft? Quick, slow?"

"Just feathery caresses. Playing with you, teasing. Running a fingertip around the head of your cock. Around and around and around."

He used his own finger and had to hold back a groan.

"I'm reaching down too," he said, "finding those full, lush lips of yours, all swollen with desire. I'm stroking soft and light, teasing you just the way you've been teasing me. You have such a sweet pussy. Do you want to open for me?"

"Yes. Oh yes," she sighed. "I want you inside me."

"All in good time. First you get a finger. Just one finger. Can you feel it? It's entering you slowly, gently, and your body is taking it in."

"It feels so good."

His finger was still circling the head of his penis and he was aching for a good, hard up-and-down stroke. "Suzanne? Will you wrap your hand around me? I want to feel you around me, firm and strong. I want you to pump up and down. Do that for me?"

"Now, Jaxon. Right now."

He locked his hand tight and gave several hard strokes, feeling the pressure building, fighting for release. How could he get so close so fast with this woman, when she wasn't even with him? He tore his hand away from his body.

Gasping, he said, "I need some wine. How about you?"

"Wine? Oh, wine. Yes, that sounds good. Let me put the phone down for a minute."

He grinned to himself. She didn't want to take her finger out of her body to pick up the glass. She'd rather put down the phone.

He slugged a couple of mouthfuls of wine and waited until she spoke again. "Mmm, this wine is so good."

"Where's my finger?" he asked.

"Your . . . Oh, it's, uh, still inside me."

He grinned more widely. "Is it as deep as it can possibly go?"

"Maybe not." The words were just a sigh in his ear.

"Go deep, and circle. Press against the walls inside yourself, find the spot that makes you moan, lover, stroke it, press it."

"Oh Jaxon." It was a sigh, a whimper. Then she said, "Is my hand still stroking you?"

"No, I . . . I had to make you stop. I was too close." He closed his eyes and whispered into the phone, "I don't want to come until I'm inside you."

"Inside me?"

"Mm-hm. Here's what I want you to do. I'm going to sit up a little, okay? And I want you to sit up too."

"So I'm sitting on your lap, facing away from you?"

"Exactly. And then I want you to lift up a little, because I'm going to slide inside you. Will you do that?"

"Oh yes."

"I'm reaching between your legs, parting those full lips . . . Are you ready for me?"

"Please. I want you."

"I'm easing inside." He wrapped a hand around his cock. "You're so hot and tight, you feel so good."

"You're so hard, so big. You're sliding in, filling me."

He imagined her fingers inside her body, mimicking his cock. "Move slowly. Slowly in, all the way. Now lift yourself, lift up so I'm almost all the way out. Then slide down again—"

"You're all the way in now, pressing hard against me and I'm pressing back against you."

"I'm reaching around, my fingers teasing your clit as I move inside you."

"God, yes."

He pumped slowly, from top to bottom, then back again, imagining the heat and friction of her body against his. He heard the slap of water against the edge of the tub and imagined the liquid slap of his flesh against hers.

Pleasure mounted as he stroked back and forth. "Suzanne, you're so good, so great," he panted. He wanted her, he was reaching into her, he longed to fill her. He wanted to move. "Faster, lover, I'm stroking faster now, I can't hold back." His hand pumped fiercely as his blood raced, heated, the climax building inside him.

"Don't hold back," she moaned. "Oh God, I can feel every inch of you. I want you so badly. I'm so close, I can't . . ."

"Suzanne! I want . . ."

"Oh Jaxon, I'm going to . . ."

"Come now!" He almost yelled the words as he climaxed,

his body thrusting out of the water, his cum spurting into the air, her voice ringing in his ears as she called his name.

His body kept spasming until finally he collapsed back into the water. Breathless, he realized the phone was still clamped to his ear. "Suzanne?" he said weakly.

"Oh my God," she whispered.

13

Dinner on Monday was at Vij's, a classy Indian fusion place where the Foursome went a couple of times a year when they were in the mood for splurging. Madly popular, the bustle and noise pretty much ensured their conversations wouldn't be overheard.

Ann was late. Across the table from Suzanne, Jenny and Rina tossed out questions about Jaxon. She sipped her India pale ale, gave them a cat-smile and said, "I'll tell you when Ann's here."

So, they spent time studying the menu and ordered four dishes to share. They knew Ann's tastes by now, including her obsession for the lamb "popsicles."

When Ann dashed in and flopped down in a chair, it was like a hurricane had hit. She jarred the table as she flung her briefcase underneath it. Then, as she twisted to peel off her jacket, her elbow caught a water glass.

Suzanne only just rescued it in time. "Slow down, calm down. We don't mind that you're late, and we've already ordered. Lamb popsicles, chicken in coconut-onion curry—"

"Sure, whatever," Ann broke in. "I haven't had anything to eat today."

"That's not healthy," Rina scolded.

"You should talk," Ann snapped. "You never eat food, you only pick at it. It drives me nuts."

Her words brought a dead silence. She slapped a hand to her forehead. "Oh crap. I'm sorry, Rina. I'm the bitch from hell today."

"You know I have a weight problem," Rina said accusingly.

"You don't!" they all chorused.

"Like the three of you would know anything about it, with your perfect figures."

"You have a great figure, girl," Jenny said. "Curvy, the way guys like. If I had a bod like yours, I'd flaunt it, not hide under all those layers."

"Time out," Suzanne said, her hands forming the signal. Rina's body image was another of their agree-to-disagree topics.

"I'm really sorry," Ann said.

Rina sighed, her Bambi eyes still looking wounded. "It's okay. Tough day at the office?"

Ann raked her fingers through her hair. "The usual. I worked all weekend, but I'm still behind. I feel so out of control, and I guess that puts me on edge."

"Oh gee, ya think?" Jenny said teasingly. "Ms. Control Freak hates being out of control?"

The waitress brought an India ale for Ann, and a basket of spicy French fries.

Ann promptly grabbed a couple of fries. "Okay, that's definitely enough about me. Suze, what's going on with Jaxon?"

Suzanne gave a mischievous smile, and dropped two words: "Phone sex."

"No way!" The signs of strain left Ann's face and she grinned widely. "I want to hear every single detail."

"I'm not going that far, you'd all be squirming in your seats. But I'll give you a summary."

They all leaned forward, heads close together, and Suzanne told them about her and Jaxon's phone-bath-sex on Friday night.

"Oh God, Suzie, why can't I meet a man like that?" Jenny moaned.

"Me too!" Rina and Ann chorused.

"I think we need a new Awesome Foursome rule," Jenny said. "When one of us finds an utterly fabulous man, she has to share him with the rest of us."

They all howled with laughter. "I don't *think* so," Suzanne managed to splutter. "Nor will you, when you find your own Mr. Hot Sex. Speaking of which, what did you all do on the weekend? Any dynamite sex of your own?"

Ann waved a hand dismissively. "No chance. When I wasn't working, I was sleeping. Alone, sadly."

"I had sex," Jenny said glumly. "With Pete. You know, the Korean guy? I used to think he was good, but damn it, Suze, you've spoiled everything. He's sure no Jaxon."

Rina nodded. "I had a date with a new guy, Sam, but when he kissed me it was just, like, okay. I'm really not—"

"That into him," the other three chorused.

How many times had one or more of them said that?

"I know," Suzanne said. "That's what it's been like for me with every other guy than Jaxon." She took a sip of ale and realized they were all staring at her. "What?"

"Oh my God, he's The One," Jenny breathed.

"Mr. Right. Your Mr. Cleaver," Rina sighed dreamily. "You've found him."

Suzanne snorted. "Get real. He's The One Right Now, okay? That's it."

"I know," Ann said softly. "You keep saying you don't even know him."

"I don't." She paused. "Though I have to say, he knows a secret few men do."

"Yeah, the location of the G-spot." Jenny snickered.

"No! Well, yes, he does, but that's not what I meant. He knows that sometimes a girl just needs to cry about something, rather than have some guy go rushing in and try to fix the unfixable. His mom taught him."

She caught their exchange of glances. "Gimme a break, so we actually had a conversation. It's no big deal."

"Very big," Rina said.

"Really, really big," Ann confirmed.

"Eight inches and growing," Jenny said.

"Aaagghh!!"

How could she now ask Ann for the loan of her apartment next Saturday night, when Jaxon would be in town? Oh well, best to get it over with. The worst they could do was tease her to death. "Ann, can I ask a favor?"

"Sure. Anything."

Suzanne had known that, underneath all the joking around, they really would do anything for each other. That's why, when Jaxon had asked if she was inviting him for dinner, she'd said yes.

"Can I swap apartments with you on Saturday night? Jaxon's coming to town and I, uh, somehow asked him for dinner."

"Somehow?" Jenny said with a lifted eyebrow.

"A romantic candlelight dinner," Rina sighed.

Ann chuckled. "God, my apartment won't know what's hit it. No one's had sex there in forever. Sure, of course we can trade. But what'll you tell your parents? Why not just bite the bullet and have the guy over to your place?"

"No way! I can't have sex with my parents just across the yard."

Ann tilted her head. "You've never had sex at your place?"

"No. The few times I've done it, I've gone to the guy's

place." Ann raised a good question though. "I don't know what to tell my parents if we trade."

"Hmm." Ann leaned forward, her brow creased in thought. "How about I don't stay at your place, I'll go to Rina's." She glanced at Rina, who nodded agreement. "You tell your parents you're getting together with us, we're having a pajama party, watching reruns of *Sex and the City* all night."

"I think I'll skip the *Sex and the City* part, but that's a terrific idea. Rina, are you okay with this?"

"My little house loves having company."

Rina had inherited money when her parents died in a car crash, and used part of it to buy a bungalow in North Vancouver. An Air Force brat all her childhood, she now loved being firmly rooted in a home of her own.

The stunning Indo-Canadian waitress arrived with platters of aromatic food and they dug in enthusiastically. Or, in Rina's case, as enthusiastically as she ever let herself dig in.

When they'd all taken the edge off their hunger, Jenny said, "So, what do you gals think about firefighters?"

"Ooh," Rina said, "now those are some hot guys. You going to date a firefighter, Jen?"

Jenny scrunched up her face. "Oh, puh-lease. Yeah, they're eye candy, but let's face it, when the sex is finished I'd kind of like a brain to interact with."

"Ouch," Suzanne said, laughing.

"It's not a date, it's a story," Jenny said.

"About the low IQ of firefighters?" Ann asked dryly. "Somehow I don't see that one selling. The public's very pro firefighters since 9-11."

"And rightly so," Rina said. "They really are heroes."

"Whatever," Jenny drawled. "But you know about the firefighter calendar, right?"

Rina fanned herself with her napkin. "Oh yeah. Definitely hot stuff."

"And the proceeds go to charity," Jenny said. "The Burn Fund and other good causes. But here's the fun thing. For next year's calendar, they're doing something new. Rather than just sell the calendars, they're going to have a competition, on stage, with the audience voting on the top twelve. Major, major fundraiser."

"Major, major fun!" Ann said.

"And a damn good story," Jenny said. "I've got an in with the *Straight*, and they'll give me a cover feature."

"Let me know if you need a research assistant," Rina said.

On Wednesday night, the phone was ringing as Suzanne walked through her door after working late at the clinic. Jaxon?

No, her sister. "Got any plans for Friday night?" Bethany asked.

Just fantasizing about Saturday night with Jaxon. "Why?"

"You know how Mom and Dad always have the kids for a sleepover on Fridays? Well, they've been invited out to an anniversary dinner, so I said, of course we'll skip the sleepover. Then Mom said maybe you could—"

"No problem," Suzanne broke in, kicking off her shoes and wriggling her aching toes. "I'll come baby-sit if you and Joel want to go out."

"Could you baby-sit them at Mom and Dad's until they get home?"

Suzanne flopped down on the couch beside Melody and Zorro and began stroking, first one, then the other. "You have overnight plans? Where are you going?"

"We sure do have plans, but we're not going anywhere. Don't you know about Friday nights?"

What about Friday nights? "I know Mom and Dad like having the grandkids for an end-of-the-week sleepover, but I don't see why it's so bad to miss one week."

"Mom says it would be setting a bad precedent."

"Uh, why?" Obviously she was missing something.

"Friday nights are for Joel and me. To be a couple."

"A couple?" Of course they were a couple; they'd been married for five years.

"*You* know," Bethany said in an exasperated tone. "Just the two of us. Romantic, sexy, playful, like when we were dating."

"Oh!" She'd never heard that part of the story before. "Hmm. That sounds like a good idea." She'd have to file it away for when she did find Mr. Cleaver.

"It's essential. When you're married, it's so easy to take each other for granted and just . . . you know, become dull and boring. Then, when you have kids, it's even harder to hang on to the pizzazz. That fun stuff that brought you together in the first place, that made you fall in love."

The cats' fur was warm and silky under Suzanne's hand as she kept stroking, thinking about what Beth had said. "Isn't it inevitable that stuff would fade? I mean, relationships have stages. The pizzazz is for the dating stage, right? Isn't marriage more about commitment, responsibility, maybe finding a deeper level of love?"

"Sure, it's all of that. But it's easier to do the serious stuff if you still spark each other's firecracker."

Suzanne thought of how Bethany and Joel behaved together. Most of the time they were absorbed in dealing with the children, but sometimes there'd be a little touch or glance that spoke of a special intimacy. She'd never imagined it came from having a sizzling sex life. "Let me get this straight. You're saying you and Joel have hot sex on Friday nights, and that somehow keeps your marriage on track?"

Her sister giggled. "Sure helps."

"Do Mom and Dad have any idea what you're doing, while they're baby-sitting your kids?"

The giggle turned to a rich, gurgling laugh. "Who d'you think suggested it in the first place?"

"Not Mom?" The idea was so foreign, Suzanne just had to get up and start pacing on her work-weary feet.

"About a year after we got married, I was kind of depressed. I don't know if you remember. Joel and I were both working hard, we'd had Krys, we were renovating the house. I felt like we'd turned into middle-aged drudges. Then I got pregnant again, and I was an elephant-sized, middle-aged drudge. Anyhow, Mom took me out for lunch and boy, was it an eye-opener."

"Mom gave you marriage counseling? Well, she and Dad do have one of the best marriages I've ever seen, so I guess she's an expert. But I can't believe she actually recommended . . . sex. I mean, she and Dad . . ."

"Yes, my naïve little sis, they do still do it. In fact, they do it quite a bit, since you moved out of the house."

"Jesus, Bethany, that's way too much information." She glanced out the window at her parents' house. Were they . . . ?

"No, it's not. Sex is a normal, healthy part of a relationship, right?"

Suzanne pulled the curtains, vowing to never walk into that house again without knocking first. "Yeah. But not our parents' relationship." She was only half-joking.

"Mom says they went through the same kind of thing Joel and I did, when you were a baby and I was in elementary school. They were tired all the time, had so many responsibilities, they were focused on being parents rather than spouses or lovers. They went to a marriage counselor."

"They did?" How could she not know these things about her family?

"They knew they loved each other; they'd just lost touch. The counselor helped them rebuild the bond of intimacy, and an important part of that was sex."

"You're saying that our parents . . ."

"Have hot sex. Yup. And so do Joel and I," she added smugly. "You oughta try it, sis."

"I have! I am!" Oh damn, Beth could always poke her buttons. She hadn't meant to say anything about her relationship with Jaxon.

"You're kidding!" Bethany screeched. "Who is he? Tell all, Suze."

Now that the tables had turned, Suzanne decided to torture her sister. "Gosh, Bethany, I hadn't realized it was so late. I've got to go. But yes, I'll sit the kids on Friday, so you and Joel can have hot sex. By the way, if you run out of ideas, you might try skinny-dipping at Spanish Banks."

She hung up the phone with her sister's squeal ringing in her ears.

Then she laughed herself silly for at least five minutes.

Afterwards, she went to check her e-mail. She and Jaxon had exchanged only brief messages this week, mainly just to confirm he could come to Vancouver on Saturday.

Tonight, she had mail from caveman. She clicked it open.

Just realized, I'll never look at my bathtub in the same light, lover. Every time now, I'm imagining your sweet body in there with me.

She smiled and closed her eyes briefly. Oh yeah, she knew *exactly* what he meant. Her tired body stirred at the thought.

Hope you're feeling better about Bondi. You can't save them all, Suzanne. All you can do is your best. And I know you did, and always will.

She stared at the screen. He'd remembered her sorrow, and said something absolutely perfect. It almost seemed as if he cared.

Was it possible? Might this Champagne-Ruled relationship evolve into something real, deep, lasting? Could Jaxon Navarre actually be The One?

No, of course not. Not only were they building separate lives in different cities, but they were opposite in many ways. A high-powered corporate lawyer and a vet? A divorced man and a woman who believed marital and parental commitments were the most important thing on earth? No, couldn't happen.

But maybe they were becoming friends. Was it possible to have hot sex with a friend? She guessed they'd find out, on Saturday.

Thanks for the thoughtful words, Jaxon. Yes, I am feeling better, and you're right. I know I can't save them all. I just want to try.

Okay, enough serious stuff.

It's been a long day and I'm ready for a nice relaxing bath. Relaxing. Hmmmmm? Is that possible, or will I close my eyes and feel your body under me, inside me?

BTW, I picked up a little something for you at lunchtime. Actually, they're for me. But you'll wear them, won't you? I distinctly recall that you didn't say no.

Oh, did I mention? They're red. . . .

Laughing, she clicked SEND. She couldn't wait to see that sexy body clothed in red silk boxers. Feeling rejuvenated, she poured herself a glass of wine and headed for the bath.

Thursday morning, she read his reply. Suzanne, you make me blush.

She chuckled and wrote back, That'll be the day. But I'll do my very best . . .

Smiling, she headed off to work.

Suzanne was in bed reading a veterinary magazine she'd borrowed from the clinic, sipping ginger peach tea and surrounded by cats, when the phone rang.

"So you wanna make me blush," a male voice said.

"Jaxon!" In an instant, her mood went from relaxed to excited.

"Is it okay I phoned, when we hadn't scheduled it?"

Did it break the Rules? Probably, but what a nice surprise. "For sure."

"I started to type a message, but decided I'd rather talk. Do you have time?"

"For you? Absolutely." She gave him her sexiest purr. "So, Jaxon, I've been imagining you in red silk boxers."

"You're not the only one. Had a hell of a time concentrating on work today."

"Oh gosh, I'm so sorry," she said in a deliberately insincere voice.

He chuckled. "You really think it's sexy for a guy to wear stuff like that?"

Ah, he was thinking he'd feel silly.

"Gee, I don't know," she said. "How do you think it'll feel, to have the caress of silk against your cock and balls, soft and tantalizing as a woman's hand? And just think how it will feel for me to run my hand over the front of that slinky fabric, feel you growing hard underneath? Hmm. Does any of that sound sexy to you?"

"Oh man."

She laughed. Then she said, "You've never worn silk?" What had his ex-wife and old girlfriends been thinking? Then she smiled to herself. Obviously, they weren't as sexy as she was.

"No. Guess maybe I'd be willing to give it a try."

"Hey, you, don't sound so noble and self-sacrificing. You know damn well you find the idea seductive."

"Okay, you got me. I confess." Then he said, "So, where are you? What are you doing?"

"And what am I wearing?" Should she make up a sexy lie? She decided on the truth. "I'm in bed, but no sexy negligee, I'm afraid. Just a long tank top over panties. I was reading about diabetes in cats. Not very exciting, I'm afraid. How about you?"

"Hate to admit it, but I'm in my office. Spent the day scheduling interviews for a big case I'm working on, and I've still got paperwork to catch up on. But I needed a Suzanne break."

"I'm glad." His words gave her a warm, glowing feeling that

was kind of nice, but kind of scary too, because the glow was closer to her heart than her crotch. Yikes, that's not what their relationship was about. Trying for breathy and sultry, she murmured, "So, big boy, you wanna talk dirty?"

He groaned. "Can't think of anything I'd like better, save having a magic carpet transport me directly into your bed. But the truth is, I do have to work. Sorry, lover, I'm letting you down."

And the truth was, she was tired too, and not in the mood for sex, and she loved that he'd phoned just to talk. Crap. Was she really heading into trouble?

If so, maybe he was too, and they could toss out the Champagne Rules. But what then? The Rules had defined them. What would they be without them? They'd avoided the term "relationship," both saying it wasn't what they were looking for. But this was turning into a friendship, and friendship *was* a relationship. And friendship plus great sex was . . .

Oh God, she was really getting ahead of herself.

But maybe it wouldn't hurt to test the waters, to find out if they really might be compatible on more levels than sexual.

"You're not letting me down," she told him. Trying to picture him, she imagined him sitting behind a big mahogany desk stacked with papers and files. "You're really busy these days?"

"Seems to be the story of my life."

That didn't sound good, in terms of compatibility. "A workaholic?" she asked, then wished she'd found a less judgmental term.

"A busy lawyer." He gave a snort. "Same thing, I guess."

"I have a girlfriend who's an associate at a big firm. I have a pretty good idea." Poor Ann was always lugging a briefcase, drinking coffee so she could stay awake to work late, suffering from tension headaches. "Every time she takes some social time, she ends up working into the small hours to make up for it."

"That's pretty much it. In fact, that's exactly what I did last night."

"You took time off?" To do what, with who? She certainly had no right to ask.

"Had some business papers to discuss with my mom, so I took her out for dinner."

She smiled with relief. "That sounds nice. What about your father?"

"Never knew him. He and Mom weren't married. She was just a kid when she got pregnant, and she and her mother raised me for the first few years. That was in Jamaica."

He'd been born in Jamaica. And wow, that wasn't how she'd pictured his family. With his innate classiness, she'd assumed rich, well-educated parents. "Was your father a Jamaican man or a tourist?"

"Jamaican. Older, a businessman. Married."

"Oh."

"He used her. She was naïve. He told her . . . Well, you can guess. And it's her story to tell, not mine."

"How sad for her."

"She was fourteen when she found out she was pregnant. Fifteen when she had me."

Suzanne shook her head, trying to imagine what it must have been like. "When I was fourteen, I'd never even gone on a date alone with a boy."

"Making up for it now, are you, Suzanne?"

"Doing my best. Thanks for helping, Jaxon."

"My pleasure, ma'am. Anything to be of service."

"Anything?" But she was actually more interested in his past than the sexy talk, so she quickly asked, "When did you come to the States?"

"I was almost four. Mom could see what life would be like for us if we stayed in Jamaica, and she wanted more. For me, especially. She met an American tourist who wanted to marry her and bring us to California."

"Are they still married?"

"No. It only lasted a few years. They were both fooling themselves. She tried to believe she loved him. As for him, he was a white guy, loved her exotic looks when he met her on holiday, but once he got her home, she didn't fit with his friends and colleagues."

"That's not fair," she said indignantly.

"Nope." He sighed. "He was an older guy, sold real estate. Wanted to entertain clients and have a wife who wasn't just a babe, but sophisticated too. Asshole. My mom's a fast learner; she could've picked up what she needed to know if he'd given her a chance."

"Jerk. So, they got divorced?"

"Yeah, and she got a raw deal because she was naïve and let his lawyer handle the settlement."

Suzanne frowned. "Couldn't she have had it reexamined? Especially when there was a child?"

"She had too much pride. Besides, it's not like I was his kid."

"But he brought you both to the States. He had an obligation." Another guy who'd taken on family responsibilities, then bailed.

"Mom said bringing us here, getting us our citizenship, was what really counted. After that, she said it was up to us to make our way." He paused, then said softly, "She'd say to me, 'Jaxon Navarre, the future's yours to make. You can be anything you want, anything white folks can be, and even better.' "

Oh yes, a proud woman. Maybe too proud, or stubborn, or maybe just too ill-informed to get what was due her and her son. "She went to work?"

"Yeah. She hadn't finished high school so the only jobs she could do paid peanuts. Often she'd work two—waitressing during the day, cleaning offices at night. I got kid jobs as soon as I could. Paper route, unloading crates at the corner store."

Her heart ached for both of them. He'd been forced to grow up early, but what choice had his mother had? "Was it—" She broke off. The only time they'd talked about race had been after the cops caught them in the playground. Should she raise the subject?

"What?"

"Maybe I shouldn't ask, but I wondered if it was harder for the two of you, being from Jamaica."

"For her, probably. She had two strikes: black and female. But Darissa Navarre's always hung on to her dignity. As for me, it wasn't too bad. School I went to had lots of black kids. I worked hard, got good marks, did well in sports, got along with the other kids. Hell, color probably worked in my favor when I got that basketball scholarship."

"Really?"

"Come on, girl, you know white boys can't jump."

She chuckled, liking the fact he didn't have a poor-me attitude. It sounded like his mom didn't either. Darissa: an interesting name for a gutsy, interesting woman. Would they ever meet? She was beginning to hope so.

"Once I was in college, though," he was saying, "it was hard getting people to take me seriously. Everyone knows jocks are dumb. Coach and the counselor kept trying to get me to sign up for the slack courses, but the whole reason I was there was to get an education."

"And you did so well in college you got a scholarship for law school. That's quite an accomplishment." She felt a glow of pride, and could just imagine how thrilled his mother must have been.

"Yeah, well. I'm a hard worker."

"Why law, Jaxon?"

"Mom brought me here to make something of myself. While I was delivering those papers, I read them too, figuring out which jobs had the status and money. Lawyers, for sure. Then I found out there was a black man, Thurgood Marshall, on the United States Supreme Court."

"One? Out of all those judges, only one?"

"Yeah. But he proved it could be done. A black guy making decisions that bound people regardless of race or social position. Who else has that kind of power? Only politicians. So I decided I'd aim for either the bench or politics, and the best route to either was becoming a lawyer."

Wow, he really was ambitious. And it seemed he wanted to make a difference in the world. Admirable, but she was selfish enough to want a man who put family first. "So, your goal is to either be on the Supreme Court, or be president?" she asked, half teasingly, half serious.

"For the moment I'll settle for making partner at my firm. Then we'll see."

Hmm. Maybe he meant he'd see what else was going on in his life then. Whether he was married again, had kids. Should she ask?

Instead, she chose a more casual question. "Where did you study law?"

"Boalt Hall, Berkeley. We were living down in L.A., where I grew up. But Mom and I both thought San Francisco sounded good—less racism, less pollution, less traffic. And Boalt Hall's a good school. I applied, got a scholarship, so we moved up."

"That's nice, that she could move with you." She liked it that he was close to his mother.

"It's worked out well for both of us."

Suzanne's brain conjured the image of a woman who looked older than her years, her body worn out from hard work, but her eyes glowing with love.

Her own mom would like Darissa Navarre. Now her mind's eye put the two of them in her mom's kitchen sipping coffee, talking about their kids, dreaming about grandchildren.

Suzanne shook her head roughly. What the hell was she doing?

Jaxon said, "You've got both your parents, and a sister, didn't you say?"

"My folks have been together almost thirty years. Dad's a history prof. Mom works part-time at a garden center and also does landscaping as a volunteer at some seniors' centers. My sister Bethany is eight years older than me. She manages a florist shop and married a high school teacher. She and Joel have a couple of young children."

She realized what she was describing: two *Leave It to Beaver* families. Not rich, but no one had ever had to wonder where the next meal would come from. Neither she nor Beth had ever held part-time jobs during high school.

"Sounds nice," he said, and she wondered if he was envious. But then he said, "We're both lucky, to have loving parents."

"That's the truth."

They were quiet for a moment, then he said, "So, how did an almost-vet from such a wholesome family turn out to be such a sexpot, Suzanne?"

She'd told him a lot about sensible Suzanne, and he still thought she was a sexpot. She grinned happily. "Lucky again, I guess." Lucky to have found Jaxon, who brought the sexy twin to life. "Sure wish you were here. I can't believe you've still got work to do."

"Law's a tough game. There's lots of hoops."

"A basketball player ought to be used to hoops."

He laughed. "Easier to toss a ball through a hoop than to jump through it yourself."

"I should let you go."

"Much as I hate to agree . . ."

"I'm looking forward to Saturday night." Really looking forward to it. For more than just sex.

"Me too, lover."

His voice, deep and husky, sent a sexy shiver through her body.

"And you do promise to wear them, right? The red silk boxers?" She hung up, laughing, before he could reply.

14

As he wound through a maze of streets and buildings between Sixth Avenue and False Creek, Jaxon was impressed by the attractive condo and townhouse buildings. How could a student afford to live here? This neighborhood was pretty far removed from the poverty-stricken ones where he and his mom had lived when he was in school.

Yeah, he and Suzanne did come from different worlds, but he wouldn't trade. If he'd grown up the way she had, he'd probably be settling for a middle-of-the-road career too, rather than striving to be the best he could possibly be. Not that there was anything wrong with being a vet, any more than there was with the kind of jobs her family held, or with his pal Rick's little law practice. Not for people like them. They didn't have anything to prove.

As for him, he needed more. He needed to go as far as he could go.

He pulled into the parking lot across from her building, feeling a little nervous. On the phone he'd felt a friendship developing, and now he was going to her home. Yeah, he was looking forward to seeing her, having sex, talking some more—but he didn't have the time or the energy to put into a relationship. If things started to get too heavy, he'd have to call a halt. It wasn't fair to let Suzanne think he could give more than he was capable of.

He climbed out of the car, collected a couple of packages to take in, and crossed to her building. It was a low rise with a brick-and-plaster exterior and luxuriant flowers tumbling from some of the balconies. He pressed the buzzer and thought about balconies. Maybe when it was dark, they'd have sex on hers.

Sex. Yeah, that's what he and Suzanne were all about.

"Jaxon? Third floor, then down to the end of the hall. Hurry up, big boy."

Just the sound of her voice made him start to grow hard. He couldn't wait to touch her, and the elevator ride took forever.

Her door swung open before he reached it and there she was, even more beautiful than he'd remembered, with a welcoming smile on that lush mouth. And clad—holy hell—in a skimpy garment of silk and lace almost the identical color to her skin.

He stood in front of her, gaping.

"Should I have dressed up?" she murmured, a wicked glint in her eye.

"God no!" He lunged toward her, dropping his parcels, sweeping her into his arms and carrying her through the door. Their lips slammed together in a bruising kiss, then parted as the kiss deepened.

She tore her mouth free and gasped, "The door," then reached behind him and shoved it closed. "Would you like—"

At this moment his body and brain were capable of only one thought. "You." He claimed her mouth again and she flung herself against him, her lips and tongue as hungry as his, her hands as greedy.

She pulled his shirt out of his pants and ran her hands up and down his back, kneading the muscles. Then she reached down and gripped his butt, pulling him against her. His rigid cock was a fierce pressure between their bellies and he couldn't wait any longer.

He reached between them and yanked open his belt buckle. As he started on the button of his pants, her hands were there too, making him even more impatient.

"Oh Jaxon," she moaned as she pulled his zipper down. "Hurry."

He yanked his pants and underwear down, freeing his erection. Suzanne was peeling off a tiny strip of fabric. If he didn't get inside her soon . . .

He swung around, taking her with him, pressing her shoulders against the closed door as he thrust one hand between her legs. Yeah, she was ready, hot and so wet his blood boiled. He gripped her waist and hoisted her, feeling her legs wrap around him. Already she was reaching down, her warm fingers inflaming him.

He shoved her hand aside, grabbed hold of his cock, found her entrance and surged inside her.

"Jaxon!" she cried and, unbelievably, he felt her body begin to spasm around him.

He let out a groan and thrust wildly, deeper and deeper inside her, as he too began to climax. He could feel his body let go, feel himself filling her, feel his seed spilling deep into her core.

Suzanne clung to him, her face buried against his neck, long tendrils of hair tumbling over both their shoulders, her breasts pressing against his chest as her breath sobbed in and out. His heart still lurched unsteadily, his hips thrust spasmodically. He bent his head, resting his forehead against her hair. His knees were weak, but he fought to stay upright and support her.

After a minute or two, he lifted his head and she did too. Her green eyes were dazed and dreamy. "Wow," she sighed.

"Oh yeah."

A typical female, she regained her breath quicker than him, and her desire to talk.

"That must be some kind of record," she said. "Even for us. I started to come the moment you entered me."

"Me too."

He lifted her gently, easing himself out, then set her on her feet. He bent to pull up his pants and briefs. And realized. "Oh crap, Suzanne, no condom."

She glanced down too, so now they were both staring at his wet, naked penis. "I didn't think either. I'm on the pill. And, uh, there's no danger of anything else. I mean, I . . ."

"I'm clean too. Honest."

For him, clean meant he and Tonya had been exclusive, and between her and Suzanne he'd only had sex a few times, always with protection. He wondered what clean meant to Suzanne. She was a sexy lady, must've had lots of lovers. They must always use condoms.

None of his business. She'd said she was clean and that was all that mattered.

Again, he began to pull up his pants. A hand on his arm stopped him.

"Jaxon? Take off your clothes. Remember, I have a gift."

Red silk boxers. Hell yeah, he remembered.

"I'll be back in a minute," she purred, gathering up the lacy scraps she'd been wearing when she greeted him.

As he finished undressing, he glanced around her living room. Nice, but not what he'd expected. Kind of ritzy and formal. This room didn't match his image of Suzanne.

What had he expected? Red satin sheets and a mirror on the ceiling? Well, he hadn't been in the bedroom yet.

He folded his pants and shirt and laid them over a chair.

"Mrrrow?"

He turned, to see a fluffy gold cat stroll toward him. Okay, this fit. Of course Suzanne would have a pet.

The cat twined around his ankles and he squatted to scratch under its chin. He wished Suzanne would come back with those boxers. Red silk might be embarrassing, but it couldn't be as bad as parading naked in front of her cat.

Cats. A battered black one eased into the room and surveyed him from a distance through narrowed eyes. If cats could scowl, this one was definitely doing it.

Suzanne came back, wearing that sexy ivory-colored outfit. She handed him a damp washcloth.

"You have cats," he said, turning away slightly as he cleaned himself up.

"You're not allergic?"

"No. But I don't think the black one likes me."

"That's Zorro. He's wary, especially of men. Poor baby had a tough life. I found him in an alley."

"You prowl the alleys looking for stray cats?"

She handed him a tissue-wrapped package and hoisted Zorro into her arms. "I'd been out for dinner and was walking back to my car. I heard a couple of cats fighting and broke them up. One ran off. Poor Zorro had his ear half torn off. I couldn't leave him there."

"Guess not." Not the girl who'd rescued all the injured animals in the neighborhood. "And how about blondie?" He gestured to the friendly cat.

"Melody's a sweetheart. She belonged to a friend who married a guy with serious allergies. Melody's been with me for years now. When I got Zorro last year, she was a civilizing influence."

"Beauty and the beast?"

She smiled. "You got it." Then she tilted her head. "Have you ever had pets?"

He unwrapped tissue and stared at the shorts. They were a red as bright as a fire engine.

"Pets? No. When I was a kid we had enough trouble feeding ourselves."

"And now?"

He shrugged. "I'm never home."

He shook out the boxers and stepped into one leg, then the other. "Having a pet is a commitment." And there were only two things he was about to commit to: his career, and his mom's well-being.

"Yes, it is." Suzanne sounded pleased by his comment.

He pulled the shorts up so the waistband rested at his hips. Could he feel any dumber? "Uh, this what you had in mind?"

"You truly are the most gorgeous man."

The heat in her eyes said he didn't look as silly as he felt. "Aw shucks, ma'am, you've got me blushing."

"Can I touch?"

Without waiting for his answer she stepped closer and ran her hands over his silk-clad buttocks, then around to the front, down his fly, checking out his package. He had to admit, the silk did feel sensuous against his skin, especially when her warm fingers pressed against it. He began to stir to life and she gave him a pat. "Later, my friend."

She turned away and bent to pick up the discarded tissue paper. Oh man, she was wearing a thong. Her creamy ass peeped out below the lacy hem of her skimpy top. He stepped forward and pressed his silk-clad front against her backside. "What about now, and later too?"

She pressed back against him, gave an erotic wriggle, then pulled away. "Dinner's all ready to go."

"Give me a minute, and I'll be ready too." But her mention

of food made him realize he was starving. All he'd had to eat was a bagel after racquetball, and a couple of bags of peanuts on the plane.

He stepped away from her and retrieved one of the packages he'd brought in. "I got you something too. I was planning to buy a red silk thong, but then I saw this and it said Suzanne."

Her eyes sparkled as she took the pink bag. And her whole face lit up when she pulled out the green silk robe.

"It matches your eyes," he muttered.

"It's lovely. So elegant." She stroked the fabric. "Thank you, Jaxon."

"Put it on. I hope it fits."

It did, draping her curves, framing her throat, revealing her chest down to the lacy top of the garment below. And it ended above her knees, baring those knockout legs.

She threw herself into his arms. "Oh Jaxon, I love it." Then she spun away. "I have to go look."

In Ann's bedroom, Suzanne stared into the floor-length mirror. Who was this woman, with her fiery hair, rosy cheeks and slim, silk-wrapped body? She looked classy, but also sexy. It was the first time in her life she'd looked in a mirror and thought of herself as sexy.

Jaxon had done this for her.

When she walked back into the living room, he was squatting down murmuring to Zorro. Her alley cat tilted his head to let Jaxon scratch under his chin. She'd never seen Zorro give his trust so readily to a man.

Her heart threatened to go all mushy on her. She cleared her throat. "You guys ready for dinner?"

Jaxon rose easily to his feet. "Can't speak for Zorro, but I'm starving." He handed her a paper bag. "Thank God for your carpet, or this might have broken when I dropped it. It's red wine. I hope that's okay. I knew I wouldn't have an opportunity to chill it, and I remembered you drank both colors."

He paid attention and he was practical. Except, he could be so overcome by passion when he saw her that he'd drop a bottle of wine on the floor.

She felt like holding up her fingers, counting off the man's attributes.

If she ran out of fingers, what would she do?

"Red's great." It was a zinfandel from a California winery called Ridge. "I don't know this wine. Is it a favorite of yours?"

"I'm no connoisseur. I asked an expert's advice. My ex-wife Tonya. She's in the restaurant business."

"Oh?" She was happy he got on so well with his ex. Really she was. How could a girl respect a guy who bad-mouthed his ex? Damn it, she'd have to overcome her stupid jealousy and give the guy another point.

She led the way to the kitchen and he followed.

"Her dream has been to open her own restaurant," he said, "and she's doing it now."

She handed him Ann's corkscrew. "Good for her. I imagine that's a tough business to get into, in San Francisco. There are lots of good restaurants, aren't there?"

"She's done her research. She's creating something a little different, and she's hired a young chef she thinks is wonderful." He chuckled. "She's even brought my mom in, as a weekend co-hostess and minor partner."

"Oh?" His mother and his ex were good friends too? This was sounding just a little too cozy.

No, that was jealousy speaking again.

As Jaxon poured wine, she took a platter of chicken satay from the fridge. "I thought we'd eat outside. I made an Asian salad and we can barbecue these while we're sipping wine."

"Asian salad?"

"Cabbage, red pepper, noodles, sesame seeds, almonds, soy sauce, ginger. Lots of goodies. Sound all right?" It was Jenny's recipe.

"Sounds wonderful."

He followed her to the patio door and glanced out toward the building across the street. "Shouldn't I put on some more clothes? It's not dark yet."

"Soon will be. Besides, you're just as covered as if you were wearing a bathing suit." Her lips twitched. "A red silk bathing suit."

She lit the barbecue. He still hovered in the doorway.

"Are you chicken?" she challenged.

"Oh hell." He strode outside, put the two wineglasses on the patio table and flung himself into a chair.

She took the other chair, enjoying the soft, humid ocean air on her skin. "Nice?"

"Yeah." He smiled a little sheepishly, then his eyes began to sparkle. He lifted his glass and raised it toward her. "A toast. To slow, lazy, sensual lovemaking. Tonight."

She touched her glass to his and was just lifting it to her lips when he said, "I'm not finished."

"There's more?"

"Tonight, on this patio."

"Oh! Oh yes, I'll drink to that."

She took a sip and had to admit the wine was great. Tonya's choice. His ex. His friend. "Jaxon? You said something earlier, about a pet being a commitment?"

"Uh-huh?"

"You got married, then divorced. Don't you view marriage as a commitment?"

He drank a little wine, seeming to reflect. "Not in the same way. A pet's dependent on you. A spouse isn't—unless there's a bad illness, disability, something like that. But normally marriage involves two completely self-sufficient adults."

She wouldn't have said *completely* self-sufficient. "It is a partnership of equals." But still, if you swore a solemn promise to each other, you should keep it. Not rationalize that it was okay to leave because the other person would survive on their own.

Not wanting to argue, she said, "Kids, though, they really are dependent."

"Sure, they're like pets." He gave a short laugh. "Sorry, that came out badly. What I mean is, having a child is the strongest commitment you can make. I'm not sure a parent ever stops feeling responsible."

"Mom says your child is always your child, even when they have kids of their own."

He nodded, then sniffed the air. "It's smelling good."

She checked the skewers and brought the salad, plus plates and utensils, from the kitchen. "It's not very fancy."

"Looks and smells great."

They took their time with the meal, and to Suzanne's surprise Jaxon asked her a lot of questions about her work and her career plans. Either he was exceptionally polite or he didn't find Suze the sensible twin to be a waste of time.

The sun set, lights twinkled in windows across the street, the stars sparkled above. The evening was relaxing—and yet Suzanne couldn't forget Jaxon's toast. Soon, they would be making slow, sensual love. Right here on the patio.

The silk of her new robe caressed her arm when she lifted her wineglass. It slid across her legs, baring her thighs. As for Jaxon—well, she had trouble keeping her eyes off that gorgeous athlete's body. Her nerves hummed with a frisson of arousal, subtle, yet as undeniable as the salty tang of the ocean air.

She finished the last sip of wine. "I'll clear up. It will only take a moment."

"I'll help."

The kitchen was bright after the balcony. Melody and Zorro pattered in to see if there were any leftovers. She'd brought the cats, not wanting to leave them alone at her place. Mouse had promptly found the computer keyboard in Ann's home office and likely would never emerge, but the other two had been exploring.

Suzanne tidied away leftovers while Jaxon loaded the dishwasher. Then she opened the fridge. "Remember that ice wine?"

She turned, and found he'd squatted down and was gently scratching around Zorro's good ear. The cat, who never purred, had his eyes slitted in bliss.

Something in her chest squeezed tight. Damn. Ann and Rina had warned her, and she'd blithely sworn she'd never put her heart at risk.

But this man understood Zorro. He believed that having children was a serious commitment. He'd bought her an elegant robe that matched her eyes, he'd fucked her like she was the sexiest woman alive and he'd asked intelligent questions about her work. He'd seen Suzanne the sexy twin and Suze the sensible one, and seemed to like both.

She pulled out the wine and fumbled with the corkscrew. She liked him too. She respected how far he'd come, from such humble beginnings. And she trusted him. Otherwise, he wouldn't be here in Ann's apartment.

They'd definitely departed from the Champagne Rules, and so far she was feeling good about it. Just a little scared. She'd always been a sensible girl who planned things out, and now she had no idea where she and Jaxon were heading.

She eased out the cork. "Ice wine?" Her voice came out choked.

"Sounds great." He bent his head over Zorro and murmured something she didn't catch, gave one final caress, then rose.

He accepted a glass of wine, then took her hand and tugged her gently out the patio door. He spread the two cotton chair pads on the floor, sprawled on one and raised a hand. "Join me?"

She sank down beside him. What now? He'd promised slow and sensual.

He reached up a hand to slide the silk robe from one of her shoulders, then the other. It dropped to her waist, revealing the ivory camisole she'd bought specially for him.

She reached for their glasses and handed him one. "You haven't tasted it."

He lifted his glass. "What's the toast, Suzanne?"

Damn it, between Tonya's excellent zinfandel and Jaxon's excellent body in red silk, her brain was too fuddled to come up with something special.

She tried to channel the sexy twin, and inspiration hit. She raised her glass. "To silk. To sensual, sexy, seductive silk. And to you wearing those boxers into your office next week."

"That'll be the day."

"You really are chicken."

He made a low, growling sound. Then he touched his glass to hers.

They both sipped. She closed her eyes, savoring the intense, peachy flavor. Essence of summer in the Okanagan.

When she opened them again, Jaxon was smiling appreciatively. "That's fine stuff."

He took another sip. "Almost as fine as you, Suzanne. Did I mention how much I like this sexy top? And the thong?"

"Do you want me to take them off?"

He put his glass down. "Not yet."

He reached out and, with one surprisingly delicate finger, traced the outline of her left breast through silk. Her nipple sprang to attention. He circled with his finger, drawing the broadest outline, then narrowing in, narrowing again, until finally he was rubbing her nipple. He joined his thumb to his finger and squeezed gently, and heat zinged down her body.

She let her head fall back, her hair hanging free. Boldly, she thrust up against his fingers, inviting him to take more, reminding him she had another breast too.

He shifted position, kneeling now, so both his hands were free to caress her. She glanced down and saw how his erection distended the silk shorts. One day, she'd like to catch him unaware, unaroused, and bring him to that state with her touch. But he was always a few steps ahead of her.

She kneeled too, cupping his head with both hands, feeling the delicious springiness of his short curls. She touched her lips to his jaw, just below his ear. She nibbled a trail upward, circling his earlobe.

He moaned. "God, I want you."

"And you'll have me." She darted the tip of her tongue into his ear. "Eventually." She drew the word out and he moaned again. "It was your idea," she murmured, "to take it slow."

He gave a rough chuckle. "Are you protesting?"

"No way. I think it's a fine idea."

"Do you now?"

He bent his head. Then his lips were on her nipple, through her camisole. He sucked, licked, sucked. It was tantalizing, having him that close but not yet touching her flesh.

Sensation zipped through her, and arousal heightened. Could she *do* slow, with Jaxon?

She needed a breather. Besides, it was time to turn the tables. Gently, she pushed his head away.

"What—"

Before he could finish the question, she had a hand on his chest, pressing him down. "My turn."

She bent over him, letting her hair tickle his chest, then his stomach. She leaned closer, to follow with her lips. He had nipples too, and she reminded him of the fact as she sucked them until he groaned.

She pressed a finger to his lips. "Ssh. The neighbors."

She felt his silent laugh against her fingertip. Then, "I'll be good."

"I'm counting on it," she whispered back. She drifted a hand across the front of his boxers, across the rigid flesh of his erection, and then away.

"What do you want, Suzanne?" And, suddenly, he was sitting up, taking control. "Do you want my lips? Here?" He leaned over and again sucked her nipple through her camisole. "Or, do you want them here?" He slid both hands into the sides of the silk garment and lifted it over her head.

"Anywhere. Everywhere."

His lips claimed her mouth and his tongue thrust inside. In and out, then circling, withdrawing, plunging in again, mimicking sex. His taste—sweet and fruity from the wine—was intoxicating. She moaned when he pulled away; then stretched back to give him better access, moaning again as his mouth moved down her body. Inch by inch. Tonguing, nibbling, sucking every bit of flesh he encountered.

"And maybe here?" His tongue swirled her navel and she gasped, "Oh yes." She pressed her shoulders and feet into the mattress, lifting her stomach toward him.

"Or here?" He breathed hot air across the front of her thong. Her thighs parted as she welcomed his touch, her pelvis writhed against him, demanding more. His tongue probed the soaking wet strip of cloth between her legs and she whimpered, feeling her body reaching, nearing the point of climax, just waiting for—

Suddenly, he drew back, grasped her by the hips, and turned her on her stomach. His finger traced the lacy line of fabric that bisected her buttocks and she writhed helplessly.

For a moment, she felt no touch at all, and she glanced over her shoulder. He was kneeling beside her, his body upright as he looked at her. More precisely, at her butt.

He bent down to nip a cheek, and she buried her face in her

folded arms, giving in to the sensation. Little nibbles and sucks that made her clench her muscles, and at the same time his finger traced the line of her thong as it disappeared between her legs. Her concentration focused, tension building between her legs.

"Jaxon!" she panted.

"What do you want, Suzanne?" He leaned down to whisper in her ear, as his finger continued its relentless pressure. Two more strokes, and she'd come. She knew it, she could feel it, she was so close and . . . He gave her one stroke, then stopped.

She groaned.

He touched his tongue to the inside of her ear. "Do you want to come now? Or wait?"

"Yes, now." How could she bear another moment of waiting? And yet, anticipation really did fuel desire. . . . "No. Oh, I don't know, I want—"

He stroked again and her body clenched, waiting for the final stimulus that would bring release. He stopped.

"I want to see your face when you come," he said, and now he had her by the hips, rolling her over on her back.

"I want you to come inside me."

"Not yet. First, let's concentrate on you."

He reached for his glass but, rather than drinking, he dipped his finger in. Then he ran the damp finger over one of her breasts. He leaned down and licked, flicking her already-erect nipple. "So that's ice wine. I like it."

Her hips came off the cushion as she pressed her breast against his lips. He sucked hard, then left her nipple and trailed his tongue down toward her navel.

His fingers tugged at the sides of her thong. He eased it down an inch or two and tangled his fingers in her curly hair, but he didn't strip the thong all the way off. He bent and applied his mouth again, to the silk at her crotch.

"Oh God!" Her body bucked, on the edge of the peak yet again.

She couldn't stand it any longer. Desperately, she grabbed his head, holding it still as she ground against him, demanding what she needed.

This time he didn't leave her. His fingers stroked, his tongue pressed the silk taut against her swollen clit, his breath was hot against her own heat. She strained upward, twisting against his mouth, and felt the climax begin to take her.

When it was finally done, her body collapsed and he followed her down, lying beside her.

After a long minute or two, she managed to roll onto her side and look at him. "Your turn?"

"No hurry."

She glanced down the length of his body, then followed her gaze with her hand, stroking his chest, his ribs, his hip through red silk. He was fully aroused, yet he said there was no hurry. Maybe this time they really would take it slow.

"Roll onto your stomach," she murmured.

15

Suzanne's small hands stroked his back in butterfly caresses, then kneaded his muscles with surprising strength. After all the hours he'd put in at his desk, the massage was welcome. For a moment, he imagined coming home every night to a woman's caressing touch.

He almost laughed. What woman in her right mind would stay up until midnight to massage a career-obsessed lawyer?

No, this might well be a once-in-a-lifetime experience, so he'd better enjoy every moment.

He was torn between the sensual pleasure of her hands and the sexual press of his engorged, silk-wrapped penis against the cushion. As Suzanne's fingers squeezed into his muscles, his body pressed against the cushion in small nudges, a tantalizing friction.

Her hands moved lower, into the small of his back, just above the waistband of the boxers and he squirmed. Would she re-move the shorts?

Instead, she caressed and kneaded his buttocks through the

silk and he had to admit the feeling was novel—as erotic, in its way, as the direct touch of her fingers.

She sure was taking her time. She moved down his thighs to his calves, and even spent a little time massaging his feet.

He knew the next gift he'd be buying Suzanne. Massage oil. And he'd be inflicting this sweet torture on her body.

She leaned over his head, her hair tickling his back. "Feel like rolling over? I'll do your front."

She would do his front. Oh man, yeah, he felt like rolling over.

When he did, her gaze went straight to his groin. She grinned. "Still with me, I see."

"Begging for attention."

"Mmm. Well, I'm not starting there." And she was back at his feet again. Gradually, she worked up his shins, then his thighs. His erection battled against its silken prison, but she ignored it. This was torture, but he was enjoying every minute.

Her deft fingers stroked between his legs, just brushing his balls, and he squeezed his thighs together involuntarily, trapping her.

He forced his muscles to relax and her fingers drifted free, again brushing him, as if by accident.

She sat back on her heels and studied his body. "Shoulders next, I think," she murmured, and he groaned with frustration.

"What's the matter, Jaxon? Weren't you the one who wanted slow and sensual?"

Oh God, he was going to get her for this. Just wait 'til he got that massage oil.

She bent over his shoulders, then made a dissatisfied sound. "It's hard to reach, leaning from one side. I think I'll have to . . ." And she straddled him, her buttocks neatly trapping his cock.

He thrust upward. She shuddered, then tapped his hip. "Settle down, I want to massage your shoulders."

She might sound cool as a cucumber, but her silken thong was saturated, her inner thighs beaded with moisture. It seemed she was torturing herself too. He loved knowing his body turned her on.

She rested her hands on his shoulders and he said, "This is familiar. From the cave. Remember?"

She smiled down. "I do. But then, you were inside me."

"I could be now," he said eagerly.

She brushed his lips with hers. "Not yet."

She kneaded his shoulders, then ran her hands across his chest, flirting with his nipples, exploring his ribs. He tried to hold still, but when she moved so her crotch pressed against his groin, he had to thrust again. Two thin layers of silk separated their most intimate parts and the musky scent of arousal filled the air.

She pressed tightly against him and squeezed his hips with her thighs. Her body began to move rhythmically, riding his erection, and her thighs clenched tighter. He glanced up, saw her hard nipples, and heard the little panting sounds she made. She was on the verge of orgasm.

He wanted her to have it, but if she kept this up much longer, he'd come himself. And he didn't want to until he was inside her. He thrust a hand between them, finding her clit.

"Oh," she moaned as he rubbed against her.

"Come, Suzanne," he murmured. "Come now."

And she did, grinding her body against his so it took all his will power to hold himself back from joining her. He gritted his teeth and locked every muscle, resisting, restraining himself, until finally it was over. Her muscles began to relax and her body drooped. He gripped her hips and eased her upward, away from him.

"Jaxon?" she murmured, her expression dazed.

"Get up," he grated out.

"Oh sorry."

She leaned down to put her hands on the cushion, shifted her weight, lifted one knee and started to clamber off him. Every movement, every change of pressure, challenged his control.

"Sorry I'm so heavy."

When she was finally off, he croaked, "You're . . . not . . . heavy."

"But . . ." Perhaps she finally noticed his clenched muscles. "Oh. I was selfish. You were close too. Jaxon, let me . . ."

She reached toward him and he grabbed her wrist. "No! I want to be inside you."

"I want that too."

"Give me a minute. If you touch me now, it'll all be over."

Suzanne sipped wine, watching him, seeing the tension in his body slowly ease. Finally, he sat up, reached for his wineglass and took a sip.

She felt the lush heaviness of physical satisfaction in her body. She was so relaxed, the wine so delicious, the stars so bright, she could almost curl up and drift off to sleep.

Except that she and Jaxon had unfinished business. She'd been saving the best for last. Ever since she'd first raised the subject of silk boxers, she had been imagining how he'd feel through silk. "I didn't finish my massage. You distracted me."

"*I* distracted *you?*"

She giggled and put both their glasses down. "Lie back."

"Do you want to use protection? I have condoms in my pants, but they're inside."

Rubber sex versus the joy of naked sex with Jaxon? "I want you. Just you. Is that all right?"

He groaned. "More than all right."

He stretched back on the cushion and she touched him gently: his hair, those tight, wonderfully springy curls; his face with its strong planes; and his broad shoulders, muscled chest, taut stomach. Then she trailed her fingers lightly across the front of the boxers. He was so big, he stretched all the way to the waistband, lifting it away from his skin. Just looking at him made her satiated body stir to life again.

She cupped his balls, felt his crisp hair through the light fabric, then again traced the hard length of him. The slippery silk, the hard heat of him underneath—the contrast was perfect, just as she'd imagined. She curled her hand, encompassing as much of him as she could, and squeezed lightly. He gave a low, shuddery groan.

"When you're in your office," she whispered, "wearing these shorts, remember me touching you this way."

She slid her hand through the front slit and gripped him, flesh to flesh. "And this way."

"Like there's any chance I wouldn't?"

She hooked her fingers in the waistband. "Off now." He lifted his hips and she eased the boxers down his legs and tossed them on the deck.

"You too. Take the thong off."

She obliged, then lay back.

"I want to be inside you, Suzanne."

"Hurry." She parted her legs and he moved between them. The tip of his cock pressed against her, tantalizing her. Then he found her entrance, eased inside and her body stretched to accommodate him. She gave a sigh of pure pleasure and he swallowed it with a kiss.

When, finally, he filled her, he withdrew slowly, almost all the way out. And then he slid back in and she pressed tight against him. Excitement built within her and she let it, guessing that he'd climax soon, not wanting to be left behind.

But Jaxon fooled her. He held on to his control and she lost track of how long the dance went on. Slow and easy, he'd promised, and man, did he deliver. Each time one of them neared the edge, he stopped moving, kissed her forehead, her nose, let them catch their breaths. And then he began again.

The exquisite tension was almost unbearable. She felt arousal peak again, and whimpered.

"Do you want to come?" he asked.

"N-no. Not until we do it together." If he could play this waiting game, so could she.

He held still, his body poised over hers, and dropped a kiss on her chin. Over his shoulder she counted stars, waiting as her body calmed.

And then he started up once more.

Their bodies were slick with sweat and she felt so swollen inside that the friction, each time he moved, was unbelievable. The sensation was so much more intense than the times they'd made love with a condom. When he slid out, it felt like he was pulling her with him. And then he thrust forward again, plunging deep into her center, touching places she'd never knew existed.

Her lover. Her perfect lover.

She ran her hands down his back, stroking his taut muscles, curving to squeeze his hard buttocks, feeling the muscles clench as he thrust into her.

He stopped suddenly, his whole body taut. "I can't hold out much longer," he gasped.

"Don't," she whispered in his ear.

"It's so good. I don't want it to end."

She touched the tip of her tongue to his ear. "All good things—"

"Oh Christ!" he groaned. His body pulled back from hers and then he surged forward. Then he did it again, his rhythm picking up, each stroke hard and demanding, faster and faster.

Her body responded to the feverish pace. A prisoner of sensation, her whole being concentrated in that place where their bodies came together, where he pounded into her, where it was no longer possible to separate one of them from the other because they were so completely joined, where pleasure was sweet agony and—

He came with a desperate thrust, a wrenching groan, and she felt his essence jet into her even as her own body spasmed helplessly around him.

"Jaxon!" she cried, burying her mouth in his shoulder.

How could anything feel so absolutely right?

And again she had the thought: *This lovemaking should create a child.*

It was crazy. Yet the idea, like their joining, felt immutably right.

His body was heavy on hers, his chest heaving as he gasped for breath. Her own chest heaved too, and she enjoyed the sweaty press of her soft breasts against his hard muscles. So perfectly female and male.

He kissed her cheek. "I've never come so hard in my life. You're amazing, Suzanne."

"It takes two."

"That's definitely the best way." Then he said, "Afraid I wasn't so quiet. Hope none of your neighbors heard."

"It's late. They'll all have gone in." She hoped it was true, or poor Ann's reputation would be ruined.

"Good. I wouldn't want anyone calling the cops." His chest pulsed against her as he laughed.

"Once is enough," she agreed.

He heaved his body off her and collapsed on the other cushion. "I can't believe we're in the heart of the city. Lying out here, naked under the stars."

"It's a good city, Vancouver."

"So you're teaching me."

She realized that, without his hot weight, she felt chilled. "It's cooling off. Want to go inside? Have a cup of coffee?"

"Sounds great." He stretched and began to rise. "I haven't had any coffee for, oh, it must be at least seven hours. That's got to be a record."

He stood above her, naked. She lay, enjoying the view, until he extended a hand and pulled her to her feet.

"You're an addict, are you?" she said.

"Seems like I live on it, some days. And the coffee at the office isn't even that good."

She picked up the collection of silk that decorated the balcony. "Want high-test, or something decadent like a latte with hazelnut syrup?" Knowing Ann had an espresso machine, she'd brought some fancy fixings.

He chuckled, a sound as dark and rich as the finest coffee. "Decadent? I just had you."

Inside, she put on her new robe and handed him the boxers. "If I'm going to turn a light on, we should be at least half-clothed. Much as I hate to see you cover up all of those yummy attributes."

He pulled on the shorts and she said, "You're not so tentative as the first time you did that."

"Okay, I admit it. Silk feels good. I could get used to this."

They decided on lattes, and took the coffees into the living room.

Jaxon settled into a corner of the couch and gave a satisfied sigh. "Here it is, eleven on a Saturday night and I'm sitting around in silk underwear, drinking a fancy latte, having just made love with the sexiest woman alive."

She curled up beside him. "Life is good?"

"Life is damn good. Normally, I'd still be at the office."

"Do you really have to work so hard?"

"Sure do."

"What would happen if you didn't?" At his puzzled look, she went on. "I mean, would they fire you?"

He laughed. "Not likely. But I wouldn't make partner." He sipped coffee, made an appreciative sound, then put the cup down. "When you join a firm, there's three ways you can go.

Out, quickly, because you can't cut it or you don't like the place. Up the partnership track, and that's where I'm headed. Or you can stay an associate. Every firm needs associates; not everyone can be a partner."

"What's the difference between an associate and a partner?" She had a good idea from Ann, but wanted to hear Jaxon's thoughts.

"Partners do more prestigious work, have a higher billing rate, have a voice in decisions that affect the firm. They make more money, have more status. The people who make partner are the ambitious ones. Some of the associates are as bright, they're as good lawyers, but they aren't ambitious. They're content to stay in the middle of the pack."

"And you're not."

He shook his head firmly. "That's not why Mom brought me to America."

Suzanne tilted her head. "I'm sure she brought you because she wanted a better way of life, more opportunity, for you, but . . . Would she really be disappointed if you didn't make partner?"

He gave her a level gaze. "That's not going to happen. I will make partner. Faster than any associate's ever done it before."

"But . . ." That hadn't been her question. Should she pursue this? She decided to go at it from another angle. "Do you see her often?"

"Not as much as I'd like, I'm so busy, but she's my next priority after work. She understands."

His mom came after his career. But then, it sounded like the career thing was partly to fulfill his mom's hopes for him.

"I bet she's really proud of you. Proud of what you've accomplished. Even if you didn't become a partner."

He shook his head. "Suzanne, you don't get it. I've got this game plan. I've had it since I was in elementary school. I learned what Americans value in a man. Career success. Power. Money. That's what I'm aiming for."

"There are more important things."

He raised his eyebrows. "Oh yeah? Such as?"

She winced at his condescending tone. "Family, friends. Health. Living a balanced life. Gaining your sense of self-esteem from within yourself, rather than from what others think of you."

"I have plenty of self-esteem," he said coolly.

Damn. She didn't want to argue, just for them to discuss this. "Good," she said, trying to sound warm and approving. "So what does it matter whether people think you're a major success or only a minor success?"

"It matters," he said grimly. "People's opinions matter. As a woman, you ought to know that. You're a member of a disadvantaged minority too."

Why hadn't she realized before? "This is about being black."

"Damn. It's about . . . being a man."

A man? Was he implying her father was less of a man because he'd never aimed for status and wealth? "Yes, it is," she said, hearing the edge of anger in her voice, but unable to hold back. "It's about what kind of man you want to be. A workaholic who has *sycophants* rather than friends, people fawning over him because he has money and power? Or a man with family and friends who love him, who has a career that means something?"

His hands were locked around his coffee cup and he didn't reply.

Was he mad, or just reflecting? She wished he'd say something.

Maybe she should leave this alone, but it was important. Besides, this was the guy whose role model was Thurgood Marshall.

She'd looked the man up, after their last conversation, and realized what a huge influence he'd had on civil liberties in the States.

"Sorry," she said, "I overreacted. I don't think I really understand what you're saying."

"It's not that complicated. I want to make it to the top."

But what did *the top* mean to him? "You said your area of law is litigation?" she asked. "Like, those big class-action suits?"

"Yeah."

"So, you represent people who are fighting against injustices?"

"No, I represent the companies who are being sued. Often by a bunch of troublemakers."

She frowned. "I don't follow."

He put his cup down. "It's a litigious society, right? People are jumping on the bandwagon, wanting to make a buck off the system. I have a case right now that's a perfect example. You know the Family Friend chain of stores? They're being sued by a bunch of employees who can't hack it in the real world, who can't compete, so they cry discrimination in hopes Family Friend will pay just to shut them up."

He sounded so harsh. And yet, maybe she could see where he was coming from. His mother had no doubt faced all sorts of obstacles, but she'd kept her pride rather than whining that she had been discriminated against. Still, if there truly was discrimination, an employer shouldn't be allowed to get away with it. Employees shouldn't have to suck it up and keep quiet. And it was more than just a moral issue—discrimination was illegal.

"So," she said tentatively, "are you saying the employees were or weren't discriminated against?"

"My client says no. That's the case I'll present."

"Don't you care about the truth?"

He snorted. "You're being naïve. Law isn't about the truth,

it's about who has the best case, which typically means the best lawyer. Family Friend has me, a damned good lawyer who's going to work his tail off for them, who has the resources of a major firm to draw on. The plaintiffs have the NAACP." He paused. "That's—"

"The National Association for the Advancement of Colored People," she said softly.

"Yeah. Surprised you know that."

"Thurgood Marshall worked for them. I looked him up. He fought against racial discrimination."

She leaned forward. "Your hero, Jaxon. He was on the other side."

"He . . . Crap, Suzanne, you don't understand the legal system. You just don't get it."

"I guess I don't," she said bitterly. Here she'd thought Jaxon was one of the good guys working to make the world a better place.

He picked up his cup, then put it down again and said, in a tight voice, "We aren't going to agree on this. We have different backgrounds, and they've shaped our goals."

That was true. What right did she have to judge?

None. Just the right to feel sad that he wasn't the man she'd hoped he would be.

She swallowed hard and touched his arm, tentatively. "You're right. I'm sorry. It's not my business anyhow."

He didn't move away, but nor did he touch her. "No, it's not."

She took her hand off his arm.

They sat side by side in silence for a few moments, then he stood. "It's late."

"Yes." She stood too, wrapping the robe around her and tightening the sash as he got dressed.

She walked with him to the door. He looked down at her

and she looked up, and neither said a word. Was this good-bye? she wondered. How had tonight gone from so right to all wrong, so quickly?

Maybe she should let it go, yet she'd felt so close to him, earlier.

"Jaxon? We're both upset, but people disagree all the time. Politics, religion, whatever. Remember the Champagne Rules? How we said we'd keep things light and fun, not get into daily grind stuff like jobs? I guess we were right."

His face softened. "We lost track of our own Rules. That was stupid."

"Let's not let one quarrel spoil things."

Slowly, he nodded. "That would be even more stupid. So, what do you think? We'd talked about a picnic tomorrow. Want to try it, or do we take some time to cool down?"

If they didn't see each other tomorrow, they wouldn't know if they could put things back together. Better to find out. Slowly, she said, "You're in town, so let's get together. I promise I won't talk about work." Or anything else meaningful.

"We'll go back to the original bargain."

"Just sex." She forced a smile. "When we stick to sex, we do pretty well."

He smiled too. "We sure do." He touched her cheek, and lifted a curl of hair. "I'll see you tomorrow then."

She caught his hand and pressed it to her lips. Then, slowly and deliberately, she took his middle finger into her mouth and sucked on it. When she released him, she whispered, "Tomorrow."

But the moment the door closed behind him, she ran to Ann's bedroom and flung herself on the bed, tears sliding down her cheeks as she mourned the loss of something that had barely begun.

16

The sun was fiercely hot on Jaxon's bare chest and shoulders, but the ocean breeze cooled the burn. He and Suzanne were sprawled on a blanket in Stanley Park, surrounded by picnic stuff they'd shopped for at a huge, colorful market on Granville Island.

Last night's quarrel hadn't been mentioned, but its residue lingered, despite their best efforts to regain their sexy spirit. Why did relationships always have to get complicated?

They'd set the Rules for a good reason, and should never have broken them. Everything had been fantastic when they'd focused on sex.

Well, things had been pretty good when they'd talked on the phone, and last night at her place, until they got into that argument. Fuck. They'd really blown it.

He looked over at Suzanne, her curls golden in the sun, her slim body looking great in low-slung white shorts and a blue-green tank top. He leaned forward and touched his lips to hers.

She smiled. "It's a beautiful day, isn't it?"

Great. Now they were talking about the weather. Earlier

they'd discussed food, the bounty of Granville Island Market, the merits of various picnic sites. Never once had they mentioned work or family. He wondered what her plans were for the rest of the day, but he couldn't ask.

Sex, he reminded himself. They should be safe if they stuck to sex.

He lay down on the rug and put his head in her lap, facing her. She started, glanced down at him, then tentatively rested her hand on his head and stroked his hair.

"You'll have to play lookout," he told her.

"Lookout?"

"Mm-hm. Unless you don't want to . . ." He slid his hand under her top and bra, found her breast, teased her nipple.

Her body tightened. "It's so public."

"We won't do anything you're not comfortable with."

He shifted slightly so he could blow warm air against the crotch of her shorts.

"Oh!"

He ran his fingers down her fly, then the center seam between her legs, back and forth until she squirmed. Then he pressed his mouth against the place where the two seams crossed, and blew hard.

"Jaxon," she hissed. "People will see."

"They'll see a guy taking a snooze, using his lady's lap as a pillow. That's all they'll see, unless you squirm around."

He waited a few seconds, then she said, "I'll have to be careful not to squirm then."

He laughed, resting his mouth against her shorts again, letting the chuckle press into her. And then, without ever undoing her shorts, he used his fingers, lips and tongue, his heated breath, to make her come. Too bad he couldn't do it without turning himself on in the process.

She showed great self-control, hardly moving at all, even as the spasms of orgasm pressed the cotton of her shorts against his lips.

A few minutes later, she tugged on his ear. "Sit up."

"Or we could do it again."

"Or I could do it to you."

His cock throbbed. She couldn't. That really would be impossible, wouldn't it?

He sat up and glanced around. They were on a slight hill, facing Vancouver Harbor. Below, on the seawall, people streamed in both directions—walking, roller-blading, cycling. But that stream was a couple hundred yards away.

"You're hard," she said.

"Oh yeah."

"I could do something about that," she said in a husky, sexy voice.

Other picnickers dotted the grass, but there were none within at least fifty feet. People did stroll across the lawn occasionally, though, and they'd even seen a couple of Mounties ride by. The cops, again.

He couldn't let her do it. But . . . "What did you have in mind?"

"I thought I might take a nap with my head in your lap."

"God."

"Put on your T-shirt."

He obeyed, letting it droop down to cover his shorts. He was growing harder by the minute, anticipating what she might do.

She lay on her side with her head across his thighs. "Mmm, black T-shirt to match your shorts. How handy. No one will notice if I . . ."

Deftly, she eased down his shorts, freeing his cock under his T-shirt. Her hair fanned out over his groin, her breath was warm on him—and then she tongued his balls.

He almost shot into the air.

"Jaxon! Hold still."

"Then don't make any more sudden moves."

"I'll only make teeny, tiny moves." She suited action to words and began to nibble the base of his cock.

Christ but that felt good. Her head moved only fractionally, yet her tongue and lips were working magic. Now her hand was under his T-shirt too, holding him firmly as she nibbled up and down.

She said something, her words muffled.

"What?"

"Are you keeping a lookout?"

He jerked his head up. He'd completely forgotten. But no one was any closer than before.

"All clear. Carry on, by all means."

Her shoulders shook as she chuckled. Then her tongue drifted up his shaft and circled the head. She closed her lips around him and began to suck. Her hand stroked his length. She swirled her tongue. She slid her mouth up and down, and he could imagine he was dipping in and out of her pussy, ready to let the climax build, to move faster and deeper. He was close. . . .

He heard the chatter of voices and glanced over his shoulder. A tour bus had parked, and a group of Asian people was starting across the sweep of grass, heading, he guessed, for the seawall. They'd likely pass within ten feet of him and Suzanne.

He pressed a hand to her head. "Stop. People are coming. Stay still."

She froze, but her breath tickled him. Orgasm was so close.

He clenched every muscle, recited basketball statistics in his head, but still he could feel her.

Sweat broke out on his forehead and he fought against the urge to thrust.

The first of the Asian group passed by. No one paid the

slightest attention to him and Suzanne. They were chattering away, referring to guide books, lifting cameras.

In agony he waited. How many people were on that damned bus? The stream seemed never ending, and all the time Suzanne's hand gripped his shaft and her breath was warm against the most sensitive skin of his body.

The last of the group passed by and he waited, grinding his teeth together, until they were safe on their way down the hill.

"They've gone," he grated out.

"We're all alone?" Her breath teased him.

"Yes, and I'm—"

"Ready?"

"Dying!"

"Well then." She licked the tip of his cock. "We'll just have to do something—"

The orgasm was coming; no force on earth could stop it. With his last conscious thought, he reminded himself to stay still. Her mouth was there, circling him, just in time to catch the first drops that poured out of him. He couldn't thrust upward or he'd give himself away, but she seemed to know what he needed, moving up and down just a little, sucking. Swallowing.

Oh man. He felt almost giddy with the relief of physical release.

And yet, a few minutes later, he felt an inexplicable sense of letdown. Last night, outside on her balcony, it had been so much more. He wondered if they'd ever have that again.

He wound a few golden curls around his fingers and tugged. "Come up, before the Mounties come back."

She lifted her head, grinning and licking her lips like a cat. "You taste good."

She settled beside him. "Who went by?"

"An entire busload of tourists."

A laugh erupted from her. "Honestly?"

He pointed toward the water. "With cameras. See."

"I wonder if they took our picture?"

He shuddered. What had he been thinking?

Well, he was with Suzanne. That meant his little head governed his big one.

Which reminded him . . . He checked his watch. "Time to pack up."

Silently, she began to gather things together. When everything was organized, they walked to his rental car. No Porsche this week, just the standard economy car.

He drove to her building in False Creek and parked outside. His luggage was in the car and he wondered if she'd invite him in to change his clothes, but she didn't. No problem, he could do it at the airport.

Now what?

He helped her unload the rug and picnic basket from the trunk. She stood, cradling them in her arms, keeping him at a distance whether she intended to or not.

Her face was inscrutable, and so was her voice when she said, "It's been fun, Jaxon."

"Sure has." He winced at his own false joviality. "I guess—" He'd been going to say something about getting together again, but wasn't sure what he wanted. Or how she felt.

"I imagine you'll have a lot of work to catch up on," she said evenly.

True. He couldn't afford to take more time off.

The realization hit him that, right now, he wasn't willing to sacrifice more billable hours for . . . sex. The sex had been terrific, but now he'd had enough to hold him for a while. It was time to get back to his top priority.

Plus, they didn't want this to become a regular thing. Like they'd said in the beginning, champagne should be drunk infrequently, so it stayed special.

"Right," he said. "Well, let's keep in touch. Next time one of us feels like . . . what was it? An erotic escapade?"

Her eyes closed briefly. Hiding what? Relief, or disappointment? Then she nodded.

He leaned forward and touched his lips to hers. "Bye, Suzanne."

Jax was on fire. He smashed the ball past Rick at a speed so sizzling his pal didn't even try to hit it, just backed out of the way.

"Shit!" Rick gasped for breath.

"Fifteen," Jax called. He'd won the match, two out of three games. His first decisive victory over Rick in months and he ought to be feeling great, but instead he just regretted their time was up. He wanted to whack the shit out of that ball a few more times.

"Man, what's up your ass today?" Rick asked as they headed for the changing room.

"Nothing."

Rick wiped the back of one hand across his sweaty brow. "Work all weekend?"

"Should have." If he'd worked, he and Suzanne wouldn't have messed up something great. "I have this big case, could make or break my career."

"What's it about?"

"Class action against Family Friend."

"Family Friend? Wow, that's gotta be a biggie. What's the cause of action?"

"Discrimination."

His friend stopped in the act of unlocking his locker and turned. "Racial?"

"Yeah. Gender as well, but mostly racial."

Rick nodded. "Makes sense they'd give it to you. Token black, huh?"

Fuck. He'd been resisting that thought. Damn it, he'd been chosen for his skill, not his race. Hadn't he? Fighting back, he said, "What's that mean?"

Rick shrugged. "You got a sexual discrimination case to defend, you pick a woman lawyer. Right?"

And who better to fight the NAACP than a lawyer of color?

"Okay, it makes sense, strategy-wise," he admitted. "Still doesn't mean it won't do my career a hell of a lot of good." He unlocked his own locker, and put his racquet in its case.

Rick did the same. "Gonna settle or fight it?"

"Fight." He explained his reasoning.

"Makes sense. If you win."

"I'd sure as hell better. I'm betting it's just a bunch of whiners leaping on the litigation bandwagon."

"Who've they got for counsel?"

Damn. He shouldn't have raised this. "NAACP."

Rick, pulling his sweaty T-shirt off over his head, whistled. "That's gotta hurt. You're up against an organization that helped make this a country where guys like us could get an education, have a fair shake at a decent job."

"Every client's entitled to a good lawyer," Jax retorted. "That's the number one thing they taught us in law school. What's it matter who's on the other side?"

"If you were gay, would you argue a case against a gay rights organization?"

"Why not?"

Rick stared at him, his expression troubled. "I know you're no Uncle Tom, but you ever think you're taking this whitewash thing too far?"

Crap, not again. Hadn't he learned on Saturday, with Suzanne, that a kid of the privileged middle class could never understand what life was like for him? Clearly it was too much to think Rick's black skin would make him any different.

"You ever think you should stay the fuck out of this?" Jax retorted.

They glared at each other, then Rick took a step back. "Guess maybe I should." He grabbed a towel and strode in the direction of the showers.

Jax leaned against his locker, resting his forearms against the cold metal. Heart pounding, he fought a major urge to hit someone or something.

This week's Awesome Foursome meeting spot was Favorito Pasta Trattoria on Broadway, a friendly neighborhood restaurant where the food was great and the prices incredibly reasonable.

The women ordered a bottle of chianti and each chose a different meal, so they could share tastes. Suzanne had trouble picking; she'd had no appetite since she and Jaxon had parted on Sunday. She finally settled on lasagna, because it seemed like comfort food and she could doggy bag whatever she didn't finish. Unless, of course, Jenny nabbed it first.

The moment the waitress had gone, Jen leaned forward eagerly. "So, Suze, tell all. Discover any new sexual positions?"

Suzanne forced a smile. "Saturday we'd barely even said hello then we were doing it, right inside the door. Standing up."

"Hot!" Jenny said approvingly.

"Later, we had sex on the balcony, all slow and sensual."

"I never have time to go out on the balcony, much less have sex on it," Ann said wryly.

"Sunday we went for a picnic in Stanley Park and—"

"You didn't have sex in Stanley Park?" Rina said, sounding half horrified and half hopeful.

"Well, he, uh, made me come through my shorts and I, you know . . ."

"Gave him head?" Jenny said disbelievingly.

"Yeah."

Her eyes gleamed. "In the park, in the middle of the day, with people around? Way to go, girl!"

"Well, there wasn't anyone right around us, but there were people walking the seawall, strolling across the grass."

"Wow," Rina sighed. "I can't imagine doing that."

"I couldn't have either, before Jaxon."

"Suze?" Ann said. "Something wrong? You're not sounding as perky as usual."

"Don't disillusion me and say you're getting tired of all that incredible sex," Jenny said.

"It's not that."

Ann leaned forward, eyes narrowed. "Did something go wrong? Did he hurt you?"

"No, not the way you mean. But we had a . . . disagreement."

"How could you get in a fight after that scandalous sex in the park?" Jenny demanded.

"Disagreement, not fight. And it was Saturday night."

"A disagreement on Saturday, makeup sex on Sunday, what's so bad about that?" Jen asked.

"The disagreement's still bothering you, though?" Rina said. "What was it about?"

Suzanne sighed. "Work. Its place in a person's life. He's bought into that whole American guy dream, with a double-whammy because he was a black immigrant kid. He wants power and money and status. Everything else comes second. I said there are more important things, told him how I value a balanced life and a man who puts family ahead of work."

Jenny screwed up her face. "Ouch. Head on, major clash in values."

"Yeah, but it shouldn't be a big deal. It's not like we're getting serious about each other."

"Except, you're falling for him," Ann said.

Yeah. She *had* been thinking about getting serious. That's why her heart felt like a lump of lead weighing down her chest so she couldn't draw a clean breath of air. "Okay, maybe I was starting to," she said softly.

"Oh Suzie," Rina said sympathetically.

Suzanne shrugged, not wanting a pity party. "Well, it doesn't matter, because he's clearly not the man for me. Now we're back to our Champagne Rules. Just sex, no heavy conversation. Our little spat proved we need those Rules."

They broke off as the waitress delivered huge plates of aromatic food, spooned parmesan on top and wielded the pepper grinder.

After they'd gone through the ritual of sampling each other's dinners, Jenny said, "So you're back where you started? Dynamite sex, nothing mundane, no strings attached? That doesn't sound so bad."

"No, of course not. But . . ."

"But?" Ann echoed.

"The sex was good on Sunday," Suzanne said slowly. "Intense, with a risky edge. He's gorgeous, a fantastic lover. He makes me feel like the sexiest, most attractive woman alive. What more could I possibly want?" It was the question she'd been asking herself for the last day and a half.

"All of that in a man you could marry," Ann replied promptly.

And there was the answer Suzanne had been avoiding. "Yeah, okay, it's what every girl wants. But honestly, I don't think I'm going find hot sex plus a stable family guy all in one package."

"Why not?" Rina asked. "Just because a guy's responsible and values his family, that doesn't mean he can't be sexy too. Does it?"

Suzanne put down her fork. "I don't know. I'd never thought about a sizzling sex life as being part of marriage."

"As Rina once pointed out," Jenny said, "Ward Cleaver was awfully good to the Beaver."

Suzanne swatted her. "Stop it. I'm being serious."

"So'm I," Jenny said. "Gimme a break, it was the fifties. Of course you didn't actually see Ward and June having sex, but I bet they did, and it was spectacular."

Jen actually had a point. A point that made Suzanne think about what her sister had said about her own marriage and— major yikes!—their parents'. It seemed that raunchy sex really could play a major role in a long-term marriage.

"Okay," she said slowly. "I'll give you that much. But there's a difference between lust and love, right? If you get married because you're in lust, that intense physicality will die down and you'll be left with nothing. So, sure, you need sexual compatibility, but that's just a start."

Yes, that sounded right. More confident now, she went on. "I want to marry a man who shares my values, a man I like and respect, a responsible man I can trust, who'll be my life partner. A man I can have children with, without fear he'll abandon us. Not by leaving, or cheating, or even working all the time."

Her three friends exchanged glances. Suzanne gave an embarrassed laugh. "Okay, you've heard all that before." She forked up a bite of lasagna.

"Okay," Ann said, "it's nuts to marry based just on lust. But it's possible to have love and respect as well as ongoing sexual attraction. They're not mutually incompatible."

"My sister's got that," Suzanne said. She wasn't about to mention her parents' sex life.

"That's so romantic," Rina sighed.

"And damn lucky," Jenny put in.

"It's never just luck," Ann said. "You'll never find someone who's perfectly compatible. A couple always has to work on a relationship."

"I guess," Suzanne said.

"So, let's look at Jaxon," Jenny said. "You don't like and respect him?"

Suzanne chewed another mouthful of lasagna—it really was delicious—and thought about the question. "In some ways. I can understand where he's coming from. An immigrant kid, raised by a single mom, living in poverty. He bought into the American dream and he's making it come true. It's a different dream than mine, though."

"You value your work too," Rina pointed out.

"And Jaxon does value family." Suzanne thought of what he'd said about his mom. And his ex. "And friends. But I put those things first, and he puts his career first."

"I'm not taking his side," Ann said, "but it does take an awful lot of hard work, and time, to get ahead in law. It's harder for a woman than a man, and I'm guessing it's harder still for a person of color."

"Okay," Suzanne said, "I can respect his dream. But I still want—deserve—a man who thinks it's more important to spend time with me and our children than to climb the career ladder."

"I agree," Rina said. "Kids come first. Even if both parents work, their jobs shouldn't be more important than their children."

"Nothing should," Suzanne said vehemently, thinking of her old friend Liz.

The other three exchanged glances, then Rina said softly, "Now would be a good time to tell us. If you can."

"Tell you?"

"Look, we all agree your values are good ones, but the reality is a lot of marriages are unhappy, a lot end in divorce, a lot of kids are neglected by their parents. We all think it's sad. We all hope for better."

She glanced toward Jen and Ann, who both nodded.

"But," Rina went on, "it goes further for you, Suze. This is emotional, personal. And yet your own parents seem pretty much perfect."

Personal. Yes, it was. Oh damn, it was silly not to tell her best friends. "It's not a deep dark secret, it's just hard for me to talk about."

Three comforting hands reached out to pat her shoulder, and touch her hand.

Slowly, she said, "When I was a kid, I had a best friend named Liz. We did everything together, shared our secrets. Her father was a rising star in a big company. Really into his career." Just like Jaxon.

"Liz's mom didn't have a job," she went on. "She built her life around him, played the good corporate wife. Entertained his clients or co-workers on a moment's notice. Didn't complain when he worked late. Not that he appreciated any of this. He was cheating, with his executive assistant."

"His wife find out?" Ann said.

"Yeah, and when she confronted him, the shit blamed her. He said she'd let herself go, he couldn't talk to her, she was an uneducated dummy."

"What a winner," Ann said scathingly.

"Well, she sounds like a doormat," Jenny said. "Didn't the woman have a spine?"

Suzanne sighed. "No. To be fair, I guess she never had much chance to develop one. She dropped out of college to marry him, and had no job skills or self-confidence. She was trying to be a good wife and he screwed her around."

"And your friend Liz was hurt by all this," Rina said.

Hurt. Oh yeah. "She was like her mom, always trying to please her father."

"Aagh," Ann said.

"Yeah. Poor Liz had two bad parental role models. Anyhow, I don't think her father gave a damn about either her or her mom. He left, and married his assistant. When Liz called, he was always too busy to see her. And her mom was shattered.

She went on meds, drifted into her own miserable world, pretty much stopped coping."

"They both abandoned Liz," Rina said sadly. "That's so unfair. Sure, her mom must have been depressed, angry, scared, but so was Liz. Her mom was an adult and Liz was just . . . how old?"

"Fourteen."

"How did Liz handle it?" Ann asked softly.

Suzanne closed her eyes, fighting back tears. "She blamed herself. Everything was her fault because she wasn't a perfect daughter."

"Kids do that. Feel responsible," Rina said. "Especially if their parents don't tell them otherwise. I see it all the time with my music students."

Suzanne nodded. "I tried to tell her, but she wouldn't listen. She studied all the time, trying to make straight A's. She kept saying she wasn't thin enough, wasn't pretty enough. She got skinnier and skinnier. Her mom wasn't cooking proper meals. We invited Liz to our house, but she picked at her food. Once I caught her in the bathroom after dinner, throwing up. She said she had the flu."

"Anorexia?" Ann asked quietly.

Suzanne nodded. "Mom figured it out. She called Liz's mother and said her daughter needed help. Liz's mom snapped at her and said they were both going through a rough time, they'd work it out. My mom didn't give up. She spoke to a counselor at school and the counselor said she'd follow up."

"Did it help?" Rina asked.

How could she tell the rest? Suzanne swallowed hard. Maybe her friends sensed there was an unhappy ending because none of them said a word. They just squeezed her arm, gripped her hands.

She sucked in a breath and said it quickly, all in one rush.

"She took a bunch of her mother's pills. I don't know if it was an accident or if she meant to, but by the time her mother found her, it was too late."

Rina gave a little gasp, but the others were silent, their shocked faces speaking for them.

Suzanne's eyes burned and she swiped a hand under them, catching the tears. "We all blamed ourselves. Me, my parents, the school counselor. I guess Liz's mother did too. Maybe even her dad, finally. He looked pretty shattered at the funeral. More than her mom, who was drugged to the gills."

Suzanne pulled out a tissue and blew her nose. "I get so mad, every time I think about it. I will *not* marry a man like Liz's father."

"And you'll never put your personal issues ahead of your children's needs," Ann said. "Like both her parents did."

They were all quiet for a moment, then Rina picked up her wineglass and held it up in a toast. "To Liz. I hope she's found peace."

They all lifted their glasses and clinked them against Rina's. "To Liz."

Although Suzanne's eyes filled again, she felt better. It was almost like, for a moment, her old friend was part of this warm, loving group.

"It's a sad story," Ann said.

"A woman needs to find a guy who values her needs equally with his own," Rina said. "That's why you have to talk about these issues ahead of time and make sure you have the same vision of the future." Her voice began to rise, which was unusual. "That's where so many people mess up. They don't discuss the important things. Then suddenly they're married and it turns out they can't both be happy."

"Rina?" Ann said quietly.

Rina flushed. "Sorry. My parents. Just be glad, Suze, that you and Jaxon found out before it was too late."

"Glad? Somehow that's not how I feel. But I know you're right. It's good I found out we can't be a couple. Otherwise, I might have . . ." She shrugged.

Ann nodded. "Let yourself care? Don't you already? Can you turn that off now? Go back to playing by the Rules, and not get hurt?"

Could she? Or was it time to give him up? "I don't know."

"You guys got something planned?" Jenny said. "Like, a phone sex date or something?"

"No. It's time for a break." Would she be the first to get in touch? If she didn't, would she ever see him again?

Feeling depressed, she said, "Speaking of which, you girls want to give me a break and talk about something else? Rina, have you had any luck tracking down Mr. Magic Fingers?"

Rina shook her dark head. "I've been debating whether I want to. It seems stupid. We're probably no more compatible than you and Jaxon."

"Jesus, you guys," Jenny said. "Doesn't anyone have something fun to talk about?" She stared at Ann.

Ann shrugged. "Not me. It's all up to you, Jen. Had any hot sex lately?"

"Hot sex," Suzanne warned, "is how all this trouble started." She turned to Jen. "Speaking of which, how's it going with Pete, the Jacuzzi guy?"

"It's getting old, real fast. I'm just hanging on to him until I find a replacement."

"No one else waiting in the wings?" Ann asked.

"Well, there's my Friday night arranged date. My aunt set me up with this accountant, the grandson of one of the ladies she plays mahjong with. Somehow I doubt he's going to be a Jaxon."

17

Jaxon was out of sorts all day Monday, and had trouble concentrating on his interviews at Family Friend. He'd decided to start with the managers at head office, and to visit them rather than have them come to Jefferson Sparks, figuring they'd be more comfortable and he'd learn more.

Only problem was, he wasn't so happy with what he learned.

First, there was the way most of them reacted to seeing him: shock.

It couldn't be his impeccable suit, shirt and tie, his neat haircut. It had to be his skin color.

Theirs was, universally, white. So were the pictures of family, friends, colleagues on their desks.

His last interview was typical. When he asked Wayne Bakker, the marketing manager, about the complaint that he'd promoted a white man over an African-American woman, the man said, "Some people aren't prepared to put in the time and work hard."

Jaxon agreed. However, this particular plaintiff didn't appear to be one of those people. "Ms. Zachary had been with Family Friend for five years," he pointed out, "and was the top salesperson for the last two. Mr. Norris had only been with you a year."

When he got no response, other than a sulky glare, he prompted, "Mr. Norris did have more job-related education, of course."

"Yeah, that's it. Superior skills."

Skills? Not hardly. The black lady had the skills, the white guy had the education. And Bakker was damned stupid.

"These people want a free ride," the manager complained. "They aren't prepared to put in their time and work for it."

"These people?" It wasn't the first time today he'd heard the term.

Bakker scowled into his black face. "People who don't have the skills. Education. Work habits. Whatever."

Jax had said the same kind of thing himself. People should work hard for what they wanted, not rely on affirmative action.

But he also believed that, having worked hard, they shouldn't be discriminated against. And from what he'd heard at Family Friend today, it seemed discrimination just might be systemic.

Tuesday morning he was back in his office, transforming his scribbled notes into a typed record. A record that disturbed him.

When Caitlin came in to ask a question, he snapped, "Can't you see I'm in the middle of something?"

She scowled, as much as a freckled elf can scowl. "Jesus, Jax, what's wrong with you today? That's the third time you've taken my head off."

"Sorry, I'm busy. Nothing's wrong."

"You're always busy. Boss, you need to get a life."

"I've got a life," he said grumpily. Why had he encouraged her to be so informal? His life was none of her business. But he couldn't snap at her again.

"Like, a girlfriend, was what I was meaning," she said. "You need some R&R."

He wasn't about to tell her he'd just spent two weekends having lots of recreational sex. "I don't have time to meet women, much less go out with them."

"The meeting part wouldn't be a problem. I know at least a dozen gals who'd love to go out with you. You're, like, a primo catch."

Suzanne certainly didn't think so. "I don't want to be caught."

She rolled her eyes. "If I didn't know better, I'd think you were still hung up on your wife."

"Ex. And you do know better."

"Tonya's doing well, isn't she? I saw the invitation for that dinner at her new restaurant. Sounds like it's going to be a great place. Hint, hint."

Eventually, Caitlin's brashness usually did make him laugh. Now he chuckled and said, "I'll take you for lunch when they open."

"Great! In exchange, I'll get you a date for that dinner."

Once, he'd toyed with the idea of taking Suzanne, wondering about her meeting Tonya and his mother. Now the only invitations he'd be issuing to outrageous69 were ones for hot sex. If he ever felt in the mood for it again. "I'm going alone."

Caitlin gave an exasperated snort. "Fine. Be like that." Heels clicking on the hardwood floor, she stomped out of his office.

He turned back to his computer and saw, beside it, Tonya's invitation.

Funny thing was, Suzanne would probably get along with the other ladies in his life. It was him she didn't get along with.

His mother had said she sounded like a nice girl. And, as it turned out, she was, as well as being a sexpot. A nice girl, who would end up with a guy far less successful than he. But that's what she wanted.

It wasn't that he'd spent his life trying to be better than the other guy. Well, maybe he had. Not better in some obnoxious way—at least he hoped not—but trying to prove he could be anything that a white guy could be.

And Suzanne would choose a low-achiever white guy.

Not that he wanted her to choose him, not for marriage and all that crap. So why did it piss him off that she rejected the goals he'd been working so hard toward?

Because it meant she was rejecting him. Who he was as a person. She'd happily take him as a lover, but not as a person.

He heaved a sigh. Damn. He and Suzanne had actually started to develop something worthwhile. Now, exhausted and stressed, it was the friend he missed, more than the sexpot.

But it was when they'd ventured into friendship that their relationship fell apart. It seemed that, for them, sex and friendship weren't compatible.

So, fine, they'd learned a lesson. Why was he obsessing like a girl?

He picked up the phone, dialed Tonya and RSVP'ed that he'd be attending her dinner party alone.

"You can escort Darissa," she said.

"Mom's not bringing a date?"

"You ought to know she doesn't mix her personal life with business."

"Yeah, guess I oughtta. Hell, I didn't even know she was dating until she told me a week or so ago."

"She's a private person." Tonya paused, then said, "Jax, you're really okay with her being a partner in my business?"

"Why wouldn't I be?"

"A new business? It's risky. I know how strongly you feel about her financial security."

It was true, yet somehow he'd never questioned that aspect

of the new venture. He had to smile when he realized why. "I have faith in the two of you. You'll make a go of it, she'll do okay."

But her comment about finances made him remember things Suzanne and Rick had said. He bit his lip. "Am I too hung up on money?"

"It's natural to want to look after your mom."

"Yeah, but I mean . . . in general. In my own life, my career."

"Um . . . Hung up on money? No, I wouldn't say that." But her tone was wary, like there was something else she *would* say.

He didn't want someone else dumping on him, but he valued Tonya's opinion. In many ways, she knew him better than anyone else did. "But?" he prompted.

"You're really driven to make something of yourself."

"So are you."

"Well, I want to run my own restaurant, do things my way, make my customers happy. But it's for personal satisfaction, you know? Not for . . . glory."

Her comment was so unexpected, it made him chuckle. "You think I want glory?"

"You're out to prove something, Jax. To yourself and to the world."

He sure the hell was. "You saying that's bad?"

"It makes you concentrate on your goals, pretty much to the exclusion of everything else. It's how you get things done."

Sure. He'd learned that technique as a kid, and it had always worked. Except . . . "I didn't do so well with our marriage."

"No. You didn't see it as an important goal, or at least not as important as work."

Damn. He'd loved her, but she was right. Building his career had mattered more. "I let you down. Hurt you."

"Yeah." She sighed again. "Oh damn, it's not fair to let you take all the blame. I'm at fault too. I knew how hard you worked, knew your goals. You had trouble making time to see me when you were articling, so why did I think you'd change? I loved you, Jax, but we both should've realized marriage wouldn't work for us."

Yeah. If the two of them had ever had the kind of conversation he and Suzanne had had on Saturday, they'd never have married. "I loved you too," he said softly. "Thanks for being so understanding."

She was quiet for a moment, then she gave a chuckle. "Instead of bitching at you like I usually do? Sorry, guess there's still some old hurt hanging around. Crazy, because I'm so happy with Benjamin. So grateful I was free when he came along."

"I'm glad it's working for you, this time around."

"Me too. This time, I knew what I was looking for. Benjamin and I are lovers, best friends, partners. We share our lives. We talk about our jobs, help each other out, and we always make sure there's time to talk, make love, laugh."

Yeah, Suzanne and Tonya would get along. They had the same values. Just like Rick.

Was he the only one in the world who was trying to live the American dream?

Or had he ever truly understood that dream?

When Jax rose on Wednesday, he wondered if racquetball was still on. He'd expected an e-mail saying Rick couldn't make it. When it hadn't come, he'd thought of sending one of his own. But hell, that would be admitting something, and if Rick wasn't going to, then nor was he.

No Rick in the changing room at the club.

Slowly, Jax took his racquet from its case. If they stopped the regular games, he'd have to find some other way of getting exercise. All those hours at a desk really took a toll on the body.

A few minutes later, the door crashed open and a breathless Rick rushed in. "The BART was late."

"No problem." Jax bent to retie his shoes.

Why did he feel relieved? He told himself it was just because he needed the exercise, and their familiar three-day-a-week routine was the easiest way.

They played in silence, but for calling out the score. The play was hard and fast, both of them sweaty and short of breath. Jax won the first game, Rick the second, and the third was hard fought until Jax made the final point.

"Good match," Rick panted.

"Yeah."

Neither spoke again. Not until, showered and changed, they hit the street together.

"Hope the BART's back on schedule," Jax said.

"Yeah."

"Friday?"

"Yeah."

Okay, fine, it wasn't like he needed conversation from Rick. Their relationship was all about keeping fit.

Still, this not-talking crap was awkward. He could call Rick, apologize. But hell, Rick had overstepped, taking that whitewash stuff from teasing to serious. He was the one who should apologize first.

Suzanne had apologized.

And look where that had gotten them. To a spot where, unless he felt like proposing crazy sex, he didn't feel like he could even e-mail her.

By Thursday night, Jax was going through serious Suzanne withdrawal. He couldn't do this cold turkey, he had to hear her voice.

It was around ten when he picked up his cell and phoned from his office. His hello was met with a long silence.

Then she said, "Jaxon? How are you?" She sounded wary.

He went for honesty. "Tired, overworked. The same old me."

She gave a soft laugh, and when she spoke, her voice was more relaxed. "Another rung or two up the partnership ladder?"

He listened hard, but there was no undertone, no jab. Damn, it felt good to hear her voice.

"One can only hope." He glanced at the stacks of files on his desk, the notes from more crappy Family Friend interviews—this time at a branch store—waiting to be transcribed. "There must be some reason—" He broke off.

"Reason?" She sounded so gentle, like she really wanted to know.

"I was going to say, 'reason I'm killing myself like this.'"

"You know the reason, don't you? I mean, you sounded pretty sure when you talked about your goals."

"I—"

"Look," she interrupted, "it was shitty of me to attack your priorities. I should know better. I have these three girlfriends, we get together every week, and the wonderful thing about our friendship is that we can disagree. We discuss, give our opinions, sometimes just agree to disagree, but it's not an attack. We support each other, we care."

Imagining the four of them made him smile. "I'm not so sure you were attacking," he admitted. "Yeah, it felt like it, but you hit one of my hot buttons. Maybe I overreacted."

"I know *exactly* what that's like," she replied eagerly. "That's why I came across so strong myself. My hot button is fathers who put work ahead of their kids."

He pushed his chair back, resting his sock feet on his desk. "That's a good hot button. I agree with you. Hell, I had a father who didn't acknowledge I existed, and a step dad who'd have preferred I didn't."

"Oh Jaxon, I never thought of it that way. What an idiot I am."

"Don't go feeling sorry for me. My mom always put me first."

"She sounds wonderful."

Oh yeah, Suzanne and his mom would definitely get along.

"So, what about you?" she asked. "Will you have kids one day? You didn't mention a family when you talked about your goals."

He'd never really thought about it. When he and Tonya married, they'd agreed children were an issue for way down the road. But . . . if he couldn't handle marriage and a career, he sure as hell couldn't have kids and do right by them.

Why had he never figured this out before?

"I guess . . . probably not," he said.

His brain said it was the right decision. But . . . He'd never be a dad. Never help with homework, teach his kid basketball. Never break the pattern and be a real father, unlike his dad and step dad.

And his mom would never be a grandmother. She sometimes teased him about getting married, making her a grandma, but he didn't know if she was serious.

"Too bad," Suzanne said. "All those great genes not getting passed on."

"Great genes?"

"Handsome, intelligent, athletic. You're the perfect man."

He frowned. "You don't really think that. You think I'm a workaholic."

"Well . . . You are, aren't you? But that's not genetic."

"My mom worked hard."

"Yes. But for survival, and to make a good life for you."

"She taught me anything is possible, if you work hard enough."

"It's a good lesson. Each person has to decide what they want to work for. You've done that, and now you're making it happen. That's something to be proud of."

She wasn't attacking him now, she was suggesting he should be proud. Why didn't he feel better?

He leaned back in his chair and rotated his aching neck. What he'd give to have her fingers massaging his shoulders. "Hey, Suzanne, you said your hot button is fathers bailing on their kids? But your father is there, for you and your sister. Isn't he?"

"It's a long story."

And obviously not one she wanted to share. Silly to feel hurt. "It's okay, forget I asked."

"No, it's just hard to talk about. But I've done it already this week, with my girlfriends, and I feel better for it." She gave a little sigh, then went on. "When I was a girl I had a best friend . . ."

He listened as Suzanne told Liz's story. When she got to the end, he said, "Poor Liz. And poor you. It must've hurt to know your friend was in pain, yet wouldn't let you help her."

"It did. I still feel like I let her down."

"You did everything a friend could do."

"We all knew her mom was taking pills. We knew Liz had access to them, knew she was upset, feeling guilty and depressed. We should have guessed."

"That's hindsight. I bet, at the time, you did everything you could think of. I know you."

"I sure tried."

He had a flash of insight. "Suzanne, what's your most important goal in the world?"

"I guess . . . to be a caring person. A good daughter, sister, friend. Wife and mother, when the time comes. A good vet. I guess—this sounds kind of silly, I know—to be a good citizen of the world."

"You're already there. I'd bet you never let your family or friends down. And when you're a mom, you'll always be there for your kids."

She didn't say anything, but he heard her sniffle.

"You need a shoulder again? Wish I could give you one." He meant it too. Yeah, tears were hard for him to deal with, but he'd really like to be touching her, offering his support.

"Y-you really are the sweetest man."

"Hell, I care about you." As he said the words, he realized how true they were. "Just because we have different goals, it doesn't mean we can't be friends. I like you, my sexy lover. And I respect your opinion, even if I don't always agree."

"Just like the Awesome Foursome," she murmured.

"The what?"

"My group of girlfriends."

Her closest friends. He was flattered to be included with such company. "You know why I called?" he asked.

"Uh . . . Phone sex?" she said cautiously.

He laughed. "Nope, not this time. I missed you. I missed our friendship."

"Friendship," she echoed. And then, "I've just realized, we've been breaking the Rules again. Except, this time we aren't arguing."

"Thank God!"

She chuckled. "We've been talking about me, Jaxon. Now tell me something about you, your life. Maybe a case you're working on, or your mom? Or—wait, tell me about your heritage." Her voice sped up with excitement. "I don't know much about Jamaica. What about reggae music, that's Jamaican, isn't it? And jerk chicken? What is that, anyhow? We have jerky, that horrible dried meat, and I'm sure that's not what jerk chicken is like."

And this was why he didn't tell people where he came from. He was American, not Jamaican. He no more ate jerk chicken than she did, and he'd never cared for reggae—not that he had time to listen to any kind of music.

Stifling impatience, he said, "Jerk isn't dried, it's spiced."

"What's 'jerk' mean?"

"Poking with holes. In the old days, the meat was poked all over, spices were stuffed in the holes, and then the meat was cooked in a stone pit, with green wood burned to add even more flavor. Now, mostly people just use a marinade and basting sauce."

"Sounds good."

"Don't remember. Haven't had it in years." Since his step dad had told his mom she was American now, and should learn to cook American food.

"Really. Why not?"

The woman didn't have a clue. "I only lived in Jamaica a few years, as a little kid. Why should I be interested in Jamaican stuff? I'm American." So American that he tuned out any time his mom reminisced about her own life in Jamaica.

"Sure, but it's your heritage."

They were friends. They were supposed to be able to talk about things without getting mad. He didn't have a hell of a lot of experience with that, but he'd give it a try. "Look, I don't know how to say this politely, but I'm feeling a little, uh, stereotyped here."

"Stereotyped? You think I'm being racist? Jaxon!" She made a huffy sound. "It's not racist to celebrate having a cultural heritage, and be curious about someone else's. My background's Irish and English. That means Dad teaching us Irish pub songs and Mom teaching us English ones; the superstition that leprechauns lurk in the garden; a proper English tea with Devonshire clotted cream when strawberries are ripe; and that's just a start."

What the hell could a guy say to all that? And in fact, he didn't have to decide, because she was going on.

"If anyone here is racist, Jaxon, it's you."

"Racist!? What the fuck are you talking about?" Hadn't she noticed the color of his skin?

"You're the one who thinks you can't get ahead if you're black. You have to pretend to be white."

Rick's words hung in his skull. *You ever think you're taking this whitewash thing too far?*

"Case you haven't looked closely," he bit out the words, "I'm never going to pass for white."

"That's not what—Oh damn, we're doing it again. We really do need those Rules."

They sure as hell did!

Then Jax took a deep breath, forcing down the anger. No, he didn't really think Suzanne was racist, and he'd bet she didn't think he was. He remembered what she'd said about her girl-friends. "Maybe we don't need the Rules," he said. "Seems to me we've just hit a couple more hot buttons. Doesn't mean we have to fight."

"Yes!" she said eagerly. "You're right. We can calm down and agree to disagree. Even better, we could talk some more, really try to understand each other's perspective?"

Talk further about being Jamaican? He should hook her up with his mom. "Maybe one day, but not tonight. Okay?"

There was a pause, then she said, "Yes, of course. We all have things we're not ready to talk about. Like I was, about Liz."

"Thanks. And it's getting late too. I should go." He thought of mentioning that he still had work to do, but figured she'd have guessed.

"Call me again when you get a chance."

"Sure." In fact, maybe now they'd kind of pulled things back on track, she might be in the mood for a little play? "So, sexy lady, feel like making a date for phone sex?"

The pause was short. "Love to." Then, in a seductive tone, "Have you worn the boxers to the office?"

Damn, she had to remember the boxers. "No way."

"Tomorrow," she said firmly. "Wear them tomorrow. And call me tomorrow night, after everyone's gone home."

Friday morning, he'd just gotten out of the shower when his cell rang.

Rick said, "Can't make racquetball today."

Damn. And next week Rick would end up being too busy too. It was his way of saying he was pissed.

"Too bad," Jaxon said stiffly. Should he apologize? Wasn't it really just another case of hot buttons, and overreacting?

He was trying to figure out how to begin, when Rick, his voice ragged, said, "It's sheer hell here. Jase caught something at day care." He broke off to cough. "Rosa was sick all night and I think I've got it too. Feel like crap."

Sick? So it wasn't a brush-off. Relieved, he said, "That's rough. Anything I can do?"

"Nah, thanks anyhow." Rick coughed again. He really did sound bad. "We're all going to stay in bed. Should be okay by Monday."

"Let me know."

Poor guy. Rotten way to spend a weekend.

Weekend. Wait a minute. "What about your Saturday b-ball thing? Got another coach?"

Rick gave another cough. "No. You volunteering?"

He wasn't going to Vancouver this weekend. He could make up the time by working even later. Besides, he needed the exercise. And Rick needed the help, the kids needed a coach, and the truth was, he actually wanted to do it. God knew why.

"Yeah, okay." He toughened his voice. "But you're gonna owe me. Maybe one of Rosa's home-cooked meals, when you guys are all bug free again." And he was looking forward to that too, he realized. A family meal.

Living vicariously, experiencing the kind of life that would never be his.

Not that he wanted it to be, of course.

Rick gave a surprised laugh, choked out another cough, then found his voice. "You're on."

Jax hung up, then opened a dresser drawer and reached automatically for a pair of dark boxer briefs. A flash of red caught his eye. Damn, he'd promised Suzanne.

Thank God he wasn't going to the club this morning. Rick would've killed himself laughing if Jax had stripped off his pants to reveal red boxers.

He slid them on. Yeah, silk really did feel good against his skin, and every inch of this silk held a Suzanne memory.

He pulled on a pair of suit pants, his cock hanging loose down the left leg rather than being anchored firmly across his belly. As an athlete, he'd spent a fair bit of his life in a jockstrap, and he tended to favor security when it came to his private parts.

Other men wore boxers all the time.

But, he knew from years of locker rooms, other men usually didn't have so much equipment to stow inside their pants.

If he could suffer through this today, he'd have his reward when he phoned Suzanne tonight.

His apartment was only a few blocks from the office. Today, as he strode down California Street, he had to admit the silk shorts felt way sexier than anything he'd worn before.

He glanced down. Christ, when his left leg went forward, his pants molded to his body and you could see his cock. He broke stride immediately, then experimentally took shorter steps. That was better; the fabric draped loosely rather than stretching across him.

He almost laughed aloud. Jaxon Navarre, star athlete, was shuffling along like an elderly cripple.

What a relief to make it into the office and sink down in his desk chair. He glanced down to see the bulge of his unrestrained package.

"Morning, boss," Caitlin's cheery voice called from the doorway.

Hurriedly, he shoved his chair closer to the desk, so his torso pressed up against the edge. "Morning."

She frowned. "You okay?"

"Fine, just fine."

"Don't like my new hair?"

He hadn't been paying attention, but now he noted that she'd traded orange for a color he could only describe as banana. She and her hairstylist must be going through the fruit basket. "Uh, it's different. Interesting." And what the hell was wrong with natural, like Suzanne?

"Oh God, all this flattery will have me blushing." She rolled her eyes and departed.

After she'd gone, he moved his chair back out again and surveyed his lap. It wasn't really that bad. If a person wasn't staring at his crotch, they likely wouldn't notice. Would they?

He could imagine Suzanne gazing at his crotch, his cock hardening under her scrutiny, pressing against the red silk, straining upward. . .

"Coffee's on," Caitlin called from the door.

He darted his chair under the desk again. "Thanks, I'll get some in a while."

She shook her head. "You are definitely working too hard." She disappeared from his doorway.

He spent the day feeling self-conscious. He had never, outside of a sexual situation, been so aware of his genitals. The silk was both seduction and torture. He felt like a different man than the usual work-day Jaxon Navarre. He was Suzanne's lover; the silken caress was a constant reminder.

The office cleared out early, it being Friday. He went out to pick up a Mexican chicken wrap for dinner, collected a Coke from the fridge in the kitchen, then went into his office and closed the door. Finally, he could relax. He took a couple of bites of his takeout meal, then a long swallow of cold pop.

Leaning back, he rotated his neck, imagining Suzanne's touch. Then he glanced down at his lap.

If she was here, she'd run her finger along the fabric that covered his cock. He did it himself, and the bulge grew bigger. Then he unzipped his fly to a dazzle of red. He studied the garment that had been tormenting him all day.

He reached down to cup his balls through the silk, then slid his hand farther, to hold his cock, to feel it harden and try to lift. He eased it free from his pant leg and caressed it lightly, making the silk slip and slide across his engorged flesh.

No. This was for later. To share with Suzanne.

He withdrew his hand and forced his zipper closed. For now, he would finish his quick meal and do another few hours of work. Then he'd phone and collect his reward.

"Time to head home," Suzanne told her dad, drying the popcorn bowl and hanging up the dish towel.

She'd accepted her parents' invitation for spaghetti dinner and a video with her niece and nephew, who, because it was Friday night, were sleeping over.

"Don't want to take your turn with a bedtime story?" her father asked. Her mom had already taken the kids up, while she and her dad tidied the house.

"Next time." Normally, she'd love to, but Jaxon would be calling, and she wanted time to shower and get in the mood.

She hugged her dad and went down the back steps. The dusky garden smelled of roses and Melody and Zorro were at the door to welcome her, but she barely noticed. Her mind was full of Jaxon.

Tonight they'd have phone sex, and her body was already humming with anticipation. But last night had been amazing too. They'd talked like real friends, and had figured out how to disagree without fighting. No sexy play, yet she'd felt a warm glow of connection.

Should she be scared? Her excitement dimmed a little, thinking of Rina's and Ann's concern that she'd get hurt. But she could handle this, and guard her heart. It wasn't like she was hoping Jaxon would change. He'd made it clear that wasn't in the cards.

Definitely not Mr. Cleaver. But for this stage in her life, he was great.

In her apartment, she took a luxurious shower, then slipped into the jade silk robe he'd given her. Under it, she wore only a black thong. These sexy undies took a little getting used to, but she liked the erotic sensation of the silk robe brushing against her bare backside. Is this what Jaxon had felt all day, in the boxers? Or had he been so involved in work he'd forgotten he was wearing them?

She poured a glass of wine, lit a few candles, then closed the cats in the bedroom and settled on the couch. When the phone rang, she grabbed it eagerly. "Jaxon?"

"Suzanne."

"I love the way you say my name. I love your voice."

"My voice?"

"Mmm, it's so masculine. Like dark chocolate, all rich and sinful, with just a hint of something spicy. That's it, you're chocolate-covered ginger."

"You like chocolate ginger?"

"Very much."

"Like putting it in your mouth and sucking on it?"

Aroused already, she gave a choky laugh. "As you well know."

"Oh yeah."

She tried to picture him. "Where are you? Still at the office?"

"I'm predictable."

Yes. But he was her friend and lover, not her future mate, and she'd try to be understanding. "How was your day?"

"You haven't asked if I'm wearing the boxers."

"Oh!" It hadn't occurred to her that he wouldn't. "You are, aren't you?"

"I am. And it's made for one weird day."

"You felt really uncomfortable? I'm sorry, that's not what I wanted."

"It wasn't all bad. Kind of . . . interesting, in fact."

"Tell me more."

"I'd be doing my usual lawyer stuff, but when I moved, I could feel the silk on my skin. When I looked down I could see . . ."

"I can imagine."

"Jesus, Suzanne. Don't tell me you notice, uh . . ."

"Do I look at men's crotches? News flash, Jaxon. All women do. Don't tell me you've bought into the myth that all we're interested in is the size of your brain? Or your wallet?"

He chuckled. "I'm shocked."

"You shock *way* too easily."

They shared a laugh, then he said, "The thought of you looking makes me hard."

"What are we going to do about that?"

"You tell me, lover."

"Hmm." The obvious thing was sex at his desk, but she wanted to be more creative. "Are you alone, or are others working late too?"

"Probably a couple of students in the library, buried in work."

"What's the layout of the office?"

"Lawyer offices around the outside, the fanciest being Jefferson's, the senior partner. Then there are workstations for staff. Library, two boardrooms, three smaller meeting rooms. Kitchen, photocopy room, supply room."

Silk called for fancy, didn't it? "Tell me about the senior partner's office."

"It's a huge corner one and his taste runs to antiques. Mahogany desk, couch and chairs, original artwork, his own bathroom."

"Does he keep the door locked?"

"Jesus! I can't go in there."

She sighed regretfully. "No, I guess it would be tacky, having phone sex in someone else's office."

He was quiet for a few seconds, then he said, with a mischievous undertone, "A boardroom, though."

"Now you're talking."

"There's one next to Jefferson's office that he uses when he meets with us lowly associates. Many times I've gone in there with my knees shaking, wondering if he was going to praise or criticize." He drew a loud breath. "And now I'm imagining going in next week, with memories of tonight."

"You'll have a whole new attitude."

"I'll call you back in a couple of minutes, from the boardroom."

She grinned, sipped wine and waited.

When he called back, he said, "I'm here and the door's locked."

"What's the room like?"

"Dimly lit. I've just got one lamp on a credenza turned on. Huge cherrywood table with a black border, about a dozen chairs around it. Jefferson always sits at the head."

"Go sit in that chair."

"Jefferson's chair?"

His disbelieving tone made her chuckle. "It's just a chair, it's not a throne. So, are these leather chairs, or what?"

"Soft, expensive, black leather."

"Bet it would feel nice against your skin. Almost as nice as silk."

"You want me to strip?"

"Not yet. Just your shirt. Then lean back against that soft leather."

She heard a rustle, then, "I really need to get a headset for this cell phone. Suzanne? Where are you, and what are you wearing?"

"I'm wearing the robe you gave me. And a black lace thong. I'm on the couch, the lights are off, a sandalwood-scented candle is burning."

"The couch? Wouldn't you rather be in the bedroom? Your living room is . . . classy, but is that the mood we want right now?"

"Oh!" Of course, he was picturing her at Ann's. She didn't want to deceive him. "Last weekend, that was a friend's apartment. I borrowed it."

"Borrowed? Oh, you have a roommate?"

What the hell, why not make a full confession? "No, but my place is a converted garage, across the yard from my parents' house."

He began to laugh. "Oh man, I get the picture." When he stopped laughing, he said, "I didn't think that place really suited you. It was kind of formal. Except for the cats."

Jaxon was right. Ann had great furniture, but because she so rarely had time to relax at home, or to shop, she hadn't added many personal touches.

"My own apartment definitely isn't formal. It's homey. Small, a little cluttered."

"I wish I was there." He chuckled again. "If we could arrange for your parents to go away for the weekend."

"Yeah, that would definitely be a requirement." She shook her head. "Sorry, that was a real mood-buster, but I wanted you to know. Let's get back to what we were doing."

"I won't object. Okay, lover, I'm in Jefferson's chair with my shirt off. Now what?"

She closed her eyes, trying to imagine the scene. "Acres of big cherrywood table, right? Let's pretend I'm sitting on that table, right in front of you."

"In the robe and a thong. Let the robe open a little, so it splits above and below your waist, just held together with the sash."

She parted the robe, wishing he could see how the candle-light played over her skin. Imagining his eyes on her, she felt a growing ache of arousal.

"Spread your legs." His voice was a husky whisper.

"And you take off your pants but leave the boxers on."

She heard rustling and imagined how he'd look. Red silk against that chocolate skin, his erection blatantly obvious.

"What now?" he asked.

"Touch yourself. Isn't that what you want to do?"

"I want you to touch me. But, failing that . . ."

"Caress yourself through the silk, pretend your hand is mine."

"And you put your fingers between your legs, rub gently against that tiny scrap of silk."

She had wanted to before, but held back. Now she obeyed, feeling her moist, swollen lips through the crotch of her thong. "If I was looking at you now, what would I see?"

"I'm leaning back with my legs spread out. My balls are bulging against the silk. And my cock is pushing against the fly. Almost escaping, but I won't let it until you tell me to."

Under her stroking fingers, her body swelled and throbbed as she imagined him. "Leave them on, they look so sexy."

"Take off that thong, and come sit on my lap. Facing me, in this big, soft leather chair. Feel the silk of your robe draping your back and thighs, and the silk of my boxers under your sweet ass. The only thing between our naked bodies is that one thin layer."

She stripped off the thong and closed her eyes, pressed her palm against her mound, her fingers between her thighs. "I can feel you, hard against me, with just that silky barrier between us. I want . . . Jaxon, slide your hand into the fly of those boxers and pull your cock out so I can feel it better."

"Run your hands up and down my shaft. Oh yeah, your fingers are even better than the silk."

She imagined that dark shaft, rising out of the front of his boxers, and pressed harder against her own hand. "I want you inside me," she gasped.

"Slide your fingers inside." His breath was coming in little pants. "Pretend it's me."

Her fingers were so small compared to him, but imagination transformed them.

"Lick your fingers," she told him. "Make them all wet and slippery. Then curl them around yourself and slide up and down. Pretend you're thrusting into me as I sit on your lap, riding you."

"Oh God, yes. Your pussy's so wet, so tight. I love being inside you."

Her body clenched as her hips rocked forward and back, up and down. Fingers circling, pressing and releasing. Tension rising, need growing. "Oh Jaxon, you feel so good. I'm so close."

"Me too. I can see you riding me, your breasts bouncing up and down, your skin flushing with passion. This is what I've been wanting all day, Suzanne. To be inside you." He was gasping for breath.

"No condom." Her fingers trembled as they stroked wildly. "Just you and me, naked together. I want to feel you spill into me when you come."

"I want . . ." And then he groaned loudly.

She caressed her clit and tumbled over the edge with him.

When she opened her eyes again, she was sprawled across the couch, the phone on the floor beside her. She picked it up. "Jaxon? Are you there?"

"Just barely," he gasped. "How about you?"

"Oh wow." Her body was slowly relaxing. "You're one heck of a lover, even long distance." And how she wished he was there, so they could curl up in each other's arms. Talk nonsense talk, discuss their days, drift into sleep together.

"You too."

They were both quiet for a bit, then he said, "Damn, I'd better clear out of the boardroom. The janitorial crew will be around soon."

So he was saying good night. She didn't want to let him go. She heard creaks and rustles. "Are you getting dressed?"

"Yeah."

"That's a pity."

"Want to talk some more? I could call you back from my office."

Did he want to talk, or was he just being considerate? "Sure, that would be nice. If you have the time."

"Oh yeah. I'm not ready for my Suzanne break to end yet."

She'd given him an out, and he'd chosen her over work. Feeling pleased, she used the time to release the cats and refill her wineglass.

When she picked up the phone again, he said, "Did you have a good day?"

"In addition to the great sex, you mean? Yes, really good. When I got to the clinic, a four-month-old beagle had just been admitted. Hit by a car. The mom was there and this poor little boy, sobbing his heart out."

"Must be rough when the kids come in."

"It is. Anyhow, the assistant who normally helps with surgery was sick today, so I was nominated. I felt kind of iffy, after what happened with Bondi, but it went great. At the end of the day, the pup went home with stitches and a cast. And one very happy little kid."

"Sure must feel good to play a role in something like that."

She curled against a pillow, wishing it was his chest. She went on to tell him about dinner with her folks. Then he talked about his workday and a big settlement he'd negotiated. They shared their weekend plans and, when she mentioned the usual Sunday night family get-together, he said, "I'm having dinner with my mom on Sunday too."

"You once said you don't see that much of her, but it sounds to me like it's almost every week."

"I've been seeing her more lately. There's papers and stuff to go over for the new restaurant."

"And it's more fun to do it over dinner, than at the office."

"Yeah." He paused a moment, then said, "You once asked whether she'd rather spend more time with me or have me make partner? Made me think I needed—no, wanted—to make more time for her. She's done so much for me, and she's my only family. And a good friend too."

Suzanne realized she'd never heard him mention friends. Maybe she and his mom and Tonya were it. How sad, not to have time for friends. The poor guy did suffer a high price, to pursue his goals. Trying to be supportive, she said, "I'm sure your mom understands."

"She tries, but I'm not so sure."

"Maybe you need to explain it better."

"Maybe I need to clone myself. Thank God I can get by with relatively little sleep, but I never feel like I've got everything done that I want to."

He sounded kind of down. So would she be, if she lived that way. But then, she'd never choose that kind of life.

"Will it get better, when you make partner?" she asked.

He sighed. "I'd like to think so, but probably not."

18

On Saturday, Jax's office felt cold and sterile as he sat behind tinted glass, with the world going on down below. He found himself reflecting on a number of things Suzanne had said—and those thoughts were no more comforting than his Family Friend notes.

Even though he'd never been keen on Rick's do-gooder basketball group, it still felt good to get out of the office. His pal had insisted on giving him a briefing, obviously not trusting to Jax's instincts. So it was with some trepidation that Jax approached the basketball court.

He knew the kids were mostly black—boys and a few girls—from low-income or welfare families. Without naming names, Rick had said a few of them were more than flirting with drugs, one's baby brother had been born HIV-positive, one boy's mom was a street worker who brought her johns home and one girl had dropped out of school to care for six younger siblings while her mom worked as a chambermaid. "And that," Rick had said, "is just the tip of the iceberg."

Sure enough, when Jax told them who he was and why he was there, he got a heavy dose of attitude.

"Okay," he said evenly, "you're pissed it's me and not Rick. Me too, I got better things to do today than hang with a bunch of smart-ass kids who're giving me 'tude. You got two choices here. We can all bail and find better things to do. Or"—he did a quick dribble toward the basket and tossed in a three-point field goal—"we can play some ball."

There were a few murmurs. Then one girl called out, "Y'ever play ball for real?"

"High school and college." He dribbled toward her, passed the ball, and she caught it and bounced it up and down. "Got myself into college on an athletic scholarship."

"Fuck, man," one of the boys shouted, "no fuckin' chance we're goin' to college."

Jax stole the ball from the girl, did some fancy dribbling around his legs. "Not if you don't want to."

"What the fuck you mean by that?" another boy asked. "Like, it sure the hell ain't up to us."

"Lots more things are up to you than you want to admit," Jax said. He stopped the ball, held it. "Like, whether we're playing ball today." He hefted the ball, and looked around. "Anyone with me here?"

"Yeah, me." The girl he'd spoken to earlier stepped forward.

Another girl joined her, then a couple of boys, and then they'd reached critical mass and the kids were choosing sides.

Jax reminded himself this was no high school team, these were just kids who wanted to hang out. So he tried for a mix of fun and discipline, along with some skill development.

By the time they'd all spent a couple of hours, they were sweaty, laughing, joking around, and he felt damned good himself. They were just kids behind all the tough bullshit. Kids living hard lives, trying to survive. Not so different from how he'd grown up. Except he'd had the good luck to have Darissa

Navarre as his mom, and a couple of teachers and a coach who'd helped him aim in the right direction.

Maybe he'd come back again, help Rick out. These kids needed an example, to prove they could pull themselves out of their crappy circumstances and make something of themselves. That was one thing he could give them better than his pal. Rick didn't know what it was like to get woken in the middle of the night by the crack whore next door fighting with her pimp. To go to the bathroom and find roaches—both kinds—on the floor.

When he got back to the office at five on Saturday, the work on his desk brought him back to harsh reality. "Crap." He was fooling himself, thinking he could juggle his mom, Suzanne and coaching ball, along with his job. Hadn't he learned his lesson when he was married? He was a one-trick pony. He could do his job, and do it damned well, but if he tried to add in any other responsibilities, he'd fail.

And failure sucked. Big time.

He worked until two in the morning, slept until six, then got up and started again.

Maybe it was this fucking case that was getting to him. He'd come to the conclusion that most of the Family Friend managers really were discriminating against anyone whose skin was darker than milk.

Not that the other clients he'd represented were all that much better. They polluted the environment, forced people out of their homes, drove their competition out of business.

But every client deserved a good lawyer. Yeah, he did believe that. That was the only way the justice system could work properly.

Except, it didn't really work that well. The people with more money got better lawyers than the poor folk. His firm's clients paid top dollar—and rarely lost. Look at him, putting in all these hours to get a win for Family Friend.

If he achieved his goal, he'd be another step toward partnership. And a major chain store would have free license to discriminate against more people of color.

Whoa. Now he was judging, and a lawyer wasn't supposed to do that. It was a lawyer's duty to do his best for his client. That principle had been ingrained in him since he'd taken a high school course on the legal system.

Lawyers presented the case, and judges made the decision.

If he was a judge, he'd do his damnedest to make sure that poor and otherwise disadvantaged parties got a fair shake in his courtroom.

The bench. Yeah, he could make it there, if he kept up the way he was going—building a good track record in the courts, making partner.

As a judge, he could make a difference. Affect the world in a positive way. He'd never thought too much about that concept before; he'd been too focused on the notions of success and status, but now it had a certain appeal.

Maybe it was worth putting up with all the crap now, so he'd be in a position to aim for the bench.

It was a relief to finally put the work aside late Sunday afternoon, and head over to his mother's. She'd insisted on cooking, so he stopped for wine on the way.

Her street was laid-back: sprinklers running in the yards, kids playing with dogs, the smell of barbecues. The tension in his shoulders began to unknot.

He knocked on her open back door and went into the kitchen, which smelled of cornbread. Today his mom wore jeans and a loose turquoise top and looked young and relaxed.

She gave him a warm hug. "It's good to see you. Hannah and Clare are away for the weekend and the house feels empty." She handed him an onion, a lemon and a knife. "Rings. Fairly thin."

He got to work. "What's for dinner?"

"Salmon barbecued with onion and lemon slices, served

with papaya salsa. I've got a salad in the fridge and cornbread, as you can smell, in the oven." She yanked the cork out of the bottle of wine.

"Sounds great. The best meal I've had since—"

"Our dinner at Rivoli?"

Knowing it wasn't wise, he still couldn't resist saying, "Had some good chicken satay and an interesting salad. Asian salad, she called it."

"She?" His mom kinked up an eyebrow. "The one you're not having a relationship with?"

"Suzanne." He did love saying her name. "We're getting to be friends."

He washed his hands and his mother handed him a glass. "Just friends?"

And hot lovers, but he wasn't talking about that. "Yeah. Won't go any further. We have different priorities."

She led him into the small back garden and lit the barbecue. "Let me guess, Suzanne's a nice normal girl who wants a husband and kids."

He sank into a patio chair. "You got it. She thinks I've got my priorities all wrong."

"And what do you think?"

Was his mom getting on his case too? "I've always known what I wanted. From the time I was a kid."

She took the chair beside him. "And now you're a man. Kids' dreams change. Not every little boy turns out to be a fireman or an astronaut."

"I wanted to be a success, and I still do." For some reason he felt compelled to say, "Suzanne has a different definition of success. She talks about having a balanced life."

"Mmm, mmm, I think I'd like that girl."

Damn. He leaned forward and caught one of her hands. "Be honest, Mama. Do you think I'm wrong? To want to get ahead?"

" 'Mama,' " she echoed, squeezing his hand. "You haven't called me that since we first got here, and you learned that California kids said, 'Mom.' You were sure a fast learner, Jax. But once you got an idea stuck in your head, seems like you never let go of it."

"I inherited stubborn from you," he muttered. "Are you saying you don't want me to make partner, then maybe be a judge or a politician?"

She tugged her hand free. "I'm saying no such thing. That's your choice to make, son. You follow your own dreams, not your old mama's dreams."

"What are your dreams?"

Her brown eyes met his. "I don't think you want to be asking that."

"Yes, I do."

She bit her lip, then lifted her chin. "Grandbabies."

"Oh . . ." He let his breath out in a whistle. "You're always teasing me. I didn't realize you were serious."

"I once dreamed of having a bunch of kids myself. But when I married your stepfather, he wanted to wait. Guess he was trying me out, not sure he wanted to commit."

And he'd always had problems with Jax—a little black stepson—and likely wasn't sure he wanted to father a mixed-race child.

"After we split up," she went on, "I didn't have time to think about anything other than keeping food in our mouths. Now it's too late for me, but then you married Tonya and I hoped . . ."

Hell. "I can't do everything, Mom. Now you're talking grandkids. Look what a bad job I did at marriage. I'm not a superman, I can't do it all. D'you realize I average more than fourteen hours a day at work, seven days a week? You ought to know what it's like. You used to work two jobs."

Even as he said the words, he realized there was a flaw in his argument.

"I did it for you," she said, chin raised. "So you'd have every opportunity to be what you wanted to be."

"I know. You told me I could be anything a white guy could be, and even better. That's all I'm trying to do."

"You're out to prove something, I know. But maybe it's time to think again just what it is you want to set about being. A superstar lawyer, or a happy, satisfied man."

"I am happy. Getting ahead makes me happy." Damn, he was sounding defensive.

"If that's what makes you happy," she said wearily, "guess I haven't done a very good job of being a mother. I meant to encourage you, help you believe in yourself, not to blinker you so's all you could see was some kind of success track."

He wasn't about to argue, not with his mom. "Sorry. I've let you down."

She stared at him a moment, then shook her head. "No!" She gripped his shoulders. "Don't think that. Oh son, I shouldn't have said those things. Look, the grandkids thing was *my* dream. A selfish one, I guess. Maybe I'm just as blinkered as you."

Were those tears in her eyes?

"But damn," she said, "I'd be one fine grandma, and you'd make a wonderful dad if you—" She broke off, released his shoulders, and went to put the salmon on the grill. He saw her raise a hand, like she was wiping her eyes.

"If I what?"

She stood still for a moment, then slowly turned to face him. Her gaze met his across the tiny patio. "Find what you're looking for. Believe in your heart that you're as good as any other man."

"I am!"

"I know that, son. Are you sure you do?"

* * *

On Monday night, Suzanne chose Greek again, this time opting for Athene's, where the Foursome could sit outside in the sun. They ordered wine and their usual favorite here, a huge dinner platter for two that was plenty big for the four of them.

As they waited for the food to arrive, Suzanne gave her friends an update.

"Okay," Ann said, "you're now officially in over your head, Suze."

"I'm not. I think it's wonderful that we've become friends as well as lovers."

Rina touched her hand. "You're a great friend. You're so generous and caring."

"Thanks."

"Caring," Ann said, "is the operative word."

"So? So I care about him. As a friend." Suzanne took a sip of wine. "That's all. Just like I care about you three."

"You're not thinking of having red-hot sex with us, are you?" Jenny teased.

"Sex is sex and friendship is friendship." Suzanne tilted her chin defiantly.

"Except when the person you're having sex with is someone you care about," Ann said.

"I'm *not* falling in love with him."

"Did anyone say that?" Jenny demanded.

"No, but you're all hinting."

Rina tugged on her hand, calling for her attention. "Suze? If Jaxon wasn't a workaholic, if he wanted marriage and kids, wouldn't he be the perfect man for you?"

"Uh . . . He lives in San Francisco."

"He's a lawyer," Ann said. "If he wanted to, he could practice here. He might have to article again, and do the Professional Legal Training Course, but it'd take less than a year. Or you—much as I hate the thought—could be a vet down there. If you got married, you could work in each other's countries. For heaven's sake, Suze, this is the twenty-first century. Distance isn't a reason to break up."

"Break up? We're not dating. We're just . . ."

"Being friends and having dynamite sex," Jenny finished. "I really want to believe you, Suzie Q."

"I'm—" Suzanne broke off as their waiter brought a huge platter of food.

By the time they'd all dished out a few things to start with—with the by now obligatory joke about calamari and cock rings—the conversation had turned to Rina's troubles with the too-friendly father of one of her clarinet students.

Suzanne had trouble concentrating. Sure, there'd been a point where she might have fallen for Jaxon, but once she'd learned that their priorities were poles apart, she had pulled back emotionally. Hadn't she?

If so, why was she wearing lacy bras and thongs to work, and feeling like sexy Suzanne had inhabited her body full-time? Why did she think of Jaxon dozens of times every day?

The sexual cravings she could understand. After all, sex with Jaxon was fabulous.

It was the other cravings that disturbed her. Why was he the first person she wanted to tell when something good happened? Why did she long for his shoulder when she was sad? In the past, she'd turned to family or friends. Now, Jaxon's name was the first to enter her mind.

Maybe she needed to pull back even more. Before she really did get in over her head.

19

_____

In his office, trying to work, Jax glanced at his watch for the umpteenth time. He'd known Suzanne was out with her girl-friends when he left a message on her machine. When would she get home, and would she return his call tonight?

It was almost ten when his cell rang. "Suzanne. Thanks for calling."

"Happy to. What's up? You, big boy?"

Oh God, she thought he'd called for sex. "No, sorry. I just called to talk."

"Sure, that's great."

"It happened," he said slowly. He'd called because he wanted to talk to her about it, but now he felt hesitant. "Jefferson offered me a partnership today."

Her squeal almost made him drop his cell. "Oh my God! Jaxon, that's fantastic. Congratulations! Wow, you weren't ex-pecting it so soon, were you? Oh God, I wish I was there, I'd bring champagne. Tell me all about it."

He'd left the message hours ago, but still hadn't figured out what to say. "I met with him this morning, to discuss a big case I'm working on."

Before he could go on, she said, "And he was so impressed with how you were handling it, he made you a partner? Jaxon, you must be thrilled."

"Well . . ."

"Come on, don't be modest. Tell me everything. Did he call you into his office?"

For the first time that day, he smiled. "It was our Friday-night boardroom. He took his usual chair and I remembered sitting there in those red boxers, imagining you on my lap. Imagining myself buried deep inside you and—"

"But what did he say? Come on, Jaxon, this isn't the time to be thinking about sex. Tell me, I'm dying of curiosity."

And he'd rather think about sex. Or anything else.

Jax remembered how he'd told Jefferson about the problems he was running into with the Family Friend managers and his doubts they'd stand up to cross-examination and not blurt out something to incriminate themselves.

"Are you saying you can't prepare them thoroughly?" Jefferson had said coldly.

"No, of course not." He tried to speak confidently, to not let his frustration come through. "I'm saying I could prepare them for days and some would still be loose cannons. They aren't very bright and don't have much self-control. If they're baited, they'll lose their tempers, say things they shouldn't."

"Hmm." Jefferson leaned back and steepled his fingers. "What about drugs?"

Had he heard correctly? "Excuse me?"

"There are drugs that will help keep them from flying off the handle."

Jefferson wanted him to drug their client's witnesses? That couldn't be ethical.

He opened his mouth to say that, then stopped himself. Wait, think this through. Jefferson wouldn't ask him to violate professional ethics.

Okay, a lawyer's first priority was his client's best interests. Really, it was just a matter of how you framed things. Slowly, he said, "If a witness seems anxious about taking the stand, it's reasonable to suggest he might want to take medication to help him stay calm."

"Precisely."

His mind racing, Jax said, "It might be even better if the CEO of Family Friend recommended it to him." In other words, take drugs or you're fired.

Jefferson nodded. "Good thinking."

Jax had asked to see Jefferson in hopes of getting some useful guidance. This wasn't exactly what he'd had in mind.

Crap, he was being a wuss. Lawyers played hardball. If he couldn't stand the heat, he'd never make it.

Jefferson leaned forward. "You know what to do?"

"Of course." And to hell with the fact he didn't particularly like it.

"You're doing good work for Jefferson Sparks."

"Thank you."

"In fact, I think it's time."

"Time for . . ." A bigger office? A raise?

"Partnership."

"P . . ." After years of wanting this, his dumbfounded lips couldn't form the word.

Jefferson rose, so he did too. "You've worked your tail off, Jax. Put in long hours, brought in clients, been loyal to Jefferson Sparks. It's time that loyalty was rewarded." He stuck out his hand.

Automatically, Jax took it and they shook firmly.

Loyalty. Was he being bribed to do something that cut close

to the line of what was ethical? Or should he take Jefferson's words at face value?

"I'm flattered." He managed, just barely, to speak without stuttering. "I've been working for this, but hadn't expected it so soon." And he'd rather have earned it on hard work and expertise, not loyalty.

"You've earned it. And will continue to earn it." Jefferson turned toward the door, then looked back. "I'll talk to the other partners, put something formal in writing, have it to you in the next couple of days so you can review it."

"Fine." He stared at the other man's back as he walked out the door. Jefferson had made the offer on his own, without discussing it with the other partners. Spontaneously? As a result of their discussion about the Family Friend managers?

"Jaxon?" Suzanne's voice pierced through the memories.

"Sorry, I was just replaying it."

"Well, do it out loud, for heaven's sake!"

Much as he might have valued her perspective, he couldn't tell her. The meeting had been a strategy session, and to reveal what he and Jefferson had said would be a clear breach of client confidentiality. Not to mention, disloyal to his firm.

"We talked about some details of the case, discussed the appropriate strategy. Then he said I'd been doing good work and was loyal to the firm, and it was time to offer me partnership."

"You sound so flat. Aren't you just bubbling with excitement? Shouldn't you be out celebrating? Oh, Jaxon, what did your mom say?"

"I haven't told her yet."

"Good God, what are you waiting for? Isn't this, like, the most important thing that's ever happened in your life?"

She sounded so thrilled for him, and she was right. There'd been other landmarks in his career—being accepted to law school, graduating, getting articles at a primo firm and then being kept on when he was called to the bar—and when they'd occurred, he'd been jumping up and down for joy.

"I guess I don't want to spread the news until—"

"Until you see it in writing?" she broke in. "That makes sense. But how can you keep it secret? Aren't you just dying to tell?"

Yes, and no.

Truth was, he'd already told someone else. Rick. Should've known better.

There he'd been, bursting with a—yeah, obnoxious—desire to tell another lawyer he'd made it.

And sure, Rick had said, "Hey, congratulations, man, you're getting what you wanted." But then, in the next breath, he'd said, "Guess that means you'll be too busy to come out to b-ball any Saturday soon."

"Guess so." Reality was, as junior partner, there'd be a ton of pressure to prove himself.

"Too bad. Ran into one of the kids—Mike, that tall skinny guy with the tatts and shaved head?—in the courthouse this morning and he said things went okay."

Okay? Yeah, that'd be high praise from one of those boys. "What was he doing in the courthouse?"

"Possession charge."

What were these kids thinking, throwing away their futures? Problem was, no one had taught them to dream, and how to take the steps to realize a dream. "You talk to him about that?"

"As much as he'd let me. Mike says a guy like me doesn't know what it's like. And the truth is, I don't."

The unspoken words hung between them. Jax did know. He'd have more credibility with the kid.

After a moment, Rick said, "So, anyhow, congrats again. We'll break out the champagne when you come over for dinner."

Champagne. For celebrations. Sparkly, fizzy, vibrant. Why the hell did he feel so flat?

"Jaxon?" Suzanne's voice broke into his thoughts. "I know you must have a million things to do. I'll let you go now."

"No, it's not that. I just . . . yeah, guess I have a lot on my mind. But I do want to talk to you." Trouble was, he couldn't figure out what he wanted to say, his mind was such a mixed-up mess.

"I'm not sure I'll accept." The words came out softly, but his voice didn't waver.

"What?" she screeched. "What are you saying?" Then her voice calmed a bit. "Oh, you're thinking of negotiating better terms? Isn't that risky?"

"It would be. But no, that's not it. I'm just . . . not sure I want this."

There, he'd said it out loud.

Silence at her end. Then, "I don't understand. I thought partnership was the next step to realizing your dream."

"Me too."

"So . . . ?"

"My mother pointed something out to me. About kids' dreams. They change."

"They . . . Huh?"

"I know, that's not what happened for you. You wanted to be a vet and you still do, and that's great. But other kids, like my mama said, they want to be firefighters, astronauts. Then they grow up and decide on something completely different."

"Sure. But you're like me. Your dream hasn't changed."

"Maybe it should. Maybe the price is too high."

"The price?"

"I'd always thought that, when they offered me partnership, I'd jump for joy. But today, when Jefferson said the words, I felt stunned, more than happy. Hell, you were more excited than I was."

"Because I thought it was what you wanted."

"And you care about what I want. Don't you?"

"Of course. We're friends."

He took a deep breath. This was why he'd called. This woman made him think, deeply, the way no one had before. Made him go beyond the superficial and figure out what he really felt.

"Is that all we are, Suzanne? Besides being lovers, I mean. Seems to me we've grown closer than that, even if it's been about the oddest relationship in history. E-mail and phone calls and kinky sex. But we've learned a lot about each other, and you've made me think about who I am. What kind of person I want to be."

"You're a fine person. Being a partner won't change that."

Maybe it would. "Thanks for your confidence in me. But I've been putting work ahead of people. That's hurt people I care about."

"You've always had time for me, Jaxon. If I needed a shoulder to cry on, you gave it to me."

"Yeah, well, we're friends." No, that was a cop-out, given how he was starting to feel about this woman. "For me, it's more than friendship," he admitted.

"For me too." Her voice was shaky.

Yeah, it was tough laying your heart on the line, when both of them knew they were such different people.

"Coached basketball for a couple hours Saturday," he heard himself saying.

"B . . . Basketball?"

She must think he'd lost it, leaping from subject to subject. "Yeah. Inner-city type kids. This guy I know normally does it, but he was sick so I filled in."

"That's great. I'm sure those kids really benefited from an activity like that."

"Yeah." And so had he.

"I bet it's pretty satisfying for you and you friend."

"Uh, yeah." Could she read his mind?

"More satisfying than practicing law?" she asked softly.

Damn. "More satisfying than some files. But I'm a lawyer. That's what I've trained for and I'm not giving it up."

"No, sorry, I didn't mean to suggest that. I was just wondering what things you find the most rewarding."

He grinned. "Yeah, okay, guess I'd like to go help Rick out from time to time." He'd like to, but partnership would pretty much preclude it. So where did that leave him?

"Rick? That's your friend?"

"Guy I know from college ball and law school."

"Sounds like a good guy."

Her kind of guy. "He is."

"Jaxon, what would happen if you turned down the partnership? Wouldn't Jefferson be mad?"

Furious. "It'd pretty much end my career at Jefferson Sparks," he said, feeling a bit of sadness, but more like a weight was trying to lift off his shoulders. "But God, then I'd be looking for work." For a job that'd keep paying his mom's mortgage.

"I'm guessing you're a pretty good lawyer. A firm would be lucky to get you."

"Thanks." He sighed. "Not sure where I'd look. I've been doing the same kind of work since I started."

"Do I hear a 'but'?"

Oh yeah, he was getting what he'd come to her for. Lots of painful self-examination.

"Maybe it's not the kind of work I want to do anymore. Maybe I don't want to work for that kind of client."

She was quiet for a moment, then said softly, "Those basketball kids really got to you?"

Damn, but this woman knew him. "Them, my mom, Tonya,

Rick. You. If you all think I'm nuts, maybe I should start listening."

"Listen to your own heart. Find the dream you want to follow, then go for it, Jaxon."

Just what he'd been thinking, about those b-ball kids. "You make it sound so easy."

"You've done it before. The thing is, maybe your heart's changed course, and your mind hasn't been paying attention."

Getting through the next day was agony for Suzanne.

After she'd talked to the girls last night at Athene's, she'd thought of pulling back. Then Jaxon had called, and he'd thrown her completely off balance. So off balance she didn't even want to talk to her friends about it.

When she'd left home that morning, she'd picked up the piece of abalone shell that sat on her bedside table, the one he'd given her at Spanish Banks, and tucked it in her jeans pocket. For good luck?

What if he did reevaluate his life, and decide on different priorities?

What did she want him to decide?

Was it possible they were falling in love?

Suzanne moved around the clinic in a daze. At morning break, she went into the washroom and splashed cold water on her flushed face. Life had become uncertain, and frightening.

How did she really feel about Jaxon? He was a great man, but he wasn't her dad.

Well, thank heavens! No wonder she'd never envisioned a passionate marriage, if she'd planned on marrying a clone of her father.

Not that she was anywhere near ready to be thinking about marriage. She still had vet school to finish.

One thing she had learned, though. Maybe sexy Suzanne

and the sensible twin weren't two completely different people. Her sister and even her mom managed to integrate their sexy sides into their day-to-day lives, so why couldn't she?

And why was she so rigid, thinking she shouldn't get serious about a guy yet? If Mr. Cleaver came along ahead of schedule, she'd be a fool to send him packing.

But Jaxon couldn't be Mr. Cleaver, could he? He lived in the States. He had his mother down in San Francisco, his ex-wife, his friend Rick. Those basketball kids. She had her family, the Foursome, her friends at school and the clinic.

Could two such different people ever hope to build a future?

Or were they really that different after all?

She alternated between hope and fear.

Why had he pushed her into admitting she felt more for him than friendship? Would her feelings factor into his decision? If he accepted the partnership, he'd likely have less time to see her.

Even her animal patients couldn't distract her from wondering what Jaxon was thinking. When he would decide about the partnership. When he'd call to let her know.

She was wrestling with Bly, a huge parrot, trying to get a pill down his throat, when Trish called from reception.

"What?" she called back in frustration. "I'm busy right now."

"There's someone here to see you."

"They'll have to wait. I've got a psychotic parrot trying to bite my finger off."

She heard laughter. Trish's high, ringing giggle and a deeper, darker, richer sound. It couldn't be . . .

She thrust Bly into a cage, scrubbed her hands at the sink and dashed into the reception area.

"Jaxon!"

There he stood, in a grey business suit and white shirt, a tie knotted loosely around his neck. Jaxon, the lawyer, and here she was wearing faded jeans, a Snoopy T-shirt and a lab coat dotted with cat spit, dog pee and parrot shit. Suzanne, the almost-vet.

Oh yeah, they were *very* different.

Except, she *was* wearing a thong, and a lacy demi-bra. And he *was* smiling as if she was the most beautiful, desirable sight in the world.

She looked into his eyes and suddenly it was like the first day, on the beach on Crete. She could almost feel magic dust settle on them as they reached for each other's hands. And then she'd ripped off that messy lab coat and they were out the door, walking down Fourth Avenue.

"What are you doing here?" Her heart was racing so fast she could hardly find words.

He handed her a sturdy plastic bag.

She peeped inside. "Champagne." Her heart sank, but she forced a smile. "Jaxon, you accepted the partnership. Congratulations. I'm so happy for you."

He was shaking his head, smiling. "Nope. Turned it down. I knew that would mean I had to leave the firm, so I gave notice."

"Oh my God." She grabbed his hand tighter. He'd lost his job, his income, his old dream, all in one day. "What are you going to do?"

"This guy I know—this friend, Rick—has his own practice. He says he'd take me on, if I promise to coach basketball from time to time."

"That sounds great." And it did, except where did that leave her? Would Jaxon have any time to see her?

"I'm thinking it's time you spent some time in San Francisco," he said. "The weekends you came down, you wouldn't mind if I took a couple hours out to coach ball, would you? You could shop, or even come along and watch. Rick would love to meet you." He grinned. "And my mom will go crazy over you."

He wanted to include her in his life. "Oh my God," she said again.

He tugged her hand, then pulled her into his arms for a searing kiss.

When they broke apart, he said, "I know it's early in our relationship, and there's lots of things to figure out, what with our careers and living in different cities. But what I do know is, we have something special, Suzanne."

"Yes," she agreed breathlessly. "Yes, we do. When I saw you in the clinic, when I looked into your eyes—"

"It was like Crete," he broke in. "The connection between us is too strong to be denied. So let's stop trying." He laughed. "You know, we owe a lot to those Champagne Rules."

"We do?"

"When we realized we had more fun breaking them than keeping them, that's when our relationship really began."

She smiled back. "Time for a new set of rules, I guess."

"Hell, let's throw out all the rules. Let's just go for it. All of it."

She gazed up at him. The sexiest, most handsome man she'd ever seen. Her red-hot lover and her dear friend.

Was he Mr. Cleaver? Only time would tell.

She began to smile. "Yes, let's go for it. Whatever 'it' turns out to be."

"Can you get off work early?"

"I'm betting Trish figures I'm already gone. I'll pop my head back in and confirm it, and get my purse and keys."

He pulled her back toward the clinic. "Hurry, then."

"Aren't you coming in with me?"

He glanced down. "Like this? I don't think so."

He flicked his suit jacket aside so she could see his erection pressing against the grey trousers. And then he leaned down to whisper in her ear. "Suzanne? I'm wearing the boxers."

"I'll be right back!"

"And then we'll find a hotel room, and open that bottle, and toast the end of the Champagne Rules."

Acknowledgments

I've been waiting a while to be published in book-length fiction, so I have a lot of people to thank.

The first is Nick Franson, for giving me Natalie Goldberg's *Writing Down the Bones* and helping me discover what I really wanted to do with my life: be a writer. And for believing and making me believe I could do it.

My mom, Sylvia Hart, and my stepdad, Ted Hart, were amazing, offering constant encouragement and never suggesting I find a more sensible—and lucrative—way of using my law degree. I'm just sorry my mom didn't live long enough to see my first book in print, but I'm thrilled to share this moment with Ted.

Huge thanks to my partner, Doug Arnold, not only for having faith in me but also for suffering the day-to-day trials and tribulations of life with a writer. I wish I could say things will be easier now I'm published, but the truth is, I'm going to be spending even more time off in a dream world with my imaginary friends.

Special thanks to my fantastic critique group, Betty Allan, Michelle Hancock and Nazima Ali, for their helpful insights, their fun and stimulating company, and their amazing tolerance for reading and analyzing yet another sex scene. I couldn't have done it without them. Thanks too to fellow Kensington author

Nancy Warren, who's been a friend, colleague and inspiration for many years.

One of the joys of being a writer is finding a community of like-minded eccentrics, and I'm blessed and honored to be a member of the Greater Vancouver Chapter and the Vancouver Island Chapter of Romance Writers of America.

Last, but absolutely not least, I want to thank my editor Hilary Sares and Kensington Publishing Corp. for taking a chance on a new writer and making my dream come true.

I invite my readers to visit my website at *www.susanlyons.ca*, e-mail me at *susan@susanlyons.ca* or write c/o PO Box 73523, Downtown RPO, Vancouver, BC, Canada V6E 4L9.

WELCOME TO PARADISE. IS IT HOT ENOUGH FOR YOU?

Stretch out on the sizzling sands of Pleasure Beach, the perfect escape from reality—and the gateway to your wildest, wettest seaside fantasies . . .

Pretender
McCall Lindsey needs a place to lay low—and no haven could be more alluring than Pleasure Beach, where a case of mistaken identity gives her the chance to unleash her inner bad girl with her gorgeous next-door neighbor—a man who won't rest until he explores every inch of her eager body . . .

Same Time Next Week
Kinsey Carlyle says no to her straitlaced boyfriend's marriage proposal. But when a no-strings-attached weekend with a rough-and-tumble cowboy on Pleasure Beach leads to days of bedroom bliss, Kinsey can't say anything but *yes . . . yes . . . yes . . .*

Jack of Hearts
His vacation house on Pleasure Beach is a peaceful retreat for cardiologist Jack McMillan—until the best friend of his ex's sister moves in next door. Radio talk show host Royce St. Clair has the voice of an angel . . . along with a body to tempt the devil himself. And as luck would have it, she's ready, willing, and more than able to help Jack indulge his wickedest desires . . .

Leave your inhibitions in the shade and bask in the heat of Pleasure Beach, where endless summer means endless ecstasy . . .

Her lawyer turned and strode away without a backward glance, obviously confident his orders would be followed.

And, of course, they would. She was great at following orders.

"Who'd believe you're a woman on the run?" she asked her reflection in the rearview mirror. "McCall Lindsey, honor student, Girl Scout, all-around boring and blah." Even the highlights she'd recently added to her shoulder-length, wren-brown hair hadn't helped. Instead, they gave her the look of a demented skunk.

With a sigh, she headed her beat-up Escort toward the parking lot exit. The air conditioner spit out stale-smelling, hot air while she waited for a break in traffic.

She blinked back tears. "How did you get yourself into this mess?"

Fund-raising may not have been a career she'd aspired to, but she'd been danged good at it—well, until Sunshine International charged her with embezzling the multimillion-dollar funds from the Summers Group and fired her. Now it was a safe bet she'd never work in that field again.

Seeing a break in traffic, she pushed the little accelerator to the floor mat and zipped into the flow, ignoring the squeal of brakes and honking of several horns.

Against the steering wheel, the key her lawyer had tucked into her hand bit the tender flesh. A week at the beach might not be too bad. Labor Day was over. Maybe a little seclusion was just what she needed. Time to regroup and gather her thoughts about what she'd do with the rest of her life. She gave a watery laugh.

Or to plan her suicide.

Derek Summers broke his pencil in half, then threw it at his legal advisor.

"Hank, you told me it was a legitimate and worthy cause, a good tax write-off. I hate publicity! You know that! That idiot attorney has subpoenaed me! Me!" He threw his hands up. "I don't even do interviews. No way in hell am I appearing on every tabloid by going into a courtroom!"

"Now, don't get your shorts in a wad, Derek," Hank Connors soothed. "I'll see what I can do about getting you out of it."

Derek regarded the man who'd been legal counsel for the Summers Group for three generations. The man looked older than dirt, but if he said he'd do something, it usually got done.

"Why don't you go home, now, Mr. Summers?" Hazel, his almost equally ancient secretary, asked from across the room. Hazel had been Derek's father's secretary and knew more than he'd ever care to know about the family business. "Have you taken your blood pressure medication today?"

"Damnit, Hazel! Don't coddle me! And for your information, I went off the pills almost a year ago. So stop asking. I'm fine."

The two employees exchanged looks, which set him off again. "I saw that! You two think I'm overreacting."

"Mr. Summers, calm down." Hazel flipped through the appointment book she always carried. "You were scheduled to leave for your beach house this morning." Through the magnified lenses of her rhinestone-encrusted glasses, her brown eyes stared meaningfully at him. "Why don't you head on out before the traffic gets any worse?"

His shoulders slumped, all fight gone. "Whatever." He jumped to his feet and jerked his navy sportscoat from the back of his desk chair. "When I get back next week I expect you to have things worked out, Hank."

"I'm already on it, boss," Hank assured him. "I'm checking into the background of the prime suspect." He looked down at the paper in his hand. "A Miss McCall Lindsey."

McCall's *service-engine* light blinked on by the time her car wheezed to a stop beside the rental beach house on South Padre Island. Trying to ignore its possible implications, she focused on the house looming above her.

Made of redwood and glass and surrounded by decks on each level, it was easily three times the size of the little house she rented in the Heights section of Houston.

Her ring snagged the side of her best skirt when she climbed out of her car. Dang. Why hadn't she changed before heading out?

She looked down at her hand. Her eyes filled with tears. The miniscule diamond was missing from the promise ring Joel had given her three years ago.

It hadn't been all that valuable, and Joel had long since moved on and even married someone else. But that tiny gold ring had meant something to her. It meant someone had once thought enough about her to promise to think about proposing. Not much in the grand scheme of things, but it had been all she'd had.

And now it was gone. Along with everything else in her life.

Listless, she tugged the ring from her finger and stuck it in the zipper compartment of her nylon wallet. When she found her next job, she would see about replacing the stone. After all, besides the diamond studs Hattie Brubaker gave her, it was her only other piece of jewelry that was worth anything.

The handle broke off her rolling suitcase when she attempted to drag it from her cramped trunk.

"Great," she grumbled "No job, no husband or even a significant other, no good jewelry and now this. On a scale of one to ten, I'm a minus."

Unzipping the bag enough to slip the tips of her fingers inside, she dragged it through the sand toward the steep steps that led from the parking area to the back deck. When that failed, she yanked on the suitcase until she came to the steps.

Drag, plop. Drag, plop. Dang suitcase wasn't going to defeat her. It was slow going, but she finally reached the deck.

"Wow." Waves rolled to shore, their sound soothing her. In the distance sea gulls called. A faint tinge of pink showed on the horizon.

She looked around the spacious deck. In the far corner, closest to the sliding doors, sat a hot tub that would easily hold six adults. She peered into the churning water, impressed by the thoroughness of her lawyer's preparation.

"Death by hot tub. . . . No." She shook her head. "All that hot bubbling water would bloat my body. It would be nice to leave a good-looking corpse."

After fumbling with the key, the heavy glass door slid open on its well-oiled track.

The cool darkness of the interior greeted her. When her eyes adjusted, she took in the decor—well, what there was of it.

The large room held an array of massive furniture, some leather, all overstuffed. Great fieldstone fireplace, although who would build a fire at the beach? She shrugged and walked into the kitchen.

"Nice," she noted, liking the way the sunset gleamed off the stainless-steel appliances. "Good to have in case I'm overcome by a Martha Stewart moment."

Dragging her suitcase to the curved staircase, she dragged the bag up the stairs until she walked into what had to be the master suite.

"Oh my gosh." Her fingers released their death grip on top of the suitcase. It fell with a soft thud, spilling its contents across the plush sea-blue carpeting.

The curved outer wall was entirely glass. She picked up a remote control and pushed a button. With a soft whir, the glass parted, allowing the surf to echo, giving the illusion of being held within a giant seashell.

The huge, round brass bed beckoned her. Taking an uncharacteristic hop backward, she sprawled on it, rubbing her hands and now bare feet against the raw silk spread. The warm dusky-peach color of the spread glowed in the impending sunset.

Feeling hedonistic, she rose to strip off her sensible business suit and fling it across the room. Her serviceable white cotton bra and underwear followed. Of course she would just have to pick them up and put them away later, but for right now, she would live her fantasy.

Being a good girl never got her anywhere. It was time to discover her inner wild woman.

She opened the bottle of sleeping pills Hattie insisted she bring with her and popped two in her mouth. So what if they always made her sleep like the dead? What did she have to wake up for, anyway? There was no job to get to, nothing and no one to meet.

Naked, she padded to the open window and looked over the stretch of beach to the Gulf. Below her was the edge of the lower deck, some rocks and sand. Lots of sand.

"Death by sand diving. . ." She rubbed her arms and stepped back. "Too abrasive," she said to the sunset.

A huge yawn escaped her. Stretching, she walked to the bed and climbed onto the sinfully decadent spread, wondering if it had satin sheets.

She yawned again. The long drive caught up to her, causing her muscles to ache, eyelids to droop. The sound of the surf beckoned her. A sunset swim before the pills took effect would be great.

Maybe she'd just rest a few minutes before she put on her bathing suit.

Her hand stroked her nudity from breast to hip and she smiled. No one would believe goody two-shoes McCall Lindsey was experiencing her wild side.

"Yeah," Derek spoke into the mouthpiece of his cellular headset as he flipped on his turn signal. "I'm turning in right now." His Porsche Boxster purred to a stop in the garage of his beach house. He turned off the ignition and scrubbed his face with one hand while he stretched. "Jack, I appreciate the thought, but I'm beat. I had a long drive and traffic was a bitch."

He stepped out of the car and popped the trunk. "My birthday isn't until next week, but thanks." He set down his suitcase and sighed. "What's the hurry about me getting the birthday present you left at your place?"

A push of his remote button turned on the exterior and interior lighting of his house. A soft click told him the doors unlocked as well.

He dropped his suitcase inside the back entry hall, then punched the LOCK button. "Okay, if it's that important, I'll head over there now and pick it up before the renter gets there. The master bedroom. Got it." He walked back toward the car. "Key still in the same place? Thanks, pal, I'll give you a call when I wake up."

Another beep unlocked his car door and he threw in the phone before heading down the beach toward his friend's place to pick up his gift.

"Oh, Jack, my man," Derek whispered from the doorway of his friend's master suite. "You have outdone yourself this time."

When his fiancée broke their engagement, Derek had been relieved. Unfortunately, his friends thought he was desolate and took up a crusade to find him a replacement.

All had failed.

Jack was the only friend who hadn't tried to fix him up over the past year, for which he was profoundly grateful.

Derek rested his shoulder against the door jamb and grinned. And now Jack had given him . . . this . . . for his birthday.

He'd been celibate for way too long. Jack must've known he was ready to experience something new.

To walk on the wild side.

His eyes caressed the nude perfection of the woman spread before him on Jack's *orgy* bed while he stripped with more eagerness than he'd felt in longer than he cared to remember. He snagged a handful of condoms from the mess on the floor on his way to collect his birthday gift.

Good old Jack, he thought as he climbed up on the bed with his personal nymphette.

He bought me a hooker.

Don't miss this sneak peek at Susan Lyons' HOT IN
HERE. Our hero: a firefighter calendar model,
Mr. February. Also known as Scott. Also known as *hot*.
Coming from Kensington in August 2006 . . .

1

Backstage, pacing, Scott Jackman heard the raunchy music swell, the crowd whoop and roar in appreciation. He groaned. What the fuck had he got himself into?

Who'd have guessed that his lifelong ambition to be a firefighter would land him here? Yeah, he'd known that, as a rookie, he'd be the butt of a bunch of stupid jokes. But if he'd ever figured he'd have to wriggle his ass across a stage in front of hundreds of screaming women—not to mention gay guys, the gang from good old Firehall 11, and his little sister—he might have . . .

Hell no. Whatever his parents might wish, he'd never been cut out for the farming life in Chilliwack.

He was a firefighter, through and through. And firefighters were tough. If he could risk his life in smoke and flames, he could bloody well get through three minutes on stage.

Scott had made the first cut, based on photos submitted by a couple hundred guys. He was one of twenty-four finalists for twelve firefighter calendar spots. If he didn't win a month, the guys at the firehall would never let him forget it.

Beyond the curtains, the last notes of music were swallowed up in a thunder of applause. Crap. The audience was voting with their hands, feet and voices, and it sounded like this guy was sure to make the calendar.

The curtains parted and a panting, laughing man burst through. He'd gone out wearing full firefighter turnout gear and was back minus the helmet and jacket. His muscled upper body gleamed with oil and sweat, and he was hauling his turnout pants up over leopard-print briefs. There was a fire hose slung over his shoulder. God knows what he'd done with the hose on stage.

Whatever it was, the audience sure the hell seemed to have got off on it.

Shit, shit, shit. What had he been thinking, trusting his little sister Lizzie to put together his act? Tap? Fucking tap dance? In front of an audience that clearly wanted raunch?

Was it too late to change his plan? There were still a few people ahead of him, he had time to work up a new routine.

Nah. Lizzie'd kill him. She'd put a lot of time into coaching him.

But the guys at the station would rib him to death if he made a fool of himself.

'Course, it wasn't like they didn't already.

The next competitor strutted toward the curtain, wearing turnout gear and—oh, great—carrying an axe. His music started up. More of that hip-grinding rhythm.

Scott groaned again, then clapped the headphones of his iPod to his ears and cranked up the music Lizzie had chosen. He closed his eyes, settled into the beat, imagined the steps, riffs, the way his hips and arms would move to the music. The sultry notes of the sax began to heat his blood. Man, this kind of music always made him feel like sex.

Speaking of which . . . If he focused on the music, went out and sold his number and made the cut for the calendar, there was a damned good chance he'd be going home tonight with one of those screaming firefighter groupies. Preferably one with a killer bod and long blond hair.

The other women were clapping but Jenny Yuen lifted her digital camera and snapped a final shot of the latest . . . *contender* had to be the only word, the way the guy'd clasped his hands together over his head like a victorious wrestler. His body was a wrestler's too. Gross!

"Any guy with overblown muscles like that has to have a tiny dick," she told her girlfriends. "That's why he brought an axe; it's his penis substitute."

The Caprice nightclub, packed with a few hundred very warm bodies, was a noise machine. Everyone was yelling and Jenny, at five foot nothing in her kitten-heeled pink sandals, had to scream even louder. Fortunately she never had a problem pumping up the volume.

The club was set up with tiny tables, packed closely together. Jenny'd come early and made her case that a midget reporter doing a cover story needed a down-front vantage point to shoot photos. As a result, she'd scored a primo table for her and her best gal-pals, the Awesome Foursome.

"Isn't it balls that shrink from steroids?" Suzanne Brennan shouted back.

The applause finally died down and they all settled back in their seats.

"Yeah, it's testicles," Ann Montgomery said. A lawyer, she was a stickler for accuracy. "And a reduced sperm rate, and erectile dysfunction."

"Oh yeah?" Jenny said. "Could've sworn it was dicks."

"Doesn't exactly matter, does it?" Rina Goldberg was the fourth member of the Foursome. Her naturally soft voice had grown hoarse from all the screaming. She took a sip of her lemon drop martini. "The guy's not going to be much use to a woman, either way."

"True enough," Jenny said, as her mind flagged a possible story idea. Obviously there were a lot of misconceptions about the side-effects of steroids, and this was stuff young women—and men—really needed to know. Like, if the people in this audience knew the truth, would any of them be cheering for Mr. Muscle-Bound? How could a guy be sexy, if unwrapping his package was going to lead to a major let-down?

She reached for her own chocolate martini. Man, was that great! Almost as good as sex—with a guy with a functioning package.

Better than sex with Pete, the guy she'd recently dumped. He'd functioned, but the sex had, after the first few times, turned out to be pretty ho-hum.

Pete, from Korea, had been the latest in a string of dates and lovers she kept secret from her majorly old-fashioned family. For them, only Chinese guys rated as date-worthy.

For her—third generation Canadian and a thoroughly modern Jenny—race, culture and religion were irrelevant. She wanted a guy who was hunky, smart and sexy. And, while some of the family-approved Chinese guys had turned out to be good company and stimulating conversationalists, not a single one had ever turned her crank.

And her crank was getting rusty from a month's disuse. Being in this room was both heaven and hell, for a sexually frustrated girl.

Because, no two ways about it, sexy was what tonight was all about. The people in this room were on a mission: to choose the men who would grace the Greater Vancouver Fire Fighters calendar for next year. Civic pride was at stake. Vancouver simply had to have the hottest guys on their calendar.

Besides, the hotter the guys, the more people who'd buy the

calendar, and the more money that would be raised for charities like the Burn Fund and Cancer Lodge.

Music began again, calling her attention back to the stage as the next competitor sauntered out. He was dressed in full turnout gear, the way most of the others had started out. When this one peeled off his helmet, she saw he had silver in his close-cropped hair. No question he was handsome, though. She snapped a shot.

"This is more like it," Ann said, leaning forward.

"Too old," Jenny shouted.

"Old enough to know how to handle his hose," Suzanne chimed in, and they all laughed.

The man was gyrating to a classic rock number with a sexy, throbbing beat. He peeled off his bulky jacket, revealing a white tank-top stretched over taut muscles.

"Oh yeah," Ann said. "No steroids here, and I bet this guy's package is fully functional." She fanned herself with her hand.

"What's this thing you've got for older men?" Jenny asked, clicking away busily.

"It's not *age*, it's about appreciating quality," Ann shot back.

Jenny studied the man. Nah. Had to be damn near forty. To a twenty-three-year-old like her, that was definitely *old*. Really old.

Still, she had to admit the silver fox had a better body than the limp-dick steroid guy, and a more handsome face. And he did know how to move. In fact, Jenny's pulse was pounding in time with that sexy beat, her body was starting to sway, and she pressed her thighs together, feeling the ache of arousal between them.

Okay, so maybe she wouldn't kick this fox out of bed, just for having silver hair.

When he finished his number, she leaped to her feet and joined her friends in cheering loudly. "My vibrator's going to get a workout tonight," she shouted to her friends.

"I know *exactly* what you mean," Ann called back.

Then Jenny climbed up on her chair, tugged down her denim mini, and turned to take some crowd shots. The club was packed. Most of the women and some of the guys wore bright, fun clothing, and the lighting should make for interesting effects. Beyond the superficial, though, she hoped she was a skilled enough photographer to convey the throb of sexual energy in the air, the buzz of excited conversation, the musk of sweat and hundreds of different perfumes, colognes and assorted toiletries.

Young women had turned out in droves, but there were lots of men too. Funny to see the trendily-dressed West End gays shoulder to shoulder with burly dudes who could only be fire-fighters, come to cheer—or jeer—the competitors.

Music started up and she slipped back into her seat. Ooh, this was different. Same old, same old on the music, but this competitor had on a Zorro mask as well as the standard helmet.

A little shorter than most of the guys—a couple of inches under six feet?—and slender, this man sauntered slowly to center stage then began to move to the bump-and-grind music in a mesmerizing, hip-swaying motion. Hands went up, the helmet came off. A head shake and—

"Oh, my, God!" Jenny shrieked. "It's a woman!"

Long, gleaming red auburn hair tossed every which way.

"Woo-hoo!" the crowd shrieked, with the women yelling variations of "Go, sister!" and the guys—the straight guys—beginning to chant, "Take it off!"

The woman on stage gave a wide, sultry smile and began to take off her turnout coat. Like the silver-haired guy, she was wearing a tank, but hers was hot pink, almost the same shade as the crop top Jenny was wearing.

"Wow," Rina said admiringly, "she's sure toned."

"They have to be strong," Ann said, "to be able to drag people out of burning buildings. Right?"

"Gotta envy those boobs," Suze said. She, like Jenny, was barely a B in a good bra.

The performer, her nipples erect under the skin-tight top, was definitely a braless C.

Jenny clicked away, knowing one of these shots would make it into the *Georgia Straight* for sure. The woman peeled off her giant boots and baggy turnout pants to reveal black tights, slung low on her hip bones.

As she did, two men in black toted something onto the stage then disappeared behind the curtain.

It was a pole, mounted on a platform.

"A fire pole," Ann yelled. "That beats an axe or a hose."

The audience howled approvingly, drowning her out.

The volume increased as the masked woman twisted and twined her way around that pole. Man, that looked sexy. Hadn't Jenny heard somewhere that pole-dancing lessons were a new craze for bachelorette parties?

Cool. Another story idea, and the research would be a blast.

The woman finished her act and the audience was on its feet, cheering, stomping the floor, wolf-whistling loud enough to burst eardrums.

"Good for her!" Ann yelled, clapping furiously. "She's definitely going to win a slot on the calendar. Gotta love how she busted the all-male stereotype."

Jenny had her camera to her eye when the woman reached up to pull off her mask, revealing a laughing, strong-featured face, then flung the mask into the crowd. A tall dark-haired woman grabbed it out of the air, the lights went off and the woman on stage was gone.

The audience was still buzzing, even more energized than before.

"A tough act to follow," Suze commented.

"Yeah. Pity the next guy," Jenny said.

The stage remained dark.

"He chickened out," Rina said.

Music started up, but it wasn't the kind they'd been listening to all evening, with a throbbing, fast-driving beat. Instead it was—

"Saxophone." Rina didn't have to yell, the room had gone so quiet that even her whisper carried. "Also known as sultry, sensual, seductive." A musician herself, she knew all about instruments.

"Sexy," Suzanne sighed on a slow breath of air.

A light came on, but rather than the floodlights used in the previous acts, this was just one blue spotlight, and the stage was . . . smoking.

"Dry ice?" Ann murmured. "Effective."

Into the smoky blue spot, walked a man clad in turnout gear. No hose, no axe, no props at all. He stood quietly, lifting his head as if the music was seeping through him. Then, with minimal movements he removed his helmet, turnout coat, then the boots and finally his pants.

The audience sighed and murmured.

No in-your-face undies on this guy, but his costume was even more appealing for being subtle.

He wore slim-fitting tuxedo pants, a black tux vest and a black bowtie. No shirt, just tanned arms with exactly the right amount of musculature.

"Take a picture!" Ann ordered.

Damn, Jenny'd been so caught up in watching, she hadn't taken a single shot. Hurriedly she lifted her camera and took a few full-body shots, then zoomed in on his face. Strong planes, vivid blue eyes, sandy hair. Serious, not smiling or flirting with the audience as the others had done.

In fact, it was almost as if he was unaware of the audience. As if it was just him, listening to that sultry music as wisps of smoke curled up around him.

His head moved just a little, then his upper body, all in time with the music, and then, finally, he stepped forward and began to dance.

To tap dance.

She'd never seen anything like it. His shoes were tap shoes, but this was no slick Gene Kelly *American in Paris* type tap, nor was it the Celtic *Riverdance* style. It was slow, almost shuffly, bluesy. And very, very sexy.

She squeezed her thighs together. Way sexier than the silver-haired guy.

The man on stage would take a kind of scuffing step, hip thrusting forward and out, then do a kind of muffled drum-roll of taps, heel to toe. His posture was perfect, but graceful and fluid rather than tense, and his arms moved sensually, in opposition to his legs. He made Jenny think of a tango dancer with an imaginary partner.

Tap, tango, blues . . . Whatever you called it, this was the sexiest dance ever invented.

"Is it hot in here?" she gasped, torn between staring, mesmerized, and taking pictures. Awesome pictures, what with the smoke, the blue light, and the man.

"That's amazing," Rina sighed. "Don't you just want to take him home?"

Take him home, for her own private dancer. Oh, yeah. No question about it. Well, not home, where she lived with her family. But somewhere, anywhere, where she could be alone with him and leap those beautiful bones.

A minute or two into the number, he slipped off the tux vest and tossed it casually on the pile of firefighter clothes.

There was only one word for his torso. No, two. Holy shit!

It was perfect. Firm pecs, a drift of damp hair plastered to his body, arrowing down a lean abdomen. Her fingers itched to touch him.

The tux pants shifted and clung as he moved, and Jenny

zoomed in with her camera. Oh, man, he was getting turned on just as much as she was.

Had she said beautiful bones? Try beautiful *boner!*

It wasn't just her fingers itching now.

She licked her lips. "Nothing dysfunctional about that guy's package," she told her friends.

She zoomed up to his face. His expression was intense, focused. Focused on the saxophone, or on his own arousal? Definitely not on the audience. It was as if he didn't see the hundreds of people whose attention he'd captured so completely. The crowd was silent now, but for an occasional whisper, the rustle of clothing, the clink of ice cubes.

It was as if none of them mattered to him.

Somehow, this man's bearing, his distance from his audience, was far more arousing than the in-your-face lewdness of the other guys who'd performed.

Arousing.

Oh, God, her black silk thong was soaked and her pussy was throbbing with need.

"Mr. February," she announced to her friends. No question, the bluesy tap-dancer, the smoky saxophone guy, would win the most coveted slot.

"There's still six more to go," Suzanne murmured.

"Not relevant." Didn't Suze get it? No-one could top this man.

The music ended and the blue spotlight shut off, making the audience gasp. The dancer was gone.

But then the spot came back on, and he was standing quietly, hands clasped in front of him—hiding his erection? For the first time he made eye contact with the audience, and they were yelling the roof off. He smiled—kinda lazy, kinda cocky, definitely sexy.

Damn, he was hot. Normally Jenny went for the intellectual type, but tonight she was into the purely physical.

If she was trapped in a burning building, she'd want a guy who was strong, capable, physical. And now she was trapped inside a body that was burning up with lust, and she knew just the firefighter who could rescue her.

Yeah, she wanted this guy. She wanted those hot, sweaty muscles, she wanted that supremely functional dick. She wanted him to concentrate as intensely on her as he had on the music, to be even more turned on, to move inside her the way he'd moved to that saxophone.